GOBBELINO LONDON & A WORRY OF WERES

GOBBELINO LONDON, PI: BOOK 5

KIM M. WATT

For further information contact www.kmwatt.com

Cover design: Monika McFarland, www.ampersandbookcovers.com

Editor: Lynda Dietz, www.easyreaderediting.com

ISBN 978-0-473-62976-2

First Edition May 2022

10 9 8 7 6 5 4 3 2 1

CONTENTS

To Jon,
who shares a little of Gobbelino's bluntness,
but only when strictly necessary.
Thank you.

1

RABIES IS THE LEAST OF OUR WORRIES

THE BEST THING YOU COULD SAY ABOUT THE DAY SO FAR was that I hadn't been eaten yet. Unfortunately, emphasis was on the *yet.*

I skidded across the cracked tile floor of a discount supermarket, paws scrabbling for purchase, muscles bunching as I tried to turn the skid into a sprint. For one precarious moment I thought I was going to lose my footing entirely, then I recovered and did a hard turn into the next aisle. A snarl behind me would've set my hackles up if they hadn't already been standing to attention, and I abandoned the floor as a bad job and leaped for the shelving.

I was going too fast to make the top in one jump, but I caught the edge of the next shelf down with my front paws and launched myself up again without pausing, packets of pork rinds scattering in my wake. The top shelf was crammed with bulk boxes waiting to be unpacked, and I briefly considered trying to hide in among them. I was panting from the chase, which had already taken us through the crowds of a Friday morning market (leaving the canvas wall of a fishmongers' stall in tatters behind us, as well as an overturned cart of cabbages and a man screaming about damages to stock while his discounted post-Christmas puddings bounced across the pavement), in the front of one early-doors pub, out through the optimistically named beer garden, and over and around far too many parked cars to count. Hiding was starting to feel like a valid method of attack.

Heavy paws hit the shelves below me, and a long, snake-like tail tipped with a bristly tuft of hair plunged in among the boxes, flinging them away effortlessly.

"Bad dog!" I yelped. "Sit!"

The dog gave a snarl which indicated it was perfectly happy being a bad dog, and the tail lashed out, trying to get a grip on me.

I reverted to the *run* plan.

THE VIDEO HAD SHOWED a burly dog running through the streets of Leeds, howling. It wasn't a particularly big dog – Rottweiler-size perhaps, all muscle and power, but nothing exciting. People video anything these days, and we probably wouldn't have even watched the clip, but the magician who sent us the link had added the note, *One of yours?* Which, no, we're not dog people. But we have been known to tidy up other people's messes, and as the camera zoomed in, Callum and I said, "*Ohhh,*" together.

Because the dog had a few quirks. Namely, three more eyes than normal, a fang-filled overbite, a ridge of cartoon dinosaur spines down its back, and a tail that was three times longer than your average dog's curling in the air behind it. The human who posted the video was wondering aloud if it was off a film set, or if it had escaped from some top-secret experimental lab – all while leaning out a window, apparently not interested enough in internet fame to get any closer to something with jaws like a Great White.

The dog loped off screen, still howling, and Callum said, "We'd better get that."

To which I made various points about us not being monster handlers, as well as our current plans to keep a low profile, and also how a dog like that likely had the sort of owners who'd take a dim view of us snatching their prize monster off the streets. Callum countered that the dog was evidently not your average pooch, and was drawing attention to itself, which was no good for anyone. The average human just isn't equipped to deal with the reality of a whole other magical world of non-human Folk existing alongside them, and though they're very good at not seeing what's right in front of them, you can't rub their noses in it.

So someone was going to have to Do Something, before some human tumbled to the fact that the dog was neither a film set escapee nor a genetic experiment. There's an organisation called the Watch that ensures humans and Folk stay separate, of course, and this would technically be their job, but the last thing we needed was them sniffing around our neighbourhood because of a runaway pooch. Even though it was nothing to do with us, every party that declares itself to be the law needs someone to blame when things go wrong, and for some reason we seem to tick a lot of scapegoat boxes. Well, me, mostly. The Watch has a nasty habit of bringing my lives to a premature end, and I had no desire for yet another repeat performance.

I still wasn't keen on tangling with a shark-toothed dog, but then Callum pointed out that there might be a reward for the beast's safe return, and we were one day off being late on our rent again, which always has knock-on effects for the standard of tuna in our cupboards.

And so here I was, racing along the length of the shelf, swerving boxes and leaping multipacks, the dog keeping pace with me below while its tail tore at the shelves, leaving packets of crisps and corn chips and weird puffed soybean things in our wake. I was going to run out of shelf any moment, so I threw myself sideways instead, hurdling a box of Monster Munch and arriving in the next aisle over.

"Gobs!" Callum yelled. I couldn't yell back, given all the humans in here, but it gave me somewhere to aim for. I leaped to the floor and took off down the aisle even as the dog surged around it from the other side of the shelf, colliding with a tower of Twiglets and sending them cascading across the shop floor, but not slowing it appreciably. It charged after me, eating up my narrow lead, and I hurtled out of the end of the aisle with a yowl, making a Lycra-clad man clutching a sports drink scream.

I tried for a hard left turn, hoping to head back out of the shop, but all I did was slide across the slick tiling, claws finding no grip at all. Paws thundered after me, and the monster dog gave a *whuff* of triumph, far too close for comfort. The man screamed again, a woman shouted something about wild animals, and Callum appeared out of the next aisle at a dead run. He snatched me up mid-sprint and legged it for the front of the shop, not even slowing. The dog's bark gave way to a yelp as it slid across the floor behind us, having as much trouble as I'd had finding purchase, and as I peered around Callum I saw Lycra-man scramble up the shelves of tinned goods like an acrobat while the dog found its feet and plunged after us, foam flying from its toothy jaws.

Just another day for G&C London, Private Investigators.

THE SHOP DOORS stood open on a cold grey day, grimy snow edging the streets and collecting in the gutters. Callum bolted past a handful of people filming the excitement from the shelter of the checkouts and straight across the pavement, diving between two parked cars and popping out directly into the path of a snub-nosed yellow Nissan that was luckily maintaining old-person cruising speed. I squawked, Callum yelped, and I caught a glimpse of a toothless old man staring at us over the wheel with his mouth and eyes wide in horror. I flew free of Callum's grip as we bounced across the bonnet, twisting to spot my landing and dropping to my haunches without too much of a jolt next to someone's half-eaten sausage roll. Callum rolled with the fall, coming back into a crouch just in time to look up and see the dog hurtling toward him.

"Oh—" he started, but before I could add to my store

of human curse words (surprisingly few of which are to do with vegetables), the old man flung his car door open. The monster hit it with a startled yip and stumbled back a step or so as the impact slammed the door closed again. Callum started to straighten up, and the dog refocused on him, its head dropping low as it started to growl.

"Good dog," he said. "*Good dog.*"

The old man opened his car door again, more cautiously this time, and the dog swung its heavy head toward him. He hesitated, and said, "Are you alright there?"

"Stay there," Callum said, and I wasn't sure if he was talking to the man or the dog. Only one of them listened, and unfortunately it wasn't the one with all the teeth. The dog was advancing, shoulders hulking up, its snaky tail whipping from side to side irritably. Its growl was a terrible, heart-shaking thing, and Callum's throat was far too close to its tooth-level for comfort.

"Hairballs," I mumbled, gathering myself into a crouch. I was going to regret this. I really was. But one has responsibilities.

I launched forward, ears back, coming in fast from behind while the dog's attention was still on Callum. I leaped straight to its back, my claws slipping on the slick hard surface of the spines, but I got in some good scratches and at least one nip before I went straight over the top and kept running. Behind me, the dog broke into a volley of barking so deep I could feel it in my bones, and tore after me.

"*Gobs!*" Callum shouted, but I was already sprinting down the street, brakes screeching and horns blaring as cars tried to avoid us. This really was the very definition of not keeping a low profile, but it totally wasn't our fault. The dog started it.

An alley loomed to one side, a couple of big commercial bins on wheels leaning against one wall, and I dived into it, not stopping until I was under the nearest one, smelling stale grease and spoiled meat. The dog shoved its nose after me, growling, but while the bin shook and rocked, it didn't move from its spot. The dog heaved, trying to get its shoulders under the bin, but it was too low and too heavy. So the beast just sat there panting and snarling, drool dripping from its jaws and smearing the cobbles. I was surprised it wasn't burning holes in them, to be honest. Given the other weird body modifications, it had to be some sort of damn pixie dog, and it was a bit uncharacteristic for them to miss the chance of giving it acid drool.

The dog backed off suddenly, and I heard Callum. "Gobs?"

"Here," I called back. "Uneaten."

"Good start."

"Could be better."

"Fair point." He made smooching noises, and the dog growled.

"Don't smooch at the thing. It's not a bloody chihuahua."

"Here girl," he said, and I heard the unmistakable sound of biscuits being shaken in a bag. "Good girl."

The dog stopped growling and gave a questioning little whine.

"Are those *my* biscuits?" I demanded. "They better not be my biscuits."

"What other biscuits would I be carrying?"

"That's my lunch!"

"Would you rather be *her* lunch?"

I huffed. "*Her,* now, is it? You can't adopt a pixie dog. Or any dog. I refuse."

"It's a bit rude to keep calling her *it.*" He shook the biscuits again. "Come on. Yummy bikkies!"

"No dogs or weres. Company policy."

"You also said it was company policy not to take imp or pixie cases."

"Yeah, and look what ignoring *that* got us. A trashed apartment and an infected bite on your hand."

He sighed. "Well, I'm not adopting her anyway. I'm just trying to get hold of her."

The dog whined, shuffling back so her bum was pressed right against to the bin. For one moment I wondered if she had some sort of noxious gas attack planned, then her tail snaked in through the debris with the tip lifted off the ground, pointing as if it could see me. For all I knew it could. The pixies could've put infrared sensors or anything in among the weird tuft of hair at the end. I scooted back until I hit the wall behind the bins, and yowled, "*Callum!*"

"I'm trying!"

The tail couldn't quite touch me. It danced across the ground, curling around a slimy lettuce leaf and discarding it, investigating a crusty can of baked beans and dropping it again. I shuffled to my left, and it slid after me. I went right, and it did the same. If I ran, it'd know exactly where

I was going, and the damn dog'd be right there waiting for me. So I did the only other thing I could think of.

I bit it.

The dog squalled like a goblin having its toes pinched, and shot away. Callum thoroughly expanded my vocabulary, and I charged out from under the bin with every hair pouffed out to its fullest extent, yowling the fury of a cat who's trodden in at least two rotting potatoes and has a fermenting tomato stuck to their belly. Callum had his tatty old coat gripped like a matador's cape as he lunged side to side, trying to keep the dog trapped in the alley, while the monster dashed about with her tail lashing wildly, alternately howling and whining. A woman paused on the street outside and said, "What on *earth* are you doing to that poor dog?"

Callum yelled, "RSPCA! I think it's rabid!" and the woman's concerns for the dog's well-being vanished even more quickly than she did. Which was lucky, as the dog chose that moment to try to rush past Callum. He tackled the beast, bundling her up in the coat while she thrashed and howled to the accompaniment of tearing cloth. He added a few more swear words to things, then the dog's tail socked him in the face. He yelped, his grip faltering, and rolled to the ground as she surged away, still wearing his coat.

I leaped over Callum, planting myself in the dog's path and putting everything into a good snarl. Gratifyingly – and somewhat unexpectedly – the dog stopped dead in her tracks, wobbling and rolling her five eyes. Slobber still dripped from her jaws, shining up that excessive collection of teeth, and, as if reminded that she weighed about ten times what I did, the monster opened her massive jaws and lunged for me.

There was no time to run, so I made use of my new words of the day, rising on my hind legs to meet the beast with my claws out and my teeth bared, and decided that I had to do more to enforce company policy. This was ridiculous.

I WAS at least 99 percent sure that I was about to be a cat-sized serving of Pedigree Chum, but I did harbour a smidgen of hope that Callum would get his gangly great form off the ground in time to tackle SharkDog before she removed my head. I mean, that's what partners are for, right? But even as those terrible teeth bore down on me, powered by what looked from my point of view to be about an ox's worth of muscle, something *shifted.*

I don't mean I did. Cats *can* shift, can step out of this world into the space that runs between all things and back out again somewhere else entirely, a metre or a mile or a country over, in the time it takes to draw breath. But due to one of my unfortunate altercations with the Watch – the one that ended my last life – the beasts that roam the Inbetween have my scent. They follow me on their side of the fragile membrane that holds our world, and if I step out of it, I'll end up as Pedigree *Monster* Chum. Which, having done it once, I had no desire to repeat, even if SharkDog was the alternative. So no, I didn't shift. But something did.

Reality rippled. The traffic beyond the alley, Callum's

shouts, even the snarling of the monster dog became abruptly muffled, as if someone had thrown a blanket over the world. Everything dimmed, the colour running out until all was shades of grey, and movement slowed. SharkDog was still moving toward me, but I could see a thread of drool swinging from one of her great fangs, moving with the slow ponderousness of a glacier cruising toward the sea. Callum was behind her, in some sort of half scramble, half lunge, drifting to the ground with his face twisted in a shout and his overlong hair moving like sea anemones. Despite the stuffy sounds of the world my ears were clear, and I caught a whisper of soft movement, bare feet or cloth or gentle paws on hard floor. There was the catch of an indrawn breath, all of it somewhere three times removed from where I was, and someone hissed, "*Gobbelino.*"

But I wasn't really listening. Fear surged in my chest, something unrooted and all encompassing, because what if it *was* the Watch? There was no logical reason for it to be, not right now, on this snow-stained winter day in a filthy alley in Leeds when we were just trying to *help,* but who else could it be? And the Watch didn't need logical. They just needed *because.* I knew that somewhere in the centre of my horrified being, knew that no matter how careful I was, I could never be careful enough, because authority has its own rules. They could simply decide I'd been *wrong,* in this life or a previous one. Just as they always did.

Maybe the dog was a trap, to draw me out or place me at fault for interfering. To give them a reason they could show to others, like a note for the teacher. It didn't need to be truthful, it was just something to have. And now they were going to grab me, drag me off to the Inbetween again, hold me to the beasts a second time and punish me for this life's indiscretions and my last lives' rebellions, to stop me before ... before whatever had happened to cause their fury happened again. I could taste the memory but not see it. Not that it mattered – this could be the time they took *all* my lives. I could taste the cold and the nothingness and the hot acid of my own blood.

And then, bizarrely, with my head still racing in hamster-ball panic, I hit the ground. I'd been mid-jump when the change had come over the world, and everyone else was still in achingly slow motion, but I'd been leaping up to meet the dog, and now I plummeted back onto my hindlegs, staggered, and plopped to the ground on my side. I had time for two hard, sharp breaths, then someone said, "*Gobbelino,*" again and there was a touch on my back, cold and feather-soft.

I surged to my feet, shooting sideways, my mouth dry and wordless but my head screaming *nononononono,* the panic too raw and metallic to form anything more coherent. There was another sound, a door slamming or a chair falling, and a curse that was sharp and short and vaguely familiar, then colour and movement rushed back into the world.

I'd fetched up with my flank pressed into the wall of the alley, the brick rough and cold and beautifully, wonderfully *real,* and the dog's snarl turned into a startled yelp as she realised I wasn't in front of her anymore. Callum fell after her, managing to grab her back legs with both hands and jerk her to a halt, while the snake tail ignored him entirely, casting about the place in search of me. It finally spotted me, and pointed so hard it looked physically painful, but by that point Callum had both arms wrapped around the dog's hindquarters, holding her in place. Or trying to, because she scrabbled at the cobbles wildly, claws like talons tearing dusty streaks from the stone, and started to drag herself toward me with him in tow.

I'd never been so happy to be under attack by a pixie dog.

2

A BRUSH WITH SOMETHING VAST & DISTANT

Relatively happy, anyway. My heart was still so loud in my ears that I could hardly hear Callum shouting at me to make myself scarce so he had a chance to get the dog under control, and I wasn't entirely sure I could stand without the wall to hold me. But I straightened up anyway, muscles twinging from the tension of the fright, and glanced around the alley. It was just us. Just Callum and the damn dog, and *I hadn't done anything wrong.* Not this time. Maybe not even last time, although the sudden, unfocused wash of memory that had come with the almost-shift was fading, and I couldn't tell if I'd actually been remembering something from before my last death, or if it had been simply a panic response. Not that it mattered right now. The important thing now was to get this bloody dog sorted, because if the Watch weren't the ones already breathing down our necks, they soon would be. And I wasn't having any of it. Not again.

So when SharkDog managed a furious bark, still dragging herself and Callum toward me, I charged forward and slapped her three times on the snout with one paw.

"Bad dog!" I snarled, and hit her again to be sure she got the message. Which would've been perfect if she'd had the sense to listen, but her tail shot out and slapped me at least twice as hard as I'd hit her, sending me tumbling across the cobbles and into the wall. I rolled to my feet and charged back, ears flat and teeth bared, and the dog and I snarled at each other.

"Gobs!" Callum shouted. "What're you *doing?* Just get out, can't you? I'll hold her!"

"Bloody dogs! Bloody pixie bloody useless soggy pumpkin Sasquatch dogs!"

"What?" he asked, and the dog tipped her head to one side, her tail forming a question mark above them where they both sprawled in the alleyway.

"Just … behave!" I snapped. "Heel! Sit! Do something *useful* and stop drawing attention to yourself, you lentil!"

"Right now I'm not even sure if you're talking to her or me," Callum said, far too reasonably.

"Both of you!" I yelled, and, to be fair, I might've been overreacting a little, but I was fairly sure someone had just tried to grab me by the scruff of the neck and turf me into the Inbetween, and while I might've suspected the Watch, I didn't actually *know* who it had been, or why, so my tolerance for SharkDogs and reasonable partners was not at an all-time high.

I gathered myself to rush the dog again, but before I could launch back into the fray, a small green snake slithered smartly between the beast's paws, straight into her line of sight, then raised his head up and tilted it rather severely at her.

The dog would've taken a step back if Callum hadn't been holding her. She whined.

The snake tilted his head a little more firmly, and the dog attempted to tuck her own snaky tail between her legs. Callum was in the way, though, so she just thumped him mercilessly on the shoulders.

"Ow," he said, trying to fend off the rogue tail.

I ambled over and stood by the snake, who glanced at me, then back at the dog. The dog whined again, and the snake stuck his tongue out. The whine turned into a yelp, and SharkDog tried to become a lap dog, bowling Callum over as she pushed back into him in a panic.

Callum held her off as well as he could, pushing himself up onto his knees and brushing vaguely at the mucky front of his jumper. It was black, but that didn't do much to hide the mud and broken eggshells he'd rolled through.

"What'd you say to her?" I asked Green Snake, but he just tipped his head at me.

Callum got to his feet and picked his coat up off the ground, inspecting the new rips in it while the dog cowered behind his legs. "I'm glad someone knew what to say to her."

"Was it the tail?" I asked Green Snake, but he just dropped to the ground and slithered back to Callum, who picked him up and put him in a pocket of his coat. SharkDog whimpered and scuttled over to sit next to me, dropping her belly to the ground and shooting me alarmed glances out of her five eyes. "I am not your friend," I told her, and she whined.

"I don't know," a new voice said. "You look pretty cosy there."

SharkDog spun around with something far too close to a roar, raising all the hair on my back just as it had started to settle down, and charged for the mouth of the alley.

"Stop her!" Callum shouted, already lunging into pursuit, although he'd have been better to chuck Green Snake in front of the beast for all the luck we'd had.

SharkDog's roar was met with a snarl that, while quieter, was still more than enough to set small creatures quaking in their burrows, and the monster put the brakes on so hard that her hindquarters hit the ground and I swear I saw sparks rising from the cobbles under her claws. She skidded to a stop with her front legs locked straight and her head straining up and away from the cobbles, her five eyes rolling desperately. I padded to the side of the alley to see a large, brindled tabby cat sitting between the beast's paws, regarding the monster looming over her with vague interest. She flicked her tatty ears and yawned, and SharkDog scooted backward until Callum grabbed her by the scruff of the neck.

"*Tam,*" I said. "What I wouldn't have done to have you here ten minutes ago."

The big tabby examined me for a moment, then inspected a paw.

"Not that I'm not pleased to see you now, of course. But ten minutes ago would've been even better."

Tam yawned again and shook herself off. She gave the

distinct impression that she'd never quite got the hang of personal grooming, but I doubt anyone would be too quick to say it to her.

"She's really come out of herself," I said instead, to the cat standing next to her. She had her ears back, and fresh scars stood out on her pale, hairless flanks as she examined the dog.

Pru shifted her attention to me, eyes narrowed in amusement. "Not everyone talks as much as you, Gobbelino."

"People miss out on so much."

"Whereas I couldn't miss out if I tried," Callum said, shrugging into his tatty coat. "Hi Pru, Tam."

"Callum," Pru said, and Tam raised her chin slightly.

"So, you here to see us in action?" I asked. "The excitement of the hunt and all that?"

"It certainly has its entertainment value," Pru said.

"Yet is ultimately successful," I pointed out.

"You have lettuce in your whiskers," Tam said, startling me.

"Camouflage," I said, shaking it off, and she snorted.

"Not that it's not wonderful to see you both," Callum said, "but we need to get this dog out of here before anyone really does report us to the RSPCA."

"Why would they?" I demanded. "We're performing a public service here."

"Public disruption, more like," Pru said. "We went past the pound shop and the police were already there."

Callum groaned, and rubbed his face with his free hand. He'd taken his belt off to use as makeshift collar, and SharkDog was straining against it, intent on the street beyond the alley. She was trying not to look at Tam, but her eyes seemed to work fairly independently, and at least two of them kept straying back to the big cat. Tam exposed one broken tooth and huffed in amusement when the dog tried to back away from Callum, almost ripping the belt out of his hands. "Unhelpful," he said.

Tam shrugged, and looked at Pru. She examined Callum and me, then said, "We're here on business."

"What business?" Callum asked.

Pru started to speak, and suddenly I wondered how she and Tam were both here, just after the Inbetween had tried to grab me, because the Watch is cats. Only cats, always, and for one horrifying moment the world shifted around me again, darkening at the edges, and I felt vast beasts turning their endless, patient attention toward me as the membrane thinned. I backed up, not even sure where I was going, then squawked as I bumped into the dog and she licked my head.

"*No!* Bad dog!"

She whined and tried to lick me again, and I stumbled away, my heart too fast and spots in my vision, but the world feeling more solid.

"Alright?" Pru asked, watching me with pale eyes.

"Sure. Fine. What business?" My heart was harsh in my ears, and I was aware I was speaking too loudly over it, but I didn't care.

"Claudia," Pru said. "We've still not been able to find her since the whole thing with the necromancers. We wanted to ask Ms Jones, but we can't find her, either."

Claudia was very much Watch. Although she'd never actually tried to kill me, which put her over and above almost every other Watch cat I knew. She had, in fact, helped me, more than once. I closed my eyes for a moment, but that was too close to the void I'd felt – could still feel – behind me, so I opened them again and returned Pru's cool gaze instead. She was watching me with her wrinkly forehead even more furrowed than usual, and Tam had stopped looking bored.

Due to my *issues* with the Watch, I didn't take up with too many other cats. Not all cats are Watch, but any cat can work for them. And will, when it suits their own needs, or if the Watch demands it. The Watch doesn't *ask*. But if I trusted anyone, I trusted these two.

Not even a couple of months ago, there had been *the whole thing with the necromancers,* as Pru put it. The whole thing being a bunch of necromancers who weren't even technically meant to exist anymore – not with proper power, anyway – performing a ritual that would raise an Old One, an ancient necromancer of a kind that had been so powerful they were just about gods. The Old Ones had been banished centuries ago by the Watch, when the Watch had actually been doing things other than terrifying blameless PIs, and were now more myth than reality. Or so we'd thought, until Tam, Pru, and I, as well as a bunch of other cats, had all ended up trapped in cages and intended for use as Old One snacks. The ritual would've taken all our remaining lives at once, if it had succeeded. We'd got out, and had ultimately sent the Old One back where it belonged, and Pru and Tam had been beside me all the way. The Watch hadn't even shown their noses.

So I supposed the odds were good that they hadn't

turned up in the alley to chuck me into the Inbetween when they could've just let the Old One eat me.

"Okay," I said, finding I could talk a little more steadily. "Why ask Ms Jones?"

Pru shifted her paws slightly. "She and Claudia were close. I don't know the details, but I think they were helping each other somehow. So Ms Jones might know where she's gone. But there's no trace of her anywhere that we can find, either."

Ms Jones was our lovely yet terrifying local sorcerer, who might, maybe, possibly, carry a teeny tiny grudge against us for throwing her book of power into the Inbetween. Well, I had. But in my defence, it had been stolen by her useless dentist boyfriend, then had gone feral and was about to rip reality apart. So I still maintain it had been good thinking under pressure, and just what was expected of an enterprising PI.

"We haven't seen her since before the necromancers either," I said, and shivered. She'd sat in our car with a whisky bottle in one hand and the other on my back, and she'd almost made me remember my last death. I was sure the beasts had been closer since then, had held to my scent more firmly.

"And you don't know where she lives?"

"We don't, but we can find out," Callum said.

"Yes, we'll just look up *sorcerers for hire* in the Yellow Pages," I said, trying to get back into the spirit of things.

"If it were that easy we'd have already found her," Pru said.

"And deprived yourselves of our company?"

Callum had pulled his phone from his jeans, and now

he hit dial and trapped it between his ear and shoulder as he patted his coat pockets. He fished out a crushed packet of cigarettes, then took the phone away from his ear, shaking his head. "Straight to messages."

"But it's not disconnected," I said. "That's something."

"I suppose. I'll keep trying." He selected a cigarette that didn't look too bent and went searching through his pockets for his lighter. "I hate to say this, but … if we haven't seen Claudia since the necromancers … do we know she *survived* the necromancers?"

Tam growled, and I gave her an uneasy look. We hadn't been the first cats the necromancers had trapped, and I doubted it had been the first time they'd attempted their ritual. We were just the first ones that had escaped.

"Not entirely," Pru admitted. "But we have to at least try. We can't just give up on her. And I'd've thought you'd be pretty keen to find her too."

"Why?" Callum asked, when I didn't.

Pru shifted uneasily and looked at Tam, who watched me with a bright and electric green gaze. For a moment I thought she wasn't going to speak – after all, she'd already about used her quota of words for the day, going from past experience. But then she said, "Because Claudia was the one thing keeping the Watch proper off you."

Everything was silent but for the panting of SharkDog and the cars passing on the road outside, and I felt the world stop again, even if it was more in memory than reality this time.

"Hairballs," I said, and hoped my voice was steadier on the outside than it felt on the inside.

"ARE YOU SURE?" Callum asked, and Tam shifted her gaze to him, arching her eyebrow whiskers. "Not about the Watch thing, that makes sense—"

"Does it?" I asked. "I haven't *done* anything. And I'm just one cat, exceptional though I may be. There must be plenty of others they can worry about."

"Not too many others running about the place poking their snouts into Folk business," Pru said. "Most of us just hang out and confuse humans."

"And help stop the zombie apocalypse," I pointed out. "The Watch told you to leave it, but you helped us, remember?"

"I can't exactly forget my human scarfing raw chicken hearts on the kitchen floor."

I shot a sideways look at Callum, who'd put a good effort into scarfing raw meat himself during a small spate of zombification. Luckily it had turned out to be reversible, and Claudia had helped us with that, as had Ms Jones. They *had* seemed to hit it off pretty well.

"Look, we're *helping,*" I said. "The Watch should be dealing with things like runaway pixie dogs charging through the local pound shop and drawing attention to themselves. So we're doing their work here."

Pru looked at Tam, but having spoken twice in the space of five minutes the big cat was evidently still recovering. "The Watch should also have been dealing with zombies, and necromancers, and unicorn dust weapons, because they're all actual threats to humans, not just at risk of drawing attention to Folk. But they're not. And I know Claudia was trying to figure out what was going on, but now she's gone."

I licked my chops, tasting dust and emptiness somewhere on the edge of my senses, and almost thought I heard a whisper of *Gobbelino* again. I wanted to say, *But is this our business?* but I couldn't. The words wouldn't come, and the yawning void lurking just out of sight reminded me that Claudia had pulled me out of the Inbetween when I'd taken the sorcerer's book there to destroy it. She'd literally ripped me away from the beasts of the void, and we bore matching sucker scars to prove it (which look just as cool as they sound). She'd told me more than once to keep a low profile, too. I had the impression that she led some shadowy branch of the Watch that was trying to keep the more megalomaniacal tendencies of the Watch proper in check. Apparently that wasn't going so well.

Callum hunkered down next to the dog, the hand holding his cigarette resting on her makeshift collar and smoke trailing over us. Tam sneezed.

"Sorry," he said, and looked at me. "We can find Ms Jones."

I started to speak, swallowed, then tried again. "If this is Watch business, then we're really sticking our paws in the custard bowl."

He nodded, rubbed his chin with his free hand, then said, "I think we've been doing that anyway."

"And we could be wrong," Pru said. "Maybe Claudia's just lying low for a bit, and Ms Jones really is on holiday."

"What?" Callum and I both asked.

"We spoke to the dentist, what's his name – Toddler, or something."

"Walker," Callum said. "Or Malcolm."

"Right. Him. He said she was on holiday."

Callum frowned. "I'm having trouble seeing Ms Jones sitting on a beach somewhere sipping on a fruity rum drink with an umbrella in it."

Pru blinked at him. "How big are these drinks?"

"What?"

"To fit an umbrella in it," I said. "Can even a sorcerer drink that much fruity rum drink?"

"It's not—" He shook his head. "Never mind the umbrella. Last time we saw her she didn't look like she was going on any sort of holiday."

Last time we saw her, a magician had trapped her in the walls of his house, and she was *not* happy, even after we let her out.

"And the last person we know definitely saw her was your friend Ifan," Pru said, her snout wrinkling as she said *your friend.*

Callum gave her a sideways look and took a final puff on the cigarette, stubbing it out on the cobbles. Ifan was the son of the magician in question, who everyone had thought was dead. Turned out he was just hanging out in Mustique, probably drinking giant fruity rum drinks with umbrellas in them. "We can ask him," Callum said.

"And I'm sure he'll be entirely truthful."

I looked at Pru, her naked tail twitching and curling in that unsettling way, and Tam sitting next to her with her own tatty tail curled over her toes, and said, "Let's not get magicians of any variety involved just yet."

Callum looked at me. "It's the obvious place to start."

Except that he lies. Although I had a feeling Callum

knew that better than I did. "Why don't we start with Walker? See what the deal is with this whole holiday thing, maybe get a home address for Ms Jones off him. He might be more likely to tell us than two cats he doesn't know."

Callum got up, tugging SharkDog with him as he went to flick the cigarette butt into the bin. "Alright. Seems like a plan."

I looked at Pru, trying to ignore the loom of the void behind me, and said, "G and C London are on the case."

"Well, I feel so much better," Pru said, but she shoulder-bumped me gently as we followed Callum out of the alley, his ripped coat swinging around his legs and the spiky-spined dog pulled close to his side. Tam fell into step with us, and we headed into the streets of Leeds together, in search of sorcerers and cats and other deadly things.

It still felt safer than the alley.

3

THE HIDDEN RISKS OF DENTAL VISITS

Walker's mobile went unanswered, and when Callum called his surgery, the receptionist just said he was unavailable and that we could leave a message. We didn't. We decided to make a house call instead.

The dentist's nondescript shopfront nestled among a row of other nondescript businesses, one of those odd oases of retail that pock residential areas. There was a dry cleaner's and a kebab shop, and a convenience store with no windows. On our side of the road there was a cafe where I happened to know the waiter looked kindly on cats, but we weren't going there, more's the pity. I could've just done with some bacon after narrowly avoiding being eaten by both SharkDog and an unexpected void.

Callum pulled around the back of the shops and parked next to an ancient, pale blue VW beetle with crocheted seat covers. Pru, Tam and I were crowded onto the passenger seat of our old car – well, Tam was sitting solidly in the middle with her paws tucked under her chest, and Pru and I were trying not to crowd her too much. Callum looked at us and said, "You lot can't come in."

"Tam and I did," Pru said. "We just shifted straight into his office."

"He doesn't have shift locks?" I asked.

Tam snorted, and Pru said, "He had some of those market stall shift locks. Couldn't keep a dormouse out."

Callum glanced at me. "Well, I can't do that," he said. Which was diplomatic and all, but of course Pru and Tam already knew I couldn't shift. Not unless I wanted to end up as void monster snacks. "Why don't you three stay here, and I'll go and talk to him?"

"Not a chance," I said, at the same time as Pru and Tam gave remarkably similar snorts.

"It's a *dental surgery,*" Callum said. "I don't think cats are welcome."

"Blatant speciesism," I said, and tipped my head toward the back seat. "Besides, I'm not a dog sitter."

SharkDog whined, and panted at us. I'm not sure if she was more afraid of Tam or the possible reappearance of Green Snake, but she was behaving herself. It could've been me, of course, but while I may have confidence in my own abilities, I'm not delusional. The other two were far scarier.

Callum looked at the dog doubtfully. "She might trash the car if we just leave her here."

Pru, Tam and I looked at each other, then at him, and I arched my whiskers at the sagging headlining, ripped seats, and the bits on the floor that were rusted through and let the water from the road come in on rainy days.

Callum sighed. "Fine. Come on."

"Meet you in there," Pru said, getting up. She stepped sideways off the seat and vanished. Tam followed her, giving me one green-eyed wink before she was gone, leaving behind a soft cloud of cat hair and a whiff of something wild and amused. I shivered.

"Coming?" Callum asked.

"Stay," I said to the dog, and jumped out of the driver's side door into the damp grey chill of a Yorkshire winter's day.

CALLUM LED the way around the line of shops toward the street, his hands in the pockets of his tatty coat and his skinny shoulders hunched against the cold.

"You really think we need to worry about Ms Jones?" I asked, trotting next to him. There had been snow last night, and though it hadn't stayed, the pavement was slick and wet with the melt. "I mean, she's a sorcerer. A proper one. Nothing that bad can have happened."

Callum took his cigarettes from his pocket, plucking one from the packet and pausing to light it. "We did destroy her book of power."

Sorcerers are ancient creatures, soaked in so many years of magic that they're barely second cousins to human anymore. But for all those muscular, sedimentary layers of power, they're also discreet. They sink their excess magic into books, binding them in strange vellum and questionable inks, until the things are all but sentient, and the sorcerers themselves can almost pass as human.

They generally do, to actual humans anyway, since humans are so convinced that magic doesn't exist that they can rationalise away pretty much anything – like a small outbreak of zombies or the ability of cats to appear in locked rooms. But sorcerers remain careful. After all, to them, the witch trials weren't so long ago. And fire still burns, if you're bound tightly enough.

"*Destroyed* is a strong word," I said now. "*Removed* might be better. Anyway, she's still got loads of power without it." Even Ms Jones, who did a fairly good impression of still being human, wouldn't have put *all* her power into her book. She'd have kept plenty handy, and however sorcerers build magic, she'd have been doing a lot of that ever since. I wasn't sure I ever wanted to know what that entailed, though.

"Is she, though?" Callum asked. "Lewis trapped her."

Lewis, who was Ifan's dad and had also been the most powerful magician in the county – if not the *country* – until we'd pushed him into another dimension. Which is starting to sound like a pattern, what with the book, but it had actually only happened twice. Well, three times, technically, but the head necromancer had been pushed in at the same time as Lewis, so that really made it only twice. And it had been them or us, as Lewis had been working with the necromancers to pull the Old One into this world, and as well as indulging in cat sacrifices, he'd got Callum briefly possessed.

So the only aspect of the situation I felt bad about was the fact that we weren't *entirely* sure we'd pushed Lewis and the necromancer into the Old One's dimension when we'd banished it. I mean, it couldn't have happened to nicer people, and I much preferred the thought of Old Ones using their ears as crudité bowls than I did the idea that they were still hanging about somewhere with designs on *my* ears.

Now I said, "Lewis trapped her in his house, which is where most of *his* power was held. Is there anyone else strong enough to do that sort of thing?"

Callum shook his head. "I don't know. But do you really think she's just taken a bit of a holiday?"

"Given the dentist, I'd be inclined to do a vanishing act, too."

Callum snorted, and stopped in front of the frosted glass door to the dentist's surgery, examining it.

"What?" I asked. "Come on, my paws are cold."

"No one's there." He tapped the door with the hand holding the cigarette, scattering ash onto his coat sleeve. "*Back in five minutes,* it says."

"Sod that. I'm not standing out here for five minutes."

He looked at me. "Want a lift?"

"Not if you're going to breathe smoke all over me. Let's try the back door."

"Breaking in's not exactly going to set the tone for a friendly chat."

"Pru and Tam are in there already. And it's not like we're strangers. Better to get in when he's not working on anyone, anyway."

Callum regarded me for a moment then said, "You just want to get inside."

"My paws are really very cold."

"Come on."

He stubbed his cigarette out and flicked it into a bin

on the way back around the building, and a moment later we were examining the scuffed, dirty white back door. Callum tried the handle. It turned easily, and we looked at each other.

"That doesn't seem great," I said.

"Not really." He pushed it slowly open, revealing a little back room with cardboard file boxes stacked on the floor and shelves to one side, and a compact sink, fridge, and a couple of kitchen-y type cupboards to the other.

I started over the threshold then paused, sniffing the air. There was something lurking under the mingled scents of antiseptic and mouthwash and tooth-dust. Callum looked down at me.

"What is it?"

"I don't know." I caught the lingering whiff of expensive talc and cheap cologne, and someone had reheated a curry for lunch, by the smell of things. That seemed like an unwise choice for anyone who spent their time leaning over other people's faces, but no one had ever accused the dentist of making good life choices.

Callum nudged me with his boot. "Get inside so I can close the door, at least."

"Don't dismiss my instincts. I've got an excellent nose."

"Of course you do." He nudged me again, and I padded inside, stopping on the rough hessian of the welcome mat. He stepped over me and pulled the door shut, then headed for the interior door.

"Wait," I said, and he looked back at me. The fur was bristling on my spine and tail, for no good reason that I could fathom. There was just that *other* in the air, less scent and more … something. Presence. Suggestion. But now I was having trouble distinguishing it from the pure fright of earlier, from the weight of the void that seemed to be following me.

Callum placed one hand on the internal door, long fingers splayed, and pushed it open very slightly. We were both silent. I could hear my breath whispering in my nose, and cars passing outside, and beyond the door the tinny music of one of those radio stations that play all the songs you wish you've never heard of.

"I can't hear anything," Callum said, his voice low.

"I can *smell* something."

We looked at each other, then he shrugged. "There's no point waiting out here. And wouldn't Pru have come to find us if there was a problem?"

Unless she was in the process of fighting with the problem, I thought but didn't say. Instead I just said, "Fine. But you can go first."

"I'd expect nothing less."

He opened the door cautiously, and I crept up to hover behind him as we both peered through the gap. The little reception area was empty. No one waiting in the chairs, no terrifying receptionist glaring at us over her glasses and demanding to know what we were doing in her file room. Not that I could actually remember if the receptionist had been wearing glasses the first (and only) time I'd come in here, but I did remember that she'd been terrifying, and seemed like she *should* be wearing glasses she could peer over. The reception desk was empty, and the magazines on the waiting room table were lined up so neatly they looked as if someone had used a ruler to do it.

Callum straightened up and pushed the door wide,

leading the way into the room slowly. I followed, my nostrils full of the strange scent I'd found in the back room. I still couldn't place it. It wasn't human, I knew that. And nothing that belonged completely to their world, either. It had a rank, feral flavour to it, and the hair on my spine was lifting.

"Check the back?" Callum suggested, and I shrugged.

"May as well." We crossed to the door that led to the dentist's treatment rooms, and Callum eased it open with the same caution as before. The short hall was empty, but the unfamiliar scent was thicker back here, stronger. Expensive cologne, not the cheap stuff from the back room, and something strange and musky.

Callum pushed open the first door onto an empty treatment room smelling of leftover curry but not much else. He peered inside while I hurried to the next door, my heart going too fast and my breath too quick. The scent felt like it was seeping under my skin, demanding attention, and I almost fancied I could feel it lining my throat, slick and greasy as old bacon.

The door was ajar, and as I nudged it open there was a flash of movement beyond. I jumped sideways into the room, back arching and tail pouffing out, and found myself nose to nose with Tam. Her teeth were bared and her own fur was standing up at all angles, making her easily twice my size. I squawked and scooted back the other way, fetching up against something warm and skittering away from it before I realised it was Pru. She hissed and backed away, her eyes wide and her pupils enormous, and the three of us stared at each other, all breathing a little too hard and with our spines high. Then the door swung wide, hitting me, and I spat at it as I went sideways into Pru, who hit me with one outstretched paw, before we both stumbled into Tam, who made the sort of noise that would've put a mountain lion to shame.

"Jesus," Callum said, looking down at us. "Are you alright? What happened?"

"Can't you smell it?" Pru asked, her voice shaky.

Callum made a slightly helpless gesture. "Not personally."

Pru turned her wide gaze on me. "You can, though."

"What is it?" I asked. "I don't recognise it, but it's ... it's not right." *It makes me want to run,* is what I wanted to say. *It makes me want to run until my legs won't work, or hide in the smallest, tightest space I can find, or curl into the tiniest ball and just pretend I don't exist, because I won't if the owner of that scent finds me.* But I could see that I didn't have to say it. Not to either of them. Just the way you don't have to have previous experience with a goblin war party to know that the marching, singing, blood-smeared mass of fighters waving axes and severed heads are best avoided, I didn't have to have smelled this before to know I wanted nothing to do with it.

Pru started to say something, then shook her head. "I don't know, exactly," she said. "But it's not ... even the necromancers didn't smell this bad."

"There's nothing here now," Callum said. "It's safe."

"Not with that stink," I said, and Pru huffed agreement.

"Weres," Tam said, her voice a low rumble that lit the edges of the room, and suddenly that strange, unfamiliar scent fell into some instinctive recognition.

"Hairballs," I said, something closing down the back of

my throat and making the word a gasp. "Oh, stinking werewolf hairballs with bells on."

Callum stared at us, then said, "This seems bad."

"No baby goats."

And for once Callum didn't try to tell me I actually meant *no kidding,* which just shows that even humans know how serious weres are.

WE DIDN'T WASTE a lot of time checking the dentist's rooms after that. It was clear no one was about. Surprisingly, there were no gnawed femurs piled in the corners, or blood splattered liberally across the walls, or territory-marking puddles. The place didn't even look as though it had been turned over, despite the stink. The desk in the corner of the room was covered with drifts of paper, but I remembered that from last time. Walker evidently wasn't the organisational type. There were various horrifying-looking implements lined up on a tray in the corner that I didn't like the look of, but Callum assured me they were just dentist tools and not devices for extracting information from people.

"Where is he, then?" I asked. "And shouldn't he have victims or whatever?"

"Clients," Callum said.

"Sure, clients. Don't see you rushing to book an appointment."

Callum ran his tongue over his teeth without answering, then said, "The receptionist isn't here, either. But she answered the phone just before."

"Probably working remotely. I would, if I had to work for him."

Tam had vanished out the door to follow her own mysterious leads, but Pru was pawing through the papery debris spread across the desk, and now she looked at us with narrowed eyes. "Are either of you going to do anything useful, or just stand there yammering?"

"We're not *yammering,*" I said. "We're discussing the situation."

"Can you discuss it while looking for any clues to where Ms Jones might be?"

"Something's really wrong here," Callum said. He pulled out his phone to check the time. "It's early afternoon on a Friday, and there's no one around. Dentists are always booked. Always."

"Not by you," I said.

He looked at me for a moment, then said, "Shall we discuss the fact that your breath smells like dead things?"

"I'm an obligate carnivore. It'd be weird if my breath *didn't* smell like dead things."

"Old Ones save us," Pru said. "*Do* something, would you?"

"I wouldn't pray to Old Ones," I said. "Not after meeting one. It didn't seem very helpful." But I jumped onto the desk and prowled through the drifting Post-its and scattered business cards, my nose full of the hairy stink of the werewolf. The expensive cologne it had layered over the top really didn't help at all.

THE DESK DIDN'T REVEAL MUCH. If the dentist had a diary, it wasn't here, and given the amount of Post-its with things like *Mrs Davis root canal,* or *Ms Patel polish & clean* written neatly on them, I had doubts there was one at all. Or maybe he was all electronic about such things, in which case we needed to get into the computer. Callum had obviously had the same idea, as he was entering passwords on the home screen, long fingers quick on the keyboard.

"Try *magic hack,*" I suggested, and he looked at me.

"Really?"

"*Tooth hack?*"

"He might be a very good dentist, for all we know."

"Sure. That's why he's working out of an old drycleaners'."

"We can't talk. We don't even *have* an office." He went back to trying password combinations.

"We do. It's merely good economic sense to combine it with our home, since we spend so little time there anyway."

Pru looked up at us, shaking a pink Post-it off one knobbly paw. "There's nothing here. Shouldn't we go before anyone gets back?"

She said *anyone,* but I heard *any weres,* and judging by the size of her pupils it was what she actually meant anyway.

Callum started to say something, probably about *gathering evidence* or *examining the scene,* since he'd found a bulk lot of police-type books the library had been getting rid of and that was all he'd been reading recently. Then he looked at the size of my tail and Pru's eyes, and nodded.

"I've used up the password attempts anyway. We'll take a quick look in reception, then we can try his house."

I wasn't sure I agreed with that idea, but I did agree on getting out of here. I was already heading past him into the hall, Pru prowling next to me.

So we all heard it very clearly. The door chime going as someone walked in.

Callum waved us back and hurried down the hall to the reception area, pulling the door mostly closed behind him. I looked at Pru, and she shrugged, her ears pricked forward. We padded to the door and peered around it, spotting Callum standing in the middle of the floor with his hands raised placatingly. I could hear his dimples from here.

"We just came by to make an appointment, and there was no one around," he said. "I'm really sorry – I didn't mean to scare you."

"You didn't *scare* me," a woman said. "How did you get in? It was locked!"

I eased a little further out of the door, getting a better angle. It was the receptionist, her hair still pulled back so tightly that I half-expected there would be a *ping* as one strand broke and her whole face collapsed forward. One hand was braced on her hip, a little brown takeaway bag clutched in it, and she had a travel mug printed with pink flamingos in the other hand. No glasses, though, so I'd got that wrong.

"Sorry," Callum said again, and I knew he'd be giving her the full force of that dimpled smile that always seemed to render him harmless and charming in the eyes of a certain portion of the population.

"I'll get the appointment book," she said, crossing to the desk and setting her lunch down. "Have you been here before?"

"No, first time," Callum said, glancing around at us as he followed her. He twitched his head – *go on, get out* – and Pru and I looked at each other.

"You go," she said softly. "I'll get Tam and we can shift out. One cat's less obvious than three."

"Fair enough." I stayed where I was as she slipped away, watching the receptionist with my ears pricked and waiting for my chance. She seemed like an irritatingly observant sort, so I'd have to be—

My train of thought was cut off by a *surge,* and I had one moment to think, *Oh, hairballs,* before the world vanished.

4

EVERY DAY'S AN ADVENTURE

It was the alley again and not, a roar of darkness rolling around me as if all the lights in the building had snapped shut and a starless night descended. Sounds stopped, the silence plugging my ears until the rattle of my breathing was the only thing I could cling to.

I backed up fast, looking for a wall to put my haunches to, ears back as I strained to see through the darkness. A pressure wave was building, thrumming in my chest, and I turned to run, but I was too late. Something vast and unseen crushed me to the floor, pressing my jaw into the cheap laminate flooring, squeezing the breath from my lungs and tightening brutally around my head like a vicious hand, sending sparks spinning across my vision. Suddenly I was less afraid of being cast into the void than I was of the possibility that the life was going to be wrung out of me right here, in the hall of some discount dentist, with the whiff of antiseptic and were still in my nostrils.

I tried for one last, panicked push against whatever force had me, muscles screaming with effort, eyes squeezed half shut and teeth bared in something that was less snarl than desperate horror. The terrible pressure pushed back, and my body collapsed under it. Some awful wall of lost memories surged up toward me, and I clawed to hold onto consciousness, and in that moment the reek of the surgery faded. It was displaced by a muscular scent that held a memory of violets and salt, lightning on sand dunes, fierce and focused all once. I had the momentary, half-coherent thought that in my next life I was adding dentists to the list of creatures to avoid, and then everything *stopped*.

The nothing that followed was so huge, so all-enveloping, that I couldn't quite comprehend it. I couldn't hear the receptionist or Callum. I couldn't hear traffic on the road outside. Light had crept back, thin and unfocused, painting the hall in shades of ghostly grey, but it wasn't real light. It was the memory of it, perhaps. The door to the reception area had nothing but darkness beyond it, and I couldn't even smell anything other than that whiff of power. No mouthwash, no weres. Not even my own familiar scent. The air was frozen and sterile around me, and I couldn't quite feel the floor beneath me.

I stayed where I was, aware that I was panting too desperately to catch a proper breath, sprawled on my side with every muscle singing like someone had run an electric wire through them. I gagged, swallowed, and pulled my tongue back into my mouth, rolling onto my belly and shaking my head gently. It felt like bits of my brain might fly out of my nose if I wasn't careful.

Everything stayed where it was, though, and so did I. I didn't trust my legs to hold me just yet. I stared around the empty, silent corridor, and when someone spoke, I was less surprised than I might've been, simply because I was using up all my surprise on being alive.

"Took your time, didn't you?" the voice asked.

I craned around and found myself looking at Ms Jones. She was hunkered down in a crouch, her elbows resting on the worn knees of her skinny jeans and her hands hanging loose between them. She was wearing old red Doc Martens, and the smile she gave me was faint and unconvincing.

"Me?" I managed. "Rumour is you've been gone for months."

"Still am," she said, and her grin looked slightly easier as she waved at herself. I blinked, and struggled to my feet, staggering slightly as I did so and putting a little more space between us. She might be smiling, but you never knew with sorcerers. It could be an *I'm going to make cat handwarmers* type smile. I blinked another couple of times, and realised I could faintly see the floor through her boots.

"So that's weird," I said. "You're not actually here?" That seemed promising on the handwarmer front, but I had the unsettling feeling that she'd just plucked the corridor up and moved it somewhere we wouldn't be disturbed. That couldn't be a good thing.

"Neither are you," she said, and pointed at the floor next to me.

I looked around, then skittered sideways and dropped into a half-crouch. There was a black cat with their fur puffed out in an undignified fashion lying on the floor on their side, paws curled and eyes half-open. "Old Ones *take* you! Did you kill me?"

She clicked her tongue like I was disappointing her, even though she was the one carelessly leaving my body lying about on the floor. "*No.* Honestly, Gobbelino. I've known you this long. I'd have killed you by now if I was going to."

"Fair point." I couldn't stop staring at the cat – at myself. The hazards of the PI lifestyle meant I had a couple of bald patches on my tail that were being slow to grow back, and the sucker scars on my shoulder were brutal and raw. Plus my tongue was hanging out. It wasn't my best look, I had to admit.

"Pay attention."

I looked back at her finally, my ghost tail twitching. "What's going on? What is this?"

"A very short window of time." She glanced behind her, but she wasn't looking at the blank grey wall. She was looking at something else, wherever she was. "You have to find Malcolm. Keep him safe."

"Where are you? Are you with Claudia? Is she okay?"

"*Listen.* He's not at home, and I can't find him. You have to, do you understand?"

"Are *you* okay?" She looked okay, in the sense that everything seemed to be attached to the normal places, but there was something deeply unsettling in the way she kept checking behind her, and in the anxious set of her shoulders. She was a *sorcerer.* She was what the rest of us checked over our shoulders *for.*

She fixed me with those odd eyes, dark one moment and light the next, her smile gone. "I'm …" she hesitated, then shook her head. "I don't have time. Find Malcolm. Keep him safe. You do that, and I'll keep you safe from what's coming."

"What? What's coming? Necromancers? The Watch? What?"

"Just find him. His safety means your safety, and you're going to need all the help you can get."

"*Us?* Why?"

She started to say something, then looked behind her again and swore. "No time. And don't trust—" She stopped, still craning over her shoulder.

"Who? Don't trust *who?*" She didn't reply, and I took a hesitant step toward her. "Ms Jones?"

As if my motion had set it off, the sorcerer crumpled. It started at the top of her head, her dark hair collapsing down into her scalp, then her head sprayed outward in a fine silver dust, taking her shoulders with it. The collapse accelerated across her body, hands imploding in soft puffs of glittering powder, legs and arms turning to fine sand that sparkled gently across the floor. I scooted backward, trying not to breathe. I didn't want to know what sort of effect inhaling sorcerer dust would have. My scoot turned into a slide, and I looked down at my paws in time to see them turning to sooty smudges on the floor.

"Gods dammit," I managed, just before everything went black.

I WOKE to the blare of a bus horn outside, a puddle of drool under my jaw and my tongue stuck to the floor. I spluttered, hauling my head up and rolling onto my belly. Everything felt unsteady, and I stayed lying down for a moment, staring around the hall and making sure I wasn't going to be stepping out of my body again any time soon. Then I staggered to my feet and wobbled toward the door to the reception area, which now had delightfully boring and familiar cold white light washing over the threshold.

I peered around it, shaking my limbs out as well as I could, and spotted the receptionist clicking something on her computer, frowning, as she asked Callum if he preferred a morning or afternoon appointment. I supposed that meant my little side trip to see Ms Jones had either taken a lot less time that I'd thought, or that her *pocket of time* had different rules.

"Is he not here today at all?" Callum asked. "I'd just like to talk to him first. Bad dentist experiences, you know."

She gave him a severe look. "He's not. And he's a very good dentist, so don't worry."

"When'll he be back?"

She hesitated, concern twisting the corners of her mouth. "I'm not sure. He must've been called away suddenly."

"Oh?" Callum matched her concern. "How worrying for you. When did that happen?"

"The day before yesterday. He said he had to go out urgently, and now I can't reach him."

"Not at all?"

"He just texted to say he was taking some personal days, and wouldn't be on his phone." She straightened her shoulders, forcing a smile. "But he'll be back very soon, I'm sure. Let me take your details, Mr …?"

I'd pushed myself into a full-body stretch, spine cracking, trying to feel like I was inhabiting my body again, but my balance was still a bit off. I stumbled into the door and it swung wide, and the receptionist turned around, smiling. She must've expected Walker to be bustling through in all his dentist glory, but her gaze fell on me and her eyebrows shot up. I was surprised they had anywhere to go, given that her hair looked as if it should have already pulled them as high as was physically possible.

"What is *that?*" she demanded, pointing at me with one imperious finger.

Callum looked at me. "Emotional support animal?" he suggested, and clicked his fingers. I narrowed my eyes, but ambled over to stand by his legs, trying to look more emotionally supportive and less like I'd just had an out-of-body experience.

"A *cat?*"

"I live in an apartment. No room for a dog."

"I've never heard anything so ridiculous."

I lifted my lip to show her a fang, but she just scowled at me, unimpressed.

"I've got a permit," Callum said, flashing his dimples and digging in his pocket as if he actually had something to show her.

"It's a *dental surgery,*" she snapped. "I don't care what permit you think you've got. It's unhygienic."

I spent a moment wondering whether to keep working on the supportive look or to try for an endearing one, then just gave up and edged toward the back door, my legs feeling rather more like they belonged to me again.

Pru and Tam should be out already, so all we had to do was outrun one tightly wound receptionist.

"Get it out," she said to Callum.

It? I bared my teeth at her properly, but she ignored me.

"*Out,*" she repeated. "Filthy thing!"

I hissed. No matter how much fancy talc she'd smothered herself in, it was no comparison to the amount of time *I* spent on personal grooming.

"I'm really sorry," Callum said, still holding on to the dimples. "We'll go."

"I should *think* so," she said, her face twisted in distaste. She glared at me as if she were about to hiss herself, then frowned and examined Callum more closely. "I remember you," she said suddenly. "You were here last year – that *cat* was here last year!"

"No, it's my first visit," Callum said, which was true enough. I'd been the one sneaking into the dentist's office in search of the book of power he'd stolen from the sorcerer. It hadn't gone entirely to plan. There had been an altercation, a chase, and I'd almost been smothered in the bosom of a well-meaning bystander before making my escape.

"It *was* you," the woman said. "That cat was in the treatment rooms! It caused a huge amount of damage!"

I had not. Or I might have, but I'd also knocked a suction thingy to the ground to save a patient from asphyxiating, which one would think would more than make up for it.

Callum spread his hands. "I've honestly never been in here before."

"That *thing* has." She glared at him, almost as fiercely as I was glaring at her. "I'm calling the police."

"That's not necessary," Callum said. "We're leaving." He took a step toward the front door, and she leaped in front of him, flinging her arms wide like an opera singer about to break into song.

"You're not going anywhere!"

Callum and I looked at each other, and I jerked my head at the back door instead. Enough pretending innocence about what we were doing or how we got in. We had to go.

"Stay right there," the receptionist said, shaking a finger at Callum. "Don't you move!"

"You've mistaken me for someone else," he said.

The receptionist held a hand out to him in a firm *stop* gesture, and leaned over the desk to grab the phone from its cradle.

Callum took a step backward, and the receptionist shouted, *"Stop!"*

Callum shook his head. "I haven't done anything."

"Then you can just stay right here and let the police sort it out." She darted to the front door and turned the lock, saying "Police, urgent," into the phone as she did.

I scooted for the back door, and Callum turned to head after me.

"I said *stop!*" the receptionist yelled, and Callum gave a startled exclamation.

I spun around to see she'd grabbed the back of his jacket, jerking him to a halt with astonishing ferocity. I could faintly hear the operator shouting something on the other end of the phone as she dropped it and it clattered to the floor. Callum twisted away, trying to pull himself out of the woman's grip, but she grabbed his arm and did something fancy, and the next minute he folded to his knees with a strangled yelp that was part pain, part astonishment.

I stared at the woman. She had the same serious look on her face that I imagined her using to deal with clients who hadn't paid their bills on time, and not a single tightly drawn hair had popped out of place. She twisted Callum's arm even further behind his back, forcing his body down over his knees.

"Stop it!" he managed. "I haven't *done* anything!"

"We'll let the police decide that," she said, trying to hook the phone toward her with her foot.

I looked at my paws. Old gods, creatures from other dimensions, zombies, even bloody unicorns – we'd faced them all. And now Callum was being held prisoner by a woman in sensible shoes and tasteful pearl earrings.

And I was going to have to bite her.

Which I did. I attacked from the side, growling and hissing and giving her plenty of warning, and she stuck one hand out and slapped me sideways across the floor so hard that I rolled twice before I found my feet. I swallowed the things I wanted to say about her ancestry and sprinted back, teeth bared and ears flat, and she shouted, "I will *not* tolerate this!" as if she were the one that had just been thrown across a dentist's waiting room.

"Gobs, *stop,*" Callum shouted, trying to twist out of the receptionist's grip, and she turned her attention back to him, leaning all her weight on his back and hauling harder on his arm so that he swore and stopped struggling.

Green Snake chose that moment to emerge from Callum's pocket and hiss at the woman, who promptly grabbed him and threw him across the room with as much fury as she'd thrown me.

"More animals!" she shrieked. "This is a respectable establishment!"

I batted Green Snake out of the air as he sailed past me, then flung myself at the woman again. I was ready for her to hit me this time, and I folded around her arm, latching onto it with my front paws and teeth and raking with my back legs. She said something that you don't expect to hear from well-groomed women in sensible shoes, and tried to shake me off, still not letting go of Callum.

"This thing's rabid!" she shrieked. "Call it off!"

"Let me go," Callum countered.

"*No.*" She wedged a knee into his back and scrabbled for the phone with her free arm, even though I was still hanging from it. I kicked harder, and she told me some fairly unpleasant things that she intended to do to me, then managed to snag the phone. She punched the speaker button. "Hello?" she shouted. "Are you still there? He's set a wild animal on me!"

"A *cat,*" Callum shouted, muffled by his twisted position. "It's a cat!"

"A unit's on its way," the disembodied voice on the phone said. "Are you safe? Are they threatening you?"

"*She's* threatening *me!*" Callum yelled.

"His animal's attacking me!"

"She's breaking my arm!"

"Alright, I need everyone to calm down," Phone Person

said, and I let go of the receptionist's arm and launched myself at the phone, tearing it away from under her fingers and mashing on the buttons with both front paws until it went dead.

"You *monster,*" the receptionist hissed, and I was on the verge of talking just because I was tired of being called a thing when her gaze shifted to the door behind me. "There's *more?*" she demanded, and I looked over my shoulder. Tam and Pru stood in the door to the little hallway, Tam with a green Post-it still stuck to her shoulder, staring at us. Pru looked at the ceiling, and Tam started growling, the sound a reverberating shudder.

"You can't scare me," the receptionist said. "You're just *cats.*"

Tam sank on her haunches and took a deliberate step forward.

"No," the woman said. "*Stay!*"

Tam showed her teeth, and at that moment the door to the back room opened. We all turned to look at it, startled, and SharkDog shoved her heavy head into the room, rolling her five eyes and panting toothily.

"That is *enough!*" the receptionist shouted. "This isn't a *zoo!*"

Tam made a scoffing noise, but apparently SharkDog was even more offended by the suggestion that she belonged in a menagerie, as she bounded into the room and charged for Callum and the receptionist with her snaky tail waving and her spines gleaming in the fluorescent lighting.

"*Sit!*" Callum yelled. "Stay! Good dog!"

SharkDog ignored that entirely and threw herself at

the two humans, sending them both sprawling to the floor. The receptionist was still clinging to Callum's arm and shrieking for the police, but when the dog planted two heavy paws on her shoulders and started licking her face enthusiastically, her shriek became a scream.

"No! *Nooo!* Oh, you horrible creature! Oh—" She was cut off by another slobbery attack, and Callum rolled away from her and onto his feet as she turned her attention to fending off the dog.

"Go, go!" he snapped at us, snatching up Green Snake. We'd been watching the dog with enormous interest, but now we spun and sprinted for the back door, Callum right on our tails. SharkDog gave a happy *whuff,* abandoned the receptionist, and bolted in pursuit.

The receptionist was as alarmingly fast as she'd been handy with an armlock, and she charged out of the building right behind us, waving a furled umbrella above her head. Tam swerved back toward her, ears pricked, and the rest of us kept running.

"Stop!" the receptionist shouted, then squawked as she tripped over Tam.

One of the car's back doors hung open, and SharkDog, showing unexpected evidence of brain cells, jumped in, her snaky tail grabbing the door and slamming it shut behind her. Callum wrenched the driver's door open and piled in, scrabbling with the keys while Pru and I leaped over him to the passenger seat. The engine roared into life just as the receptionist disentangled herself from Tam and raced toward us. She grabbed the driver's door handle and hauled it open again, but Callum was already shoving the car into reverse. He backed away fast, ripping the handle out of her hands while the dog barked hysterically and the receptionist shouted, then he slammed the brakes on. Tam leaped through the open door as he shoved the car into gear, the door swung shut under its own momentum, the engine revved wildly, and we pulled onto the road in the path of a delivery van that laid on its brakes and horn in equal measure. The receptionist snatched up her umbrella and hurled it after us, and as we made our clattering escape, I could see her through the back window stomping her feet and waving her fists about, her face pink. Her hair was still very neat, though.

We rattled down the road for a couple of blocks, the car belching alarmed exhaust smoke in protest at the rough treatment, and eventually Pru said, "That went well, then."

"About normal," Callum said, easing the car back to a more sedate pace.

"I suspected as much."

"Welcome to G and C London, Private Investigators," I said. "Every day's an adventure."

Tam snorted. "*Adventure.*"

Which I decided to take as a compliment.

5

LET THE WERE HUNT BEGIN

"Everyone alright?" Callum asked.

"Relatively speaking," I said. My hackles still hadn't entirely settled down.

Callum glanced at me, frowning. "What's up?"

I considered it. *Don't trust* … who? Presumably Ms Jones didn't mean Walker, since she wanted us to protect him. If she meant Callum, well, too bad. But might she mean Tam? Pru? Ridiculous five-eyed dogs?

"Gobs?" Callum said. "You okay?"

"I need custard," I announced. "That dog ate my breakfast."

"You had breakfast."

"Then she ate my lunch."

"There are more important things going on here than your belly," Pru said.

"Few things are more important than my belly."

"Weres?" Pru suggested. "How about them?"

I huffed.

"Yeah, what about weres?" Callum asked. "Sounds like

Walker's been gone for two days. The receptionist can't get hold of him."

"That must've been right after we talked to him," Pru said. "We didn't smell weres when we were there."

"So we're not far behind. That's good."

Pru wrinkled her snout. "Is it? We're after Ms Jones and Claudia, not a dentist. We should look at your magician again."

Callum *hmm*-ed. "We can't just not do anything about Malcolm. We need to make sure he's okay."

Pru sighed. "Maybe it was unrelated. Just a routine visit. Polishing their canines or something."

Callum took his cigarettes from the doorless glovebox and shook one out, dislodging Green Snake from the packet. Green Snake hissed at him. "I doubt it. Weres stick more with humans or other weres rather than Folk. I can't see them dealing with a dentist who's partners with a sorcerer." He pawed around in the glovebox, looking for his lighter. "Stop it, you."

Green Snake had wrapped himself around the lighter, and kept trying to bite Callum's fingers. Callum gave up and hunted in his jacket instead, coming up with a different lighter. He gave a grunt of satisfaction, lit the cigarette, and fell back in his seat as we eased to a stop at a red light. A man in a flashy Audi next to us gave our car a horrified look, then noticed the three cats on the front seat and the dog on the back, and stared. I bared my teeth at him, and he looked away.

"We do need to find him," I said. "He's still our best lead."

Pru gave me a puzzled look. "Ifan was the last to see

Ms Jones, and you said his dad imprisoned her in the walls of his house. That seems like a decent lead."

"I know, but Walker's her human." It didn't sound like such a convincing argument even to my ears, so I looked at Callum. He was scrolling through his phone, and now he hit dial. We all heard it ring a few times then go through to messages.

"You've reached Doctor Malcolm Walker. For appointments please call—"

"Doctor," I said. "That's about as good as him calling himself a sorcerer's apprentice or whatever he reckons he is."

Callum hit disconnect and tried another number. It went straight to messages. "Still nothing on Ms Jones, either."

"So now can we get lunch?" I asked, and Pru growled.

Callum tapped his fingers on the wheel. "Could you tell anything about what happened in the surgery? From the scents, I mean. Did he go with them?"

"We're not *dogs,"* I said, and we all looked at SharkDog. She whined, her tail twisting anxiously.

"So you couldn't sniff anything out?" Callum asked, and I looked at Pru. Much as we hate to admit it, tracking's possible. Cats don't like to let on that we can do it, and it's a fickle art that uses other senses than our nose, but it's possible. You need the Inbetween for it, though, so I was out.

Pru sniffed. "There was too much interference from the weres to pick anything else out. And no point trying to track *them*. They know how to hide themselves. It's pretty much second nature when you're the Watch's public enemy number one." She looked at me. "Second nature for most people, anyway."

"It's a very unfair vendetta they've got."

"Weres probably think the same thing. What did you *do* in your past lives?"

I shrugged. "No idea. Don't remember."

Pru blinked at me. "What, at all?"

"No, of course not."

Tam and Pru looked at each other, then Pru said, "You must. Everyone does."

I scratched my jaw with a back paw. "I don't, okay? Very traumatic deaths." My stomach was doing nasty, twisting things, and I could feel the cold at my back again. "We were talking about weres, anyway. It kind of seems like they took him, or at least scared him out of his surgery. But why? Bad root canal? What?"

"Bait?" Callum suggested. "Drawing out Ms Jones?"

"Why would weres do that?"

Callum flicked ash into an old takeaway mug wedged between the seats. "Weres'll do a lot if the price is right."

Pru was still watching me, but she just said, "So who's paying them?"

Callum flicked the indicator and moved us over into another lane, the sky low and grey above us, threatening more snow to come. Taillights painted red exclamations ahead of us, and the shops spilled warm yellow glows over the pavements. It felt like it should be early evening already.

"Not even a sorcerer would walk into a were pack just because of a dentist," I said finally. "You'd have to be three fleas short of a worm bath to try that."

"Maybe Walker's working *with* the weres," Pru suggested.

We all looked at her, and Callum said, "What?"

"Maybe he's looking for Ms Jones too, and is using them to do it."

"Or he's using them for something else," I said. "Don't forget that mangy parsnip stole her book of power and keeps trying to pretend he's some sort of sorcerer in training." Which would explain why she couldn't find him. He was actively hiding from her.

Callum frowned. "I think Pru's idea is more likely. I mean, never mind that he was so worried about Ms Jones that he agreed to help us with the necromancers, but, as you keep pointing out, he's a dentist."

"A dentist who stole her book of power, and who hasn't been in contact even though she's stayed missing *since* the necromancers. Maybe the weres are to ensure she doesn't come back at all. Or he's preparing for when she does."

"They seemed to be getting on fine after the whole book incident," Callum said.

"I still fail to see what an ancient, terrifying sorcerer is doing slumming it with a cut-rate dentist."

"She likes him."

I wrinkled my snout. "She must still be a bit too human. You lot have terrible judgement."

"Yes," Callum agreed. "Look at the company I keep."

Pru, Tam, Green Snake and I all glared at him, and SharkDog whined from the back seat. Callum just grinned and blew smoke through the gap in the window.

"We have to find Walker," I said.

"*Why?*" Pru demanded. "Why are you so keen on finding the bloody dentist? It's Claudia we need."

"And your best lead for her is Ms Jones, and our best lead for *her* is Walker."

"Which means weres," Callum put in. He was still driving, wending our way through the veins of the city. The cars had their headlights on as they whisked around us, the gritted roads dark with slush. "And that means Dimly."

"Are you sure?" I asked him. "Do we really want to go there?"

"No. But it's the fastest way to find weres."

Pru sighed. "Your investigative technique is very eccentric."

"Yet effective," I said.

She gave me a look that might've indicated she disagreed.

"This tastes weird," Callum said, examining his cigarette.

"Well, they're not meant to taste nice," I pointed out. Green Snake lifted his head out of the glovebox and tilted his head at me. I lifted my chin at him. I didn't really want to know what he'd done to the cigarettes. "You should just quit."

"The last time I tried to quit, someone opened a portal to another dimension, and I got possessed by an ancient god."

"Pretty sure those events were unrelated."

He shrugged. "It's just not worth the risk, if you ask me."

Pru sighed. "I'm not sure why we came to you for help, really. You have no focus when it comes to the job at hand."

"We do," I protested. "We even have a plan. We're going to Dimly."

"Isn't Dimly where you got into some mess with unicorns last summer?" Pru asked.

"Unicorns, a river god, and Komodo dragons, among others," I said, then hesitated. "Last time we saw Claudia was there, too."

Tam looked at me, her eyes narrowed, and I stared back at her. I *wanted* to tell them about Ms Jones. Or I thought I did. Pru, anyway. But Tam gave nothing away. She could've been some sort of Watch supreme leader, for all I knew. Although I'd have expected better grooming, if that were the case.

I looked away first, and turned my attention back to Callum. "Sure you want to hit up Dimly? Last time we were there your sister tried to kill you."

"It was just business." He slowed as we caught up to a small car pulling a far too large caravan, toiling optimistically along the slushy road. "Besides, I've been back since."

"You haven't. When?"

He gave me an amused look. "You sleep a lot."

"You don't sleep enough."

He shrugged. I was right, though. His sleep was short and fractured, and you could see it in the shadows under his eyes and the lines that bit into his cheeks sometimes. Not that my sleep was all that much better, but what one lacks in quality one must make up in quantity.

"Why were you in Dimly?" I asked. Dimly was a pocket town, one of those strange little places where magic still existed, and Folk could walk the streets without hiding their *other*ness. Pocket towns were old and rare, and too often crushed and scattered under the advance of human cities. Those that survived were mostly in more remote stretches of the country, at the end of potholed roads where street signs vanished and tourists gave up and went in search of more authentic and less potentially farmer-with-shotgun related experiences. Some pockets did still persist in towns and cities, though. They were on the streets humans didn't turn down, at the ends of alleys no one even remembered seeing. Magic has its ways of protecting its own, and Dimly had been old before Leeds even came into being. Its defences had deep, savage teeth.

"Round Dimly, really. Not so much in. Visiting Gerry." Gerry was the current mayor, a troll with a penchant for a nice summer dress and a good cream cake.

"So will he know about weres?" Pru asked. "Or Claudia?"

"He will," Callum said, and offered her his hand. She sniffed his fingers, then let him scratch the back of her head. "We're on it, Pru. Really."

She looked at him with pale eyes, and I could see the tension strung under her bare skin. She should be home in front of the fire, sitting on a fluffy blanket while her human fed her the sort of treats I'd never even stolen, let alone been able to come by legitimately. She was the sort of cat that should never need to so much as think about the Watch, because her path should never cross theirs. She was *safe.* But instead she sat here in our shuddering car, nestled next to Tam for warmth, with were stink on her paws and the scars of the necromancers' dog on her flanks. I still hadn't worked out quite why, and now Ms Jones' warning scratched at me, an irritant in my fur. *Don't trust* ... someone.

"I'm filled with confidence," Pru said to Callum, and he snorted.

"Of course you are," I told her. "We're professionals." I turned my attention to Callum. "Does Dimly really allow weres? I never heard of any."

"They're allowed," Callum said. "But most don't choose to live there. There's the prejudice for a start—"

"What, because they have a tendency to turn into ravening monsters?"

"Because people say things like that, yes. But also the bylaws are pretty restrictive. It used to be that they had to wear silver ankle cuffs all the time, to stop any unexpected transformations."

I wrinkled my nose. Ravening monsters they might be, but the silver didn't just stop the transformations. It'd also cause massive allergic reactions of the sort that make your hair fall out and your eyeballs ache. "That's harsh. Even the Watch didn't try that one." Probably only because they couldn't figure out how to force weres into bracelets, though. It was easier just to drop the creatures straight into the Inbetween, where the monsters could gnaw on their bones. The Watch was fond of doing things like that, and as only cats, gargoyles, and faeries can shift at will, it was a handy way to get rid of problems.

"Which is why most of them stay clear of pockets, and particularly Dimly. But Gerry'll have heard something, or at least know where we can start looking. Or someone will. Dimly always had use of weres."

Meaning his dodgy family always had use of them, I guessed. That didn't surprise me. I hadn't known much about Callum's past until the last year, when it had started encroaching on our lives. His family – the Norths – had run Dimly for years, some Yorkshire criminal dynasty that traded in everything from imported American breakfast cereals and spectacularly off-brand cigarettes to Atlantean curses and the sort of weapons that need hermetically sealed cases just so you can survive being in the same room as them. Not to mention a pretty hefty line in illicit substances that Callum had been a bit too keen on sampling in the years before we'd met.

I still found it strange that Callum had once been part of the sort of family that smart people crossed the street to avoid. He gives off the air of being about as *other* as a cabbage, and for a long time I'd believed it, even though there was always a scent to him that just didn't sit right. Something wild and strange and hidden. But I didn't ask about the things he chose to hide, any more than he asked me about the times I woke pressed into a corner of the room, scratching and hissing at something that wasn't there. Some things are ours alone.

"Can we re-home the dog while we're there?" I asked. "It's starting to stink in here."

"I knew you shouldn't have had sausages for breakfast," Callum said, and Pru snorted.

"Rude," I muttered, but my heart was only half in it.

Mostly I was thinking about weres, and the strange streets of Dimly, and missing sorcerers.

And the constant threat of the void, leaning over my shoulder and whispering promises and threats.

DIMLY WAS on the edge of Leeds, hidden down a tangle of streets that started out stolidly suburban, all semi-detached bungalows standing in gardens that ranged from unkempt to derelict, strewn with old cars lurching on three wheels, washing machines with missing doors, and, for reasons that always escape me, abandoned shoes. They're ubiquitous in places like this, like some sort of urban tumbleweeds.

The bungalows gave way to blocks of grey, stained flats rubbing shoulders with hard looking warehouses, all red brick and broken windows, and abandoned loading yards with chain-link fences padlocked against the world. Regeneration hadn't come to this part of Leeds, and it was unlikely to. It probably barely showed up on the maps in town planning offices, partly due to the influence of Dimly seeping into the human world and protecting its boundaries, and partly due to the way some parts of town get hit with a *too hard* label. Some places are simply forgotten. It's like the area under the fridge where all the debris of life ends up, uncared for and unthought of.

And it's the perfect place for a pocket town to loiter.

You feel a pocket town before you see it. If you're human, your eye slides away from the street you were trying to look at, and you can't for the life of you imagine *why* you wanted to look at it in the first place. You're also filled with a burning desire to be *elsewhere,* even if the burned-out shell of a car crouching outside a graffitied, metal-shuttered off-licence wasn't enough to make the little, primeval mammal still living in the back of your mind sit up and scream. And if you're not human, your hackles rise and your ears get twitchy, and even though you know it's just the charms guarding the town, you put some serious thought in as to just how much you want to walk through them.

Pocket towns are serious about protecting themselves.

Callum slowed as we drove over the border, all of us shifting uneasily in our seats, and the dog gave a mournful little howl. There was nothing visible to mark the change, but we could feel it. Magic lifted the hair on my spine and made my paws itch, and Pru sneezed twice. And then we were driving down the same streets as we had outside, only instead of broken washing machines and abandoned shoes the gardens were decorated with shattered altars and the crumbling remains of effigies.

I mean, *some* of them were. Some of them were so sweet and tidy and twee that you expected bluebirds to flit around the softly smoking chimneys, and bunnies to prance across the lavish, curiously un-wintry flowerbeds, while red gingham curtains framed unnecessary amounts of baked goods resting on windowsills to cool. The waft of power coming off those houses was much nastier.

We didn't linger for either the gingerbread houses or the rather more familiar ones. Instead, we headed straight into the heart of Dimly. The streets were quiet and grey, festive lights still showing in windows here and there, and the few people on the pavements were bundled heavily against the cold. We didn't pass more than a couple of cars, and there were plenty of parking spaces when we pulled into the town square and parked next to the faded green of a compact park that ran down to the river. It was cold and innocuous looking, but just last summer I'd been attacked in it by two elderly booksellers. They'd first imprisoned me in words, then, in a rather undignified manner, inside a wicker basket. I cast a baleful glance at the bookshop sitting on one corner of the square, carts of books flanking the door.

"We're not asking in *there,*" I said.

"No," Callum agreed. "We'll go straight to Gerry. Hanging around Dimly isn't good for anyone's health." He swung out of the car, pulling his tatty old coat tightly around himself and scanning the quiet square as if waiting for someone to jump him. I didn't feel much different. Along with the booksellers, there had been sewer monsters, Komodo dragons, and coconut crabs, plus some crows who took the collective term *murder* a little too seriously. And that was before his sister – well, technically, one of his sister's friends – tried to kill us.

I jumped out of the driver's side door, looking up at him. "Reckon he's at the pool?" Last time we'd seen Gerry, he'd been dressed in a rather fetching ruffled swimsuit and matching cap.

Callum shrugged. "Probably not at this time of year. We'll try the old town hall. He should be about today."

Pru and Tam followed me out, Pru sniffing the air with her ears back and Tam giving the place the belligerent look of the local hardman walking into an unfamiliar pub.

"Nice spot," Pru said. "Atmospheric."

The clouds had thinned out a little, but everything still felt damp and bone-achingly cold, and the light painted Dimly in stark edges and muted colour. The stone buildings that lined the square were a mix of old stone and roughly whitewashed render, damp and cold and stained in places, the windows small and dark. Grit and old snow were pushed against the kerbs, and a little reluctant sun had crept out. It cast our shadows winter-long and deep to our sides, the only things that felt certain. Someone slammed a window closed, and my tail twitched. Tam growled softly. SharkDog let herself out of the back of the car and scooted over to Callum, wrapping her tail around his leg and whining. He patted her on the head. "I know someone who'll look after you."

"Silver linings and all that," I said. "Let's go, then."

Callum shut the car door and locked it, then we headed off into the depths of Dimly, feeling exposed in the empty square. I could feel eyes on us, people watching from windows and sharper eyes peering from the rooftops, all marking the strangers in their midst. The *cats* in their midst.

"Doesn't feel much like last summer," I said.

"No," Callum said, and then we fell silent. Pocket towns have more ears than human ones, and they listen more closely. We couldn't pass unnoticed here.

"Welcome to Dimly," I said to Pru, and she huffed, her bare flanks as cold and grey as the streets.

6

ALL THINGS TEND TO CHAOS

I COULDN'T SEE ANYONE ACTUALLY WATCHING US AS WE crossed the square, despite the itchy feeling on my spine. A couple of kids stuffed into snowsuits were scrambling up the frames in the playground, looking like brightly hued pandas, and the parents watching them never seemed to glance in our direction. They were both on their phones. "Callum—"

"I know," he said, and kept walking. "We were never going to get in unnoticed."

"Should we even be here?"

"Do you have any better ideas?"

Not being here would be a start, but if this was how we found weres, this was where we had to be, at least until we figured out if Walker really was tangled up with them. His safety was our safety. I checked the sky again.

"At least the damn crows have made themselves scarce."

"That's something," Callum agreed.

It was. Although it wasn't like they were the only citizens of Dimly to get my tail prickling – about the only creatures in this town that didn't were the anarchic rats, and that was only because I suspected that they thought I wasn't worth wasting their anarchy on. But I'd take what I could get at this point. We headed down one of the larger streets leading off the square, leaving the car parked where it was. None of us mentioned the fact that it seemed like a good idea to have it somewhere that gave us a straight shot out of town, but I'd guess we were all thinking it. Except the dog. The dog was just thinking *walkies,* as far as I could tell. She galloped ahead of us to investigate the winter-empty pavements, rushing back to safety behind Callum's legs every time a shop door opened or a person emerged out of a side street.

"She should be on a lead," Pru said. "She'll run off and get lost."

"This is a problem?" I asked.

"It is if we have to waste time finding her."

"She's fine," Callum said, clicking his fingers at the dog. She dropped her chest to the ground on the pavement ahead of us, her tail whipping and her eyes wide and happy. Then a faun in plaid shorts and a leather jacket backed out of a shop proclaiming itself as The Happy Herbivore, the bell jangling behind him. He raised one arm to defend himself from a hefty block of tofu that sailed out after him, and yelled, "This is *terrible* customer service! I'm giving you one star on Yelp!"

A dryad appeared in the doorway with her mossy hair lassoed into a pink headscarf, a shopping basket clutched to her chest. "Carnivore!" she yelled, and threw a cabbage at him.

"It's a *jacket!*" the faun shouted back. "And it's vintage! Reuse and recycle, yeah?"

The dryad hefted an unwashed carrot at him, and it left a splatter of mud on the offending clothing. "Hypocrite!"

"*Me?* You literally *eat* your cousins!"

The dryad put a hand on her hip. "Are you saying I'm a vegetable?"

The faun opened his mouth, shut it, then snatched up the tofu and bolted.

"*Thief!*" the dryad shrieked, and took off after him, her bare arms strong and dark and gnarled with the soft patterns of bark.

The dog ran after her.

"See?" Pru said.

I looked at Callum. "Dude. I hope she doesn't think that dryad's a stick. That's the sort of inter-species conflict you do *not* want kicking off."

Callum swore, and sprinted after the dog. We watched him go, then I looked at Pru and Tam. "Want to see if we can get some local knowledge while we're here?"

Pru shrugged. "May as well. He could be a while."

I wandered along the street a little further, looking for drains. There was one not far from the shop, and I caught the reassuring whiff of rats from it. Not that it meant anyone would be close enough to hear me, of course, but you never know. And given how closely the anarchic rats had monitored things in Dimly before, I was willing to bet the arrival of three cats hadn't gone unnoticed.

"Patsy?" I called. "You about?"

There was no answer, just the echo of my voice drifting into the depths of Dimly. I waited, then added, "I've got ..." I looked around, then added, "A cabbage?"

There was silence for a moment longer, then a small, harsh-edged voice said, "A cabbage."

"I mean, I can probably get something else, but right now, yeah. A whole one, though. And probably organic. Oh, and there's a carrot."

I heard the soft rasp of rat laughter, and a shadow moved under the grating. I stepped back, and the sleek brown form of a rat emerged, squeezing through what looked like an impossibly small gap. She slipped onto the road and sat back on her haunches, regarding me from her one good eye. The other was milky and clouded, and the scar that ran across it lifted her lip in a permanent sneer.

"What more could I expect from you, Mogs?"

"Endless good humour and the occasional rescue from Komodo dragons."

"The Komodos I wouldn't have been anywhere near if not for you?"

"Yeah. Those ones." I stepped down onto the street so that we were eye to eye, not that she seemed bothered by the size difference. Patsy was a true believer in the irrelevance of stature. Most rats are, to be fair, but she elevated it to an art form. "How goes the anarchy?"

She shrugged. "We had a bit of a hiatus there when your troll buddy took over the town. Thought we might be able to retire."

"But?"

"But all things tend to chaos, Mogs." She looked past me at Pru and lifted her chin. "Ay up."

"Morning," Pru said.

I checked on Tam. There are treaties in the Folk world just as there are in the human world, to ensure there isn't all-out war between kinds. But, just as in the human world, they're often open to interpretation, and certain individuals don't always feel they apply. But Tam was emerging from The Happy Herbivore with a wedge of soft, stinky cheese in her jaws. She ambled over to us and set the cheese in front of Patsy.

"Nice," the rat said, and Tam shrugged.

"She's not much of a talker," I said.

"Well, when held to your standard, who is?" Patsy said, and Tam snorted.

I decided to ignore that obvious slur on my sparkling conversational skills and said, "So what's the latest chaos, then?"

Patsy sampled the cheese, her whiskers twitching appreciatively. "Let's just say that the bucolic days of summer didn't last long."

I wondered if the cheese would be enough compensation for me picking the rat up by the scruff of the neck and giving her a little shake. Not to hurt her, just to get her to start talking in actual specifics. But I didn't fancy my chances of emerging from that with my whiskers intact, so I said, "Have things started up again? With the crows patrolling, and rats and cats being kept out of town and so on?"

She *hmm*-ed. "Hard to say if it's the same thing starting up, or just the simple fact that if you create a vacuum, something will fill it. When you remove an old power, you don't know what will take its place. It's not always what you want."

"Hey," a voice said from around my paws. "You sending that cheese down, Pats?"

"Yeah, yeah." She pushed it to the grate, and it was tidied away into the darkness beneath.

"Ernie?" I asked.

A grey, whiskery face appeared and blinked at me myopically. "We thought it was you. We've been following you since you arrived. Seems like a bad sign though – last time you were about, we ended up in a warehouse brawl."

"Good to see you too," I said, and lowered my nose to meet his. I could smell the age on him. Rats don't live long, and Dimly rats would be no exception. Patsy's three-pawed lieutenant had done well to last as long as he had, especially given the other things that lived in Dimly's sewers.

"You here to sort out the pest problem?" Ernie asked.

"What pests are those?"

"Cats," he said, and peered past me at Pru and Tam. "Present company excepted, obviously. None of you look inclined to eat an old rat."

Pru wrinkled her nose at the very idea, and Tam just looked bored.

"Are you saying cats have been *eating* you?" I asked. I knew some cats would happily ignore the treaties where they could get away with it, whether for their own reasons or simply for the horrifying sport of it, but a thinking animal doesn't just *eat* another one. I mean, we're carnivores, but no one wants their dinner to talk back.

"We don't know for certain," Patsy said. "No one's openly attacked us. Life was actually pretty cheery over summer, and I even put the word out for some of the old crews to move back in, that things were looking better. A few came back, but by the end of autumn it was all starting to give at the edges again. Less ice cream vans and swim clubs, more nasty charms and strange packages. Then we started losing rats. Not a lot, just here and there. But too many for it to be accidental, and we never find the bodies. The Watch are everywhere. Them and the bloody crows. A smart rat doesn't leave her sewer."

"Pats, I'm sorry," I said. "I thought it'd be better with Gerry in charge."

She shrugged. "Some things can't be dug out so easily."

"Do you mean the warehouse?" I asked. "Is it still there?" The warehouse had been sunk into the earth below the brutal concrete structure of Dimly's seat of power, a labyrinthine expanse filled with the sort of things that required careful storage but didn't get it. Ghast eggs and bottled storms and the tightly rolled portals to unknown dimensions, all thrown carelessly in together where the damp and the anarchic rats could slowly eat away at their bonds and set them free.

And that was without even mentioning unicorn horn, which shouldn't be stored *anywhere*. When ground to dust it can be used as a drug that turns the user's world – and sometimes the user – inside out, and weapons tempered with it can kill anything. They'll take down a troll, an ogre, probably a damn sea serpent, if you could get it through the scales. And they'll destroy every one of a cat's lives in a single blow, no takebacks. The Watch was meant to have outlawed it, of course, but the little faith I'd had in that organisation was going the way of unicorns themselves. Highly endangered, unpredictably stabby, and pretty flaky.

"It's there," Patsy said. "But the honourable sludge puppy didn't just drown it. She *buried* it. I checked."

"Is there a new one, then? A new stash?" My mouth was dry. All those unicorn horn weapons. All that death. All that *power.* The sludge puppy – more properly known as a river spirit, and also the previous mayor – might have buried it, but there were plenty of creatures who'd go digging in magical soup to reclaim the sort of treasures that had been down there.

"Not like before," Patsy said. "But this is Dimly. Things tend to resurface of their own accord, or are burrowed down to. There are always nasty little summoning charms being worked in cellars and magic-workers dowsing for power. And magical things make their own way, too. Things turn up in the roots of carnivorous plants growing in the reeds, or someone finds a vein of unicorn dust at the edge of the river."

"Hairballs," I said softly. "What about Gerry? Is he still in charge?"

"He's still mayor," Patsy said, which wasn't really an answer.

"Things not going so well there?"

Patsy made a non-committal noise. "Ez hasn't been as easy to contain as Gerry might have hoped."

"You don't say." Ez, Callum's sister, hadn't only taken

on the family business. She'd also been the power behind the mayor until we'd upset the pumpkin cart last year. Gerry had set her up as his community liaison, intending to reform her rather than giving her a more suitable punishment. Like life imprisonment on a rocky island somewhere. Although even then she'd probably have started a business running hallucinogenic seaweed to sprites or something. You couldn't fault her entrepreneurial spirit.

"The Norths are slippery creatures, and she's got plenty of support. More than Gerry. His plans for the town have met some resistance."

"In what way?"

Patsy cocked her head at me, her teeth bared by the twisted scar. "In all the Dimly ways, Mogs. Things go wrong. Sea serpents infesting swimming pools. Basilisks nesting in community centres. Sinkholes in the middle of fundraising fêtes. I'd like the anarchy of it, but it's all going in the wrong direction."

I sighed. "We're on the way to see Gerry. Maybe we can help."

"Really? Think you can push back entropy?"

"It's not on the job description, but not much is," I said. "You'd be surprised."

Tam grunted, and I looked around to see Callum hurrying back along the road, being half-dragged by the dog. He'd taken his belt off to use as a collar again, which meant he had to pull his jeans up every few steps. There was a cigarette hanging out of his mouth, and the dryad had evidently hit him with a tomato from her shopping basket. There were still bits of it stuck to his jacket.

Patsy huffed laughter softly. "Yeah, I reckon I would. Mind how you go, Mogs. And don't expect too much from Gerry. Heavy is the head that wears the crown and all that."

Then she slipped into the grate and was gone. I looked at Pru. "Crown? I thought mayors wore those fancy chains."

Pru blinked at me, then said, "I don't know. Maybe it's a rat thing."

"Or a troll thing. Maybe the chain doesn't fit the aesthetic." I looked up at Callum as he arrived next to us, hitched his jeans up, and took the cigarette out of his mouth. "Alright?"

"Just bloody marvellous," he said, brushing at the tomato stain and managing to smear ash on his coat along with it. "You?"

"The anarchic rats feel the town is falling to entropy."

"Oh, good."

"Chaos is reasserting itself."

"Even better."

"And Tam stole some cheese, so we should probably go. It looked expensive."

Tam growled, and Callum looked at her, then sighed. "And I thought one cat was bad enough."

"I'm not the one collecting green snakes and five-eyed dogs," I pointed out, and the snake in question poked his head out of Callum's pocket to give me what I assumed was an indignant look.

"Can we just go to the town hall already?" Pru said. "Tam and I aren't hanging around for the pleasure of your company, you know."

"That way," Callum said, adjusting his grip on the belt and nodding deeper into town.

"The company's part of it, though, right?" I asked, as we headed into the narrow streets of Dimly.

Pru didn't answer. Tam just huffed and said, "*Mogs,*" so softly that I almost missed it. I narrowed my eyes at her and she looked back at me with her eyebrow whiskers arched.

"I knew it was," I said.

THE OLD TOWN hall was on the edge of a market square, still populated by a few tatty stalls on a Friday afternoon. One was selling pre-packaged charms that would encourage your potatoes to grow faster, or your hair to curl, or not curl, and shift locks to keep cats out, and electronic repellents in bright packaging showing terrified pixies fleeing with their hands over their ears. I was willing to bet they'd work just as well as the charm labelled *The Whiff of Love*. *Work* in the sense that they'd relieve shoppers of their money, and probably bring them out in a nasty rash.

The next stall was all herbs and spices, but not the sort you put in your curry. Not unless you want to run the risk of more side effects than a bit of chilli burn, anyway. Some of them were strapped into hefty glass jars with ratchet-down lids, and the stallholder was just putting on heavy welder's gloves and safety goggles to open one up as we went past. Callum gave the stall an incurious look and kept going. I suppose when you grow up in Dimly, these things are commonplace, the Folk intertwined with the human.

We rounded a final stall, this one the compulsory crappy phone case supplier (although with a few tweaks, such as anti-possession runes on the cases, and a couple with weird toothy surrounds that made me think stealing them would be a bad idea), and found ourselves in front of the long, shallow steps leading up to the town hall doors. It had obviously been modelled on some sort of European hall somewhere, all big windows and colonnades by the doors, and a steep, swooping roof, with the Dimly coat of arms carved in stone above the entrance. It dated from the days when coats of arms were intended to strike fear into your enemies and remind them of your might, so there were a lot of tentacles and dripping teeth going on. Also a hamster, for no reason I could see.

But despite all the fanciness, the hall was also small, like someone had taken the model and scaled it down to fit the space, or the budget, or the level of importance Dimly placed on duly elected leaders. It gave the impression that it was huddling among the blockier, more traditionally English buildings to either side as if hoping to avoid drawing attention to itself. The windows were old-school, with about twenty little panes in each, and the one to the left of the door had three of the panes replaced with cardboard. I could see the name of a popular baked beans brand printed on one of them.

Callum climbed the steps to the doors, which were newly painted a glossy green that didn't quite disguise the fact that the old, sickly yellow paint hadn't been removed properly from underneath, and it was peeling badly.

There was a big brass knocker in the centre of the door, and a round brass handle that looked new as well. No good for paws, I noticed, which seemed inconsiderate. There was no shifting in pocket towns – even if there weren't shift locks on the town itself, it was considered rude to just pop up in people's business. And cats can't get away with such things around Folk the way we can around humans. So having a doorknob we wouldn't be able to open seemed unnecessarily restrictive. We'd have to wait to be let in or out, which is the sort of thing only humans think is acceptable.

Tam was obviously thinking the same thing, because she glared at the door and growled. Callum glanced at her, then shifted his grip on the dog's makeshift leash, tugged his jeans up on his skinny hips, and tried the handle.

It didn't turn. He frowned, and jiggled it a couple of times, as if it might be stuck, but the door was resolutely unmoved.

"That's weird," he said.

"Long lunch?" I suggested. My stomach rumbled, suggesting it supported the idea.

"So they close the whole hall?" He lifted the heavy knocker and slammed it into the wood of the door a few times, setting up an echoing knock inside that spoke of marble floors and high ceilings and dusty, unused spaces.

"No use," someone said behind us. "No one's there."

Callum closed his eyes, not turning from the door, but I spun around with my hackles already rising. She was leaning on the post at the bottom of the stairs, a takeaway coffee cup in each hand, the fickle sun picking out the copper highlights in her brown hair that matched Callum's so exactly.

Callum turned, sighing like he'd finally found the serial killer he'd been expecting in his closet. "Ez."

"Hello little brother," she said, and smiled at him. She had the same dimples, too.

7

A TROLL TEA PARTY

"I BROUGHT YOU A TEA," SHE SAID, RAISING ONE OF THE cups. The cafe logo had a hamster on it, and I was starting to wonder about Dimly's relationship with small fluffy rodents. "You learned to drink coffee yet?"

"Only under duress." He looked under duress now, his back to the door and his eyes wary. "Where's Gerry?"

"Dunno. Day off or something, I suppose. Probably off at a cooking class or seamstress workshop. Or taking elocution lessons."

"As opposed to being on community service cleaning sewers?" I asked her. "How's that going?"

She smiled at me. "I appealed. A jury of my peers felt I'd been unfairly persecuted."

"Obviously. The weapons stash, drugs supply, and army of goons under your control would've made anyone feel persecuted."

"Goons? Does anyone really say that anymore?"

Callum took his phone out and squinted at it, then put it back in his pocket. "We're not getting anywhere here.

Let's go." He headed down the steps, and SharkDog growled at Ez as they passed her.

"We can walk and talk." She fell into step with him, taking a sip from one of the cups. She had the same lanky build as he did, but she held herself differently, her shoulders back and her eyes quick and sharp as she watched the street. I had an idea she didn't miss much. "Were you really going to come to Dimly and not even say hi?"

"I was, actually."

"I'm wounded." She tucked the spare cup into the crook of her elbow and put a hand on his arm, but he shook her off, more with a dogged sort of stoicism than anger. "Cal. We're the only ones left. Can't we give this a rest?"

"I don't know, Ez." He looked at her finally. "Why do you want to? So you can get me back into the business? So you can feel better about yourself, that you tried to reach out to your baby brother? So you can keep an eye on me, make sure I'm not *threatening* the business? Which is it?"

Pru and I glanced at each other as we trotted to keep up. Her eyes were narrowed with suspicion, and she hadn't even been around to see Ez playing with her unicorn horn.

Ez snorted. "How about I'd like to have *some* family left?"

He stopped finally, and they stared at each other. She was smiling faintly, but there were dark shadows under her eyes and her fingernails were bitten to the quick. Her hair was gathered into a bun that looked very much as if she'd slept in it, and not in the sense that it was styled to look like that.

"Why?" Callum asked. "Why now?"

She hesitated. "I suppose I've just had a chance to think about some stuff."

"And?"

That hesitation again, and she looked down at us, standing on the pavement close enough to listen, but far enough away that we could almost pretend we weren't. Not that we were – Pru and I were both examining her with our ears up, and Tam had her nose wrinkled like she could smell something bad. "Do we have to do this with an audience?"

"Don't mind us," I said. "As you were."

Ez looked back at Callum. "Three cats? Really?"

"I don't exactly get a choice in the matter."

"Besides, we hear you're a bit chummy with certain cats, anyway," I put in. "Isn't that how you survived the North family massacre?"

"Seriously?" Ez demanded, more of Callum than me, and he said, "Gobs."

Pru shifted her gaze to me. "That was off."

I looked at Tam, who shook her head sadly. "Right. Sorry. North family ... demotion?"

Ez rubbed her face with her free hand. "I made an arrangement. That was all. You would too, if you didn't want to be thrown in the bloody Inbetween."

The fur crawled on my spine, and I caught a whiff off her, sleeplessness and frayed edges and self-medication. "Did you see it?" I asked, without thinking.

"I felt it." She caught my gaze, the brown of her eyes flecked with darker spots. "There's nothing to see in there."

My joints did some weird thing that suggested they wanted a bit of a break, and I locked them in place by sheer will alone, while the void loomed behind me, and I heard that whisper again. *Gobbelino.* "Sucks, huh?" I managed.

"Yeah." She looked at Callum, who had a tight, unhappy look on his face. "It did. And then there was just me."

No one spoke for a moment, then Callum said, "What do you want, Ez?" His voice was gentler than it had been.

She started to say something, stopped, and offered him one of the takeaway cups. He took it, and they both stared at each other. Then she looked at us again. "A little privacy with my brother?"

"No," I said.

"He stays," Callum said. "He's family."

"And the other two?" She waved at Tam and Pru. "Who're you?"

"Interested parties," Pru said, and Tam yawned, then turned around and ambled off. Pru watched her go, then sighed and added, "Although apparently not that interested. Fine. We'll be over here." She followed Tam up the street, heading in the direction of the car, her bare flanks pale in the low light.

"Thank the gods for that," Ez said. "The naked one was giving me the creeps."

"*You* give me the creeps," I said. "At least she's not likely to have unicorn horn in her pocket."

Ez spread her free hand, the fingers long and slim. "It's just business."

"I'd still like to know how the Watch let you get away with having *unicorn horn,*" I said.

"I'm sure you would. But it's Callum I wanted the word with, Chatty McChatface."

Callum snorted, then bit down on it, trying to look serious. "He's got a point. How did you get away with it?"

"Because they let me," she said simply. "That's not important right now. You're still hanging around with the magician. Ifan." It was a statement, not a question.

"Sometimes. Why?"

She shook her head. "Look, it was better when he was off pretending to be dead—"

"You knew he wasn't actually dead?"

She sighed, tipping her head to one side as she looked up at her brother. "*Callum.* It's Ifan. Precisely no one who's known him over the past few years thought he was actually dead. We all knew he'd got himself into some bother with necromancers and had to get out of it."

"I didn't," Callum said.

"You should've been around more."

He made a non-committal sound, and I said, "I thought it was his dad he was in bother with."

"Probably because he was in bother with necromancers," she said. "Irrelevant, anyway. Steer clear of him, Cal. He's bad news."

Callum nodded. "Maybe. But he's never told me the only life I was allowed was a North one. Never given me gear when I was trying to get clean."

To her credit, she didn't look away from him. "I'm sorry. I was wrong. I should have helped you, not tried to keep you here."

"Thanks."

They were both quiet for a moment, then she said, "I'm serious about Ifan, though. The necromancers he was in with weren't some Ouija board players. They've got power. And his dad's not around to intervene now."

"Right. I'll take it under consideration." He hesitated, then asked, "You seen any sign of them recently? Since old Lewis vanished?"

"Since you shoved him into another dimension, you mean?" She grinned, showing neat white teeth. "Your reputation's getting around."

"That's not good," I muttered.

She glanced at me, her grin fading. "No, it's not, actually. But I haven't heard much since then. I'd guess they're being a little more careful."

"What's happening with the Watch around here, then?" I asked. "My sources are a bit jumpy about them."

"We're all jumpy about them. It's just how they like it." She glanced down the street, then back at Callum. "My advice would be to go back to a low profile, Cal. That's all I wanted to tell you. You're drawing too much attention to yourself, and you need to *stop.* Stay away from Ifan. Stay away from Dimly and Gerry and anything to do with stray bloody cats. Let it all play out."

"What's *it?*" he asked.

She shook her head. "I don't even know yet. But something's coming. You did well to get out. Don't get dragged into anything else." She raised her cup in a salute. "Now get out of here. I've got a business to run, and no one'll want anything to do with me if they're worried about my little brother chucking them through summoning circles."

She flashed that grin again, then turned and walked away, low boots scuffing on the old cobbled road.

We watched her go, and I looked up at Callum.

"I don't know," he said, before I could ask. "I don't know anything."

And I couldn't even think of a smart reply, which I blame on the lack of lunch.

CALLUM WAITED until Ez was out of sight behind the market stalls before he dropped his cup in the nearest bin and said, "Come on."

"Come on where?" I asked. "Come on leaving?"

"No."

"Dammit."

He hurried down the nearest side street, his stride long, forcing me to lope to keep up. The street was all leaning buildings and old cobbles, the uneven walls of the houses jutting over their bases toward each other, close enough that people could've shaken hands across the street from their upstairs windows if they'd wanted. It was dark and close and smelled of old secrets and ground in magic and baking bread, and when I glanced back, the open space of the market square was already dwindling behind us. More reassuringly, though, the mismatched forms of Pru and Tam were running to catch us.

We dived down another side street, this one even smaller and tighter than the previous, the houses a mix of stone and old plaster and huge timber slabs, lights glowing from small diamond-paned windows, and shop signs swinging from brackets above doors. A lot of them seemed to be pubs or apothecaries, but that was hardly a surprise in Dimly. What was more surprising were the coffee shops and raw food bars, and the fact that the few people we encountered seemed to be heavily invested in a return to natty waistcoats and flowing skirts.

"What is this?" I asked. "Hipster Dimly?"

"Something like that." Callum came to a stop outside a narrow, two-storey building with rough expanses of salmon-pink plaster between the dark-stained wood of its ancient beams, wedged firmly between a pub advertising organic beer brewed on site and a shop with a blackboard threatening wheatgrass smoothies. "Here we are."

I blinked at the pink building, the view of the interior heavily distorted by the small panes of thick, rough glass in the windows. "Are we?"

"Yes." He pushed the door open, letting out a wash of warm air and the mixed scents of cake, coffee, and troll.

Pru had stopped next to me, and now she took a step back, one paw raised. "Is that …?"

"It's okay. I think we know these trolls." But my hackles were raising of their own accord. No amount of cinnamon and ginger can quite drown out the feral, rage-filled reek of troll. Not even modern trolls.

"Coming?" Callum asked.

"I suppose." I followed him into the interior, warm and low-ceilinged and washed in golden light, a bell jingling cheerily to announce our arrival.

The little front room was crowded with two small, round wooden tables and one larger, long one, with benches and chairs squeezed around them. The furniture was sturdy, solid stuff, softened with cushions in a clutter of cheerful hues, and the walls were filled with a curious mix of old food advertisements in frames and homemade posters offering dogs, rabbits, and small chimeras looking for good homes. Someone had added pink stickers to them, which read *NOT FOOD!!!*

In front of us, on the left-hand side of the room, stairs led up to the next floor, and to the right a counter cluttered with cake stands and biscuit jars and menu holders and a large vase of fresh flowers divided the kitchen from the shop floor. A faery was doing a crossword at one table, scribbling her answers out furiously and muttering under her breath while a large bowl of soup sat uneaten in front of her, and at another an elf and a faun leaned across the table toward each other, whispering urgently. A troll in a striped apron generously smeared with flour and cocoa looked up from painstakingly placing tiny flowers on a large pale cake and gave us a small, polite wave.

"Hello Callum, Gobbelino."

"Hello William," Callum said. "Lovely place you have here."

"Yes," William said and grinned, then quickly covered his jagged teeth as Pru backed up, hissing. He had a checked shirt on under his apron, done up as high as it could go, given his lack of neck, but there was no hiding the heavy armoured plates of his forehead or the huge muscles of his arms. "I is – am – glad you comes. You is welcome."

"Dude," I said. "You've seriously upped your cake game."

He dipped his head, his grin widening. "I makes the

cookies and the sandwiches, too. And I try pies this week. You want? I makes this morning."

My stomach reminded me again that the dog had eaten my lunch. "Do you have some tuna?"

"Yes—"

"No," Callum said, scowling at me. "William, Gerry messaged me. Is he here yet?"

"Is upstairs. Door say 'Private', but is okay. You go."

"Thanks," Callum said, and hustled SharkDog with him as he headed for the stairs.

William gave me a wink that somehow involved his whole body. "I bring tuna," he stage-whispered.

I tipped him my own wink. "You're the best of trolls."

Then we ran after Callum while the customers regarded us with varying levels of hostility. Dimly might be open to cats these days, but they evidently weren't happy about it.

THE STAIRS RAN up to another room filled with tables and chairs, with a couple of cosy-looking sofas flanking an old pot-bellied stove. It was on, belching out heat, and a dwarf was asleep on the sofa closest to it, a mug of hot chocolate balanced precariously on her belly amid her flower-bedecked beard. One of the tables was taken up by two young humans, an elf, and a water nymph, all wearing cloaks and hunched over a board game. The elf had a fancy headdress on, and the nymph had his feet in a bucket of water, and none of them even glanced up at us as we hustled to the only door marked *Private*.

Callum held the door while we scooted past, then shut it behind us and flicked the lock for good measure. We were on another set of stairs, warm with the heat rising from below and lit by dim light from above. The smell of troll was fiercer in here, and Tam went up the stairs with her head low and her shoulders hulked up, leading us out into a wooden-beamed room tucked below the roof, a couple of dormer windows letting in light and a touch of draught. The room held a heavy, troll-sized bed, a dresser, and a low, scarred coffee table made in the same chunky, hardwearing style as the furniture downstairs. Big floor cushions were scattered around it, and a truly enormous troll was rising to his feet, all hard muscle and gnarled grey skin, the sheer bulk of him filling the room as he loomed over us.

Pru hissed and backed up fast, and the dog whipped around and bolted for the stairs, ripping the makeshift leash out of Callum's hands. Even Tam looked alarmed, which I hadn't been sure was a state she was capable of. But at least she had the presence of mind to spit in the dog's face, sending the silly creature veering off to try and wriggle under the bed, both her snaky tail and her head vying to be the first to hide.

To be fair, a large troll, no matter how dapper his attire, leaping to his feet in front of you isn't a sight designed to make anyone relax. Trolls aren't known for their easy-going nature and sparkling conversational skills. They're more known for eating first, asking questions later.

But Callum just said, "Hi Gerry."

"It's *wonderful* to see you, Callum," Gerry said, and gave

us a grin that was even larger and more ragged than William's. He waved at the coffee table. "Do sit down. William's going to bring us up some tea." He frowned. "I'm sorry about the lack of seating. I'm not at all a fan of the floor cushions. Hard on the old knees." His joints gave a horrifying *groinch* sound as he sat down again, as if to illustrate the point. "And I'm quite sure trolls aren't made to sit cross-legged. This one isn't, anyway."

Callum checked that SharkDog was safely ensconced under the bed, then peeled his old coat off and sat down across the table from Gerry, his knees making slightly less alarming noises. I picked a cushion next to him, and Pru and Tam approached the table warily, Tam's tail still twitching and Pru's ears back. Callum introduced them, and Gerry nodded formally.

"Pleased to meet you," he said, his tone neutral.

"Charmed," Pru said, her ears still back. Tam just lifted her chin slightly. Both of them looked ready to bolt for the stairs at any moment, and it was true that Gerry's heavy cologne didn't really do much to mask the feral troll scent. It was enough to make anyone twitchy.

Gerry looked at Callum and me, raising his heavy eyebrow ridges. Callum nodded. "We trust them," he said, and I hoped he was right. I *thought* he was, but ... cats.

"That's good enough for me," Gerry said, and unbuttoned his suit jacket. It was navy blue and pin-striped, and he'd gone for a lilac cravat and matching pocket square. All I could think was *spiffing,* and I've never even used that word before. It didn't exactly go with his craggy, horned troll head and lack of any evident neck, but he somehow pulled it off. It wasn't his usual look, though.

"What's with the suit?" I asked. "Are skirts not so good in winter?"

"Gobs, shut up," Callum said. "Gerry can wear what he wants."

"Of course he can. But what he wants used to be twin-sets and pearls." I looked at Gerry expectantly, and Callum shook his head.

"I'm sorry. Maybe you could give him some of those etiquette lessons you've been giving William."

Gerry took his jacket off and laid it carefully on the cushions next to him. "It's quite alright. No one expects tact from a cat."

"Excuse *me,*" Pru said, her eyes narrowed. "That's a sweeping statement."

Gerry inclined his head slightly. "I do apologise. I have come not to expect it from the cats I have personally met."

Pru looked at me. "Alright. I can see why."

"It was a fair question," I protested.

Gerry straightened his sleeves. His cufflinks were in the shape of sunflowers. "I'm not sure if it's a *fair* question," he said. "One should be able to dress as one wishes without being questioned." He glanced at the door, then sighed. "But it appears that while the people of Dimly can *accept* a male troll with a taste for a nice tea dress as their mayor, there are certain portions of the population who won't *respect* said troll."

"Did you try knocking their heads together?" I asked. "That does the trick for most people."

"Of course not. I'm not a monster." He frowned at me, and I wondered if the lilac cravat was really making much difference. I had a feeling that the portion of the population he was referring to wouldn't respect much short of a beer-swilling, fist-punching, unthinking reflection of themselves.

"How's Poppy?" Callum asked, and the conversation descended into small talk about the other young troll who, together with William, Gerry was bringing up to be very un-troll-like. Or new-troll-like, as Gerry insisted. Trolls with good diction and table manners, which was at least as unexpected as a troll in a cravat. Tam set to cleaning her paws, and Pru gazed around the room with cool green eyes, then looked at me.

"What's the mayor doing having meetings above a teashop?"

I shrugged. "Probably the same thing we are. Avoiding lurking Norths. And the Watch."

"Fair," she said, and we waited for the niceties to be over. One can't rush such things with modern trolls, it seems.

8

SOMETHING'S ROTTEN IN THE STATE OF THE WATCH

CALLUM AND GERRY WERE STILL TALKING – GERRY WAS telling Callum that Poppy had held a weird animal rescue day, and other than an incident involving the Komodo dragons and the bake sale, it had gone really well, and he was terribly proud. And the funds had even covered the medical bills for the dwarf who'd lost half his beard to a small manticore who wanted it for its nest. It was all very pleasant, and civil, and not at all what we'd come here for.

I was just about to interrupt and point out that, as delighted as we were that modern trolls were flourishing in Dimly, we had slightly more pressing and hairy business, when there was a heavy knock on the door at the bottom of the stairs.

"Ah," Gerry said brightly. "Tea." He got up with a chorus of protesting joints and thudded down to let William in, reappearing a moment later with a large plate of daintily sliced, crustless sandwiches in one hand and tray of assorted cakes in the other. William followed, his tongue sticking out of the corner of his mouth in concentration as he balanced a tray laden with a teapot, a milk jug and a sugar bowl, cups and saucers and side plates, and a pretty woven basket full of packets that looked promisingly cat friendly. He'd taken his apron off, but his pleated khaki trousers were liberally dusted with flour.

"William," Gerry said, his voice mild. "I did tell you to wear an apron, didn't I?"

"Did," William said, looking at his trousers. "Not long enough."

"William is developing into a wonderful pastry chef," Gerry said, setting the plates on the table while the young troll lowered his tray, his forehead plates scrunched together in concentration. "His tea shop, as you can see, is a triumph."

"It's lovely," Callum said. "Seems really popular, too."

"Is hard," William said, his ears flushing a darker grey than previously. "Cake nice. People not nice."

"Only some people," Gerry said, and patted William on the back. William didn't answer, but his shoulders were more slumped than a young troll's should be as he turned and shuffled out again.

"Have you been having trouble?" Callum asked.

"Nothing we're not used to," Gerry said. "One always makes enemies when one takes a stand, and people are still adjusting to the idea of trolls as more than brainless oafs. It doesn't fit their image of the world. Tea?" He gave the pot a quick swirl, then peeked inside. "A little longer, I think."

I wondered how much worse it was, really. Before, Gerry and his odd family had stayed clear of Dimly, and Poppy had told me once that things had been bad for them in the town. And now they weren't just back, they were right in the middle of everything, not only drawing attention but *demanding* it. I looked at Gerry, smiling his great, broken-toothed smile, and wondered exactly how much he missed his pearls and twinsets.

Quite a lot, I imagined.

THERE WAS some fussing with plates and sandwiches and cups, all of which Gerry carried out with a certain degree of delight, before we were finally settled. True to his word, William had sent up packets of fancy tuna along with an array of cat biscuits, and Callum emptied them onto a few plates in front of us. Tam and I launched ourselves at them, while Pru just watched Gerry curiously. There was a cat who hadn't had the character-building life experience of never knowing where the next meal was coming from.

Finally Gerry set a cucumber finger sandwich on his plate, adjusted his cravat, and took a sip of tea, the cup incongruously delicate in his huge hands. "Lovely. But as wonderful as it is to see you, you wouldn't have come to the hall for a social call."

"Were you there?" I asked him.

"Yes. I saw you from the window, but I also saw your sister. It's best if she thinks we didn't meet." Gerry sighed slightly and popped the sandwich in his mouth whole. "And the hall is no place to talk privately, anyway."

I wrinkled my nose at him. "What's happening here? I thought you had Ez learning the error of her ways while being your assistant or whatever." That had been part of her punishment for her role in turning Dimly into her own unicorn horn–fuelled empire. I'd personally thought that if life imprisonment was off the table, leaving her with her stock when the warehouse had been flooded would've been a safer option.

He smiled slightly. "I may have overestimated my ability to force change on a North."

Callum snorted. "No one can force change on a North."

"Case in point, you're still wearing that coat," I said.

"I like my coat."

"No one can actually like that coat."

"Focus," Pru said, and we all looked at her. She raised her eyebrow ridges. "Claudia? Ms Jones? The dentist?"

"Claudia, the Watch cat?" Gerry asked.

"You know her?" Pru asked.

"I do. She was around for a while after I first stepped in as mayor. She was very helpful – seemed rather keen to make sure Dimly didn't go back to old ways, and other Watch cats were a bit scarce while she was about. But then a few months ago she just vanished, and there have been plenty of Watch cats around since. Ones with ... a different agenda, shall we say."

"What sort of agenda?" Callum asked.

Gerry tapped his fork against his plate, frowning. "Not one that holds with my idea of Dimly as a town built on community and mutual support. They seem to be rather intent on encouraging a return of the Norths and other unpleasantness. No offence."

"None taken," Callum said.

"It's made a lot of good people nervous, even if they're doing nothing wrong. I end up using this place for business rather a lot."

"Shift locks," Pru said. "I thought I felt them."

"But no one can shift in a pocket town," I said. "And no one's meant to have personal shift locks. It interferes with the town ones, or something."

"So the Watch say," Gerry said, tipping his cup at me.

I blinked at him. "*Oh.*"

"The Watch had laws passed years ago, preventing locks being set into new builds," Callum said. "But they can't do anything about the old buildings. We used to use them all the time for that reason."

"Exactly," Gerry said. "And though the old hall's got locks on a couple of rooms, it's watched all the time."

"So Ez really is working with the Watch?" Callum asked. "It wasn't just a few rogue cats turning a blind eye to what she was doing?"

Gerry spread his hands. "I don't know. But she certainly had her own dealings with them then, and seems to be re-establishing them now. And so much of the Watch is rotten that it's hard to tell where they stand on anything."

"Other than what they do to those they disagree with," I said. "They seem pretty united on that front."

"It's who they disagree with that keeps changing," Gerry said, and sighed, picking up a custard tart on a delicate china plate and poking it with his fork.

"That's true enough," Pru said. "I've been to a few different Watch cats about Claudia, thinking I could get some help to find her, but they all just say the same thing. *Claudia's business is her own.* I don't trust any of them."

I looked at her, the tuna suddenly faintly rancid in the back of my throat. "Claudia was never just Watch. You know that, right? She was the Watch's Watch, or something."

Pru met my gaze steadily. "I know that. All the more reason for legitimate Watch to worry about her going missing."

Gerry set his plate back down again, the tart untouched, and glanced at the window as if expecting avian eavesdroppers. It was entirely possible in Dimly. "They won't help you, or they've warned you off?"

Pru hesitated, shifting her paws slightly. "Well. It was suggested by more than one of them that it might be bad for my health if I poked around in Watch business too much."

I stared at her. "*Pru.* You did *not* tell us this."

She shrugged. "It just means that she's on her own. No one's going to look for Claudia unless we do. So sod the Watch." Her voice wasn't quite even, but her chin was up and her ears back, daring us to disagree with her.

I licked my chops, hearing the roar of the Inbetween rubbing against the membrane of the world, close enough to touch. Close enough to drag me in. "They don't mess around, Pru. You know what they did to me."

"So we know what they might do to Claudia."

I took a deep breath and looked around at the low, stained table with its troll-sized floor cushions and clutter of afternoon tea plates and cups and cutlery, ridiculous and civilised and utterly, utterly beautiful, holding back chaos with a finger sandwich and loose-leaf tea. The Watch. The Watch, and weres, and necromancers, and a damn sorcerer with her fingers on my back. There are many things that a resourceful cat can handle alone, but also some that no one ever can. And if Ms Jones had meant I couldn't trust the people in this room, then I likely couldn't trust myself, either.

"We have a sorcerer problem," I said. "And it all starts with the dentist."

Which I felt was suitably dramatic, but all Gerry did was blink at me, then look at Callum and say, "Weren't we talking about the Watch? Have you been giving him nip?"

"I'm not responsible for his poor life choices."

"It's not nip."

"Nip would explain a lot," Pru said.

"I'm not on nip."

"Sharing would be polite," Tam said, and I thought that while I was fairly sure I could trust them, I wasn't sure I always *liked* them.

"So I'm not sure we've got a sorcerer *problem,*" Callum said, once I'd told the story of Ms Jones and her unscheduled visit. His hands were tight on his knees. "But we definitely have a dentist one."

"And she said nothing about Claudia?" Pru asked.

"There wasn't time." I shivered, seeing the cold emptiness of the hall again. "She just said we had to find Walker and protect him."

Pru and Tam looked at each other. Tam shrugged, and

Pru shifted her pale gaze back to me. "Alright," she said. "We're in. Even if you sort of neglected to mention this *all* afternoon."

"She tried to tell me not to trust someone," I said, looking fixedly at the tuna packet. "There could've been eavesdroppers."

Tam gave a sceptical huff and Pru said, "We trusted you enough to come to you for help."

"After basically announcing to the Watch what you were up to."

"It seemed the most logical place to start. Anyway, you keep hanging around with Ifan, and for all we know he's still working with necromancers, *and* did something to Ms Jones."

"We don't know that," Callum said.

"I still don't trust him," Pru insisted. I agreed with her, but I didn't say so aloud. Callum had already reduced two paper napkins to shreds, since it seemed like a non-smoking sort of place.

He sighed and took a large slurp of tea. "We don't have anything to suggest Ifan's involved."

Pru snorted. "If you say so. But fine. The dentist first, then Ms Jones, and we'll find Claudia that way."

"You should just let us find Walker," I said. "Hanging around with me is likely to get the Watch even more interested in you. We'll let you know if we find out anything about Claudia."

"I've seen the pace of your investigations. Claudia'll die of old age before you find her if you're left to your own devices."

"We're very efficient in our own way."

"Sure you are." She lifted her chin. "Besides, I meant it. Sod the Watch."

"Seconded," Tam said, then added, "Definitely no nip?"

"No."

Gerry popped a morsel of tart in his mouth and chewed thoughtfully. "Are you sure there's weres involved? I can't see them tangling with anything like this. Not if it meant going against a sorcerer. They're smarter than that."

"They were definitely about, though," I said.

Callum nodded. "Even if they're not behind it, they're the best lead we have."

Gerry frowned. "I haven't heard anything about missing sorcerers or dentists, but I'll keep my ear to the ground. As for weres – well, they're still not that welcome in Dimly. But if you go to the Green Wolf in Bradford, Yasmin may help. She's a good sort." He checked his watch. "And you should be leaving. We don't want to draw any more attention to you."

"Fair point," Callum said, and drained his cup. "Thanks, Gerry."

The big troll nodded. "I'll see what I can find out and be in touch. But things are delicate. I can't be seen to be asking the wrong sort of questions."

"Understood."

We said our goodbyes, Gerry holding his enormous hands out to each of us to sniff or shake, depending on our disposition. He smelled of weariness and anxious thoughts, and a cold, grinding resolve that set a shiver into my spine, and made me less worried about William and his unpleasant people than I might've been.

And it also made me wish Gerry could be seen to be doing more than just asking the wrong sort of questions.

IN SHORT ORDER we were back down the stairs, minus SharkDog, whom Gerry had promised to take to Poppy. She'd have the monster washed and groomed and doing tricks within the week, if her ability with creatures as unruly as unicorns was anything to go by. Callum waved at William as we hurried through the tea shop, which had gained a few more customers while we'd been ensconced upstairs. They watched us go without making eye contact, and I was quite sure that even if we hadn't been exactly drawing attention to ourselves, our meeting hadn't gone unnoticed. And it probably wouldn't go unreported, either. The only question was to who. Ez? The Watch? Or was that the same thing now?

Between the early winter dusk and the leaning buildings the street outside was fully dark, and lit with a motley assortment of mismatched streetlamps that looked as if they'd likely been nicked from a variety of the nicer towns around the place. Light also spilled from the windows of the shops and pubs to turn the cobbles golden, and Callum dug in his pockets to find his cigarettes as we headed back the way we'd come, threading our way through a growing swell of shoppers and walkers. Dimly definitely had nocturnal tendencies.

I waited until I was sure no one was close enough to hear us, then said, "So now we're actively going against the Watch rather than just sort of not quite going *with* them. As well as having weres to deal with."

No one spoke for a moment, then Callum said, "At least we're going *with* a sorcerer. That seems like a positive."

"I think our understanding of positives might've got a little squiffy."

"Possibly. But it's the best we've got."

"Weres, then," I said with a sigh.

"Weres," he agreed.

"Joy. All my Halloweens have come at once."

"They might not be so bad. They've never thrown you into the Inbetween, after all."

"I still don't want to hang out with anyone who takes on the worst traits of both humans and dogs."

"Never mind," Pru said. "Could be that it'll all come back to your magician, anyway. Might be they're *his* weres, and he's having another try for Ms Jones."

"Fantastic," I said, and skirted someone's dropped beer can. "Just brilliant."

"I like Halloween," Tam said.

THE LONG JANUARY night was creeping out from the shadows by the time we got back to the car, the riverside park beyond it melting softly into darkness, and the sparse streetlamps on the square only working intermittently, stuttering old-fashioned yellow light across the pavements. Someone was leaning against the car waiting for us, hands in the pockets of his coat, and I recognised his smell before I even saw him properly.

"Talk of the wallaby," I said.

"What?" Callum asked.

"You know. They always turn up. Or is it wombats? Koalas?"

"Devil," Callum said.

I blinked at him. "That's not an animal."

"A Tasmanian devil is. But it's a saying, anyway, not an animal. Talk of the devil."

"You just said it was an animal. Do they really turn up all the time, though? I've never seen one."

Callum started to say something, then just shook his head and raised a hand. "Ifan. What're you doing here?"

"I was wondering the same thing about you. I spotted your car on my way out."

I looked around the square. "Way out where? Where's your car?"

"I got a lift." He grinned at us. "Now I need another one. Thought I was going to have to walk out and grab an Uber."

Pru growled, a rumbling little sound, and Ifan looked at her and Tam. "Hey."

They both stared back at him, then Pru said, rather grudgingly, "Hey."

"You been visiting Ez?" Ifan asked.

"I saw her," Callum said, unlocking the car.

"That's nice. Reconnecting with family and stuff."

"Not really." Callum frowned at him. "What're you doing in Dimly? Doesn't everyone here think you're dead?"

He snorted. "It's Dimly. People are more surprised if you *stay* dead."

"People, or necromancers?" I asked. "They wouldn't be too surprised by the walking dead, I imagine."

"It is one of their defining characteristics," he agreed. "But I kind of got put off them when they tried feed us to an Old One."

"Fair point," I said, although I wasn't sure I believed him. Which was pretty much my rule of paw when it came to Ifan.

Ifan shifted his attention to Callum. "Lift, then?"

Callum shrugged, and opened the car door. Pru, Tam and I jumped over the driver's seat to settle on the passenger's side. "Sure."

Ifan looked from Callum to us and back again. "Really?"

"You can try moving them, if you want."

Ifan peered in the window at us, and Tam lifted her top lip to show a single yellow fang. He sighed. "Never mind."

I snorted, and turned to say something to Callum as the men got in. But as Ifan tucked his coat around him and swung into the back seat I caught a whiff of something. Not weres, not magician, not even the uneasy pulse of low-level magic that ebbed and flowed around Dimly, keeping the town secret. It was something cold and high and strange and not unfamiliar, something that tickled the hackles on my spine and made me think of vast beasts moving through an un-empty void. I stared at him, and he met my eyes for one unguarded moment, the lines of his face tight and drawn. Then he grinned, and both the moment and the scent were gone.

I dropped back to my haunches as the magician sprawled across the seat and announced that there was more room back here anyway, so we were welcome to the front.

"Alright?" Pru asked me, her voice low.

"You smell anything odd?" I asked her quietly.

Her gaze shifted to Ifan. "No. But I never liked the smell of him."

"No," I said. "I suppose not." If she couldn't smell that strange scent, then maybe I was imagining it. Maybe the mix of weres, and the disjointed meeting with Ms Jones, and the sudden, stomach-turning proximity of the Watch had me too much on edge. Maybe it was nothing more than the smell of magic and dark Dimly places.

But, either way, the fur on my spine was as unsettled as it had been in the dentist's surgery. And I had a feeling I was going to have to get used to it.

Callum got the car started on the fifth attempt, just when I was wondering aloud at what point an automobile should be put out of its misery, and after a moment of idling while we waited to see if the engine would actually keep running, we pulled back onto the road that led out of Dimly.

"So what's Leeds' weirdest PI team doing in Dimly, then?" Ifan asked. "Investigating dodgy love charms that make your bits fall off? Looking for missing children in gingerbread houses?"

"It'd be a brave magic-worker who let children into

their gingerbread house," Callum said. "That never ends well."

"Fair point. What've you been up to, then?"

"Re-homing a pixie dog," I said, peering at him through the seats. "You?"

He yawned. "Chasing up some old contacts."

"Why?"

He grinned at me, broad and infectious. "Because hanging around that old house on my own all the time gets boring. And kind of creepy. It's still got Dad vibes everywhere. I wanted a bit of fun, you know?" He yawned again, and rubbed his face with one hand, stubble rasping on his dark skin. "It may have been a bit too much fun, to be fair. I left the car in bloody Harrogate on Wednesday. Not going that way, are you?"

Callum glanced at him in the rear-view mirror. "Not right now, no. Drop you home?"

"Sounds good." He stretched, and I smelled weariness on him. That much was true, at least. I wasn't sure what else might be.

9

NO ONE TOUCHED THE CORGIS

"Seems a long way to come to re-home a dog," Ifan said, as we shivered across the town's boundaries and into darker, less threatening streets. "And I know Dimly's not exactly your happy place. What gives?"

"Private PI stuff," I said. "Client confidentiality, you know."

Ifan gave me an amused look. "Did you steal one of the queen's corgis or something?"

"Not even the Watch mess with the corgis." Cats come and go through Number 10 and other halls of power as they wish, eavesdropping on the creaking machinations of human government, and no one thinks to stop us. But, much to the disgust of the Watch, the corgis are a problem. The constant presence of the dim-witted little dumplings at the queen's side means she remains off-limits. And no one knows where the bloody corgis came from - they just happened. Not even the Watch can control everything, which is a reassuring thought for some of us.

"So, what, then?"

"Why're you so interested?" Pru asked. She'd been watching him with narrowed eyes. "Not your business, is it?"

He spread his hands, still smiling. "Just asking. It's what friends do. Take an interest, you know."

"Take an interest. Fake their own death. Run off to the islands," I said. "The usual."

Ifan regarded us, his smile fading, then looked at Callum. "Am I missing something here?"

Callum sighed slightly. "We're looking for Ms Jones, and we haven't seen her since we let her out of the walls of your dad's house."

"Ms Jones?" Ifan asked. "The sorcerer?"

"The sorcerer last seen by you," I said.

"Ah. The one who threw me off the beach in Mustique." Ifan nodded. "She hasn't come back, then?"

"No," Pru said. "Funny, that."

Ifan shrugged. "I barely even spoke to her. She just said I had to go home, and we had … words, let's say. I ended up in the water, then before I could get my guard up, Dad had summoned me, and I was back in the basement with all hell breaking loose."

All hell breaking loose being his dad teaming up with a particularly unsettling necromancer called Sonia to bring him back from his fake death, and in so doing almost unleashing the Old One on the world. Which seemed like a bit of an overreaction, but that apparently ran in the family, considering Ifan claimed that the reason he'd faked his death and run off in the first place was all down to the familial demands of being the sole heir of the most powerful magician in Yorkshire. Talking about it might've been easier, but they were British.

"What sort of words?" I asked.

"She just said I had to come back, I said absolutely not, and then she threw me in the water." He rubbed the back of his head. "She's not much for small talk."

"And that was it?" Pru asked. "You *stink* of magic, and you just let her throw you back?"

Ifan met her gaze for a long moment. It was easy to forget who he was. *What* he was. The last of his line, with a house soaked in generations of questionable magic, and his own patchy history of mucking about with necromancers to foot. To shoe? Whatever. And also Callum's oldest friend, although I still hadn't figured out the strange connections of their intertwined pasts.

"She's a sorcerer," Ifan said finally. "I'm just a magician, and I hadn't exactly been practicing much. I didn't want to draw any unwanted attention. So yeah. I might've tried to fight back more, but Dad latched the summoning onto me right then, while my guard was down. I never had a chance."

There was silence for a moment, then Tam said, "Diddums," and Callum gave a snort of startled laughter. Ifan looked at Tam, that grin creeping back over his face, and Pru shook her head slightly.

Callum took his cigarettes from his pocket and plucked one out, his wrists resting on the top of the steering wheel as we slipped down the darkened streets. "Anyhow, that's who we were looking for. Ms Jones."

"Wish I could help," Ifan said, watching Callum flicking his lighter ineffectually. "I'd never even come across her before that. I could ask around, though, see if anyone knows anything."

Callum gave the lighter an irritable shake. "No, best stay out of it."

Ifan clicked his fingers, a little silver flame springing into life above them, and leaned forward to offer it to Callum. He grunted, and lit his cigarette from the twisting fire.

"Don't enable him," I said. "Some friend you are."

"Well, you won't let me do anything else to help."

Callum looked at me, then back at the road, and none of us spoke for a moment. Then Callum flicked some ash into the old mug between the seats and said, "You know of any weres?"

"Weres? What d'you want with them?"

"Just something we're looking into."

"To do with the sorcerer?"

"That's classified," I told him, and Pru sighed. "What?"

"Well, that's basically just saying *yes,* isn't it?" she said.

"Not until you said that," I protested. "It could've been a completely different case."

"Not now it couldn't."

Tam shook her head and put her chin on her paws.

"Right," Ifan said. "Look, I just won't ask. But you know weres are always about. Not in Dimly so much, but your family always knew how to find them."

"I'm not asking Ez," Callum said.

"No, but not much changes." Ifan hesitated. "You probably don't want to go looking for them, though."

Callum glanced at him in the rear-view mirror, his jaw tightening. "Why?"

"It's the old business," Ifan said. "Never mind Ez. You don't want to put yourself back there again."

Callum didn't answer for a moment, and Tam gave me a curious look. I didn't say anything. People's pasts are their pasts, and their stories belong to them. Even I didn't know just how bad things had been for Callum. When he'd crashed into my life to rescue kitten-me from both the beasts of the Inbetween and beasts in human form, he'd been strung out on whatever human drugs stopped him feeling and filled the void that the Folk drugs had left behind. I wasn't sure what void he'd been filling in the first place, but these days tea, cigarettes, and coverless paperbacks rescued from the bins outside charity shops seemed to fill it. Or to make it manageable, anyway. There was no shame in any of it – don't we all have our own voids that we're always seeking to fill? – but his story was still his story.

"I'll go," Ifan said. "Tell me what you need, and I'll go."

"You don't have to do that."

"It'll be perfectly safe. I can be like your undercover agent. Who's going to mess with a magician?" Ifan grinned, suddenly delighted. "I'll go in, buy a bit of pixie juice—"

"Gross," Pru and I said together. Pixie juice wasn't actually made from crushed pixies, although it was rumoured to have been in the good old days, but it was still some sort of fermented monstrosity that the elves had come up with. And, elves being as they are, there was no guarantee it *wasn't* made from crushed pixies. That's what happens when you look like you've just stepped out of a shampoo ad. You get away with pretty much anything. Pixie juice was up there with imp dust as one of those things that weren't legal, but plenty of people still got their hands on. Not as contra to all treaties as unicorn horn, but definitely not what you wanted in your pocket if someone with any sort of legal standing was asking you questions.

The problem being, of course, that while all kinds have their own rules, the main *law* in the Folk world was the Watch, and cats don't really care that much if you're frying your brain on dried faery wings. They *do* care that the faeries would probably rather keep their wings, though, simply because faeries don't take such things lightly, and a Folk war would risk attracting too much human attention. So things are still illegal, but mostly only when a cat can be bothered to follow up. Which all depends on how discreet you're being, and what exactly you're using in the first place. And what you might have on offer to convince a cat to look the other way.

Ifan shrugged. "I didn't say I'd *take* it. Look, it makes perfect sense. Just tell me what you want me to find out."

"Are they really going to trust you?" Callum asked. "Given that you're meant to be dead? The weres'll have wind of that, and you know they're jumpy at the best of times."

"If everyone who was rumoured to be dead around here actually was, an entire financial sector would collapse."

"I don't think I've ever heard it called a financial sector before," I said. "Is that the polite term for *drug gang* these days?"

"*Drug gang*'s a bit limiting," Ifan said. "Weres are into a lot more than that. In fact, the drugs are usually run by someone else. They're more facilitators, among other things."

"Great. So the weres use business speak before they tear your head off?"

"It makes the tearing of heads pleasant in comparison."

I huffed, and Callum glanced at me, the corner of his mouth twitching in something that was nearly a smile. "Pixie juice or not," he said. "We still can't ask you to do this."

"I'm offering. Besides, I've been up for two days already. Hitting up a were club seems like a great idea at this point."

"They have clubs?" I asked. "What, do they all get together to swap notes on flea treatments? Or take turns throwing sticks for each other? Do they sniff—"

"You're definitely not coming," Ifan said.

"Wouldn't want to."

"And you can't come, either," Ifan said to Callum. "You two are known these days. No one's going to think you're there casually unless you're using."

Callum nodded, that muscle twitching in his jaw again, and I wasn't entirely sure if it was an itch of desire or distaste. They can sit pretty close together sometimes. But he just said, "It's a nice offer. But this is our business, Ifan. We'll drop you home."

Ifan opened his mouth to argue, looked more closely at Callum, then shrugged. "Sure. The offer stands. Just don't go hunting out a club alone, Cal. Don't risk it." He patted Callum on the shoulder and dropped back in his seat.

Callum didn't answer, just stubbed his cigarette out, his face pale and tired looking.

THE STREETLIGHTS on the tree-lined roads outside the tall gates to Ifan's house were casting smooth yellow light over the pavement, and the after-work rush was in full swing. In this part of town that meant fewer buses, more big 4x4s that had never been off-road in their lives, unless you counted bumping over a kerb to get the best spot in front of the hipster coffee joint. Our old Rover attracted some suspicious looks, but we were mostly ignored. They probably thought Callum was a gardener or something.

Ifan clambered out of the car with a promise to call later, then vanished through the gates of his fancy house with a wave. Callum pulled his phone out to check the time. "If it's a cafe, the Green Wolf'll be shut by now," he said. "And if it's a bar it'll be too busy. We'll have to try tomorrow."

Pru shifted on the seat and gave us both a narrow look. "Really? *Tomorrow?*"

"Well, why don't you nip down there and try interviewing Wolfy yourself?" I asked. "You can report back."

She considered it for a moment, then shook her head. "Weres and the Watch don't get on. She probably won't trust two cats on their own. She's not going to talk to us."

Tam huffed.

"She's not going to talk to two cats who *ask nicely,*" Pru amended, looking at Tam. The big tabby she-cat looked at the roof of the car in obvious disdain.

Callum rubbed his face with one hand. "We *can* go, but even if it's open, it's going to be a bad time to talk. Which doesn't seem like the best way to get the help we want. How about we meet first thing tomorrow?"

Pru and Tam looked at each other, and Tam shrugged. "Alright," Pru said. "You seem impervious to being hurried up, anyway."

I thought of Ms Jones' hand on my back, and shivered. Hopefully *she* wouldn't take it in her mind to hurry things up.

"Pretty much," Callum agreed. "You need a lift?"

"We'd rather shift," Pru said. "No offence."

"None taken," Callum said, but he patted the dashboard lightly as if the car might be the one to have taken offence.

I lifted my chin at the other two cats. "Later."

"Later," Pru said, getting up. She stepped sideways off the seat and was gone.

Tam looked at us for a moment, as if she were about to say something, then just lifted her chin instead. Then she was gone as well, and we were alone in the gathering dark of a long winter night, the cold already creeping in around the doors despite the labouring heater.

Callum and I looked at each other. "Home?" he suggested.

"Home," I agreed, not without some misgivings.

HOME HADN'T IMPROVED since the book of power–related incident, when reality went a bit squiffy. Although, to be fair, not everything could be blamed on that. We'd always had problems like the creaking sash windows not closing properly, the lights sometimes dimming inexplicably, and, judging by the yells from the shower most mornings, hot water that tended to be pretty iffy. But now we also had, among other things, cracks in the stairs that led to different dimensions and cupboards that sometimes opened on tins of baked beans and sometimes on murky abysses, crawling with half-glimpsed things. That kept things interesting. As did the constant threat of being ambushed by threateningly large landladies wanting rent or clients who weren't so happy with the outcome of their cases. It was astonishing how many people paid for the truth, but took a fervent dislike to it as soon as they got it. And liked to express said dislike by trying to take their payment back in inventive and potentially painful ways.

But home is home, even when it's cold enough to see your breath, and the mysterious stink of boiled cabbage that often lurked in the hall outside had sneaked in to fill our little bedroom/living room/office like a physical presence. All was familiar and as it should be, but my fur still wouldn't lie flat. I padded around the corners of the room, checking scents and looking for something I couldn't quite place – peace, maybe – while Callum switched on the portable radiator and went to heat the microwavable pad for my bed. He waited until it had dinged off before switching the kettle on. The fuses had a tendency to blow when he tried to do both at once.

Before long he was back in his creaking office chair behind the desk, cradling a cracked mug of tea, and I was trying to push Green Snake out of my bed. Snakes are hard to push, though. He just shaped himself around my paw and looked at me out of his flat green eyes, then stuck his tongue out.

"Same to you," I said to him, and climbed into the bed with him. "You could go and sit on Callum, you know. It's not weird for *you.*"

Green Snake just moved over a little, then as soon as I was settled, he curled himself against me.

"Honestly, *ew.*"

"You're warm," Callum said, pulling a towel out of the gap in the window and lighting a cigarette.

"I know I am. I'm warm and engaging, but I still do not want a snake sleeping with me."

Callum blew smoke in the vague direction of the window and squinted at me. "I mean your body temperature. It's warmer than mine."

"I didn't ask for that."

He snorted, and tapped ash into an old can that was serving as an ashtray, then reached for his tea. "Anything more from Ms Jones?"

"No." I shivered. "I'm hoping to avoid a repeat of the whole out-of-body experience, really."

He frowned. "I wish she'd given us more to go on. All we have is the weres at the moment. And I can't see how they'd be involved with Claudia. But could that really be a whole separate thing?"

"Seems like a bit of a wild coincidence that she's missing separately to Ms Jones and the were situation. But weres hate the Watch. They'd never work with them."

"Alright. So, say Malcolm got mixed up with weres on

his own. Could the Watch be responsible for Ms Jones *and* Claudia going missing?"

I shivered again, my spine tight with the anticipation of icy fingers, and Green Snake lifted his head to look at me. I ignored him. "Claudia? Yes. I don't know what the Watch is up to these days, but I know it doesn't tolerate … dissent, I guess." I wondered if I should be trying to remember more about my previous lives, more about why the Watch was so keen to end them. But how could I? Other than knowing they kept killing me, things were pretty fuzzy. I'd just thought that was how things worked – after all, dying and being reborn as a mewling, helpless kitten does kind of take it out of you. And we don't get any sort of memory back at all until after we're weaned, anyway. There's something in the milk that keeps us in kittenish innocence, which is a good thing. I mean, it'd be pretty weird otherwise, wouldn't it?

"And Ms Jones? Could the Watch take on a sorcerer?" Callum asked.

I thought about it. "Maybe? If you listen to the stories, sure. But no one knows how much of the history's truth and how much of it's myth."

"Sounds like history in general," Callum said. "What do you think, though?"

"I'd've said no one would take on a sorcerer, but Ifan's dad did, with the help of that bloody necromancer. They even drained some of her power off for themselves. And we've no idea where those two ended up." I was still hoping for the sucked-into-another-dimension outcome.

Callum stubbed his cigarette out and rubbed his face. "And weres?"

"I hate weres," I said.

"I think I've got that bit."

I sighed. "You know as much as me. They tend to run in packs, but for the most part they keep their heads down. The Watch has no love for them. They're too *obvious,* and even if the whole full moon thing is just convenient human myth, you lot still know a were when you see one. It gets all your tiny senses tingling, or something."

"Spidey senses."

"You what?"

He shook his head. "Doesn't matter. But it does look like they took Malcolm, and why would they do that other than to bring Ms Jones out of hiding?"

"But why would they risk that? She could tear them apart."

"Maybe they want some leverage to get her to do something. Maybe the Watch is threatening them, and they want her help."

I thought about it, then conceded, "Maybe. But why's she in hiding in the first place? Who does a sorcerer need to hide from?"

We looked at each other, and Green Snake tucked himself a little closer to me. I wished I hadn't said it. Some questions shouldn't be out in the open like that. Even the familiar, if tatty, embrace of the little apartment felt off tonight. I couldn't stop sniffing the air, as if the void might give me some warning before it swallowed me.

Callum took a sip of tea. "I wish we knew if Ifan's dad and the necromancer escaped or not."

"Well, we don't know," I said. "And we can go and chase down the necromancer minions, but I think they renounced the whole thing when they realised it wasn't just a particularly edgy goth social club."

Callum nodded. "Well, we're not going near the Watch whatever happens, so we do what Ms Jones asked, and we keep following the weres. Ifan was right about them being open to most jobs. They don't get a lot of choice as far as legitimate work. Humans are unnerved by them, and Folk are no better. We can see what this Yasmin knows."

"See if she can string a sentence together." I hooked a biscuit out of the bowl on the table with one paw. It was too cold in here to move out of the bed unless I really had to. Plus Green Snake would just take it over. "What d'you think Ifan was really up to in Dimly?"

Callum tapped his fingers on the mug, considering it. "I don't think it's anything to do with Ms Jones or Malcolm," he said eventually, which didn't answer the question.

I crunched on the biscuit then said, "Well. I suppose we're going to a wolf cafe tomorrow."

"Looks like," Callum agreed.

I just hoped they weren't looking to put something new on the specials board.

10

CAT PEOPLE & CREEPING UNEASE

THE SNOW HAD RETREATED BY THE NEXT MORNING, LEAVING a grimy crust of dirty ice on the edges of the roads, and the pre-dawn dark revealed the faintest glimpse of stars beyond the streetlights. It was going to be one of those sunny Yorkshire winter days that look beautiful through a triple-glazed window from a well-heated room, but were less than idyllic when waking up in a damp, unheated flat with a steady draught coming from somewhere. I figured the walls just leaked at this stage, as the gaps around the window and door were as well-packed with second-hand towels as Callum could manage. I poked my head out from under the blanket, the chill stinging my nose and making me snuffle.

Callum opened one eye, looked at me, and said, "How come it's weird to sit on my lap, but not weird to sleep on top of me?"

"It's cold," I said.

"It's uncomfortable," he replied, and pushed me to one

side as he sat up, swinging his legs off the armchair that unfolded into an almost acceptable bed. He stretched, and I heard his spine crack. "You're heavy."

"I'm positively svelte."

"Still heavy." He grabbed his jacket from the rickety client's chair in front of the desk and pulled it on as he headed for the tiny bathroom.

"I want bacon," I called after him. "It's too cold not to have bacon."

"I want a tropical holiday," he said. "Not much hope of that." He pulled the door shut behind him and Green Snake poked his head out of the discarded blankets, tilting it at me.

"*You're* alright," I said. "You just hang out in people's pockets all day."

Green Snake tilted his head a little more, which I assumed was agreement. Nice for some. I shook my fur out against the cold and looked around the apartment, lit a watery orange from the lights outside. We'd tried covering the window against the cold at one point, but had quickly found it more useful to have some light in the case of unexpected and unwelcome visitors than it was to stay warm. Although that seemed like a toss-up right now, given the fact that I felt like I had frost on my whiskers.

I shifted slightly, examining the room. Everything looked much the same as it always did, the battered metal filing cabinets leaning against the stained wall, Callum's desk chair pushed back under the window, and the top of the desk cluttered with old books and pens and forgotten receipts. But it didn't *feel* as it always did. It wasn't as simple as things being out of place, or a new leak appearing in the ceiling, or even a suspicious scent among the myriad creeping to us from other apartments, but something was off. I was sure of it.

Or almost. It seemed like things had been off for a while, that the stomach-twisting thinning of the world in the alley, whether Ms Jones had been responsible or not, had been less the shock of the unexpected than the horror of the inevitable. Waking to the unease here had the sticky, familiar taste of fights you just can't win, but there was still nothing I could put my snout on. I closed my eyes, letting my senses drift out in search of something more concrete, but the jumbled scents of yesterday seemed stuck in the back of my nostrils, and every time I thought of the Watch I felt like coughing up a hairball, so I wasn't exactly at my most calm and observant.

I opened my eyes and looked at Green Snake. "Any thoughts?"

He stared at me, then vanished back under the blanket.

"You're not wrong." But I didn't follow him, as tempting as it was. I jumped to the desk instead, and sat there in the freezing air drifting off the glass, my nose twitching and the tip of my tail moving restlessly of its own accord. The street outside was empty, but I watched it anyway. Watched, and waited for something unknown, that maybe wasn't coming. That maybe wasn't even out there at all.

And hoped that weres would prove to be the worst of our problems.

It was too cold to even think about staying in the apartment once we were up. Besides, the only thing in the fridge was a quarter-full bottle of milk and some sardines that had been left too long. There were always cans of tuna (or, more often, "tuna", with quotation marks included and weird blurred labels that almost–sort of resembled actual brands, but not quite) and so on in the cupboard, but I'd had one for dinner, and I wanted something hot for breakfast, which I kept telling Callum until he abandoned his half-brewed cup of tea, wrapped a multicoloured scarf that our across-the-hall neighbour had made for him around his neck, and stomped out the door, muttering about complaining cats.

"I'm not complaining," I said, following him down the stairs. "I'm simply communicating my needs in a clear and firm manner."

"You have to stop reading those magazines Mrs Smith gives us. Besides, is bacon really a *need?*"

"It feels like a need."

"Of course it does." Callum jumped over the stair with the gap to another dimension tucked under it, and I followed suit. There was a tangle of feathers and a small bell lying next to it, and I didn't stop to sniff them. Like I said, certain things had never healed after our building's brush with Ms Jones' book of power.

We walked through the pre-dawn dark to the local greasy spoon, with its familiar hard plastic chairs and torn lino floors, and the comforting stench of old fried breakfasts and slightly burned toast. The pavement was cold beneath my paws, still rimed with frost, and above us the sky was the bleached undark of every city. The cafe was only a couple of blocks over, and its big windows were opaque with condensation but glowing with yellow light that washed across the pavements and promised an oasis of warmth and processed meat.

We let ourselves in, the door clattering shut behind us, and found half the tables already full, mostly with big men whose stomachs were as broad as their shoulders, all tucking into dishes piled with baked beans and eggs and meat, with fried bread on the side for variety. Callum went to the counter to order, and I found a corner table, jumping up onto a chair and curling my tail over my toes, my nose twitching with the scents. A man with a huge beard and tattoos running up his neck did the *pspspsps* thing at me, and I ignored him. I could probably scrounge some bacon off him, but I wasn't up for head scratches today. The fur on my spine seemed to be having its own thoughts on how to behave, no matter how many times I groomed it, and every clattering pan made my ears twitch. I sank down on the seat, my muscles tight.

Callum came back and sat opposite me, stretching his legs out under the table. I wriggled my ears at him, but neither of us said anything, even though it wasn't like this was the sort of place where anyone would be that surprised by someone talking to a cat. They had a pretty varied clientele, and right now I could see one of the large men feeding a rat who was sitting on his shoulder. The rat gave me a suspicious look and I lifted my chin at him in acknowledgement. I was fairly sure *that* wasn't up to food hygiene standards. Not that I was sure much was, but the prices were good and the plates were large. Plus Petra, the woman currently carrying an enormous mug of tea toward us, always sneaked me bits of cheese. No, the only thing wrong with this place was the fact that it might be okay with people talking to animals, but it was still a very *human* place. A cat talking back would likely be noticed.

I sometimes think that's why Callum likes coming here so much.

Petra set the mug in front of Callum and scritched me between the ears. "Hello, handsome," she said. "What's happening?"

I just purred and arched my neck. Petra had seen some odd things around us, although she seemed to have forgotten them well enough. Rationalised them away, as humans do. But her fingers smelt of bad dreams and restless nights.

She dropped a couple of pieces of cheese in front of me, gave Callum a wary smile, and went back to the counter. Callum sighed and pulled his phone out, disentangling Green Snake from it and setting him on the table, then hitting dial. A moment later I heard, *"You've reached Doctor Malcolm Walker. For appointments—"*

Callum looked at me and shrugged. I wrinkled my snout. I hadn't expected anything else.

We didn't linger over breakfast. Despite the delights of being in a warm place that smelled of food, it was crowded and the thought of facing a were – even a Gerry-approved were – was making it hard to concentrate on my breakfast. And that same prickling sense of unease, of things being just one degree off *right,* still persisted. I wolfed my bacon, and shifted my attention to the sausage Callum had chopped into manageable pieces. Green Snake kept sneaking around to investigate my plate, and I bared my teeth at him. I was pretty sure snakes didn't eat sausages, and he certainly wasn't starting with mine.

The large *pspspsps* man leaned over and said, "He shouldn't be eating that."

Callum looked up from his phone, and I swallowed my mouthful of sausage, licking my chops. Green Snake took advantage of my momentary distraction to snatch a piece in his fangs, then promptly tried to shake it off again, hissing.

"Sorry?" Callum said.

"It's not good for them, all that processed stuff." The man's shoulders were straining the seams of his T-shirt, and I could smell diesel and sweat under the scent of coffee on his breath.

"It's a treat," Callum said.

"It's not right, though," the man insisted. "I was reading this article, see, and all the salt – it's way worse for them than it is for us."

Callum nodded. "I'll bear it in mind."

The man frowned, evidently feeling Callum didn't sound convinced, and folded his heavily tattooed arms. "If you have cats, you've got to take responsibility for them. They're not just accessories, you know."

Callum scooped some beans onto his toast, nodding.

"And you can't just let them eat what they want, neither."

Callum looked at me. I bared my teeth at him. "He's very particular," he said.

"He's a bit scrawny, to be honest," the man said, and I huffed.

"Not sure how," Callum said. "He eats plenty."

"Might be it's the wrong sort of food," the man said, raising his eyebrows. Callum didn't respond, so he continued. "I've got some cat food in the truck if you want. I buy it in bulk when I do a run to Germany. They've got good cat food, the Germans."

I blinked at him. Callum just said, "Good to know."

The man fumbled his phone out. "I'm not trying to sell it or nothing. It's for my girls, see?" He showed Callum the lock screen on his phone, which was a photo of six cats piled together on a sofa. Three of them were asleep, two were in the middle of attacking each other, and the third was staring at the camera with a bored look on her face.

"Lovely," Callum said. "Nice cats."

"This is Millicent," the man said, tipping the phone a little so he could point them each out. "I found her in a truck stop in France. And this is Daphne, she was—"

I tuned out and went back to my sausage. At least he didn't seem inclined to take my plate away. And this was just the sort of thing Callum deserved for favouring cafes where cats couldn't talk.

We didn't linger much after that. Beardy man turned out to have most of his phone given over to photos of his cats, photos of other people's cats, and photos of cats he'd met along the road and had re-homed elsewhere. He was certainly the sort of man you wanted to run across if you were a small cat doing it rough, but only if you were prepared to put up with a lot of fussing and a very strict diet. He had a lot of photos of him with cats on his shoulders, or snuggled against his beard. Most of them looked either resigned or startled.

Callum waved to Petra as we left. She waved back, giving a small smile. She didn't seem quite sure about us these days, which seemed a little unfair. It had been *her* dog who had dug up an arm and set us off on a zombie chase last spring, after all. Just because we'd proven maybe more comfortable than she expected with spare body parts was no reason to have reservations.

The sun was up somewhere beyond the buildings, shedding grey light over the narrow alleys, and the streetlights (the ones that weren't broken) had winked off while we were breakfasting. The shadows persisted, though, feeling too deep and too *full.* Callum looked at me.

"Bradford?" he asked.

"Home of the were cafe," I said, wrinkling my nose.

"Gerry wouldn't send us anywhere dangerous."

"You do realise that Gerry's version of a dangerous situation is probably a lot different to ours? I mean, not even the most rabid were's going to take on a troll."

He pulled his scarf up around his neck, puffing wraiths of warm breath into the day. "True. But we're just asking a few questions."

"Well, *that's* alright then. That sort of thing *never* gets us into trouble."

Callum snorted, and we ambled down the street to where we'd left the old Rover slumped wearily at the kerb around the corner from our building, dribbling oil onto the stained tarmac. We found Pru crouched on top of it, hunkered on her haunches with the bones of her shoulders sharp against her bare skin.

"Morning," I said. "You should've joined us. We just had sausages."

"I just had wild salmon in some sort of seaweed *jus*," she said. "I remain unconvinced that a cat should eat seaweed, but the salmon was good."

"Can't be as good as sausages," I said, although I wouldn't have minded being able to at least make a comparison.

"I went up to your apartment," she said, as Callum unlocked the car. "It smells weird."

"Oh? Was it the creeping damp or the tears in reality?"

She wrinkled her snout. "Neither. Different weird. Not like last time I was there."

I wanted to say something effortless about Woo-woo Lady upstairs and her smelly oils, or the as yet unidentified boiled cabbage culprit, but somehow I couldn't find the words. The uneasy sleep of the night before was a suddenly physical weight, and the blank eyes of the buildings, boarded up and not, loomed all around us, abruptly hostile. I licked my chops while Pru examined me curiously, her ears pricked forward.

"Maybe it was the seaweed," I managed finally.

"No," she said, still watching me.

Callum swung the driver's door open and looked from one of us to the other, frowning. "Where's Tam?" he asked.

"Chasing your magician," Pru said, looking away from me finally. "Just in case he's up to magician-y things."

"You have no faith," Callum said, taking his cigarettes out of his pocket while I jumped in past him.

"I don't. Where's our next were, then?" Pru asked.

"Bradford," I said. "Coming for a ride?"

"In your car? Wouldn't miss it for the world." She padded across the driver's seat to join me, and Callum persuaded the car to start, mostly through sheer willpower alone, as far as I could tell, then left us inside with the heater running while he scraped frost off the windscreen. By the time we pulled away from the kerb my ears were numb, but the vents were coughing out air that was marginally above zero.

The streets weren't too busy, the work rush already gone and the pre-school one just dying out, and Callum took the quickest route to Bradford he could, nipping through grey suburbs and rough industrial areas and past the sudden, startling stretches of green parks. We weren't worried about waiting for Tam – she'd catch us up. Even if she didn't know where we were headed, there's that particularly feline version of tracking, a way of slipping into the Inbetween and out again, following the faint traces of people's scents where they pass through the world. It's a tricky and painstaking job, especially if you're not sure where your quarry's going, or how they're travelling, but it's possible.

Many things are possible, usually far more than we realise, and so there was nothing to say that Pru *hadn't* just got a whiff of Woo-woo's latest diffuser blend.

Then again, in my experience, if there are two possibilities, the one with the most teeth is also the most likely. It's one of many laws of the world that convince me the universe is essentially one of those eternal schoolboys to whom snapping someone with a wet towel is the height of humour.

Luckily, most of those schoolboys are pretty easy to outsmart, outrun, and generally shed on. Which was a thought that kept me going a lot more than it probably should.

11

THE WAY OF THE MODERN WERE

BRADFORD GREW UP AROUND US IN LAYERS OF TIRED suburbs with desultory attempts at tree-lined streets, all pebbledash walls and net curtains and the sort of gardens that make estate agents talk about "potential". Those gave way to tighter coils of red brick terraces that were a mix of homes and offices, interspersed with corner shops sporting posters advertising that week's specials on already cheap booze. It was a once-rich textile town gone to seed, and everywhere were the spires of old fabric mills and startling glimpses of worn yet well-groomed green spaces, and the elegant sweep of grand houses given over to shops or apartments, the beginning of a regeneration that was working for the usual 10 percent.

The good thing about Bradford was that its regeneration hadn't got so far that the parking charges had caught up. We parked in a half-empty lot in front of the usual retail park suspects of furniture stores and cheap sports stores and pound shops, and Callum looked at Pru and me.

“Are you coming?” he asked.

“I can’t let you go alone,” I said. “We don’t know what sort of place this Green Wolf is. What if it’s a bookshop? You’ll never come back.”

“I have no problems letting you both go alone,” Pru said. “But I’m here now, so I might as well come.”

Callum lifted Green Snake out of his pocket. “What about you?”

Green Snake coiled himself around Callum’s fingers, tipping his head slightly.

“At least someone’s actually got my back,” he said.

“You don’t know that,” I said. “That could mean anything. It could mean he thinks you’ve got a book problem, too.”

“At least he’s not so vocal about it,” Callum said, and stepped out of the car into the harsh chill of the day. Even with the sun up, it was cold enough that I shivered, my fur pouffing out in all directions, and Pru hesitated on the seat, one paw half-lifted to her chest.

“You alright?” I asked her. Meaning, *are you going to be okay running around with no fur on,* but I wasn’t quite sure if that was offensive or not. Probably, but she *was* naked.

“I can give you a lift,” Callum said, already unwinding his scarf from his neck. He shivered as the thin breeze stuck its fingers down his collar, then folded the scarf a few times into a chunky, multicoloured bed and offered it to Pru. She looked at it, then at me.

“I don’t mind,” I said. “Not much use if you freeze your paws off, is it?”

“And I really don’t fancy telling Katja I let you get frostbite,” Callum said.

"Fine," she said, and stepped onto the scarf. Callum tucked the loose ends over her back and settled her against his chest, then locked the car door.

"We all set?" he asked.

"Your coat stinks," Pru said.

"I've told him that," I said. "He still wears it, though."

"It doesn't *stink.*"

"It does," Pru said. "It smells of cigarettes and loss and empty nights and broken magic."

Neither Callum or I said anything for a moment, then he said, "Well, it's warm," and headed across the car park with his long, slouching stride. I trotted next to him, my ears back against the wind, and wished he had a second scarf. It might not be dignified, but it'd be a whole sight warmer.

THE WERE HAD her place in the arches, a part of town that had grown up in the roaring days of industry, before the mills had gone and so much had fallen derelict. The whole area was rising again now, the dim, low-ceilinged passageways as windowless as a castle's dungeons, the clean-scrubbed brick walls lit by caged orange lights and oddly barren between the businesses encased in the walls. There were cafes with tattooed waitstaff and menus that heavily featured the word *organic*, and coffeeshops with bearded baristas and twelve different kinds of plant milk, and bars with old barrels instead of tables and neon signs that Callum said were ironic, although they looked like regular neon to me. There were a few shops, too, all vintage tin signs and ancient typewriters in the window displays, with racks of second-hand clothes that cost a whole lot more now than they had new.

We picked our way through the tangle of brick passages and stairs, decorated here and there with framed signs for live music and open mic nights, and finally found a bar with heavy wooden double doors standing open onto the passageway. They looked like they belonged behind a portcullis, and the rest of the place was decorated to match. Heavy metal light fittings made from huge old gear wheels, stone-flagged floors, and wood and metal tables that didn't look like anyone would be throwing them over in a fight. We'd reached the outer edge of the arches, and there were three big windows inside the bar, looking out over the streets below where the hill sloped away under the buildings. They were protected by iron bars that might've been original, or might've been aesthetic. I wasn't sure – it can be hard to tell with humans and human-like Folk. The bar counter was long and high, with bare orange bulbs hanging from cables above it and bottles lining the wall behind. It was crowned with a huge coffee machine and a sign that said, *No biting.* The sign had a stylised bite mark out of one side. At least, I assumed it was stylised.

I looked at Pru. She wriggled, and Callum put her down, clutching the scarf in his hand as we peered over the threshold.

"Anything?" he asked in a low voice.

The floor was freshly mopped, and I could smell lavender and tea tree oil and something vaguely sunny emanating from it. Deeper in there was coffee and a faint whiff of slow-cooked onions, and someone laughed from somewhere off to the right, startling me. I'd been braced for the soured beer and old pain and stale sludge of regret that was ground into the bones of every pub I'd known, but there was nothing of that here. There was a sense of something quick and light and sharp, and I couldn't place it.

But I could place the hairy whiff that accompanied swift soft footfalls running up stairs in the direction the laugh had come from. A woman swept around the corner, her thick dark hair piled high on her head, and stopped so suddenly that she almost dropped the basket of croissants and pastries she was carrying.

"Sorry!" she gasped. "I didn't see—" She stopped, nose wrinkling, and her gaze dropped to me and Pru. Her smile vanished. "You," she said. "I've no business with you."

"Dude, I wish we didn't have business with you either," I said.

She scowled at me, then at Callum. "You're not welcome in here with them."

"Are you Yasmin?" he asked. "Gerry said you might be able to help us. You know, from Dimly."

"Gerry should keep his flat nose out of my business. I don't deal with cats."

"We're just after some information."

"No. I don't want any cats in here stinking up the place."

"Hey," I said. "Uncalled for. At least we don't smell of wet dog."

"No, just rotting fish," probably-Yasmin shot back. "And Watch."

"They're not Watch," Callum said.

"And I'm supposed to just trust that?"

"Gerry does."

"Gerry's a soft touch," she said. "Everyone knows that. And I can't have cats in here. My clientele are not the sort to frequent anywhere that welcomes cats."

"Can we talk somewhere else, then?" Callum asked. "It'll only take a moment."

"I don't have time."

"What about if just I come in?"

She looked at him, then at Pru and me. "You'll still have the smell of them on you. And I told you – I don't deal with cats. And that extends to those who associate with them."

Pru and I exchanged glances, and I put one paw over the threshold, not putting it down, just holding it mid-step.

"*Don't,*" Yasmin said.

"Think you can catch me before I stink the place up?" I asked. Pru had joined me, her paw hovering over the spotless floor. "Catch *both* of us?"

"I'll bloody *skin* you," she hissed, her lips drawn back from her teeth, the canines just a little too long and too sharp. Her hands were clamped hard on the basket, the muscles of her forearms smooth and defined against her brown skin.

"Gobs, don't," Callum said, and I ignored him.

"It'll take days before you get the smell out," Pru said. "How much business will you lose?"

"I think I'm shedding, too," I added. "And with that damp floor? Well. It's going to *stick.*"

Yasmin growled, a furious noise in the back of her throat that set the hair on my spine shivering to attention. "*Fine,*" she hissed. "Gods-damned cats. Just wait out there, can't you?"

"Pleased to," I said, stepping back and sitting down with my tail coiled over my toes. "See how easy that was?" I was quite pleased with the fact that my voice wasn't shaking. The growl was still coiling around my innards.

"I hate cats," she mumbled, and went to set the basket on the counter. "Tina," she yelled as she came back. "I've just got to pop out. Mind the front?"

There was a faint shout back from somewhere down the stairs, and the were shooed us away from the door. "Come on. Stop shedding about the place."

We let ourselves be shooed, and she led us to a door marked *No Access Do Not Use*. There was another sign on it declaring it was alarmed, but the were just pushed it open onto a narrow flight of stairs.

"Where're we going?" I asked.

"Somewhere I don't have to smell you."

"Thank the gods for that," I muttered, and dodged Callum when he tried to nudge me with his boot.

The stairs led to another supposedly alarmed door – there seemed to be a lot of nervous doors around here – which opened onto a roof terrace. Well, a roof *space,* really, probably just there to give access to the big vents that ran fresh air down to the enclosed rooms below and drew stale, greasy air out. That would've been a new addition since the age of the mill worker. No one was too worried about their air quality back then. The wind snarled around the vents and scoured the low walls on the edge of the roof, and someone had put a cheap gazebo up in one corner. It had two sides, trembling in the wind, and was reinforced with extra waterproof tarps. Astroturf ran out of its shelter and across a fair portion of the space, held down with upturned half barrels that could've been seating or low tables. Cushions were piled in the gazebo, and the were took shelter inside it, tugging her cardigan down over her arms. She had soft curves everywhere, someone easy and comfortable in her own skin. Henna tattoos danced delicately across her hands, and she had a small ruby stud in her nose. I wondered what happened to it when she changed. Did she have to remember to take it out, or did it just pop off and get lost? Or did she end up as a wolf with a nose piercing?

"You can't stay long," she said. "It's bad enough you've even been in the area – if my customers think the Watch has been sniffing about, they won't be back for weeks, if at all."

"We're not Watch," I said. "I really can't emphasise how much not Watch we are."

"And we're not your old-school weres, either," she said. "Doesn't stop you looking like a feather duster, does it?"

I shook my tail out irritably, trying to get it to calm down. "But—"

"You know what the Watch did," she said, her voice flat. "You know how many packs they wiped out. Weres were all but extinct. And the last cleanses weren't so long ago."

I didn't answer. I did know what the Watch had done.

And they could argue they'd been protecting humans from weres, and the Folk from the risk of discovery that rampant weres posed, but it came down to the fact that a whole kind had paid for the indiscretion of a few.

"They must know you're here, though," Pru said.

"I imagine they do," she said. "But we keep our heads down, and unfamiliar cats make us nervous. Even you two."

Pru and I looked at each other, and I tried to decide if that was a compliment regarding how approachable we were, or an insult to our many abilities.

"What about familiar cats?" I asked. "A certain calico cat with gloriously mismatched eyes, maybe?"

Yasmin inclined her head slightly. "Yes. Claudia."

"We're looking for her," Callum said. "Her and another friend of ours. That's all."

The were looked at him, then at us, and shook her head. "Gerry shouldn't have sent you. We don't get involved in the affairs of cats. Or anyone else, for that matter."

"He just said you might be able to give us some information," Callum said. "We're worried. Our friends are missing." His voice was quiet and level, with a touch of a plea to it. Just one lost soul searching for another.

She sniffed, unimpressed. "Gerry's too bloody soft. He thinks that if everyone's just a little *nicer* to each other, we can all go skipping into the forest together like one big happy Folk-family. He forgets weres have never been welcome. We stick to our own, and we protect ourselves by *not* talking to the likes of you."

"So if you're not an old-school were, what are you,

then?" I asked. "What do you do instead of howling at the moon and eating maidens, all that good stuff?"

"Maidens?" she asked.

"I think that's vampires," Callum said.

"They don't exist," Yasmin and I said together, and she grinned suddenly, the expression both wolfish and delighted. Then she shook her head. "I like maidens as much as the next person, but we don't eat anyone. No one ever really did, even in the old days. Most of it was just stories hunters told to scare people into paying them for protection. And these days the last thing we want is to draw attention to ourselves. So no uncontrolled changes, no attacks on humans or wildlife, accidental or deliberate. My changes are strictly when I want them, where I want them. I am a wolf of my own choosing."

She said it firmly, like a mantra that had been said a thousand times before, said so often that it had become a truth of sorts. But I didn't know if that made it a truth to her, or a truth to everyone, especially small furry animals.

"What happens at full moon, then? Do you lock yourself in a padded room or something?" I asked, and Callum nudged me with his boot. "What? It's a fair question!"

"You and your fair questions. Sorry," he added to Yasmin.

Yasmin snorted. "Gods. *Cats.* But if you're so interested, then no. We don't lock ourselves up. Denying one's nature is as much a problem as giving in to it." She looked from me to Callum. "Do none of you know about modern weres?"

"I don't think I've met one before," Callum said. He'd given up on the dejected approach, and instead just looked fascinated. He took his cigarettes out and offered them to her. She shook her head.

"I've always tried to avoid weres, as a rule," Pru said. She'd found herself a comfortable cushion and was sitting on it perfectly upright, her ears forward and her tail over her toes.

"We have associations," Yasmin said.

"Is that a fancy name for packs?" I asked, and she gave me a look that was half exasperated, half amused.

"No, that's different. These are like clubs, investment groups, whatever you want to call them. We buy land, set it aside. There's no livestock on it, nothing but wild spaces and rabbits, and anyone who wants to run can go up there and change. It's how we embrace the wild of our nature without harming others. We don't turn anyone by accident, and anyone who wants to be turned has to actually watch someone change, as well as be educated regarding the lore." She shrugged. "It's like having a taste for diving, or rock climbing. It's in us, but it doesn't control us. We indulge when we see fit."

"And so ... what? You run a nice little were bar the rest of the time, and it's all very pretty and civilised?" I asked. "No scraps and accidental maulings? Do you re-home orphan birds in your free time, too?"

She gave me a half smile that exposed one of those overlong canines. "I run an organic, alcohol-free bar," she said. "Most modern weres barely drink. It's too risky."

"How can you have an alcohol-free bar?" I asked, but she ignored me. I looked at Pru.

Pru shrugged, then said, "Have you seen Claudia recently?"

"Not for a while, no. Why?"

Pru didn't answer, just watched the were with her pale eyes narrowed. I looked at Callum, and wondered if he had some more tactful way to say, *eaten any dentists lately?* He'd managed to get his cigarette lit, hunched against the wind, and now he looked up, the wind twisting his messy hair.

"Do you know anything about a dentist called Malcolm Walker?"

Which was, as expected, more tactful than my approach, but a bit vague for my liking.

"Why?"

"He's a friend of ours, and we can't seem to find him."

Yasmin took half a step toward Callum, her head up and her nostrils flaring slightly, the ruby catching the thin sun as she examined him. I caught another whiff of her, as if the wolfishness had intensified, and my hackles rose of their own accord.

Then she stepped back again, adjusting her cardigan. There was something tight and drawn in her face. "I think we move in different circles. We have as little to do with Norths as we do cats."

"I'm not a North."

"Yet you smell like one."

"And you smell like a ravening beast, yet you run an alcohol-free bar," I pointed out. Actually, she also smelled of sunshine and wide spaces, but the musk of wild animal was strong enough that I wasn't entirely lying.

"Unhelpful," Callum said to me, but Yasmin just snorted, her expression softening slightly.

"Are you sure you wouldn't be better looking for the RSPCA rather than a dentist?"

"Believe me, some days I wonder."

I growled, and Yasmin grinned at me, then looked back at Callum. "What's so important about the dentist?"

Callum scratched his chin. "He's a friend. And there had been weres at his surgery."

"We get plaque like everyone else."

"He's not just a dentist." He hesitated, looking at me, and I shrugged. Either she knew about Walker or she didn't. And if she did know, she'd know about Ms Jones. No were would miss the lingering whiff of that sort of power. "His partner's a sorcerer. Polly Jones."

How someone who could throw you into a different dimension ended up with a name like Polly was beyond me. Why she'd kept it, even more so.

Yasmin had been fidgeting with the bracelets stacked on her left wrist, and now she stopped, looking at Callum sharply. "You're working for her?"

"In a manner of speaking."

"Why would a sorcerer need you to hunt down her partner?"

Callum spread his fingers, shaking his head slightly, and I said, "Strangely, we didn't think to question the scary sorcerer lady."

"Maybe you should have," she said, and we stared at each other in the thin winter sunshine, while beyond the rooftop traffic groaned and heaved, and somewhere a siren screamed.

12

WORLD DOMINATION FOR THE FUN OF IT

"So what can you tell us?" I asked finally, when Yasmin didn't say anything else. "You obviously know them both."

She looked at me. Her eyes were warm brown, and there was an intensity in them that made my hackles rise as surely as the growl had earlier.

"Who else have you asked?"

"Why?" Callum's voice was calm, but his fingers were denting his cigarette.

"Because some things you don't want to go poking your snout into." Her nose wrinkled. "But it's what you do, isn't it? I've heard of you two. You're some sort of trouble for hire, sticking your nose in about the place. Didn't know you were a North, though. A North and a cat. Interesting combo."

"I'm not a North anymore," Callum said, grinding the cigarette out on the edge of the roof. "I'm just Callum."

"Is a North something you can stop being?"

They stared at each other, and I wondered what

exactly she could smell. If it was something more than that old, neglected whiff of loss and magic that lingered under the scent of cigarettes and books. Callum didn't say anything, and after a moment I said, "We're PIs, actually."

The were kept her gaze on Callum for a little longer, and he just stared back, his face set and his eyes steady, the fickle wind shoving his hair in all directions. Finally she shifted her gaze to me, and cocked her head. "Is that what you call it?"

"G and C London, Private Investigators," I said. "Best magical PIs in Yorkshire." I mean, as far as I know we're also the only ones, and we were actually trying to avoid magical cases, for all the good it did us, but *details*, you know.

"Yeah, well." She looked back at Callum. "Don't go PI-ing about this. Whatever questions you've been asking, whatever you've been thinking, leave weres out of it. Or we'll keep you out of it. We're not looking for trouble, and we're definitely not looking for the Watch being in our business."

"It's the last thing we want, too," I said.

She snorted. "Good luck on that one."

"So you won't help us?" Pru's voice was flat, and we all looked at her. She hadn't moved, carved like an Egyptian god on her pillow. "If you know the sorcerer, you know she wouldn't just vanish. Neither would Claudia. Something's happened."

"Maybe they're on holiday," Yasmin said, and shrugged.

"Really?" I asked. "*Holiday?*"

"People take holidays."

"We don't."

She looked at Callum's coat and said, "Evidently. Look, you're looking for sorcerers, ask some other magic-workers." She lifted her chin at Callum. "I can smell magician on you. Ask him."

"We have," he said.

"Have you asked him about necromancers?" She showed her teeth in that smile again, and Callum tried not to look surprised.

"You can smell necromancers?" he asked.

"No, but I know whose smell that is. And there's plenty of rumours." She raised a hand before Callum could ask. "Rumours, mind. My bar's still a bar. Truth and rumour don't even touch noses half the time. But I'd still ask."

"What other rumours have you heard?" I asked. "About—"

"No." A growl touched the word. "We're done here. I'm not messing with sorcerers, and I never mess with cats. Neither will any were you talk to. We show our respect and keep our distance. You're wasting your time."

"Is there anyone else—" Callum started, and this time the growl sent my heart leaping for my throat.

"*No.* I've told you – you two are trouble. A North who won't be a North, and a cat on the wrong side of the Watch? We want nothing to do with you. Stay away from my weres, you hear me? There *will* be consequences."

Her voice was human and not, laced with a snarl that set Pru's ears back and my hackles fully up. Callum looked at her, his face still expressionless, then nodded.

"Alright. Let's go." He turned and headed for the door back into the building, not looking back.

"But—" Pru started, and I was the one who interrupted her.

"Let's go, Pru." I jerked my head toward the door, and she bared her teeth at me, but jumped off the cushion, giving Yasmin a narrow look as she went. The were didn't respond, and we left her on the roof, her long, multi-coloured skirt swirling softly around her in the breeze and her hands in fists at her sides.

"I don't like this," Pru said, as we headed down the stairs. "She knows something."

"We know," Callum said. "But she's not going to give us anything else. Pack above all."

Pru and I looked at each other, and she arched her non-existent eyebrow whiskers at me. I shrugged, and she gave a huff that indicated she wasn't impressed.

"Hairballs," I muttered, then said to Callum, "So, Ifan—"

"I know," he said. "Let's just get back to the car, okay?"

So I left it. Bloody magicians.

"HE'S NOT ANSWERING," Callum said, hitting disconnect on his phone.

"He could just be sleeping off his epic party," I said, and Pru shook her head.

Callum gave me a sideways look and swapped his phone for his cigarettes. "Maybe."

We were hurrying back toward the car, threading our

way through shoppers bundled against the cold morning, buildings looming around us in a curious mix of tatty and glossy, depending on exactly how far the regeneration had got. Pound shops rubbed shoulders with bookies and hipster cafes, while half-empty, blocky shopping arcades that had obviously started the sixties with high hopes glared at the elegantly sweeping windows of grand, pollution-stained old buildings, which in turn leaned over the flash and gleam of new, purpose-built shopping centres. The whole place was crowded with shoppers brandishing clusters of branded bags and students staring at their phones and hijab-wearing women with immaculate make-up striding about purposefully, and it also had a decent population of the sort of people that meant one tatty man talking to two cats didn't even draw a second glance.

"Or he's still in with necromancers," Pru said. She'd refused Callum's offer of a lift on the way back, and her skin looked grey and cold. "And has been all along."

Callum cupped his hands around his cigarette, trying to get his lighter to work, and said a little indistinctly, "Even if he was before, it was their fault he lost his dad. He wouldn't have wanted that."

"Are you sure? If he gets rid of Ms Jones as well, that'd make him the most powerful magical being in the county, wouldn't it?"

"He's already the most powerful *magician*, as far as I know," Callum said.

"You humans seem to have a thing for *more,*" Pru said. "Nothing's ever enough for you. And what if it's not quite as we think? We don't know that Sonia and Ifan's dad really got sucked into the Old One's dimension. What if they're just in hiding?"

"And Ms Jones would be the only one strong enough to stand against that sort of combo," I said. "They'd want to make sure she was gone for good before ... well, before whatever they're planning. And Lewis did work out how to drain her power when she was stuck in his house."

"And the weres?" Callum asked, finally getting his cigarette lit. "How are those fitting into your plans for magician-necromancer world domination?"

"Yasmin definitely knows something," I said. "Maybe they're working for Ifan, and she was just trying to scare us off."

Pru gave something close to a purr. "That fits. The weres kidnap Walker so Ms Jones will come and save him, then Ifan and the necromancers trap her and steal her power."

"Sounds reasonable," Callum said, and we both stared at him. "I mean, provided Ifan's a megalomaniacal criminal mastermind." He raised his eyebrows at us. "Which totally fits with someone who wandered off to Mustique rather than just tell his dad he didn't fancy being part of the family business."

Pru and I looked at each other, and she sighed. "I *really* don't like him."

"I know," Callum said. "And he's a bit of a muppet sometimes. But I'm pretty sure he's not plotting world domination."

"Are you?" I asked. "Not even a little bit, just for fun?"

"That would be more his style, but I don't think so.

He's pretty cut up about his dad. And he really did fake his death to get away from the necromancers."

We walked on in silence, shoppers washing around us and the stained pavements cold beneath my paws. We were almost back to the car before I said, "What about Sonia? Pru's right on that. We don't know she's really gone."

Callum opened his mouth, shut it again, then groaned. "*Necromancers.*"

Worse than magicians, really.

CALLUM LET us both into the car as he tried Ifan's phone again, then shook his head. "Still no answer." He took a piece of paper out of his pocket and unfolded it, setting it between the seats where Pru and I could see it, then leaned against the car as he tried the phone again. I sniffed the paper, which smelled of cheap home printers and wolf.

"What's this?" I asked, as he gave up on the phone and got in, coaxing the engine into life.

"It was under Yasmin's door. Someone must've dropped it."

I examined the straggly print. "DJ *Scoot?* Really?"

Callum grinned. "Weres have a slightly weird sense of humour sometimes."

"There's no address," Pru said. "Is it just for her bar?"

"No." Callum tapped a finger on the top of the page, where the words *banging beats* was printed in a tight, smudgy font. "That's part of the location. I need to look at it properly, but it'll tell us where the were club is."

"Awesome," I said, "Sounds fun. Do we bring our own bones?"

"You don't go in at all," he said, and I could smell the sort of tight, anxious scent that usually means sleepless nights. "But that's where I'm going tonight."

"Is that a good idea?"

"It's *an* idea."

Pru looked from one of us to the other, then said, "And now?"

Callum sighed, and looked at me.

"Oh, *super*. We're going to look for necromancers, aren't we?"

"Well, one," Callum said, as we pulled into the city traffic. "He's not answering his phone, either."

"Seems like a good sign."

Pru put both paws on the dashboard, looked around, then said, "Well, you two have fun. I'll find Tam. See if she's still on your magician."

"Are you sure?" Callum asked. "You're cold—"

"I'm fine," she said, and was gone before either of us could say anything more.

I wished I could follow her, but as I was still hoping to survive the day without an out-of-body experience or the threat of the void, all I did was look at Callum and say, "What're we going to do with our necromancer?"

"See if he knows anything. And hopefully get a cuppa."

"Of course. Because what we need in the face of dodgy necromancers, scheming magicians, missing sorcerers, and the damn Watch, is a cuppa."

"I'll ask if he has any tuna."

"It's the least you can do."

IT'S NOT like there's a necromancer's directory where you can pop your city in and it'll tell you the location and star ratings of all the necromancers within a twenty-mile radius. But handily, we knew one ex-necromancer who might be able to help us. Or ex-necromancer henchman, maybe. I wasn't convinced by Muscles' own abilities in the magical realm.

Even better, we weren't going to have to trek across to the other side of Leeds, either. Muscles' flat was in the tangled sprawl of villages that had been swallowed by Bradford and Leeds as they advanced on one another and the surrounding countryside, so all we had to do was put up with a whole lot of stopping and starting to get there. Callum pulled off his garish scarf as the heater started to raise the air marginally above the outside temperature, and we struggled our way out of Bradford and back in the general direction of Leeds, with the gods of traffic lights firmly against us.

Fifteen minutes or so later, and we were just starting to find clearer roads when something large and brindled hit the bonnet of the car with a thud that made me hiss and Callum swear. He jammed the brakes on, setting up a screech of tyres and some enthusiastic horns from the following cars, while Green Snake craned his way out of the heater vent, peering around anxiously. Whatever had hit us was already gone, but Callum swerved to the side of the road, pulling half up onto the pavement while the car behind us revved angrily past, the driver shouting something that even through both sets of windows I could tell wasn't complimentary.

"Was that Tam?" he asked, already opening the door to check the road, and there was another thud from above us, heavy enough that I half-expected the roof to bow in.

Callum swung out onto the street, and there was a whisper of air parting from the backseat, then Pru said, "Where's he going?"

I peered between the seats at her. "Tam's aim's a bit off."

Pru shrugged. "Moving targets are hard."

Callum leaned back into the car. "She's not there."

"Give it a moment," Pru said, and just then a large and slightly damp she-cat appeared on the driver's seat, hunkered down as if she were about to spring at someone, teeth bared. Those teeth were aimed at me, and I flinched back before I could stop myself.

"There you are," Callum said, and Tam spun around, hissing. He flinched as well. "I didn't mean to hit you."

"*She* hit *us,*" I pointed out, and Tam gave me a look that suggested she was questioning my parentage.

"You're a fine one to criticise shifting technique," Pru said, and Tam gave her a remarkably similar look to the one she'd just given me. "No offence."

"Some taken."

"Fair."

"Tam?" Callum said, and they stared at each other for a moment, then she jumped over to my side of the car with surprising grace. Pru stepped through from the back with wraith-like neatness, and Callum got himself back inside, hitting the indicator as he hunted for a gap in the traffic.

"Did you see Ifan?" he asked.

"Tam did," Pru said. "She hung out at his house the whole night, and he didn't go anywhere that she could see."

Which didn't mean he actually hadn't gone anywhere. When you play with the sort of things magicians do, you're bound to have secret passageways and escape routes.

"And today?"

"He went out earlier in an Uber. Tam tried to track him, but he's hiding himself somehow. She got nothing."

"Sneaky," I said, then added to Tam, "You think he knows you were watching him?"

She shrugged.

"He's not stupid," Pru said.

"More's the pity."

"He might not be hiding from us," Callum said. "It could be something entirely unconnected."

Pru, Tam and I looked at each other, but didn't say anything. Finally I said, "Anything else? Anyone go into the house? Did you hear anything? Smell anything?"

Tam shrugged, and looked at Pru, who said, "Not really."

"That bit I got," I said. "How did you get the rest? Is it only me and Callum you don't talk to, Tam?"

Tam just looked at me, her eyes half-closed.

"Right."

Tam shook herself off, looking around the car.

"Got any biscuits?" Pru asked. "She's starving."

Callum reached into the doorless glovebox and pulled out a packet of cat treats. Tam took it from his hand before he could open it, and promptly vanished again.

"Hey," I protested, but not very loudly. Just in case she'd only gone as far as the back seat.

"She's gone back to keep an eye on things," Pru said. "In case he turns up again."

"Thanks for the update," I said. "Anything else?"

She narrowed her eyes at me. "Have you found a necromancer yet?"

"We're getting there."

"Hurry up, then," she said, and vanished.

THE COUNCIL FLATS where Muscles lived were those sort that had been built to embrace green areas, I suppose as a means of cheering up the poor sods who had to live in them. None of the green areas were given over to gardens, of course, not even for the ground floor flats, and nobody had thought that it might be an idea to have communal flowerbeds or a bit of a seating area, anything that might actually allow the green patches to be enjoyed. What they had instead were featureless stretches of lawn, looking a little sorry for themselves in the long shadows of a dull winter day, and liberally pocked with litter and dog deposits.

The blocks of flats were square pebble dashed things, the lumpy finish left bare and multicoloured as if it were meant to convey character on the buildings. There looked to be four flats to a floor, so each side had a balcony that was just big enough to put a clothes horse out on, but not big enough for so much as a folding chair. They were like the lawn – less a case of the thought counting, and more a case of the creators of the flats wanting to be seen to be having the thought.

We parked on the side of the road, behind a Peugeot with a broken taillight and a classic Mini that someone obviously spent a lot of time polishing, even if it was made up mostly of mismatched parts. There were four blocks of flats in the little development, and we headed to the one furthest from the road. It was thinking about raining, the air heavy and chilled with moisture, and the only people around were an old woman trailing a shopping bag on wheels, and a tired-looking man trying to control three dogs and a toddler. Neither of them looked at us as Callum scanned the names at the intercom, then pressed the bell to the right flat. No one answered. Callum tried again, holding it down for longer, but there was still no response.

"Maybe he's out," Callum said.

"Could be. Plotting necromancer world domination, perhaps."

Callum tried the bell again, and shrugged. "It could be broken."

"Try calling him again."

Callum scrolled though his phone to find the number, tried it, then shook his head. "Straight to messages." He looked around. "He's in one of the bottom flats, though. Come on."

He led the way around the building, and I didn't need to see the extra-large T-shirt that said *World's Greatest Cat*

Daddy hung on the clothes horse outside to know we had the right place. I could smell the thin, confused scent of old cat, and overlaid with it cologne and shaving gel and microwave dinners.

"That's him."

"Door's open," Callum said, and we both stared at the sliding door, a heavy red curtain obscuring any glimpse of the room beyond.

"That seems bad," I said, and jumped to the chunky concrete wall of the balcony. There was no pebbledash on top, but it was cold and harsh under my paws. I watched the small gap between the curtain and the edge of the door, aware that it had started raining, falling in fat drops on my spine. From here, the lived-in smell of cat and man was overlaid with something both familiar and unwelcome, rank and wild.

"Hairballs," I said.

"What?" Callum asked.

"I smell weres."

And not just them. Underpinning their hairy reek was the rich, thick taste of blood.

"*Hairballs,*" I said again.

13

IT'S NOT BARBECUED DUCK

THERE ARE TWO TYPES OF PEOPLE. THERE ARE THOSE WHO, when confronted with an open door in midwinter and the whiff of violence lurking around the place, will beat a judicious retreat and either contact the relevant authorities or decide that it's None of Their Business. That second option, by the way, is favoured in the sort of places we tend to frequent, and is almost guaranteed to extend the life expectancy of all involved.

The second type of people are those who apparently harbour delusions of invincibility or immortality or misguided heroism, or delusions of some sort, anyway. I'm fairly sure they're the sort of people who come to tacky ends, probably somewhere behind an open door in midwinter. And despite my best efforts to dissuade him, Callum definitely belonged to that group.

"Hear anything?" he asked me in a low voice.

"No." I could smell plenty, though. Panic, and rage, and the confusion of an old cat as the world he barely understood anymore crashed down around him. "But there's definitely been weres here."

"Why would weres be after Rav? He's not even involved with the necromancers anymore."

I shot a sideways look at him, shifting my paws on the rough surface of the balcony wall. "I don't know, dude. Maybe he does a good line in dog grooming."

Callum didn't respond to that, frown lines digging into his forehead. I didn't need to point out that there was one person who knew we'd likely go to Muscles for information on necromancers. One *magician.* Judging by the way he was chewing on his thumbnail, he was thinking the same. "Anything necromancer-y?" he asked.

I hesitated. I could smell blood, and I could smell magic, mostly in the form of protective charms and shift locks, but there wasn't *blood magic.* I didn't think. Primarily there was a lot of acrid, lemon-tainted confusion, but the were stink could be hiding anything. "Maybe? There's some magic about, but mostly it just stinks of weres."

"Great," he muttered. "Years without seeing a were, and now I'm tripping over them. What the hell's Rav doing with weres?"

It didn't seem like a question that needed an answer, although it was raising my own questions about just how much time he'd spent with weres before. But that would have to keep until after we'd foolishly got ourselves involved in yet another crime scene. I jumped to the floor of the balcony, the concrete cold and faintly gritty.

Callum boosted himself up and over the wall, landing lightly next to me and pausing, both of us still straining to hear anything from inside. There were some winter-empty pots on the balcony along with the clothes horse, a small stool, and a few empty beer bottles. Callum pushed the door a little wider, then ducked inside without waiting, the heavy curtain moving reluctantly in his wake. It wasn't like we could see anything from here, and the light behind us meant that stopping in the doorway just made us into better targets.

I followed him in, nose wrinkling at the scent of mild feline incontinence and industrial strength body spray. Neither of which completely obscured the reek of panic and fright, the smell of chaos cruising in the front door without knocking. And hairy were stink, of course.

"Anyone?" Callum whispered. He'd dropped into a crouch to one side of the door while I peered around, my nose twitching and my eyes wide, searching for movement. There were no other windows, and the curtain blocked out the day behind us. A doorway to the right let in a little dreary light, and another to the left was just deeper shadows.

"Can't see anyone," I said, still trying to sort through the scents but without much luck. Muscles must've been bathing in cut-price body spray. I sneezed.

Callum stayed where he was, switching on the torch on his phone and using it to light up the room. Or he tried to – it gave us a glimpse of a cheap, shattered coffee table and bodybuilding magazines scattered across the room, then went out. "Damn it."

"You forgot to charge it, didn't you?" I said, venturing into the room a little further now that it looked like no one was going to rush us.

"I had other things on my mind." He felt his way along the wall, and a moment later the room was washed with yellow light from a single overhead bulb. It was graced with the sort of lampshade a particular generation of cat ladies calls tasteful, with dangly bits and some sort of lace stuff stuck to it. It lit the little room well enough, though. Or well enough that we could tell it hadn't been a peaceful night in the Muscles house. As well as the smashed coffee table, the sofa cushions had been torn half to pieces and scattered across the room, and the shattered frame of a set of cheap shelves lay on the tatty carpet among a muddle of forlorn indoor plants and broken pots and travel books, potting mix and old water trodden into the pages. A TV gazed serenely down from its perch on the wall, and there was still a framed print of that Greek island with all the white buildings and blue roofs hung above the destroyed shelves, but it was at a bit of an angle. There had been something else hung over the sofa, but it was reduced to a broken frame and smashed glass that glittered in the light. "Mind your paws," Callum said.

I minded them. I was minding everything, in fact, because I was half-expecting to fall into a necromancer trap at any second. Not that I was sure what that would actually entail, but I assumed it'd be painful and likely undignified.

But the more I sniffed around, the more I suspected we weren't dealing with necromancers. There was blood here, definitely, but it didn't have their sour echoes of power. It spoke more of fists than charms, and most of the magic I could sniff out was in the form of laborious shift locks and fae-guards of the sort an inexperienced practitioner cobbled together from library books and YouTube tutorials. They did the trick, but only if no one was too interested in busting through them.

Callum ducked through the door to the right, into a little kitchen with a floor of worn wood-print linoleum, and the sort of nondescript units that could've come from any DIY store on the planet. I trotted after him and peered in the doorway, spotting a small table with two stools pressed against one wall, and on the floor next to it two bowls elevated on a fancy adjustable stand, one still half-full of biscuits. My stomach rumbled despite myself. It had to be getting toward lunch by now.

"Nothing." He stepped over me and headed back across the living room to the other doorway, finding another light and illuminating a small hall, unlit and faintly damp smelling. "I'll check the bedrooms."

I let him brave whatever passed as Muscles' bedroom decor while I nosed my way around the debris on the floor, being careful where I put my paws. There was a mug smashed in among the bones of the coffee table, the tea thoroughly soaked up by a sofa cushion, as well as a plate with the remnants of some chocolate cake on it. I nibbled a few crumbs, just to make sure it hadn't been poisoned or anything, and moved on.

I found an open packet of cat treats under an abandoned hoody that had a strong whiff of were on it, and, since Callum was neither back nor shouting for help, I checked those for edibility as well. Never pass up a free meal.

They proved edible, and I was bolting the lot before Callum could get back and tell me they were treats, not a main course, when something rushed me from under the sofa. I caught the movement out of the corner of my eye, a scrambling, disjointed charge, and scooted backward with a squawk, almost choking on my mouthful of biscuits and spilling a couple on the floor as I went. Gah. I hate food waste.

I tried to yell for Callum, but my mouth was still full, and I leaped the broken corpse of the coffee table to put a bit of space between myself and whatever monstrous attack creature had been left behind after the battle. I spun to face it, and a very old, rather tatty tabby tom with his hipbones jutting at his saggy skin peered at me across the mess and gave a plaintive mewl.

"Oh, gods," I said, and swallowed hurriedly. "Gordie?"

"Who's that?" he asked.

"Gobbelino. We met …" Actually, I probably didn't want to remind him about the necromancers and the cat traps and the ancient, hungry beings busting through from other dimensions. All that fun stuff. "I'm a friend of Mitzi."

"Mitzi?"

"Yeah, you know. Your …" I had no idea who she was. Daughter? Sister? Friend? "Fluffy black and white cat who hangs around with you."

He blinked at me, his eyes rheumy. "Is it dinner?"

"Um, sure. There're some biscuits just there." I hadn't eaten them *all*. Come on, it was a whole packet. And I got chased off.

He huffed. "Don't like biscuits."

"Okay. Well, we'll find something else." I hesitated. "D'you know where your human went, Gordie?"

"Is there chicken?"

"I'll find out. Did you see who made the mess?"

Gordie looked around as if seeing it for the first time, and wheezed. For one horrifying moment I thought he was going to keel over from fright, but then I realised he was laughing. "Kittens," he said. "They don't know their own strength."

I blinked at the chaos. If kittens had done this, I didn't want to meet Mum. "What sort of kittens?" I asked.

Gordie yawned, and licked his chops. He only had about two teeth left, which made me feel better about eating his treats. He wouldn't even be able to chew them. "You know," he said vaguely, and blinked at Callum as he hurried through the door.

"The bedrooms look fine," he started, then saw Gordie. "Aw, Gordie. Are you okay?"

Gordie looked at him, then said, "Do you have any chicken?"

"I can see if there's any in the fridge. Are you alright, though? You're not hurt?"

"No." The old cat looked puzzled for a moment. "I was under the sofa. Why was I under the sofa?"

"I think there was a fight," I said. "Between your human and some others, maybe?"

"Oh." He considered it. "Oh, yes. There was."

"What happened?"

"Is it dinner time?"

Callum and I looked at each other, then Callum went through to the kitchen and a moment later I heard him say, "I've got your chicken, Gordie."

"Good." Gordie looked around as if unsure how to get

out of the furniture-based carnage, and Callum came back in.

"Can I lift you up?"

Gordie looked at him with his eyes half-lidded. "Be careful. I'm an old cat."

Callum lifted the saggy old tom gently and carried him through to the kitchen, where we watched him test his chicken, declare it too cold, and wait for Callum to heat it in the microwave. Only after he'd swallowed a few pieces whole did he sit back and lick his chops, then stare at us as if seeing us for the first time.

"What d'you want?" he asked. "I'm tired."

"Who was here?" I asked. "Where's your human?"

"I don't know. I'm not his keeper."

Callum glanced into the little living room. He'd put his back to the nearest wall, and I was doing about the same. Whether this had anything to do with missing dentists or not, anyone taking on Muscles would either have excellent backup or be someone we had no desire to meet. Gordie mumbled at another morsel of chicken, trying to get it into his mouth.

"Do you know who came to see him?" Callum asked. "Were they friends?"

Gordie swallowed painfully and lapped a little water from the other bowl. "Maybe. Humans have weird friends."

He went back to his chicken, and I was about to suggest to Callum that we weren't going to get anything useful out of him, so we may as well beat a judicious retreat while the retreating was good, when something caught on the edge of my hearing. I was on my feet without realising it, hackles rising and ears twisting toward the sound, barely hearing Callum say, "What is it?"

I couldn't answer that. Some instincts are too old to be articulated, and you don't argue with them. Not unless you've got lives to spare. But even if I didn't know what it was, I knew what we had to do. *"Duck,"* I hissed, my back arching of its own according.

Gordie said, "Oh, that'd be nice," but it ended in a squawk as Callum slammed the kitchen door, scooped him up unceremoniously, and threw the little two-person table over on its side, the top facing the tiny window over the sink. I shot straight over the table and plunged into shelter, and Callum grabbed me with his free hand, trapping both Gordie and me beneath him as he hunkered down in our questionable cover.

There was a long, breathless pause, long enough that I wondered if I'd got it wrong, if my instincts were so frayed from were stink and stray sorcerers and magicians and the ever-present threat of the Inbetween that my whiskers were just jumping at harried delivery drivers dropping boxes or kids kicking cans while they did their nan's grocery run.

Then there was the rapidly ascending whistle of an old-fashioned kettle coming up to the boil, or of a train thundering through a tube station without stopping, and the window lit up so brightly that Callum swore, and I could see the blood vessels behind my eyelids. The kitchen window shattered and the door to the living room blew in, and I heard the balcony doors collapse in a cacophony of smashing glass. I smelled magic, raw and violent purple as a bruise, and then the whiff of fire coming fast on its heels.

Callum didn't wait on niceties. He came to his feet with Gordie in one hand and me in the other, clutching us to his chest, and plunged through the living room door in a low crouch, his coat sweeping the debris with us.

"Is it barbecued duck?" Gordie asked, and we both ignored him.

The sofa was on fire, the flames spreading out from a black crater in its middle. The curtains that hadn't been torn away by the missile coming through the doors were lighting the place with some nice blue flames, and the rug was illustrating why you should always buy fire retardant material. Smoke was everywhere, a rapidly thickening fog of it, and Callum hissed, "Anything?"

"No one," I said, and he ran across the room, slipping on glass and flaming coffee table, then we were into the clearer air of the hallway and out the front door into the tatty entrance hall to the block. Callum deposited me on his shoulder and ran to each of the doors on the floor, pounding on them with his fist and yelling, *"Fire!"* Alarmed faces were already appearing on the stairs, and three different people were on their phones to the emergency services. By the time we slipped out the main door it was to join a crowd of excitable humans in a mix of slippers and onesies and tracksuits, clutching phones and pets and favourite toys, and the scream of sirens was bearing down on us.

"It's those damn kids," an elderly man in a turban said to Callum. "Fireworks all year, that's the problem."

"Could be," Callum said agreeably, and headed away to

avoid a woman with a cat under each arm. The cats looked more startled than suspicious, but you never know where the Watch has its agents. And the last thing we needed was to be implicated in a fire that tasted at its edges of raw, furious magic.

We made our way back to the car through more people flocking from the other apartment blocks, and the newly arrived police shouting at everyone to clear the area. We'd parked far enough away that we were going to be able to nip away without anyone noticing, but as we came around the corner of the building I said, "Stop."

"What?" Callum paused where he was, doing that thing he does where he just seems to fade into obscurity. It's a good trick for someone as unnecessarily tall as he is. We were still on the edge of the crowd, and in the mix of startled evacuees and rapidly arriving onlookers, he could've been just another resident, running out the door and throwing on the first coat that came to hand. One that had been set out to take to the bin, most likely.

I lifted my nose, scenting with more than just the usual senses. Muscles was gone, and there was no way he was gone willingly if he'd left Gordie in a trashed apartment. So whoever had just firebombed it hadn't been after Muscles. Or if they had, they must be a separate faction to whoever had attacked the first time, which seemed a stretch. Other than assault on T-shirt seams, I couldn't think of anything Muscles might have done to make him such a target.

We, on the other hand, seemed to be making a habit of being targets.

I was just about to say I thought it was all clear when

the car slipped by on the road, not far beyond where we were parked. It moved slow and shark-like, the tinted windows giving away nothing. It could've been anyone, drawn to the spectacle of disaster like every human in history. But it was a flash car in the part of town where flash cars were avoided, even by those who could afford them, because the police were more likely to wonder where you got it from.

And it was a *familiar* flash car, too, although it's not like there wouldn't be more than one on the streets of Leeds. It wasn't *that* flash.

But I have this thing about coincidences. And a car that looked very like the magician's, passing the site of a mystery magical bombing at an ex-necromancer's, seemed as likely to be a coincidence as Gordie was to get his barbecued duck.

"Damn it," Callum said quietly.

Which I thought was on the mild side.

14

MAGICAL FIREBOMBS & NICOTINE WITHDRAWAL

We waited long enough that we were reasonably sure the car wasn't coming back, and also so that we had more the air of *oh well, excitement's over* rather than *fleeing the scene of the crime.* Not that it was our fault exactly, but, well. Couldn't say it wasn't our fault, either, not with that car cruising the streets like a hungry predator.

Callum had smoked himself out of cigarettes by the time we climbed back into the chilly confines of the old Rover, and the grey morning had passed into grey afternoon without much fanfare. The fire engines were gone, and the police were telling bystanders with exhausted patience that there was nothing for them to see here. It was still raining on and off, and I'd spent a certain portion of the time sheltering in Callum's coat with Gordie. Callum's hair was dripping down his collar, and he looked paler than ever, the shadows under his eyes heavy smudges.

Now he swung into the car, set a half-asleep Gordie on the passenger seat, and fired the engine up to get the heater going before scrabbling around in the glovebox. He came up empty-handed and dropped back into his seat with a sigh.

"Corner shop just down there," I said, and he gave me an amused glance.

"Why, what d'you want?"

"I think magical firebombs *and* nicotine withdrawal all at once might be pushing things a bit."

"Maybe," he agreed, plugging his phone into the charger before coaxing the car into gear. "No sign of Tam or Pru."

"No. But all that means is he hasn't gone home from wherever he took his Uber this morning."

"We don't *know* it was him."

"Not entirely," I said, and then we were both quiet as he pulled out into the patchy traffic. Green Snake emerged from Callum's pocket and looked around warily, then went to curl up with Gordie. At least someone was getting some sleep.

WE STOPPED at the corner shop for chicken (it definitely wasn't the sort of neighbourhood for duck), cat biscuits, custard, and cigarettes, one of which Callum had lit before he even got back into the car. He'd also got a cup of tea from one of those vending style machines that so many shops have now, which he drank with the grim determination of someone who isn't enjoying the taste, but isn't going to waste his money, either.

"What now?" I asked, sampling the chicken. Gordie

was currently asleep, slumped against me, and Green Snake was curled around us both.

"Ifan's," he said.

"Really? Even though he might've just tried to blow us up?"

He took another sip of tea, grimacing. "Yes. I want to know if it was actually him."

"You think he'll tell you?"

"Maybe not. But I might know anyway," he said, and flashed me a weary grin. "Besides, we can pick up Tam and Pru. I don't think the car can take being hit by Tam too often."

"Fair point."

We stopped and started our way through the damp, grey-lit roads to the magician's house, the old Rover giving alarmed coughs as we pulled away from red lights and idling with a rougher purr than old Gordie's. Callum didn't go straight to the gates, but pulled into a side road and parked in the shelter of a leafless tree, turning the engine off. The Rover gave a relieved groan and settled into silence, and he rubbed his forehead wearily. I'd dozed on the way over, curled up next to Gordie, and judging by the stink in the car, Callum had been making up for the lack of sparkling conversation by taking up chain-smoking.

I got up and stretched, careful not to disturb Gordie. He was drooling, his snout planted firmly into the seat. "We not going in, then?"

Callum tapped his fingers on the wheel. "I want to know if Tam saw him go out first."

"I'm sure we'd have known if she had, but I'll go and find them."

Callum looked out at the rain, which had softened to a particularly miserable drizzle, and wrinkled his nose. "Want some custard first? See if it eases?"

"Nah. It won't, and I'll get some after."

He eyed me. "Have you suffered some unseen injury?"

"I can show restraint when needed." That, and all the cat treats I'd scoffed kept coming back on me. I'd barely been able to eat any chicken, and I was starting to see why you were only meant to eat a few at a time. But who designs a food like that?

Callum shook his head and said, "I think you must have concussion." But he opened his door and I jumped lightly over his lap and out onto the lane. "Be careful. And don't go onto Ifan's property without me, alright?"

"I have no intentions of it," I said, and ran for the corner of the street.

There were a few cars passing, spitting up spray from the damp roads, but no pedestrians, despite the broad pavements. Which suited me, as there was also no handy bush or weed cover for small black cats, just well-mowed grass verges and trees at regular intervals on either side of the wide road. There was no real option for taking cover in gardens either, as the properties were all walled with the sort of thick stone barricades that aren't designed for neighbourly chats. Not one of them was under human head-height, built to keep the world out and the privilege in. So I just trotted straight down the path with my head up and my ears forward, on the theory that people always assume cats are exactly where they're meant to be. And since we're almost always exactly where *we* mean to be, that works for us.

I found Pru sitting on one of the lower branches of the tree nearest the magician's house, one that had been home to a whole colony of nut-raging squirrels last time I'd tangled with it. There were no squirrels about now, though, and she was snuggled into a tasteful grey scarf she'd nicked from somewhere, the thickness of the branches above shielding her from the rain. Tam was curled against the trunk, snoring lightly.

Pru watched me approach, and I said, "Nice scarf," as soon as I was close enough.

"Thanks," she said. "It's Barbour."

"Any sign of the magician?"

"Nothing."

I scrambled up the trunk and sat down next to her. The scarf smelled of some delicate and doubtless expensive perfume. "Anything else happen?"

"No. And Tam's tried tracking him again, but she can't get anything. She's worn herself out." She glanced back at the matted mass, still snoring behind us, then wrinkled her snout at me. "Have you been in a fire?"

"Yep. We got firebombed by someone at Muscles' place, and saw a car taking off that looked very much like the magician's."

"Ah. After you, or after Muscles?"

"Not sure. But there had been weres at Muscles' already."

"Could be worse," Pru said.

"How?"

"Could've been the Watch."

I shivered, and we sat there together in the rain-stained day while the cars rumbled past in cocoons of warmth below us, and Tam snored on behind us, and I wondered where we went next.

I had a horrible feeling the answer was going to involve DJ Scoot.

WE'D BEEN SITTING THERE ARGUING for so long about who should be the one to risk waking Tam that I was considering asking Pru if she'd share her scarf, when the big gates to the magician's house gave a startled little click and swung open.

Pru and I looked at each other, and I got up to peer down the road. A low-slung car growled toward us, lights on and windows dark, and pulled in as the gates reached their widest. It headed up the potholed gravel drive to the house, the gates shut themselves again, and Tam yawned, sat up, and stretched. She blinked at me and lifted her chin.

"Hey," I said, relieved. I was fairly sure I'd been losing the argument, and I quite liked having both eyes in working order.

She yawned again, and looked from the house to the road. The Rover grumbled out of the side road, coughing exhaust smoke, and puttered over to pull in beneath us.

We peered down through the fumes as Callum cut the engine and got out, looking up at us. "Everyone alright?"

"Mildly asphyxiated," Pru said.

Callum nodded as if that were to be expected, and said, "Do we know where he's been?"

"Would seem not," I said. "Sneaky, slimy radish that he is."

"Right." He scratched his chin, fingertips rasping through stubble that definitely looked less designer and more *out all night*. "Come on, then."

"Come on where?"

"To see where he's been."

Pru and I looked at each other. "Why?" I asked.

"Because he might tell us, and then we can stop worrying about it."

"Or he might not, and the taxidermy army could eat us instead."

Callum considered it. "Pretty sure *taxidermy* is the key word there. Not going to be doing much eating."

"So they'll just stomp us and not bother with the eating. Besides, it's a magician's house. There's probably any number of things that could eat us. Or he could just firebomb us. Again."

"The firebombing does seem like a bad sign," Pru observed, still ensconced in her scarf.

Callum folded his arms, leaning against the car to peer up at us. "*If* he did it, and *if* we were the targets. And we're not going to learn anything more from here."

"We probably won't learn anything more in there, either," I said. "And how can you really trust him to tell the truth? About anything?"

"Maybe I can't. But he's still a friend, so I'm going to at least ask."

I looked at Pru. "Wouldn't you call this a bite first, ask questions later situation?"

"Humans," she said.

"Humans," I agreed.

Tam huffed and jumped to the roof of the car, landing surprisingly lightly for such a big cat. She twitched her ears at Callum.

"Also, yes, there's lunch," he said.

"You should have led with that," Pru said, and abandoned her scarf to join Tam.

I lingered for a moment longer, staring over the wall at the bland front of the magician's big house, its secrets hidden behind rain-streaked windows that reflected the grey sky. There was no smoke coming from any of the four chimneys, no lights on to alleviate the gloom. It nestled grandly in its neglected grounds, leafless ivy still clinging to the walls and the lawn overgrown even in the cold, smelling of old magic and disuse and emptiness.

"Coming?" Callum asked.

"Coming," I said with a sigh, and followed Tam onto the roof of the car and into the warmth within. It smelt of old cats and cigarettes, which was a sight better than outside.

IT TOOK a while for Ifan to answer the intercom and open the gates, but I couldn't tell if that was because he was shocked we were alive or if the house was just that big he didn't hear us at first. We dodged the worst of the potholes in the drive and pulled into the gravel turning circle in front of the house, avoiding the broken water feature and parking next to the corpse of an ancient Bentley. The garden had already been pretty well gone to seed when Lewis senior had been around, and his son apparently wasn't exerting too much effort to restore it. Weeds and winter flowers fought for dominance in beds half-hidden by the overgrown grass, and the trees that had once hinted at topiary were rather more cheerfully tree-shaped now.

Ifan was standing in the door waiting for us, his feet bare under expensively distressed jeans.

"Hey," he said, as Callum opened the car door and got out, then stood waiting for the rest of us to jump out on to the damp gravel. "How goes the investigative team?"

Callum shrugged and picked up Gordie, who'd tried to follow us but had somehow got tangled up with the handbrake. "Not much progress so far."

"That sucks," Ifan said, and I had to stop myself from agreeing with him. Callum headed to the front door and I slipped across to the garage, sniffing warm cars and magic above the sleepiness of winter gardens in rain.

"Where're you off to?" Ifan called, and I glanced at him over my shoulder. Callum was already inside, Tam ambling after him. I couldn't see Pru.

"Can't you give a cat some privacy?" I asked.

He lifted a hand apologetically. "Fine, fine. Come to the kitchen door then. I'm not leaving this one open. It's too bloody cold." And he pulled the door shut, leaving the garden silent but for the occasional swoosh of a car going past on the damp road outside.

I waited for a moment, then nosed around the garage

door, looking for a cat-sized gap. It was more well-maintained than it looked from the outside, though, and I couldn't find a way through, so I just put my eye to the gap and peered in. There was light coming from high, dirty windows, enough for me to see his car, still splattered with rain and oozing money and threat. I couldn't tell anything else from here, though. Not that I was sure what I was hoping to find. A large sign saying, *firebombs launch here,* perhaps.

"See anything?" Pru asked behind me, and I swallowed a yelp, turning as casually as I could.

"Nothing," I said. "I mean, his car, but that's it."

"I don't get why he'd attack Muscles."

"It might've been meant for us. Muscles was gone, and the place was already trashed. I can't see whoever did that coming back to finish the job."

"Maybe it was two sets of people after him," she suggested.

"This is Muscles. I mean, his body spray's pretty offensive, but that's about as much as you can say about him."

"You really think Ifan would attack Callum?"

I thought about it. "I don't know."

"Maybe it was another car."

"That just happens to look exactly like this one?"

She wrinkled her nose as the drizzle increased to a more determined rain. "Coincidences do exist, Gobbelino."

"I've yet to see one. He may have been trying to scare us off, not actually kill us."

She sighed, and lifted her nose at the garage. "You're probably right. But we're not learning anything here."

I shook myself off, scattering droplets of rain from my fur, and said, "No. Let's go."

We trotted around the house to the back door, and when a few scratches went unnoticed I jumped to the windowsill and glared in at Callum and Ifan, who were both leaning on the kitchen island with large mugs. Callum was buttering toast generously, and Ifan opened the door to let us in.

"Better?" he asked.

"Yes, digging holes in the garden in the rain is delightful," I said, and jumped on the island to shake myself off again.

"Jesus, Gobs," Callum said, protecting his toast with one hand.

"So what's up?" I asked, ignoring him. "You got your car back alright, then, Ifan?"

"People are oddly reluctant to steal it," he said, slurping coffee. "You want some chicken?"

"Someone did say duck," Gordie said. He was hunkered down on the island with milk dripping from his jaw. "I know someone said duck."

Callum piled marmalade onto his toast, and I gagged. He took a large bite, then said a little indistinctly, "Where did you say you left it?"

"Harrogate. Went to a bar opening up there and things got a little excessive." He stretched and looked around the kitchen, all gleaming black and white surfaces. "Worth it, though. This house ... It misses Dad. It turned my favourite jeans and jacket into matching leisurewear the other day, and all my cologne smells like Old Spice."

Callum regarded Ifan for a moment, then said, "Must be hard."

"It's not super fun." He shrugged. "But it's better when I get out a bit."

"Stop by anywhere on your way home, then?" I asked. "For breakfast, or to see anyone – anything?"

Ifan gave me a puzzled look. "No. Why? Was I meant to? Sorry, last night's still a bit fuzzy. Was I meant to go to a were club for you? I remember something about that."

"You seemed alright to me," I said.

He snorted. "In this house, I had a lot of practice at seeming alright."

There was a teetering silence, then, and I looked at Callum, waiting for him to say something, but he was frowning at his toast. I mean, I would too, with all that marmalade, but I don't think that was the reason. Then he said, "Are you done with the necromancers, Ifan? Really?"

Tam sat up from a stool on the opposite side of the island and looked at Ifan, her ears back. He looked back at her calmly, and took another sip of coffee before he replied. "I never really had much going on with them in the first place. I just wanted to know more about them – if they actually had any power or not. It seemed like something worth knowing, when they're messing about in our backyard."

"And you've definitely not seen Ms Jones."

Ifan set his mug down and spread his fingers on the island. "Just met her the once, and it was enough. What's going on, Cal?"

"I wish I knew," Callum said, his voice level, and took another bite of toast. No one else said anything, but the kitchen was screaming with a thousand things unsaid. If they'd been cats, one of them would've been growling and the other would've been showing their teeth, and at some point there'd have been the sort of scrap that ends in someone going to the vet. Or possibly both someones.

But whatever else they might've been, they were also painfully human, and so Callum just took another bite of toast, and Ifan drank his coffee, and the rest of us looked at each other and waited for someone to say something. Ifan gave Green Snake a grape from the fruit bowl, and Green Snake looked at it suspiciously, then picked it up and slithered over to drop it in front of me. I patted it with one paw, watching juice ooze from the holes his fangs had made. Green Snake nudged it toward me, and I patted it again, not sure what he wanted. He reared up, tilting his head to one side pointedly, then nudged the grape again.

"I think I like duck," Gordie said, filling the silence. "Or was it turkey?" He had a bit of chicken skin stuck to one of his remaining teeth.

Ifan waved his mug at him and said to Callum, "When did you gain another cat?"

"They just keep turning up," Callum said, finishing his toast and brushing the crumbs off his fingers.

Ifan examined Gordie. "Do I know you?"

"No," I said, before Callum could answer, and Ifan gave me a curious look. Green Snake shoved the grape at me again, and I growled at him. "Stop it, you overgrown garden worm. I'm not a bloody rabbit."

Green Snake flopped his head to the ground with every evidence of despair.

"We'd best get on," Callum said, taking a final mouthful of tea.

"You're not going to try and go to a were club, are you?" Ifan asked.

"Not right this minute."

"You know what I mean. It could be dangerous for you."

"I think I can decide that," Callum said, his voice tight.

"Not just ... I don't mean that you'd use," Ifan said. "I know you've got yourself together these days. But you don't have the protection of the Norths now. And things have changed, too. You don't know the people anymore."

Callum nodded, and got up, picking his jacket up from the chair and shrugging into it. "Sure. Thanks."

Ifan looked like he wanted to say something else, then sighed and got up as well. "You just have to tell me what you need, you know. I'll help."

"Alright," Callum said, and picked up Green Snake, who made a last-ditch effort to force the grape on me. "Thanks."

Tam and Pru jumped to the floor, and as Callum headed for the door I nudged the grape with my nose, wondering what the green shoelace was playing at.

And smelled it. Raw magic and the smoky carbon residue of fire, where the magician's fingers had rubbed across the green skin of the fruit. I scuttled across to take a whiff of his mug, and it was there on the handle as well, brutal and unfocused.

"Aw, hairballs," I muttered, and ran for the door before Ifan came back to see what I was doing.

15

PEROXIDE FIXES EVERYTHING

IFAN WATCHED US LEAVE, OPENING THE GATE WITH SOME magician fanciness to let us out. None of us spoke until we were on the road outside, pulling into the broad, quietly posh streets and rumbling off in a direction that likely had weres at the end of it. Or necromancers.

Then I said, "It was his fireball."

"What?" Callum asked, and Green Snake lifted his head out of Callum's pocket to give me a pleased little head tilt. Or possibly a *well, finally* one. Nuance is tricky when your sole method of communication is a head tilt.

"It was on his fingers. I smelt it." Green Snake stared at me, and I sighed. "Gummy Snake here must've picked it up when Ifan gave him a grape. So *he* gave *me* the grape, and I got the scent."

"Are you sure?" Callum asked. He was chewing his thumbnail again, his shoulders hunched and tight. "It wasn't just from that flame thing he does?"

I wished I could say I wasn't sure. Ifan was a shady bloody parsnip, but Callum had already lost him once, when we'd thought he was dead (or possibly zombified, but that still counted as a loss). It seemed unfair to ask anyone to lose a friend twice. "I'm sure," I said, and Callum sighed.

"So he doesn't want us going to were clubs, and also wanted to make sure we couldn't talk to necromancers."

"You don't think he was after us with that firebomb?"

"I don't think it matters much either way. If he wanted us dead, we'd never have made it out of the house. So he's just trying to stop us finding Ms Jones."

I shivered, thinking of the taxidermied animals that lined the big entrance hall of the magician's house, staring down at visitors with glassy eyes and bared teeth. They'd almost had us once already. "*Just.*"

Callum smiled faintly and took his cigarettes from his pocket. Green Snake didn't even try to stop him. "It's better than having a magician actively trying to kill us."

"True. Things are looking up."

"Positively sunny," he agreed, and lit a cigarette. I didn't miss the fact that his knuckles were white on the lighter.

"I'm rethinking my use of *eccentric* for you two," Pru said. "What's the next step on from that?"

"Heroic and dashing," I suggested, and Tam snorted so hard that it turned into a sneeze.

"No," Pru said. "Pretty sure that's not it."

Callum flicked ash into the cup between the seats and said, "Were club tonight, then."

"Is that a good idea?" I asked. "What if Ifan's warned them to be looking for us?"

"Do you have any better ideas? Yasmin won't help us.

Gerry can't. The last signs we have of Walker are with weres. And if Ifan's involved at all – which he seems to be – then we need to find Walker before he moves him, or ... something."

Or something. I shivered, seeing my abandoned body lying on the floor of the dentist's hallway again. "Hairballs. Why couldn't it be a bunny club or something?"

Callum snorted. "I think that's a different sort of club entirely."

"What?"

"I don't think it was bunny," Gordie said. "Maybe pheasant?"

"I prefer quail," Tam said.

"Pheasant's good, though," Pru said. "Organic, obviously."

Callum actually laughed then, and she gave him a puzzled look. He still looked tired and fed up and more than a little like he wanted to punch the steering wheel – or punch something, anyway – but his smile was easy as he stubbed the cigarette out in the cup. I suppose there's only so much you can stretch trust before it shatters, and when it's been thin for so long, perhaps the breaking is less loss than it is relief.

But there was still the issue of weres, and I truly didn't fancy the idea of walking into a whole pack of them. I sat back, scratched my shoulder with a back paw, then said. "What about Muscles?"

"What about him?"

"There wasn't enough blood about the place for him to have been seriously hurt. And if he's been hassled by weres and dodgy magicians, he might be up for giving us a hand. Be nice to have a heavy in our corner."

Callum considered it. "It would be handy," he admitted. "And I'd like to know he's okay."

"So try phoning him again. Nothing ventured, nothing strained, and all that."

"Gained."

"Huh. I suppose. But, you know, weres and necromancers and dodgy magicians. Strained seems better."

"Maimed seems more likely," Pru said, and we both stared at her.

MUSCLES STILL WASN'T ANSWERING his phone, which didn't bode so well.

"Try his flat?" I suggested.

"There's not exactly a lot there for him to go back to," Callum said.

"I'd like to go back," Gordie said. "I'm tired."

"You've been asleep basically the whole time," I told him.

He glared at me somewhat blearily. "I'm a very old cat."

"You are," I agreed, not without a little jealousy. I'd never made it as far as very old, and I wouldn't have minded trying it in at least one life.

"We need to get Gordie somewhere safe," Pru said. "We can't keep carting him around like this. It's not fair."

Callum scratched his chin. "Could you take him to yours? Would Katja be likely to look after him for a bit?"

"She's away, and I've got a useless onion of a cat sitter."

She thought about it, then added with no small satisfaction, "He's probably combing the streets for me as we speak. But even he might notice if an ancient male tabby appeared in my place. Besides, Gordie might get lost in the shift."

"What about Poppy?" I asked. "She'd look after him, and we could talk to Gerry at the same time. Ask if he was sure he didn't fancy knocking some heads together."

"Poppy's a good idea," Callum said. "But I don't think we can expect help from Gerry. Not with how things are in Dimly."

"We should still try," I said. "Maybe he can meet us outside Dimly or something. He'd be able to talk more freely there."

"Nothing ventured, nothing maimed," Tam said comfortably, and I purred.

Callum sighed. "I hate that your version makes more sense."

"Me too," I said.

GERRY, it turned out, wasn't in Dimly, but he wasn't at home, either. He and Poppy were out walking Strawberry, which was what Poppy had named the snake-tailed dog, and agreed to meet us on a stretch of canal that was more human territory than Folk. It was on the Leeds side of Dimly, and we parked on the verge of the road behind the cars belonging to half a dozen other dog-walkers and joggers. The sun was out patchily, casting low thin shadows among the trees, and a persistent little mist hung around in pockets of low land. The road was still wet from the previous night's rain, and there were puddles in the potholes of the lane. A cricket pitch lay dormant near the parking area, and further on I could smell horses and stables, the scent warm and vital in the chill air.

Callum tucked Gordie inside his coat and asked Pru if she wanted a lift, but she just showed him one immaculate tooth and trotted off shoulder to shoulder with Tam, leading the way down the lane and onto one of the little paths that wound through the woods to the canal.

"I'll take a lift," I said.

"You're not going to freeze."

"I might," I said, but just ambled behind him as we went in search of trolls.

We found them in a field on the less-used side of the canal, the one where the path was mud and grass rather than the well-packed gravel on the other side. Poppy was throwing a ball for Strawberry, who was sprinting the length of the field with her tail waggling wildly through the air behind her and drool flying from her jaws. As soon as she spotted Callum, she rushed to him and tried to jump up, but Poppy intervened, catching the dog effortlessly by the collar and holding her back.

"*No,* Strawberry," she said. "Good dogs no jump."

"Don't jump," Gerry said, in the tone of someone for whom correcting has just become a reflex.

"Good dogs don't jump," Poppy agreed. "Good dogs sit." She was wearing lime green dungarees over a bright orange fleece, and a large puffy yellow jacket on top. A blue bobble hat completed the ensemble, and she smelled distinctly of hay and good garden dirt and antiseptic cream. "Hello kitties," she said.

"Hey Poppy," I said. "How's the animal rescue coming?"

She scrunched her three eyes at me, wrinkling her nose. There was heavy sunblock smeared across it. "Only Strawberry is coming. Kent says is too cold to walk, and lizards is scary to walkers."

"Are scary," Gerry said, looking at us impassively. He was wearing walking trousers and a heavy jacket with the collar turned up to his chin, but the jacket was, at least, bright pink with a flower print lining, and his pearl earrings went rather well with a feathered felt cap of the sort one imagined the better-dressed lady walker in the 1920s wearing. He looked more like Gerry than the version we'd met in Dimly, even with his own warpaint of sun protection. He watched two joggers pattering along on the other side of the canal, their breath pluming out ahead of them, then said, "I'm going to guess you're not just here because of a cat."

Callum immediately looked so guilty Gerry probably thought we'd been going to ask him to declare war on the city of Leeds. "We just thought you might be able to speak more easily here," Callum said. "We're not asking you to do anything."

"Although we wouldn't object if you did," I added.

"Gobs, shut up," Pru said. "He's the *mayor*. He can't get involved."

"I can't," Gerry agreed. "I'm having enough trouble with Dimly as it is." He rubbed his face with one huge hand, and I realised I'd never considered the fact that trolls could look old and tired. Maybe I'd never seen a worried troll before. Mostly they seemed to work in two modes: hungry and angry. Anxious and stressed was a whole new area of troll behaviour to me. Gerry looked at me as if hearing my thoughts and asked, "What information are you after now?"

Callum shoved his hands in his pockets, hunching his shoulders against the wind. "Right now we're also looking for an ex-necromancer called Rav. There had been weres at his place, and someone firebombed it last night."

Gerry put his hands in his pockets and rocked on his heels, his heavy brows pulled down over his eyes. "You had a tussle with necromancers a few months ago."

"Rav was sort of involved, but he got out of it."

"He was more a goon than a necromancer," I added. "You know, hired muscle."

Poppy had gone back to throwing the ball for Strawberry, but now she inspected Gordie, who was peering blearily out of Callum's coat, and said, "Rav with muscles?"

We looked at her, startled. "Sounds like," Callum said. "You know him?"

"I knows animals," she said, and waved at Gordie. "Hi Gordie."

"Do you have duck?" Gordie asked. "No one's giving me duck."

"When did you last see Muscles – Rav?" I asked.

Poppy petted Strawberry and tussled with her briefly to get the ball back. "He asks me for medicines."

"What sort of medicine, Poppy?" Callum asked.

"For dog bites," she said, then shook her head. "*People*

bites. He say dog, but it look like people to me. No human people exactly, but no dog."

"Oh, sugared parsnips in gravy," I said. "He was bitten by a were?"

"He says dog. I say no, is people, but he go funny colour and no believe me." She hesitated. "He *don't* believe me." She beamed at Gerry, who gave her a weary, craggy smile, then she looked back at me. "Dog bites is different."

"Could you tell what sort of people?" Callum asked.

She scratched her head, dislodging her hat. Gerry readjusted it for her. "Maybe. But need a comp … compary … same thing to look at."

"You couldn't tell anything from the smell?" Pru asked. "Or the feel?"

Poppy bent down and scritched Pru very carefully between her ears with a huge finger. "Trolls no smell like cats. Or sense. You is special."

Tam purred, and rubbed herself against Poppy's legs. She was a big enough cat that she almost looked in proportion to the small troll.

Callum looked at Gerry. "You've not heard about this?"

Gerry shook his head. "I hadn't, no. Poppy runs her own business very well."

"I is business troll," she said, and grinned.

"When did he get bitten?" Pru asked.

Poppy thought about it, counting on her fingers carefully. "He come see me … eight day past. He say he go out walking, and there is fight, and he is bitten."

"Walking where?" Callum asked.

Poppy shrugged. "I no ask, because I think he tell

story. Not important, anyway. I just gives peroxide. Peroxide fix *everything.*"

I had some doubts that peroxide could fix werewolfness, but it was a nice thought. "Have you seen him since?"

"No." She frowned. "He say he come back this week so I can check bite, but he no come back."

Which could mean that he'd lost faith in peroxide, or that he'd been intending to come back right up until the point his flat was trashed by weres or other persons unknown. Come to drag him to the pack? Come to stop him telling anyone about it? Or, of course, it could just mean that he'd been overcome by wolfiness himself.

"That's all we can tell you," Gerry said, looking back under the trees as if expecting to spot lurking voters. "I can't be seen talking to you."

"You're the *mayor,*" I said. "You can do whatever you want. You've got a chain and everything."

Gerry snorted. "Dimly isn't a human town. The mayor can be removed rather quickly if they prove not to be to the taste of the populace. Quickly and uncomfortably." He sighed, and adjusted his hat. "I don't think I'll last much longer. The people who want change aren't prepared to be as … *problematic* as the ones who want a return to the status quo."

"I like Status Quo," Tam said. "The guitars are good."

There was a confused pause, then Callum said, "Okay. Thank you, Poppy. And Gerry, if we can help with anything, just tell us."

Gerry patted him on the shoulder gently, almost dislodging Gordie, who gave him a startled look. "Thank you. One soon knows who one's friends are."

"Why you no call Rav?" Poppy asked. "He has phone."

"We tried," I said. "He no— *didn't* answer."

Poppy *hmph*-ed and took a tablet from her pocket. She poked it a few times, making me fear for the screen, but it was evidently one of those ones made for dropping off buildings. A moment later we heard ringing, then a vaguely familiar voice said, "Hello? Poppy?"

"Hello Rav," she said. "How is bite?"

"Um, yeah." There was pause then he said, "Something happened last night, and now my apartment's burned up and Gordie's gone, and ... is it bad to mix peroxide and vodka?"

Poppy frowned. "You no drink peroxide?"

"No."

"You put vodka on bite?"

"No."

"I no— don't understand." Poppy glanced at Gerry, who gave her a thumbs up, then took the tablet from her and handed it to Callum. I scrambled to Callum's shoulder so I could peer down at the video on the screen.

"Rav?" Callum asked. "It's Callum—"

"Ah—" Muscles reared back, looking around a little wildly, as if expecting us to come charging in the door. I couldn't tell where he was, but his normally carefully slicked hair was standing up at weird angles and he had a shirt on that was far too tight, even for his standards. "I'm a bit busy."

"Human!" Gordie exclaimed, and hauled himself toward the tablet. "Human, is it pheasant I like, or quail?"

"Gordie!" Muscles just about shouted. "Gordie, are you okay?"

"I thought it was duck, but now I'm not sure."

"He's okay," Callum said.

"I thought—" Muscles pressed a hand to his mouth, then shook his head. "Where are you? Can I come and get him?"

"Thought you were busy," I said, and Callum tried to tap me with the side of his head, since he had one hand full of Gordie and the other full of tablet.

Muscles screwed his face up like he'd tasted something sour. "Things have got weird."

"Says the necromancer henchman. Weirder than dragging ancient beings out of different dimensions?"

"I quit all that. But this is pretty weird too."

"We better meet up," Callum said. "Where are you?"

"You're not going to arrest me?"

"Dude, do we look like the police?" I asked.

"Well, maybe not arrest me, but … you know. Tidy me up or something."

Callum and I looked at each other as well as we could at such close quarters. "Have you seen his coat?" I asked. "*Tidy* isn't exactly our area either."

"Don't think he meant that sort of tidy," Callum said.

"Yeah, I got that. Same, though. We're normally the ones people want to tidy."

"Maybe it was venison," Gordie said. "Was it venison?"

"That's not even a bird," Pru said, more to herself than to anyone else.

Muscles rubbed a hand through his hair, which stuck out in weirder angles than before. "You wouldn't turn me in to the Watch or something, would you?"

"Rav, we need your help," Callum said. "We're not turning you over to anyone."

He scratched his chin, nodded a couple of times, then said. "Okay. Yeah, okay, then. I'll meet you in Keighley."

"At the bookshop?" Callum asked hopefully.

"What? No. There's a park. We can go there."

"A park," I said. "It's *winter*. Why's everyone so keen on meeting outside?"

"Because fewer people are outside," Callum said, and hung up after telling Muscles to send the location to our phone. He handed the tablet back to Poppy. "Thank you. Really – we were completely stuck."

"Is okay," she said, patting Strawberry. "You brings me dog, and is because of you I have lizards and unicorns and am business troll. You friends, always."

"You'd have always done that," I said. "We just helped a bit."

Poppy gave me a surprisingly gentle head scratch. "You believes. Before, only Gerry believes. And"—she adopted a very loud whisper—"he is parent troll. He *has* to."

"You've got enough belief for everyone," Callum said, and smiled at Gerry. "I know things are getting sticky. Thank you for meeting up, and let us know anything we can do to help. Really."

"I will," Gerry said, and put a heavy hand on Poppy's shoulders. "Come on, business troll. William was making crumpets this morning."

"Oooh, crumpets!" Poppy exclaimed, and ran ahead with the five-eyed dog while Gerry trudged along behind her. I thought his shoulders looked marginally less slumped than they had done, though. Maybe being a parent troll was rather better than being a troll mayor.

"Right, then," Callum said. "Let's go see a man about a dog."

"Sounds more like a wolf," I pointed out, jumping back to the ground.

"Or a were," Pru said.

"Seeing a were about a wolf?"

"Or a wolf about a were?"

Callum sighed. "I need more non-cat friends."

"Yeah, look where that's got you," I said, and ran ahead before he could answer, Tam and Pru loping after me along the well-trodden track. A passing dog walker snatched her poodle to her chest as we passed, and Callum gave her an apologetic wave while the dog yapped hysterically. Tam lifted her lip to show her fangs, and we kept going.

Turns out actual trolls can really restore your faith in people sometimes. Unlike the more human types we were encountering.

16

ALWAYS HAVE A SAFE WORD

THE RAIN HAD FADED AWAY AND THE WIND HAD PICKED UP as the day plunged on toward night, a thin, petulant breeze from the north. It should have been full of the scent of high moors and bleak fells, gullies crouched under frost and streams crackling with ice. Instead it mostly smelt of chip shops and the queued cars on the main road below the park.

The park entrance was through the gates of a once-grand country house that was now home to a slightly mouldy orangery and an ice cream shop, although the age-stained walls were no less imposing for that. A dog walker bundled in what looked like a duvet hurried past, the dog straining to get back inside somewhere warm and comfortable. They're not entirely clueless animals.

And neither was Pru, who vanished briefly once we'd parked, reappearing a moment later with a mass of multi-coloured wool in her jaws. She dropped it in front of Callum as he leaned out of the car, and looked up at him.

"What?" he asked.

"Well, I can't put it on myself," she said. "And if one more person offers to pick me up and stick me in their coat, I'm going to bite them. Which is something I usually refrain from."

"Wise choice," he said, and picked up what turned out to be a tightly knitted, cat-size jumper in a cacophony of bright colours.

"Subtle," I said. "Excellent for sneaking."

"I didn't have time to hunt around," she said, as Callum helped her into it. "The cat sitter might've spotted me."

"You probably should've let them," Callum said. "You haven't been home for ages."

She shrugged. "He just wants to cuddle me all the time. It's irritating." She stepped away from Callum, resplendent in stripes of red and orange and yellow and blue and purple, and already looking distinctly more comfortable. She turned and walked toward the park gates, her head high, and Callum gave me a warning look as he collected Gordie and shut the car door. I showed him a fang, and followed Pru.

"Where can I get one of those?"

She glanced at me. "You couldn't pull it off."

"Probably right."

We headed through the gates, Callum hunched against the wind and Pru looking both comfortable and smug, and hurried through the gardens with their subdued winter foliage. The lawns were waiting for warmer weather before they sprouted again, the bushes pruned back in preparation for the spring to come, and everything looked a bit threadbare and dull. We took one of the curling gravel paths down to a little rotunda, where we could see a short but very broad form in a red jacket pacing back and forth, either in anxiety or to stave off frostbite. The lawn was tiered around the gazebo itself, offering a grassy amphitheatre for the warmer months, and some cider cans blown into the skeletal forms of the rose bushes suggested it was a popular hangout on a Friday night.

The pacing figure froze as he saw us, then ran down the steps. "Have you got him? Do you have Gordie?"

"He's here," Callum said, extricating the old cat from inside his coat and handing him to Muscles.

"Thank you. Thank you so much." Muscles sounded on the verge of tears, and he unzipped the front of his big puffer jacket so Gordie could nestle inside.

The old cat blinked up at him. "There you are, human. I'm not sure I approve of this, you know. It's cold."

"I know. We'll get inside in the warm as soon as we can." Muscles zipped his jacket up a little so Gordie could peer out of the neck, and adjusted his scarf to fill the gap. The jacket was too tight across his formidable shoulders, and hung loose around his waist. "How did you get him?" he asked Callum. "What happened?"

"Could ask you the same thing," I said, and he blinked at me, then pulled a woolly cap tighter down over his ears. Pru and Tam were prowling around him, Pru's knitted jumper bright against the dull grey of the path. She narrowed her eyes and snuffled at the leg of his jeans, and he shuffled sideways a little, then swallowed a yelp as he bumped into Tam.

"Sorry," he said, and she stared at him, unblinking. He looked back at me. "They're not Watch, are they?"

"No. Why're you so worried about the Watch?"

"Um." He wiped his mouth and looked at Callum.

"Shall we get a coffee?" Callum suggested. "We could go to the cafe up there."

Muscles shook his head almost violently. "I don't know if it's safe."

"Why wouldn't it be safe? Is this to do with what happened at your place?"

"Yes. No. Sort of." He blinked around at the deserted park. "No one followed you, did they?"

"No." Callum took his cigarettes out and offered them to the shorter man. He shook his head, so Callum lit one, tipping his head against the wind that was whipping his tatty coat around his legs. The gusts were getting stronger, making my paws itch, and Tam bounced sideways suddenly, her ears back, and lunged at a leaf spinning past. Callum put his lighter away and said, "Why don't you tell us what happened, then?"

"And just give us some warning if you're going to go all wolf-man," I added. "No one needs that sprung on them."

"I'm not going to go *all wolf-man*," Muscles said, clutching the front of his jacket. "I don't even know what you're talking about!"

"Sure you don't, Fido," I said. "How's that bite doing?"

"What?"

"Ignore him," Callum said. "He can't help himself."

"How do you even— It's just a *bite.* It doesn't mean anything!" Muscles' voice had got a little breathless and squeaky, and he was darting looks around the park as if he expected us of having contacted the RSPCA and reported him as a stray.

"Okay. That's fine. Why don't you just tell us what happened?" Callum asked, in his patented *just talk to me* voice. Muscles eyed him anxiously, hugging Gordie so tightly that the old cat grumbled a complaint.

"Sorry."

"You should be," Gordie said. "I'm an old cat."

"We know," I said, and Callum flicked ash at me. "What? He keeps telling us!"

Tam growled, and Muscles looked at her with such wide eyes I harboured doubts he actually was a ravening beast at all.

"I *am* old," Gordie said. "But I'm not silly." He eyed me with bleary hostility.

"Sorry," I said.

"I should think so. No respect." He yawned. "Anyway, it was that night." He craned his neck to look up at Muscles. "I told you anyone who runs out like that is bad news."

"You did," Muscles agreed.

"What night?" I asked. "Who ran out?"

Gordie shrugged weakly. "Some hairy guy."

"Hairy as in were?" I know, it was unlikely he meant they had a beard, but it pays to be certain.

"I don't know where," he said. "Everywhere, I assume. I wasn't going to *check*."

I blinked at him, and Callum said, "Poppy said you were bitten."

Muscles frowned. "I was. But that doesn't mean anything. It wasn't full moon or anything."

"But you were bitten by a were," Callum said.

"Um. Yes. I guess, as it turned out. But he wasn't a wolf at the time – and is that really how it works? It sounds like a bit of an urban myth to me. You know, bitten by a guy and you turn into a wolf. Like, really?" He gave a hopeful sort of laugh, and we all stared at him.

"Hang on, he was a guy when he bit you?" I asked. "As in a man? *How?* Were you fighting?"

"Um, no," Muscles said, shuffling his feet and looking everywhere except at us. "Look, I didn't realise … he just all of a sudden *bit* me, and when I yelled he freaked out and ran. I mean, he apologised, but then he took off. I don't think he meant to bite me. It was all heat of the moment sort of thing."

"How do you bite someone in the heat of the moment?" I asked. "What sort of moment's that?"

"Gobs," Pru said, and I looked at her.

"What? That's weird, right?"

Tam gave a huffing laugh and Callum just said, "Poppy said you told her it was a dog bite."

"I didn't want to tell her it was a guy. She's …" he waved slightly. "Poppy. But I figured it'd be like treating a dog bite, right? Same thing?"

"Don't let a were hear you say that," I said.

"No. Right." He hugged Gordie again. "I just … Some people get weird about stuff."

"About bites?"

"Gobs," Pru said again.

"What?"

"But he was definitely a were?" Callum asked, ignoring me.

Muscles touched his shoulder uneasily. "Yeah. Seems he is. But I'd have noticed if he'd been a wolf right at that point. Would've been kind of hard to miss."

"*Ohhh,*" I said. "Right. That sort of moment. I thought only cats did that, but whatever works. Dude, just *say*. Saves the confusion."

"Like I say, some people get weird."

"And some of us are quicker on the uptake than others," Pru said. "But no one's getting weird here. Gobs and Callum are already weird, anyway. You can't make them more so."

"Hey," Callum and I said together, and Muscles snorted.

"So what happened to your apartment?" Callum asked. "Poppy said you were bitten about a week ago. You haven't left Gordie alone that long."

"No, of course not! I just got home this morning and ... I don't know. My place is all burned up and cordoned off. The police are looking for me, apparently, but I didn't do it."

"But what happened before that?" Callum persisted. "We came to find you last night, and the place was already turned over."

Muscles shook his head. "I really don't know."

"It was your hairy buddy," Gordie said. "Well, both of you. But he started it."

"The same were?" Callum asked. "He came back?"

"He's really fit," Muscles said, looking at the ground. "And he said he wanted to make sure I was okay, and one thing led to another, and then ... I don't know. I'm not really sure what happened, but I woke up at his place, and

I couldn't find my clothes, and when I got home, someone had burned my apartment down. It's been a really hard night, okay?"

Callum stubbed his cigarette out on the ground and looked around for a bin. "Well, yeah. It's going to be an adjustment."

"To what?"

"To being a were."

"I'm not a were."

"Of course you are," Gordie said. "You stink of it."

"You do," Pru said, looking up at him. "Although that might be your boyfriend's clothes."

"He's not my boyfriend," Muscles said. "I mean, I don't think. We haven't talked about it."

I sat down and scratched my side with a back paw. "Is turning you into a were a dealbreaker? I'm not saying it should be, but you might want to take it into account."

"I think the biting itself's more problematic," Pru said. "Considering you're not cats. Unless you're into it, of course. You probably want to lay some ground rules with that."

"Always have a safe word," Tam said, then pounced on another leaf, her tail flicking.

Muscles stared at us, then at Callum. "Is this the feline agony aunt section?"

"I'd say just ignore them, but it's really hard."

Everyone was quiet for a moment, then Muscles said, "So you think I'm a were now, then?"

"You totally are," Pru said.

"Huh." Muscles looked at his free hand, the one not supporting Gordie, as if expecting it to sprout hair and claws. "So what happens now? The Watch are going to be after me, aren't they?"

"Not if you keep your nose clean," I said. "Well, in theory, anyway. But you were hanging out with necromancers before. That's way worse."

"That was just a bit of fun."

"Sure," Pru said. "Until the whole *sacrifice a bunch of cats and raise a dead god* thing."

"I didn't know that was going to happen."

Callum rubbed his face with one hand. "I don't suppose you're still in touch with any of the necromancers?"

"No. After I realised it was for real, and they were actually going to kill all of you and ... stuff ..."

"Raise an ancient almost-god and end the world," I said helpfully.

"That. I mean, that *really* hadn't been mentioned."

"I'd hope not," Pru said.

Callum sighed. "After you realised that ...?"

"Yes. Sorry. After that, I just made myself scarce. I've not heard from anyone."

"How about Ifan?"

"The young magician? Bit fit, isn't he?"

"Honestly, is a were not enough?" I asked. "You want to be messing around with magicians now, too?"

"It was just an observation," he protested.

"Gods," Pru said. "Can *none* of you stay on subject?" She glared up at the men, resplendent in her multi-coloured coat.

"Sorry," Muscles said.

"Ifan?" Callum asked again. "Have you had any contact

with him?"

"I wish," Muscles started, then glanced at Pru. "I mean, no. I only met him at the house after the whole dead god thing."

Well, there went that lead, then. Callum and I looked at each other, and I sighed. "How about the BF?"

"Gabe? I don't think he knows Ifan."

"No, but he obviously knows weres," I said, twitching my ears at Callum.

"Good point. Rav, your boyfriend, or friend, or whatever – where did you meet him?"

"At this club down in Leeds. He works there." He smiled slightly, the angles of his face softening.

Callum gave an intrigued *huh.* "Belle Isle sort of area? Maybe on an industrial estate of some sort?"

"Yeah, you know it? Great music."

"Heard of it," Callum said, and took the flier from his pocket, unfolding it. "This one?"

"That's it."

"Good. We're looking for someone, and we think he's mixed up with weres. We might be able to find something out from the club, but I'm not sure how welcome I'll be. Can you help me out?"

Muscles took half a step back. "Help you out how?"

"I don't mean get me in. But there'll be a password, something not on here." He tapped the flier. "Do you know it? Or can you find it out?"

"I know it. But what're you going to do?"

"Just ask some questions. We need to find this friend. It's urgent."

"I don't know." He adjusted his woolly hat. "I don't

want to get Gabe in trouble or anything. Or me."

I huffed. "Sharing a bloody club password is the least of your worries. Wait till the Watch find out someone's making unauthorised weres."

"Gobs," Callum said, but I ignored him, watching Muscles.

"I thought you said everything was fine as long as I kept my nose clean."

"Yeah, well, changing in a council flat with people all about the place then going haring around the streets of Leeds with your soulmate or packmate or whatever isn't exactly keeping your nose clean, is it?"

"He's not going to the Watch," Callum said.

I glared at him. "I *could.*"

"But you won't. You do need to be more careful, though," he added to Muscles. "And so does Gabe. It's the sort of thing that gives weres a bad name, and attracts attention."

"I thought weres only changed at full moon, though," Muscles said. "And how come I can't remember? Did I set my flat on fire?"

"No," Callum said.

"So how'd that happen?"

Callum and I looked at each other. "No idea," I said, before he could admit it was probably our fault. "It must've happened after we got Gordie out."

"What were you doing there?" Muscles asked, just as Gordie said, "You said there was duck."

"Looking for you, although more because of your necromancers at the time. The weres were an unexpected bonus."

"Not my necromancers," he said, looking at Gordie. "What was that about duck?"

"They said there was duck. I thought it might be barbecued."

"You've had no contact at all with any of them?" Callum asked.

"No. I was a bit worried they might not be happy that I kind of switched sides. You know, at the end."

"The rest of them ran," I pointed out. "You even looked after the dog."

Muscles sighed. "Poor Brutus. I couldn't keep him. The flat was too small."

"Probably a good thing," Pru said. "Dogs and weres seem like a bad combo."

"I think I like duck," Gordie said. "Does anyone have any, so I can check?"

Callum rubbed the back of his neck and said, "So you know nothing about Ifan or the necromancers. How about the sorcerer?"

He shook his head. "I heard Sonia and the old magician talking about her being trapped in the house, but that was it."

Callum and I looked at each other, and he sighed, putting the flier back in his pocket and fishing for his cigarettes again.

"What about the dentist?" I asked, without much hope. "He was the one on the roof of the car after we all got out of the cellar."

Muscles nodded, startling me. "Yeah, him. I've seen him at the club a few times. He's a really good dancer."

"Really?" Callum and I said together, then Callum shook his head. "When did you last see him?"

"Last time I was there. A week ago."

"Did he seem upset, or worried?"

"No, he was chatting to some of the staff. I remember thinking he was getting the VIP treatment."

"Did you see him leave?" Callum asked. "Or notice who he was talking to in particular?"

"*Hmm.* No. I met Gabe and got a bit distracted."

"A week ago," I said. "A week ago he was hanging out with weres *by choice*."

"It was the staff, not weres," Muscles said, and we all looked at him. "What? Oh. Oh, you're kidding me. They're all *weres?*"

"Humans," Pru said. "How d'you survive with those sort of observational skills?"

Muscles touched his shoulder again, an almost unconscious reflex. "They all *look* normal. Gabe looks better than normal, really. Does that mean I'm not going to go all hairy and get horrible yellow teeth?"

"Only when you change," I said.

"Cool," he said, and grinned suddenly. "This might not be too bad."

Callum patted his shoulder a little clumsily. "I'm sure it won't. Is there anything else you can tell us?"

"Not really. Do you know *anything* about the fire at my place?"

Callum opened his mouth and I spoke before he could turn us into the destroyers of a were-house. "Tell you what, you get us into the were club, we'll look into the fire."

Muscles eyed me. "No charge? I can't afford to hire you."

"No one ever can," I said with a sigh, then added, "No charge."

"Deal." He bent over and extended a fist to me, and I patted it lightly with a paw, smelling the reek of body spray and fear and something raw and muscular lying dormant below the surface. He straightened up and looked at Callum. "The password changes all the time. I'll talk to Gabe and get this week's one, then I'll text you."

"Thanks," Callum said.

"Sure. I hope you find who set that fire. I had some really nice trainers in there." He gave us a wave and headed off across the grass with Gordie still tucked inside his coat.

"How long do we have before Gordie tells him we were there *during* the fire?" Callum asked.

"Hopefully long enough to find the dentist," I said, and shivered. "Is there any chance we can be inside somewhere any time soon?"

"A were club, by the sounds," Pru said. "So we've got that to look forward to."

"Awesome," I said. "All we need is some Watch cats now. You know, just for icing on the bun."

"Careful what you wish for," Callum said, and we headed back to the gates, the wind chasing leaves across our path and ruffling my fur, and doing nothing to dissipate the tightness in my chest.

I really needed to look into a cat jacket. Preferably an armoured one.

17

NO SENSE OF SELF-PRESERVATION

CITY DRIVING IS NOT FOR THE FAINT-HEARTED OR impatient, but there are rewards for those who know the back ways and less-travelled routes. We spun through suburbs and shopping streets, ignoring the main arteries that fed the city, and eventually dived down onto a long stretch of road on the south side of Leeds that was full of cars coming and going, but very few stopping. It was lined with twenty-four-hour gyms and tyre shops, with a drive-through coffee shop that seemed to be attracting most of the custom. There were no pedestrians on the weed-encrusted pavements, and although there was a second-hand car yard and a big furniture shop, I couldn't see anyone entering or leaving them. The shops were still lifes, mere background to the rush of passing traffic.

Callum had pulled some mysterious combination of letters and numbers off the *DJ Scoot* flier and turned it into a postcode that he put into his phone, and now the bored voice of the map program directed us down a side road that was too narrow for two cars to pass each other, although there were passing bays pocked along it, like you see on country lanes. It was pinned in between a tall corrugated iron wall that hid a timber yard on Callum's side, and to mine was just a guard rail with a scraggly, litter-choked stream struggling down a culvert beyond it. The tarmac gave out about halfway down, leaving us crunching over gravel, slowly enough that I could read the plywood signs on the wall.

Luxury Party Hire, one said, the edges of the letters so curled that they'd created their own font. *Build your perfect party!* There were some blobs on it that had probably been balloons. Another read, *B.L. Evans, Tax Lawyer,* and had a set of scales on it. They were probably meant to be judicial, but looked more to me like the ones our across-the-hall neighbour still used when she was baking. There were a few others, all looking as if they'd been left behind when the businesses collapsed. Certainly none of them had been refreshed for a while.

There were newer signs too, though, homemade fliers in familiar grey print on pastel paper. DJ Scoot was in the were-house, apparently. There was no date, no location, but that was the point, wasn't it? The signs weren't for the uninitiated. They were there for those who already knew where they were going, a promise that they were in the right place. And that DJ Scoot would be blowing dog whistles, or whatever were DJs did. Shake bags of biscuits about, maybe.

We finally came off the track, finding ourselves at the bottom of a small, sagging industrial estate, enclosed in chain-link fencing. It was made up of three long, metal-clad buildings with wide roller doors, arranged in a rough arrow shape. An old garage, complete with derelict cars rusting outside it, was at the closest end of the building to our left, and another building sat almost at right angles to it on the far side of the lot, their backs to the fences. A third, wider building stuck out into the car park at an angle from the right, its long face toward us, and pointed at the gap between the other two, making the shaft of the arrow. Its far end was butted up to the fence, but the other had plenty of space between it and the other building for cars to come and go.

From the look of the doors, the buildings had each held five businesses at one point, but the remaining signs were as faded as the ones on the drive. They wouldn't have been comfortable places, not with the tin walls and more corrugated iron on the roofs. Cheap to put up, but freezing in the winter and hot in whatever summer we got. Other than the rotting frames outside the garage, the only cars I could see were a half dozen or so gathered in front of the wide building that made up the shaft of the arrow. There was still a sign there for the Luxury Party Hire store, and a mannequin in a faded pirate costume stood outside it. Pumpkin-shaped fairy lights were looped over the roller door, and the cars were all lined up in the instinctively neat way people park, even when the guidelines on the tarmac are long gone.

Callum nosed up to the garage and stopped with the rusting shell of a green Ford Fiesta between us and the party hire store, then shut the engine off. We stared across the car park, waiting for something to happen, but all I could hear was the rumble of traffic on the road behind us.

"It's too quiet to go in yet," Callum said. "We're going to have to wait."

"I can go and take a look," I said, although I had about as much desire to do that as I do to visit the vet. "There must be a way to sneak in."

"That seems like a bad idea," Callum said. "They'll smell you."

"So what's your plan?" I asked. "Knock on the door and ask them if they've welcomed the lord nicotine into their lives yet?"

He checked his phone. "I've not got the password yet. That'll be a start."

"And then?"

"I'll figure it out."

"Solid plan," I said, and we watched the blank face of the building for a while.

Finally Pru said, "Well? What're we waiting for, exactly?"

"Open doors, I'd say," Callum said, and checked his phone again, then reached into the back and grabbed a book at random out of a damp-stained box he'd picked up at some point. He leaned his seat back and lit a cigarette, and Pru looked at me.

"Really?" she said.

"Well, we *could* walk into a were club in skinny daylight with no one else around to muddle up our scent," I said. "But I'm voting wait until the club's pumping, there're loads of people about, and we're winning on the night vision front."

"Broad daylight," Callum said, not looking up from his book.

"Have you seen the day?"

Pru looked at the roof of the car. "You two have no sense of urgency."

"We do have a remarkably well-developed sense of self-preservation, though," Callum said.

Pru curled herself up next to Tam, closing her eyes, and I sat watching the club, my nose twitching with the scents of smoke and crumbling tarmac and weres. Callum was wrong about our sense of self-preservation. We needed to work on that.

"How many can they fit in there?" Pru asked.

We were currently watching a minivan disgorge far more bodies outside the Luxury Party Hire store than seemed possible, and certainly more than was legal. A faery and a dwarf were standing in front of it yelling at each other, the dwarf pointing at a damp stain on his skinny jeans and the faery waving a large glass of something about rather unsteadily, sloshing it all over herself as well as the dwarf.

The car park had started filling up an hour ago. It was still early, but it had been full dark for a good few hours, and the were club was evidently the place to be for all discerning Folk partiers. Fauns tripped down the drive in baggy jeans and skin-tight tops, laughing and shoving each other as they came. They had to be either brave, reckless, or already a few pints down. I didn't fancy looking like half a sheep in a warehouse full of weres. Faeries pulled up helmet-less on grumbling motorbikes, shaking their wings off as they stripped out of leather jackets. Elves swept up in whispering electric cars, fussing with their make-up and trying to keep their fancy shoes out of the puddles. Goblins – gah, how could *anywhere* allow goblins – arrived in cars shaking with the heavy bass of goblin music. All sorts of creatures that looked more or less human trailed down the drive in ones or twos, or pulled up in cars that ran the full spectrum from *my other car's a Bentley* to *I nicked this from a scrapyard.*

"Well. I think we can get started," Callum said. He peeled his jacket off, dumping it in the back seat then throwing his old jumper in after it, leaving him shivering in his T-shirt. It was surprisingly intact, but the print had faded to illegibility.

"Get started on what? Hypothermia?" I asked.

"No," he said. "Walking straight in the front with a big group is my best chance of not being noticed. I'm going clubbing."

"You can't just walk in there. There'll be guard dogs."

"Bouncers," Callum said.

"Same thing."

"And that's why you're not coming." He shoved his phone into the pocket of his jeans. "I've got the password. It's the best chance we've got." He swung out of the car, barely waiting for us to follow him before he slammed the door, then tucked his hands in his pockets and strode across the car park to where the warehouse door was guarded by an enormous man in a well-tailored black shirt, the pumpkin lights reflecting softly on the glossy dark skin of his bald head. Callum joined the straggly queue next to the faery and dwarf, who'd stopped arguing and were singing loudly, arms around each other. The dwarf immediately threw a heavy arm around Callum's waist, pulling him into the chorus. The enormous man at the door waved them past with the rest of the group, barely glancing at them.

Pru, Tam and I looked at each other.

"How good is he at passing as the sort of person who goes clubbing?" Pru asked.

"You saw him."

Tam looked at us both, then got up and headed along the edge of the car park to the right of the club, slipping across the drive and keeping in the shadow of the long weeds that grew along the fence. Pru took a moment to scratch herself out of her coat, then followed, and after a moment I did too. It wasn't like I had much choice.

In the damp, half-lit dark of the were car park, under the mixed scents of the club-goers, I caught a whiff of hair and blood and rage on the wind, half-smothered by the stale tarmac stink of the city. I could smell charms, too. There were cloaking ones that hid the club, protecting it from the casual gaze of Folk and humans who didn't know what they were looking at, and I caught the fractured scent of shift locks as well, trapping even Pru and Tam in here. It was normal for a place like this to have charms, but it still made me uneasy. Further off, there was the flat cold scent of water and rebellious green growth, a canal or river anchored in some bit of furtively rewilding land. I shivered.

Tam's tread was slow and deliberate as she led us around the lot, her ears twitching. The plastic pumpkin lights at the club door were the brightest part of the whole estate, and it didn't take much to keep us hidden. But in this place we were less worried about being seen than being smelled. She paused as we got to a large, water-filled pothole, took a breath, then belly-flopped into it with her ears back and her eyes squeezed shut.

"Ew," Pru said.

"Aw, no." I could smell the mucky water from here. It wasn't foul, exactly, but it was full of stale water, old oil spills painting rainbows across its surface, and as Tam kicked the mud up it blossomed with the defeated scent of ground gravel and crumbling tarmac. She rolled a couple of times, even rubbing the top of her head in the water, then stood up and stared at us both.

I looked at Pru. "You can't do that. You'll freeze."

"I'll dry quicker than you," she said, and stepped delicately into the muck. She wasn't as long about it as Tam, but she came out glistening with grey mud.

"Katja's going to kill us," I said, and flopped in before I could lose my nerve. The water splashed up my nose as I rolled, drenching my fur while the mud clogged up my claws, and when I stood up I was shivering with the chill of it. But I couldn't smell the familiar, wild scents of Tam or Pru. All I could smell was old water and forgotten places.

Tam and Pru looked at each other, and Tam gave a huff of cat laughter.

"Oh, and you look so much better," I said.

She just narrowed her eyes in amusement and turned toward the were's party shack, her shoulders rolling under her mud-slicked fur. Pru and I fell into step with her, and I hoped it was going to be enough. And that we'd know what to do when one of us, inevitably, got caught.

We slipped along the fence line to the end of the Luxury Party Hire warehouse, keeping low among the scraggly weeds on the edge of the car park. As we got closer the heavy beat of music started to shake through my bones, and I thought the sheds must be better insulated than they looked for the noise not to leak out more. I caught the faint whiff of humans and Folk and weres, but nothing strong, other than just around the corner, out of sight of the door and close to the corner of the fence, which had obviously been unofficially designated as the outdoors toilet.

"And they call animals filthy," Pru muttered as we skirted the area. Tam grunted, and I was just glad she didn't decide that this would be even better scent camouflage. Some things are asking too much, even in the cause of PI work.

The building was double-sided, and when we rounded the end to the other side, we found more roller doors with shop signs in the same state of disrepair as the others. There were more cars parked here, too, but the whomp of the music was slightly more distant. One of the doors stood open, laying yellow light across the tarmac, and a man leaned in it, drinking from a bottle as he stared at the night. We hunkered down, watching.

He was there for long enough that I could feel the gunky water on my fur drying, and my joints stiffening up in the cold. Pru was shivering next to me, and I shuffled a little closer to her, but she hissed softly and backed away. I suppose wet cat hair isn't actually that helpful.

I was just about to suggest that we tried another way when there was a sudden rush of music and someone said something from inside the building.

The man turned to look. "There's more in the back room," he said.

There was a muted response, and the man sighed. "We *can't* be out. I just picked up a whole shipment yesterday. Did Klaus look properly?"

Another mutter, and he shook his head. "Fine, fine. I'm coming." He pulled the door closed after him as he went, cutting off the light and the music, and we didn't wait to see if he was coming back. We ran along the edge of the building, three muddy shadows, our eyes on the wall above us. The reek of weres was strong back here, trodden firmly around the door and back and forth to the cars. The scent of the man we'd just seen hung acrid and hairy about us, along with a whiff from whatever he'd been drinking. It smelled like coffee.

The door handle was a round knob, the sort that's pretty impossible to get your paws on. I had a couple of goes anyway, but then we hurried on. We had to go right around the far side of the building, exposed to the car park, before we found it – one high, small window propped open by a rusting can of air freshener.

"Were toilets," I said. "Lucky us." But I jumped straight for it, anyway.

It was right on the edge of my range, and I got my claws hooked over the sill and hung there for a moment, listening for movement beyond. There was only the steady *thump, thump, thump* of the music, and water running softly. I muscled myself up and onto the ledge, careful not to dislodge the air freshener, and found myself peering into a toilet stall, the floors torn linoleum and the walls and door the sort that don't go all the way to the ceiling or floor. It stank of weres and cologne and spilt beer and pine toilet cleaner, and I shook my head to dispel a sneeze.

I glanced back at Pru and Tam, giving a quick arch of my whiskers, then jumped lightly to the seat of the loo, wrinkling my nose in preparation of the stench. It wasn't actually too bad, that piney reek drowning most of the nastiness, so I slipped to the floor and checked the room was empty as Pru scratched her way in behind me. Tam came after, squeezing her bulk through the gap and dislodging the air freshener can. The window swung shut behind her, but we were in. We could always push it open again, assuming we came back the same way.

Which was also assuming we came back at all.

THE DOORS out of the toilets were just those swing-shut kind, so we nipped through easily enough, leaving muddy smears behind and finding ourselves in a long, narrow corridor that ran the length of the building, dimly lit by orange LED candles someone had stuck in the end of garden tiki torches. I wasn't sure if that was for atmosphere or to save on the power bill. Doors marked it at regular intervals to either side – it must've once allowed access out of the back of each of the shops to the toilets without having to trek outside in the glorious Yorkshire weather. It was empty right now, but music pounded from our right, the pirate party side. The thin wall shook with it.

"We can't stay in here," Pru said. Her pupils were huge in the dim light. "The first were to pop out a door will see us, never mind smell us."

"We need to find Callum," I said.

"We need to get out of sight first."

I couldn't argue with that, and even if I'd been inclined to, Tam was looking at me in a manner that suggested I think very carefully about what I said next.

"Try the doors," I said. "I can smell booze everywhere. No one in here's going to be being that careful about shutting up behind them."

We split up, Pru trying the nearest door while Tam and I ran on. We ignored the doors to the left – the rooms beyond them were silent, and if they were the back rooms the were in the door had referred to, they'd likely be rather more carefully locked and guarded. Tam took the next door, and as I ran to the third, I heard her snarl of frustration when the knob didn't turn.

I had no more luck with the third one, which was just insulting. Drunk people are never that careful. Did they have door people on every one, making sure they were shut properly? Pru passed me, running for the next, then came to a stumbling stop as, ahead of us, a door to the left swung open, unleashing pale fluorescent light. We froze. There was no point running. They'd just see us even more quickly.

"I'll consider it," an unfamiliar voice said. It was mellow and smooth, the sort of voice that wears its shirt with the top two buttons undone and the sleeves rolled up above its tattooed forearms.

"I'm sure there will be other interested parties if you decline," a rather more familiar voice said. "I wouldn't consider it for too long."

The first speaker chuckled, and there were growling edges to it. "I don't do the hard sell, magician. Keep that for your human mates."

"Not a hard sell," Ifan said. "Merely a statement of intent."

The open door had swung toward us, hiding us from the speakers, but we could see their shadows falling into the hall ahead of them. Now one swelled, and Ifan stepped into sight. He glanced around, his gaze falling on Pru, and I saw his eyes widen. He turned back to the room.

"Perhaps I could go out the back?" he suggested. "Easier than fighting my way through the crowds."

"You can go out the same way you came in," the other man said. "I don't want you snooping around my place more than you have been."

"I wasn't *snooping,*" Ifan protested.

"Sure you weren't." A second shadow grew, swallowing Ifan, although he didn't step back from the door. I jerked my head at Pru, and she ran soft-footed back toward me. I turned to sprint for the toilet door, Tam waiting for us with her teeth bared and her tail lashing, and it seemed for an instant that we might make it.

But our luck never runs that way.

18

IT'S GOT A GOOD BEAT

One of the doors to the party room swung open in our path so fast it caught Tam and sent her stumbling across the floor. Pru and I didn't stop. We swerved around the staggering feet that came through the door, plunging into a sweating, heaving darkness punctuated by strobing lighting and sweeping spots of various colours, the beat of the music shaking my chest and stuffing itself into my ears. I looked back in time to see Tam nip around the door after us, her ears back, but the group that had just gone through didn't seem to notice her any more than they had us. They didn't smell like weres. They smelled of booze and exhausted excitement and sweat, and the sick-sweet reek of things that fill the void, even if only momentarily.

I sprinted across the floor, dodging bouncing trainers and twisting heels and stomping boots. I only glanced back to make sure Pru and Tam were still with me. We needed cover before anything else. The walls were lined with makeshift seating, sofas and tables made from pallets and drums and crates, and they were crowded with weres and humans and goblins and faeries and more creatures than I had time to take inventory of. What mattered was that a very large proportion of them would not be particularly inclined to extend a warm welcome to felines in their midst, Watch or not.

Pru smacked my haunches with one paw, claws slightly unsheathed, and I spun to look at her, almost running into a pair of furry, hoofed legs, and some smoother ones in heeled boots. Pru lifted her nose to my right, and I spotted scaffolding through the tangle of jouncing bodies. It was hung in dust cloths that had been spray painted with paws and stars and anarchy signs, and it seemed mostly unoccupied. I nodded, and we veered off, emerging from the dancers with our tails intact, although all of us were wide-eyed and panting.

I nosed my way around the edge of one of the dust cloths, and found they were disguising nothing more nefarious than stacked crates of empty bottles and sacks of rubbish. I supposed it saved carrying them out through the chaos below. I looked at Pru and Tam and lifted my chin. *Up?* They both lifted their noses at me, and we wriggled our way in among the stacked rubbish, scrambling to find a good angle to haul ourselves to the next level. Tam went first, hanging by her forepaws from the rough planks for a moment before vanishing upward. We followed her, finding a tangle of cables that coiled like serpents across the platform before trailing up to the next level. We followed them up, and emerged onto the top of the scaffolding, not far beneath the roof. It was covered with black, egg-box-like material that must've been soundproofing. The heavy vines of the cables ran off into the open metal rafters, joining the lighting and speakers in intricate webs.

From here, we had a clear view of the entire club. The five businesses on this side had been knocked into one vast, long hall, with a bar at each end and another in the middle. A DJ perched on a raised platform in the middle on the centre bar, bobbing her head happily to the cataclysmic beat, and the crowd surged like the tides in response. There were far more people in here than there were cars outside, and there was barely any floor space to be seen. The heat rose off the crowd in waves, and along with it came a wild, animal joy that almost made me want to run down and join them. They ebbed and flowed like a single organism, and in here there was no hiding. I could see wings and horns and glittering claws, bared fangs and shaking tails and pumping fists. Folk and humans in one glorious, music-drenched mess, smashing their drinks together and pressing their heads to one another and shouting their joy to the world.

Well, to the warehouse, anyway.

Tam and Pru sat down on either side of me, and none of us spoke for a moment.

Finally Pru said, raising her voice over the cacophony, "Look how much fun they're all having. It's kind of lovely."

"It's kind of loud," I shouted back.

Tam grunted. "I like it. It's got a good beat."

I blinked at her, then looked back at the dancers below. "No wonder they don't want the Watch seeing this. Look at them all. There's a goblin hugging a dryad down there, and that faun's plaiting a dwarf's beard. The Watch'd *hate* it."

No one answered for a moment, then Pru said, "Why? It's all hidden. No one's doing anything wrong."

I stared back at her without answering. I knew I was right. But I couldn't figure out why.

Some tall people are all elegance when they dance, loose-limbed and graceful, as if the music moves them the way wind moves reeds. They seem *made* to dance.

Callum was not one of those people.

And though the club wasn't exactly full of candidates for the Royal Academy of Dance, at least most of them had heard about something called rhythm and had a grasp on the theory of it, if nothing else. Even so, it took me a while to spot him, simply because of the sheer mass of people crammed onto the floor, but eventually I spied him midway between the door he'd come in and the one we had. He had a bottle in one hand and sweat already sticking his overlong hair to his neck and forehead, and he was doing some weird dance that seemed to involve little more than bobbing his head and waving his hands about like he was trying to imitate an octopus. This also served to splatter his drink over his neighbours quite liberally, and as I watched a faery yelped and wiped the back of her neck, then spun around and gave Callum a shove that sent him staggering into a human woman, who said something it was probably better I couldn't hear, and shoved him back toward the faery. Callum held up his hands apologetically and kept bopping in the direction of the back doors.

"Dude," I mumbled.

Pru put her snout next to my ear and said, "Can you see the magician?"

I scanned the crowd as it bounced and surged under the sweeping lights and multicoloured spots, looking for Ifan's dark coat. Even given the dim lighting, it'd stand out here, among all the bare shoulders and chests. But I couldn't see him. "Maybe he went out the back way after all," I said to Pru, my voice raised to be heard over the insistent *whomp* of the music. It was starting to grate on me, my ears twitching with it.

She gave me a look that indicated she thought he was likely up to something questionable at the least, if not downright dodgy, and I couldn't disagree with that. In fact, I was certain of it, but he wasn't my main concern right now.

"I'm going after Callum," I said. "I don't know what's going on back there, but he's useless on his own."

Pru nodded as if that was a given, and started to say something, probably *we'll come with you because you need all the help you can get with that one,* and at that point the door to the back hall swung open in front of Callum. He tried to duck out of sight, but a knot of goblins who had apparently been watching a lot of those sort of movies where breakdancing is deadly currency were arranged in an immovable barrier around one of their buddies, who was lying on the floor pretending to be an upturned beetle. Callum twisted away, wriggling through the crowd with his head down as Ifan emerged from the door with a were behind him. Shirtsleeves-and-tatts looked exactly as he'd sounded, with the addition of a well-crafted grey beard. He was tall and broad-shouldered, and his eyes went straight to Callum, drawn by either his hurried movement or his scent or something else – crimes against dancing, maybe.

"Oh, hairballs," I muttered, as the tall were lunged forward and grabbed Callum by the back of his shirt. Ifan started to raise a hand and the were turned back to him, placing one big hand around the base of his neck. I had no idea what he was saying from up here, but other weres were materialising, standing up from the seating along the walls and slipping through the crowd, which seemed to part magically around them. A moment later Callum and Ifan were bundled back through the door and it was pulled shut behind them. The goblin on the floor got up, staggering, and his buddies erupted in cheers. The DJ moved seamlessly into another track, and my ears twitched.

Tam looked at Pru and me and said, "*Eccentric,*" then turned and started back down through the scaffolding.

I followed her. I didn't know what we were going to do, but staying here was getting us nothing but a headache.

IF ANYTHING, the dance floor was more crowded and feverish than it had been when we'd first arrived. The music seemed to have cranked up a notch, the dancers stomping harder and flailing their various limbs and wings and tails about with even more abandon. The beat was in my chest, shaking my joints and sending my ears flat as it swamped everything, even thought. It crushed us beneath it, and by the time we'd made it halfway to the door I'd had my tail stood on, beer spilled on me, and someone had tripped over me hard enough that my ribs were stinging. I was panting, and ahead was nothing but a forest of stomping legs, all seemingly designed to flatten a small but well-proportioned cat.

I turned back, finding Pru right behind me. Tam was a ball of damp, muddy fury beside her.

"It's too much!" I bellowed. "We can't get through!"

They both stared at me, and I realised I couldn't even hear myself. We were being jostled on all sides by feet and hooves and paws, and I staggered as someone's boot caught me a glancing blow. I nodded back the way we'd come, and we turned to make a struggling retreat toward the comparative safety of the scaffold.

Tam bulled her way through the tangle of legs as if she could make them move out of the way through sheer willpower, but even she was being jostled off course, once losing her footing as a fancy, immaculate trainer caught her in the chin and made her stagger. Pru followed in Tam's wake, someone's drink dripping off her muddy flanks, and as I fought my way through the mess after them a foot caught me, hooking right under my belly and hefting me off the ground. I snarled, rolling off with my teeth bared, and dived into the crowd again, scrambling for cover before anyone realised what they'd tripped over. By the time I landed I'd lost sight of Pru and Tam, and there was no way I was finding them again. I'd been turned around by the fall, and with the constantly surging feet all about me I couldn't tell which direction I'd come from, or glimpse the scaffolding or the doors or even the bloody *ceiling* from here. I took the first gap I could find, scrabbling desperately through the revellers, every surge of music translating into an answering pound of dancing limbs that sent me spinning off in a different direction, trying to keep my tail and toes out of harm's way wherever I could.

It seemed to last forever, a world of thundering feet and hammering music, and I couldn't tell if my ears or my sides or my paws or my tail were having the worst time of it. But finally I ran up against an upright surface that wasn't a wall, not the way it leaned out over me. I took cover under the slight overhang and scooted along it with my flank pressed to the corrugated iron surface, panting in the reek of stale beer and the sharp stink of spirits, and avoiding the nastiest of the puddles.

A gap appeared in the barrier, and I shot into it gratefully. Even under the overhang of the not-a-wall, people had been shuffling their bloody great feet into the space, grateful for a little more room themselves, and with no thought for sneaking cats. The gap let me straight into an open area where I stopped short, my breath hard against my bruised ribs, and stared around at what was very clearly one of the bars, tended by half a dozen rushing weres. It was lit by the glow coming from a mismatched row of glass-fronted fridges as well as some spotlights hanging over the top, and I'd evidently just walked straight out of the dance floor and into the snacking gallery. I spun to plunge back into the punishing crush of dancers just as someone yelled, "What the *hell?*"

I didn't wait to see if he was going to follow the shout with action. I threw myself into the tangle of feet, leaping over boots and diving through legs, while someone shouted behind me, "*Stop!*" and those in earshot turned to see what was going on.

I just kept running. At least I'd been able to get my bearings, after a fashion. I headed for the closest door, one that would let me out on the front of the building, hoping Pru and Tam were well ahead of me. The music was still pounding, and the shouting had been drowned beneath it. In fact, the music seemed to be getting louder, if anything, as if determined to turn everyone's attention back to the party. I could feel ripples of unease washing around the room, though, the rhythm of the crowd faltering as they tried to see what the disturbance was.

Some instinct made me glance back. It was more than curiosity, because I knew there was nothing I could see among the tangle of people, not from my admittedly disadvantageous vantage point. But I looked back anyway, and I saw the wolf on my trail. There was a channel opening in the crowd between us as it shouldered people aside, leaving the way clear for its pursuit. The dancers seemed more intrigued than concerned, watching the beast slip through them with its heavy shoulders rolling under its thick pelt, pale eyes fixed on me. When it saw me look back it growled, exposing the sort of teeth that are just unnecessary. It was moving with perfect, focused economy, the crowd making way for it, and no one was doing the same for me. I bolted.

Admittedly, it was more of an attempted bolt that an actual one. It was like trying to sprint through a forest of trees that refused to stay in one spot, and which jumped into my path at every possible opportunity. I couldn't get any speed up. I was bounced from one person to another, and by this point my claws were out, so there was a trail of outraged yelps following me. I wasn't even sure I was heading for the door anymore, but that didn't matter – all that mattered was staying ahead of the inexorable approach of the wolf-were. My fur bristled against the mud and my tail braced for the feel of the beast's teeth on my hindquarters, and I flung myself into a complicated zigzag, as if that could throw the creature off its pursuit. My breath wheezed, my throat too tight, and my heart was competing with the music to drown everything, even thought. All I could see were those pale eyes and terrible teeth, and there was *nowhere,* dammit, *nowhere* for a cat to hide, or climb, or *anything*. So I simply plunged on wildly, right up until I almost ran straight into the were at the door.

The crowd had expanded to fill every bit of space, and I came out of it at a stumbling sprint, catching the whiff of tarmac and damp air drifting from beneath the door just before I hit it. It smelled glorious. I rebounded off the door, spotted an enormous were still in human form stooping to grab me, shot between his legs, and found myself trapped in a corner under a folding chair.

The big were, the same one who'd let Callum in the door earlier, bent down to look at me, his bald pate shining. "Puss, puss," he said, rubbing his fingers at me encouragingly.

"Oh, as if," I snapped, panting, and the wolf-were emerged from the crowd with its head slung low between its shoulders, staring at me. It licked its chops, and glanced up at the bouncer.

"We should call Anton," the bouncer said.

The wolf opened its mouth, drool descending from its tongue.

"I know, but eating them's kind of bad form." The bouncer bent over to look at me again. "Any more of you in here?"

"No," I managed, not even having to work to sound a little squeaky and harmless. "And I'm not Watch, if that's the problem. I'm just looking for my silly human."

"Aw. That's cute."

The wolf snarled.

"It is. He's worried about his human." The bouncer peered at me and said, "Did they leave you home alone, puss?"

Gods. If it wasn't for the wet hair stink of the man, I'd be thinking he was just another cat person. "Yes," I said, swallowing hard and trying to get the panting under control. "That's it exactly. And he can lose *days* in a place like this."

"Some people do," the bouncer said, with the sort of sigh that said it wasn't right, and he didn't like it, but he had a job to do, and people had to help themselves.

The wolf looked at the ceiling, shaking its heavy head slightly.

"We don't allow cats, though," the big were continued. "You should know that. You *could* be Watch, and just lying to us."

"I'm not."

"Well, you would say that." We stared at each other, then there was a horrendous cracking sound, a howl of pain, and the wolf-were melted. I said something that made the bouncer blink at me with far more astonishment than he showed the collapsing animal behind him. I guess he'd seen it all before, but I hadn't. The creature's fur rushed off its skin, sucked inward or dissolved or just plain vanished, and everything else *reformed.* There was no simple lengthening of limbs and reshaping of the torso, no gentle redistribution of muscle and sinew. There was no grace or beauty involved at all. For one moment the creature was nothing more than a clumpy pile of flesh and bones, a sort of build-your-own monster, then in the space of a breath it all rattled back together again, and the gloopy mess morphed into a woman, standing pale and naked in front of us with her hands on her hips. The bouncer took a dressing gown from a rack of them hanging by the door and handed it to her without comment.

She snatched it. "It's a bloody *cat,* Xavier. He's not here for a nip fix."

"I'm looking for my human," I repeated, not really thinking about it. I was wondering what happened to your internal organs when you melted like that. Did they keep working? What if bits went back together wrong, and your lungs were where your liver should be? What if *everything* went back together wrong, and you ended up with your brains on the outside? And what about the muck on the floor? What if you reformed with a paper cup in your face? It seemed like a risky way to do things.

Messy, too. "That was seriously gross," I said, and only realised I'd said it out loud when the bouncer gave me a disapproving look.

"That's rude," he said.

"Sorry."

"What are you really here for?" the woman asked.

"I really am here for my human. Tall, bad dancer." I hesitated, but no cat just follows their human into a mess like this without good reason. "He's had some issues with … a few substances before," I said. "I was worried."

"You see?" Xavier said. "You judge cats as if they're all the same, Lani."

"It's no different to how they judge us." She tied the dressing gown firmly around her and stared at me. I stared back, trying to look like a poor lost little cat, simply searching for his irresponsible human. I found it was pretty easy to pull off when trapped in a corner by two weres.

And it might even have worked if a young were with long braids hadn't emerged out of the crowd, holding Pru aloft by the scruff of the neck with one hand, and supporting her hindquarters with the other.

And even *then* we might have got away with it, if Tam hadn't chosen that exact moment to attempt to free Pru.

"Aw, hairballs," I muttered as the big she-cat appeared out of the shadows and flung herself straight into the young were's face. The young were shrieked, Lani tore off the dressing gown and melted, and Xavier gave me such a reproachful look I almost felt bad.

Not bad enough to stop me biting him when he tried to grab me, though.

19

JUST LIKE CATERPILLARS

ANGRY CATS ARE NOT EASY TO GET HOLD OF. *LARGE* ANGRY cats, aiming at your face, are just plain terrifying. So as Tam bore down on her startled target, the young were dropped Pru, bringing her arms up to protect herself. Pru twisted as she fell, landed lightly on all fours and threw herself out of the path of Lani the wolf-were, who had reformed again out of her gross flesh puddle and lunged into the fray.

I feinted left, then right, then shot straight through Xavier's legs and laid some decent clawing into one of Lani's back legs, so that she left Pru and spun around to face me. Which was both what I wanted and exactly what I *didn't* want, as her teeth were just as big close up as they'd looked when she'd been stalking me at a distance. Tam flung herself off the other were and onto Lani's back, and the wolf snarled, twisting and snapping wildly as she tried to reach the big tabby. Pru and I plunged into the scrap, trying to keep those teeth away from Tam and avoid the other two weres at the same time, who were still in two-legged and slightly less terrifying form. They were still plenty big and grabby, though.

And all the time I was wondering how in the name of small sainted invertebrates we were going to get out of here, even if we got away from the weres. I somehow doubted anyone was going to just open the door for us.

Then someone did just that.

The door was pushed wide, unleashing the intoxicating scent of damp and mud and industry-stained sky, and Lani just about roared her frustration as Xavier ran to slam it shut. He wasn't fast enough to stop three cats who know they're one nip away from losing their tails, though. We shot out past the newcomer, Pru in the lead, and Lani charged in pursuit. I caught the crack and crunch of shattering bone behind us, and wondered if that was Xavier or the young were changing.

As we shot past, our rescuer said, "*Stop,*" in the sort of voice that's used to being obeyed, and has contingency plans for the rare occasions it's not.

We worked on the assumption that she wasn't talking to us, and that cats don't take direction well anyway, and kept running until we were sure no one was close enough to bite us, scattering across the car park. I stopped next to a boy-racer style Mazda, ready to scoot under its low-slung frame for cover if needed. Tam and Pru had made similar choices. A Land Rover's no use when being chased by a were.

"*Lani,*" our rescuer snapped, and crossed her arms over her chest. Yasmin, her hair still caught in a messy bun, with a long purple puffer coat zipped to her chin. It almost reached her knees, and underneath it the soft, multicoloured cloth of her skirt flared out in pleats and whorls. It gave her the impression of being an upside-down flower just about to bloom.

Lani stood on the muddy tarmac with her head low, glaring at Yasmin. Another wolf-were slipped out of the door, stalking around to take up a position just out of Yasmin's line of sight, and Xavier hovered in the doorway, plucking at his black shirt anxiously. His arms were heavily muscled, all dark smooth skin and the intricate whorls of tattoos.

Yasmin glanced at the second wolf-were, and looked back at Lani. "Don't play silly buggers."

"Hi Yasmin," Xavier said, and she barely glanced at him.

"Hi Xavier."

"I did say we should just take them to Anton."

"That would've been sensible." Yasmin checked on the second were again, then glared at Lani. "And it's what we're going to do now, isn't it?"

Lani snarled, stalking forward a step, and the second wolf-were did a little scuttle toward Yasmin, teeth bared.

"Oh, very clever. Let's have a full-on scrap in the bloody car park."

I was as close to certain as I could be that the other weres weren't going to listen to Yasmin. That's what makes weres so bloody tricky. In human shape, they're as reasonable as any human (which is to say, it completely depends on the situation and on the person as to how reasonable they're going to be), but in wolf form it's not just their shape that changes. Or so common wisdom goes, anyway. Which meant Lani wasn't thinking politics or sense. She was thinking that Yasmin had just deprived her of the joy of tearing apart three small felines, and now she was spoiling for a fight, reasonable or not. Her priorities had shifted from *deal with the intruders* to *fight fight fight.*

It was an ideal time to beat a hasty retreat, while everyone was otherwise engaged. Xavier looked like he'd probably jump in on Yasmin's side, and she *was* a were, so it wasn't like we were leaving some helpless human to be torn to bits. We should fall back, regroup, and then figure out how the hell we were going to get Callum out. But as the two wolf-weres circled closer to Yasmin, I didn't move, my claws testing the gravel beneath me. She was looking from one to the other with her eyes narrowed, and I glanced at Tam. The big she-cat was creeping forward, careful not to draw attention to herself. She hadn't even met Yasmin, so I wondered if she was just in much the same mind frame as the wolves.

"Hairballs," I muttered, as Lani dropped lower into a crouch, and Yasmin said, "You don't want to start this, Lani."

I ran forward before I could think any more about it. We weren't going to make any difference in a fight, no matter how big Tam thought she was, so we needed to stop it before it started. "Hey, Fido!" I yelled, skidding to a stop in the middle of the aisle of cars. "Wanna play fetch?"

Lani didn't move out of her crouch, but she did swing her head toward me, those formidable teeth gleaming in the low light.

"Here, girl! Or shall we do obedience – sit! *Sit,* and you'll get a treat!" The second wolf was growling now, the sound reverberating around the cars. "Roll over," I offered. "Play dead?"

"What the hell, cat?" Yasmin demanded.

I bounced about a few times, just for the hell of it, and also because my nerves were singing so much I couldn't stay still. "Two stinky dogs in a foul car park, can't do tricks and they just won't bark!"

"Oh, Anubis preserve us," Xavier said, with a wondering tone in his voice. "Have you lost your little mind?"

"*Woof, woof!*" I shouted at them, and the second wolf broke first. She rushed me and I bolted, hearing Lani snarl behind me, a terrible reverberating sound, and the thunder of big paws on loose gravel as they charged. I was ready for them, but they were so *fast.* I could all but feel their breath on my tail, and I plunged below the first car I could. I didn't stop, though, just kept running, out of shelter and back into it, one car, two, three, the wolves' heavy bodies slamming into the chassis above me and shaking the vehicles on their shocks, sliding them across the gravelly tarmac as if it were bulls hitting them instead of overwrought dogs. Dimly, I could hear Yasmin and Xavier shouting, but it was mostly drowned out by the snarls and growls that surrounded me.

I shot from the cover of an ancient Volvo estate and under the sort of car that's definitely been retrofitted with blue lights that shine down onto the road, all glittering chrome and massive alloy rims and probably a furry steering wheel. It was a hideous orange colour, but it was also so low to the ground I could barely get under it. The wolves certainly couldn't, and they weren't going to roll it over either. I hunkered down with the car's undercarriage brushing my ears and stared at the snapping, foaming muzzles that tried to shove themselves after me. The car shook and rocked with their assault, but the tyres were fat and they couldn't slide it far. I just shuffled with it to keep myself well under cover.

"Good dogs," I said, a little breathlessly, and swallowed hard. My mouth was horribly dry, and my heart was so loud in my ears it was almost like being back inside the club.

The snouts retreated, leaving just big paws and long legs stalking around the car, and I closed my eyes.

I really hate weres.

IT SEEMED AN INORDINATELY long time before the paws were joined by two pairs of trainers, one set barely visible under a long skirt.

"Puss, puss," Xavier said.

"Oh, come on," I said. "Really?"

"You alright under there?" Yasmin asked.

"Well, I'm uneaten, anyway."

"Despite your best efforts to the contrary." But I could hear a smile in her voice. It faded as she said, "Lani, Angela, human up, please."

Both wolves gave matching growls.

"Come on. This is a joke. Chasing cats around car parks? Even if they're not bloody Watch, this is the sort of thing that'll get the Watch's attention."

A couple more growls, then I got a floor-level view of

dissolving wolves. I gagged as they reformed and vanished upward again, leaving me staring at bare feet and wondering how much gravel was embedded in their internal organs.

"You can come out now," Yasmin said.

"I realise that you pose the most danger as wolves," I said, "but I'm still not super-keen on your buddies there as humans. They looked kicky."

"No one's going to kick you," Yasmin said. "We're all going to be sensible Folk about this, aren't we?"

"Yes," Xavier said.

"Oh, lick her bloody feet, Xav, why don't you?" Lani snapped.

It was wet and mucky under the car, and all I could see were human feet beyond it, so I slipped out from under the far side and jumped to the roof of the next car along. I examined the weres. Xavier had obviously carted some more dressing gowns out with him, as both Lani and the one Yasmin had called Angela – and who was also the young were that had grabbed Pru in the club – were wrapped in fluffy robes. Lani's had yellow rubber ducks printed on it.

"Styling," I said.

"Don't push it," Yasmin said, as Lani lifted her lip to show one overlong canine.

"I'm serious," I said. "As a cat I know cosy when I see it."

"Gods," Lani said. "How can you even stand to talk to the insufferable creatures?"

"That was a compliment," I protested.

"Gobs, shut up," Pru said, startling me. I looked

around. She and Tam were perched on two different car roofs, all of us watching the weres with same caution cats the world over offer packs of dogs. We might be fast, but they were bigger and stronger, and there were more of them. Plus, with the shift locks in place there was no chance of cat-specific getaways. Even Pru and Tam would have to rely on the more traditional version of flight, if it came to it.

"*Gobs,*" Angela said, and giggled. She was only a teenager by the look of her, strong and broad-shouldered. She looked like she got picked first for all the sports teams and were hunts.

"Yeah, well. At least I don't dissolve into goo at a moment's notice."

"It's no different to being a caterpillar."

"A really hairy, carnivorous one?"

"Yeah." She grinned at me, and as toothy as it was, there was no malice in it. No more than a dog's cruel when they chase a rabbit. Doesn't help the rabbit much, though.

"What're you doing here?" Yasmin asked me. "I told you lot to stay clear."

"Callum's in there," I said. "He went looking for a friend, and now they've both been taken out the back."

Yasmin looked at Lani. "You know about this?"

Lani shook her head. "Damn cat just showed up in the middle of the bar. How the hell did you even get in?"

"Skills," I said, and Tam huffed softly.

"No one *different* about, then?" Yasmin asked, and I thought of her saying, *You're a North,* with that flat hostility.

"Some magician came in and wanted to talk to Anton," Xavier said. "He anything to do with you?"

Yasmin scowled at me. "You brought your magician?"

"No. But we saw him in there. He's not our favourite person right now, either, if that helps."

"Not particularly."

"You know this lot, Yasmin?" Lani demanded. "What the hell are you doing, talking to cats?"

"They turned up at my bar," Yasmin said. "I came here to warn Anton they were poking around."

"We have these things called phones, you know," Lani said, her head titled.

Yasmin didn't smile. "Some discussions are best had in person."

"About cats?"

"And other things. But now we have a magician."

"Bloody magicians," Xavier put in. "They're a right pain. Last one that came in kept magicking out her empty bottle with fresh ones from behind the bar and passing them round. Made no bloody money at all for a whole week till we rumbled her."

"That does sound like Ifan's style," I said. "Magicians, huh?"

"Exactly," Xavier said, with feeling.

"Ifan?" Lani asked, and looked at Xavier. "You didn't say it was bloody *Ifan*."

Xavier scratched his chin. "I didn't think it mattered which magician it was. They're all as bad as each other."

I was starting to think weres might be more than just teeth and brawn, given that they seemed to have a far more accurate view of magicians than most. "He seemed to be having a good old chat with one of your pack mates in there."

Yasmin looked at me, and I caught the wolf in her dark eyes, just for a moment. "Who?"

"How do I know? Tatts and shirtsleeves. That's all I've got."

Yasmin looked at Lani. "Anton's meeting with the magician? Why?"

Lani shrugged. "I didn't know about it. But you don't get to ask those questions, anyway."

Yasmin considered the other were for a moment, then shook her head. "I get to ask any question I want. But not of you." She shifted her gaze to me. "Come on. Let's go and see what's happening with your human. You other cats coming?"

"Wouldn't miss it," Pru said, and jumped to the ground, wrinkling her nose at the splatter of mud.

"You can't just—" Lani started, and Yasmin growled. It was a restrained noise, but it was strung about with fury.

"Think very carefully before you continue that sentence, Lani."

Lani scowled. "They're not welcome. You know that."

"I do. But I'm quite sure Anton and I can discuss that ourselves. You're not the gatekeeper of this pack."

Lani didn't reply, and the two women stared at each other for a moment, until Angela said to Pru, "Aren't you cold?"

"Yes," Pru said simply, and before she could react Angela lifted her up and bundled her into her arms, holding her against the fluffy front of the dressing gown.

Pru was on her back, legs stuck up in the air, and she blinked at the young were in astonishment.

"Aw," Xavier said.

Pru looked as if she was about to start fighting her way down, even though I could see the greyish tinge to her skin and the tremble in her ears. "Hey, I'm cold, too," I said. "Don't I get a lift?"

"You've got fur," Angela said.

"*Wet* fur."

Pru looked down at me, then up at Angela, and said, "This is very undignified."

"Sorry," Angela said, and shifted her grip so that Pru was up the right way, but still ensconced in fluffy dressing gown glory. "Better?"

Pru started to say something, and I said over the top of her, "Alright for some, eh Tam?" The big she-cat looked at me, then at Pru, and did an astonishingly good impression of a poor-me cat, all big eyes and slumped shoulders. I looked at Yasmin and said, "Let's go and find Callum, then."

"I can give you a lift if you want," Xavier offered. He was looking at me in that way people do when they really want to pet the kitty, but are also aware that the kitty has more sharp edges than not.

"No," I said. "Cheers, though." I saw his gaze shift to Tam and added, "I would not recommend it."

He subsided, his shoulders slumping in disappointment until they almost matched Tam's, and Yasmin said to him, "You two better get back to stations."

"Are there any more of you?" Xavier asked me. "Honestly, this time?"

"Not a sausage. Cross my heart and hope you die."

"Hope *to* die," Xavier said.

"What?"

"The saying. Cross my heart and hope to die."

"But I don't hope to die," I said. "I mean, I don't really hope you do, either, but rather you than me."

Lani snorted, then shook her head and walked back to the club door, muttering about cats and magicians and menaces. Xavier followed, stealing little glances back at us.

"That dude has some cat issues," I said.

"He has cat tattoos," Angela said, using the sleeve of her dressing gown to clean some of the muck off Pru. "And cat earrings. And cat T-shirts. And cat socks. I think he probably sleeps in cat pyjamas."

I blinked at her. "That's really unfortunate for a were."

Angela nodded and looked at Pru. "Are you warmer yet? Only I can put you inside the dressing gown if you want."

Yasmin looked at me, the corner of her mouth twitching. "Such natural enemies."

I shrugged. "Look, I only know what I've been told about weres."

"And therein lies the problem with every kind. We far too often rely on what we've been told about what makes others *other,* and never ask what – or who – the story serves."

I wrinkled my snout. "Your Lani there did try to eat me."

"I believe you called her a stinky dog."

"Before that."

"You mean when you were trespassing?"

I looked at Tam, who shrugged, thought about it, then said, "The rhyme wasn't subtle."

Everyone's a critic. Yasmin inclined her head and led the way around the building, holding her skirt up with one hand to keep it out of the worst of the puddles. Her legs were smooth above her trainers, a floral tattoo snaking up one calf, and she still smelled of cleaning stuff and musky perfume and wild, savage things. She was certainly *other.*

But I wasn't exactly sure what that meant anymore. If I'd ever known.

20

PLENTY OF MOUTH SPACE

THERE WAS NO SNEAKING THIS TIME, SINCE WE HAD A WOLFY escort. Yasmin led us around the building and straight to one of the doors about halfway down the side. It had a still mostly complete sign that announced itself as a marine upholsterer. *Deck cushions – awnings – foam bunk mattresses!* it proclaimed proudly in blue writing on white board, and had a little anchor in one corner to assure the buyer that yes, they really meant boats. I supposed the Leeds-Liverpool canal wasn't that far away, so maybe having a boat upholsterer in the middle of Yorkshire wasn't as far-fetched as it seemed. Then again, their shop was now occupied by partying weres, so it obviously hadn't been the best business model.

The shop had the same big roll-up garage door and smaller regular one to the side as the others, and Yasmin knocked sharply on the regular door. There was a pause, then Tatts-and-shirtsleeves opened it and looked at her without surprise.

"Yasmin," he said.

"Anton."

"Haven't seen you around for a bit."

"I understand we have an issue with an undead magician, plus an interloper."

Anton looked over his shoulder, scratching his beard with one hand. He had hard blue eyes, and smelled of sweat and heat and salt under the wolf. "Not just any interloper. A North. Not sure which one's the main issue yet, but I'm not liking the combo."

I'd slipped along the wall, keeping my side as close to it as I could as I tried to peer around the door and see if Callum was inside. The were hadn't exactly thrown the door wide, though, so all I could see were some crates of beer and a filing cabinet. I went to scoot through the door and Yasmin clicked her tongue.

"Hang about, cat," she said. "No sneaking."

Anton's gaze dropped to me. "You're keeping some strange company, Yas." His voice was mild, but the hot scent of him intensified.

"I just stopped Lani tearing them apart," Yasmin said. "She needs to work on other forms of conflict resolution."

"Agreed on that," I said. "But, to be fair, we had the situation under control."

Yasmin snorted. "Keep telling yourself that, puss."

"It's Gobbelino." I shifted my attention to Anton. "I don't think much of your staff, dude. Distinctly light on the hospitality part of the hospitality trade."

Anton raised his eyebrows. "Cats aren't known for wanting to do anything in were bars but shut them down or start fights. Sounds like you're upholding part of the tradition, at least."

"I didn't start a fight," I protested.

"You did," Angela said. "Well, the big cat did. She jumped me." She wrinkled her nose at Tam, who half-closed her eyes in satisfaction.

"You were waving Pru about by the scruff of the neck," I pointed out.

"You were," Pru agreed, still snugly ensconced in Angela's arms. "It was quite uncomfortable."

"I'm sorry," Angela said, and scritched the back of Pru's neck. I could see Pru trying not to purr.

Anton looked from one of us to the other, shook his head, and said, "I don't even know where to start. Come in."

He pulled the door wide, and Yasmin led the way into a room that was part office, part some sort of staff room. There was a big computer desk with an old desktop and over-full filing trays to one side, under a cork board covered in fliers and postcards. The rest of the room was given over to a few big, sway-backed sofas with worn cushions, a couple of coffee tables that looked distinctly like someone had been chewing on their legs, a table tennis table without a net, and a couple of big fridges against the wall by a small kitchenette area. It was tidier than I'd expected, no empty bottles left on tables or bones scattered on the floor, and someone had put up a sign that said, *Clean your own mess!* A second one read, *You shed, you vacuum.*

Callum was sitting in one of the sofas, cradling a mug of tea, and Ifan was sprawled in another with a beer in one hand.

Callum blinked at me. "Gobs? Are you okay?"

"Sure," I said, giving Anton a suspicious look as I padded past him. "Not as good as you, though, evidently."

Callum looked at his mug almost guiltily. His T-shirt was torn at the neck, but it had been going that way anyway, and otherwise he looked better than we did.

"Explain," Anton said, taking a couple of bottles of apple juice from one of the fridges and handing one each to Angela and Yasmin. Pru jumped down and shook herself off.

I looked at the bearded were. "Well, see, he's sitting here with a cuppa while we've been rolling in the mud, having our eardrums almost burst, running from wolves—"

"Not you," Anton said.

"Why not?"

He ignored me and looked at Callum. "You, North. Explain what you're doing, and why you brought three cats here."

"What about magic boy?" I demanded. "He was here first." And I almost added, *What were you two talking about? What are you going to **consider**?* But I bit down on the words at the last moment. Ifan had seen us, had even given us space to get away, but he didn't know we'd heard him. And I wasn't sure I wanted him to know. Not until I had a better idea of what he and the were had been discussing.

Ifan took a swig of his beer before answering. He looked perfectly comfortable, leaning back in the sofa with his heavy coat undone, one ankle over his opposite knee and his arm flung along the back. "Anton knows why I'm here," he said. "Sometimes working magic leaves you a bit too much in your own head. It's good to get out." He thought about it. "And a little chemical help doesn't hurt."

"Really? Then what're you doing back here instead of out there?"

"Bit hard to have a conversation out there," Ifan said.

"What's conversation got to do with getting off your head?"

"Gobs," Callum said.

"*And* I heard you weren't that welcome here, so interesting choice of venue."

Ifan spread his free hand, smiling. It didn't quite reach his eyes. "It's familiar. That enough for you?"

"Familiar doesn't mean safe."

"You're fun," Anton said, sitting down on an old leather pouffe that had seen better days. "How the hell do you put up with cats all day, North?"

"How do you put up with smelling like wet dog all day?" I demanded. "And his name's *Callum,* not *North.*"

Callum shook his head and looked at Anton. "Sorry. Civility is a foreign language."

"Evidently."

I showed them all a fang, and Anton answered with a grin that was all teeth. It set the hair on my spine bristling, and Pru growled softly. Tam was patrolling the edges of the room, and she looked around with her ears back.

Yasmin and Angela had sat down in the third sofa, and Anton said, "Ange, aren't you on bottle collection?" His voice was softer when he spoke to her, and she shrugged.

"I was due a break anyway. And then there were cats."

He nodded. "Well, go and find your clothes, then take your break next door, okay?"

She wrinkled her nose. “Can’t I stay?”

“No,” he said firmly. “Next door. And make sure you drink that juice. You need the sugar after a change.”

“Yes *Dad,*” she said, giving Yasmin a look that plainly said she was far too old to be treated as a child, and would appreciate some intervention. Yasmin just smiled at her, and Angela got up with a sigh, then padded barefoot out the door.

“Child labour?” I asked. “Putting your own kids to work in a bar? Smooth.”

“She’s seventeen, and not actually my kid.”

“She shouldn’t be changing in a room full of people,” Yasmin said. “No one should, but she’s too young for that.”

Anton nodded. “She’s not meant to. And there’ll be a discussion about that later, too. But you know how young weres are. If she saw Lani change she’d not have been able to stop herself.”

“She shouldn’t have been in that situation in the first place.”

Anton raised his hands and let them fall back into his lap. “This isn’t the time, Yas. Can we go back to discussing what three cats, a dead magician, and”—he waved at Callum—“*you* are doing in my club?” He glanced at Yasmin. “Also you. How long’s it been?”

“It’s not about me.”

“My appearance is purely recreational,” Ifan said. He was smiling a lot, and I wondered if he’d been telling the truth about recreational-ing.

Callum gave him an odd look that I couldn’t quite interpret, then said, “We’re looking for someone.”

“So you came sneaking around my place?” Anton

asked. "This isn't North territory. At the least you should've had the courtesy to come to me directly."

"I'm not a North anymore," Callum said, his voice flat. "I'm just looking for a friend."

"You smell like a North."

"You smell like wet dog," I snapped. "Yet you're not one, are you?"

Anton turned that hard blue gaze on me, still wearing the same mildly amused expression as he had all along. Only when he'd spoken to Angela had it slipped a little, exposing something rawer yet more gentle beneath. We stared at each other for a long, stretched moment, and I could smell old beer and damp coats and the slow rust of the walls, and the heavy were stink over everything. My muscles ached with cold and tension, and I almost wanted him to lunge at me, to do something that would mean we could be out of here and gone, putting this whole thing in the *too risky* pile and leaving Callum's messy past and weres and the magician behind us.

"A dentist," Callum said, shattering the moment, and we all looked at him.

"A dentist," Anton repeated.

"He's missing. Weres have been at his surgery."

"And what would a were want with a dentist?" Anton asked.

"Dog breath's pretty vile," I said. "I'd want to keep on top of that, too."

Anton snorted. "If we want to see a dentist, we go the NHS, same as anyone else."

I cocked my head at him, his slight smile exposing the tips of those characteristic canines. It seemed unlikely that a regular, human-type dentist wouldn't notice those, and who knew what else was done to teeth when they reformed themselves into fangs on a regular basis. Anton raised his eyebrows slightly, as if daring me to challenge him, but I didn't.

"Do you know a sorcerer?" Callum asked, drawing the were's attention back to him. "Goes by the name of Ms Jones."

Anton spread his hands, still with that mild, amused smile on his face. "I've run across her. Does she need a dentist?"

"The dentist's her partner. And we can't find either of them."

"Maybe they're on holiday," he suggested. "Or just not interested in being pursued by cats."

"Why's everyone so fixated on holidays?" I asked. "Who ever heard of a sorcerer on holiday?"

"They're still *people,*" Anton said.

Yasmin dropped her jacket on the back of a chair and leaned against the bench in the kitchen area to open her apple juice. "I told you it was nothing to do with weres. I told you to leave it." She scowled at us, swigging from the bottle.

"You led this lot here?" Anton asked, his tone still level.

"Of course not. I warned them off. Looks like their magician led them here." She and Anton both looked at Ifan, who raised both hands.

"I really didn't. Maybe they just like my company."

"We don't," Pru said, and eyed Anton. "We're missing a cat, too."

The were's smile faded. "We have nothing to do with

cats of any sort. We keep our heads down, and out of the way of the Watch wherever we can."

"She's not that sort of Watch," I said. "And she might've been hanging around with the sorcerer."

Anton shook his head and got up. "You'll have to go. There's a room full of pups next door, and if they get a whiff of cat, it'll be all on."

Callum nodded, took a final mouthful of tea, and got up. "We appreciate the help."

I wanted to ask, *What help?* but there was a current in the air, a tension that spoke of many things unsaid. Callum looked at me and tipped his head toward the door. I glanced at Yasmin, who just looked back at me, her face expressionless.

"Sure," I said. "The welcome was delightful."

Anton snorted, the smile resurfacing. "Next time I'll lay on the kibble, shall I?"

"You can get it when you stock up on chew toys."

"And you wonder why cats aren't welcome."

He ushered us out of the door ahead of him, Tam appearing from the shadows of the room and slipping silently out, Pru padding along next to me. Yasmin stayed where she was, and Ifan watched us for a moment, then when Anton turned to look at him he said, "Oh," and pushed himself out of the sofa. He followed us out into the sharp, hard-edged chill of the night. It had started to drizzle while we were inside, a bored, resentful splatter that ticked off my ears and made me shiver.

Anton leaned in the door and examined us for a moment, then said to Callum, "I'm no fan of Norths, but if you're out of the business and keeping your nose clean these days, you can come back. Sans magician. And cats."

Callum looked at me. "I'm not sure that's an option."

"It's for the best," I said. "No one needs to see your dancing."

Anton lifted his chin to Ifan, who gave a wonky half-salute, then the were pulled the door shut. I looked up at Callum and said in a low voice, "Shall I see what I can hear?"

Callum shook his head, then turned to make his way back around the building, Ifan joining him. I looked at Pru, but she was following the men, her tail ticking restlessly and her ears back against the rain. Which left Tam and me outside the door.

"Anything?" I asked her.

She shrugged.

"Successful night, then," I muttered, and we trailed back to the car, the rain at least washing a little of the mud off us as we went. Even a small win's a win, I suppose.

WE DIDN'T TALK on the way back to the car, and it wasn't until we reached the Rover that Ifan looked around and said, "I best be off, then."

Callum opened the car and took his jumper and coat from the back. "No," he said. "I'll give you a lift."

Ifan shook his head and took his keys out of his pocket, bouncing them in his hand. "I'm not drunk. Just a bit mellow."

Callum examined Ifan for a moment, pulling his jumper back on. Green Snake emerged from one of his coat pockets to glare at us all in evident disgust at being abandoned in the car before vanishing again. "No. Get in. We'll get your car tomorrow."

Ifan opened his mouth as if he were going to argue, then took another look at Callum's face and shrugged. "Fine. Bet I can still drive better than you."

"Let's not find out."

We took up our usual places in the car, Tam and I pressed against either side of Pru in the front seat while the heater slowly wound itself up to a cranky, spluttering heat. The roads were quiet, and the trip back to Ifan's house passed in a strange silence until he finally said, "Well, I did try. But I didn't find anything."

Callum glanced at him in the rear-view mirror. "Tried what?"

"You were looking for Ms Jones. I figured I'd try to help."

I sat up and peered back at him. "What were you talking about with Anton when you were in the back? He didn't sound like you'd asked him about Ms Jones."

"I was just buying a little product. Playing the part, you know."

"They let you in the back to do that?"

Ifan shrugged. "Seems so."

I watched him for a moment longer, then settled back into my seat, and we were quiet until Callum pulled up outside the gates to the magician's house. Ifan got out, and Callum said, "You need a lift back to get your car tomorrow?"

"No, all good. Thanks, though." He patted the top of the car and ambled to the gates, which swung open obligingly ahead of him. Callum pulled out again, and drove down the road to the next intersection, where he pulled into a side road and parked behind a skip. Someone was evidently renovating with a capital R. There was an entire bathroom suite hanging over the top.

I sat up and watched him as he pulled his cigarettes out of his coat pocket. He lit one in silence, then looked at us.

"Well?" he said.

"Well what? Love the scenic stop, but what're you thinking?"

He opened the door a crack and waved the smoke out. "How much was he lying?"

"A lot," Pru said, her voice soft.

"But about which bits?"

We looked at each other, and I shrugged. Callum made a wordless sound of frustration and beat one fist softly against the top of the steering wheel.

"Bloody magicians," he said, and none of us spoke for a moment. It wasn't like we were going to disagree, and given the way he was glaring at the hapless steering wheel, saying *I told you so* didn't seem like it was going to help much.

"You don't think he was there to help us?" I asked finally.

"No. I think that was just an excuse because we found him there."

"You think he's behind the whole thing?"

Callum's face twisted like he'd tasted something sour.

"It's really hard to tell. I still don't know why he'd want Ms Jones back here, if he does." He sighed. "Dammit. I keep *wanting* to trust him, but ..." He trailed off, and went back to smoking like the cigarette had personally insulted him.

"I suppose him using doesn't help, either," I said, once it seemed he wasn't going to continue.

Callum gave me an amused, sideways look. "He wasn't using. He wasn't even drunk."

Pru and I looked at each other. "But you wouldn't let him drive home," she said.

"He wanted me to *think* he was too messed up to drive. Too messed up to be of any use. I thought maybe it was just a show for the weres, but turns out it was for us, as well. For me." He took the cigarette out of his mouth, examined the end, then stubbed it out, half-finished. "And I don't know why."

I added it to the list of *don't knows* we already had about the magician, along with the faked death and necromancer connections and Ms Jones. Oh, and why the cemetery he'd been buried in had become the centre of a zombie outbreak. That one was still unanswered, too, and it made the hair on my spine crawl just as bad as the weres did. Worse, maybe, since so far the scariest were we'd encountered had last been seen wearing a yellow duck dressing gown. Toothiest, anyway. Not that Yasmin had been bothered, facing Lani and Angela down in her purple puffer coat with the utter certainty of a pillar standing against the tide. The more I thought about it, actually, Lani wasn't the one we had to worry about. She just about had a *warning, will bite* label on her forehead.

Yasmin you wouldn't see coming until she took your head off.

"You always said he had his own agenda, even when you were kids," I said finally. "Is it really that surprising?"

"No," Callum admitted. "But it is disappointing. I thought, maybe, with his dad gone he could step into the magician role and make it count, you know. Like Gerry is in Dimly. Maybe even help settle things down a little around here. Because doesn't it feel like it's all gone a bit weird over the last year or so?"

"*Yes,*" I said, with feeling. "But Gerry's a bit of a high standard to hold anyone to. It's the dress sense, for a start."

Callum snorted. "True. And the only other person I know with such a good doily game is Gertrude."

"The *reaper,*" I said. "Aw, man, we should introduce them."

"I'm not sure how social Gertrude is."

"But they could talk about cakes and things. Swap recipes and whatever. And that would seriously be a tea party to remember."

Callum actually laughed at that, and reached a hand out to me. I headbutted it, and let him scratch me between the ears. I could smell the exhaustion on him, even under the stink of the cigarettes.

"That's all very nice," Pru said. "But we're no further forward."

"No," Callum agreed. "It was kind of a wash out."

We sat in silence for a moment longer, while Callum frowned at his half-finished cigarette and lit another. It didn't seem like the time to point out that stepping up his smoking was unlikely to help matters. Not with magicians and necromancers and weres and so on all about the place.

Then Tam coughed once, softly, and spat something onto the seat.

"Gods, *gross,*" I yelped, and backed away from it. Pru went with me, raising one front paw as if to bat the thing away if it rolled any closer. But Tam just looked at the roof of the car and shook her head.

Callum squinted at her, then stuck the cigarette in the corner of his mouth and fumbled for the torch on his phone. A moment later he spotlighted Tam, and the name tag lying on the seat in front of her.

Dr Walker, DDS, it said.

"Holy broken mouse toys," I said. "How did you keep that hidden?"

She just yawned, displaying a lot of teeth and plenty of mouth space.

21

THIS IS WHAT SMOKING GETS YOU

I LOOKED AROUND THE CAR EXPECTANTLY. "WE'VE FOUND him," I informed the air in general. "You can pop back and deal with things now."

There was no response, just the dull splatter of rain on the windscreen.

"Really," I said. "None of us are exactly equipped to infiltrate a were pack, so we'd appreciate some help."

Still no response, so I looked at Callum, who had his elbow braced against the door and his head resting on his hand. "She's not answering."

"I'm astonished," he replied, and took his phone out instead, scrolling through it. He tried one number, then another, then shook his head. "And she's still not answering her actual phone, either. Neither's Malcolm."

"If she'd been able to answer her actual phone, I rather doubt she'd have bothered with displacing me from my body. Seems like a lot of effort."

"Muscles, then," Pru said. "He can get in and sniff around."

Callum frowned, tapping his fingers on the wheel. "That's a lot to ask. He needs that pack now."

"And we need a break," I said. "All he has to do is figure out if Walker's still there, and where they're holding him if he is, so at least we're not going in blind."

Callum *hmm*-ed, then nodded and went back to his phone. "He might do that."

"He owes us. We did look after Gordie."

"We also got his flat firebombed."

"We still don't know if that was definitely aimed at us."

Callum gave me a sideways look, and hit dial on his phone. Fair enough. It's generally good practise to assume any incidents of magical fire attacks to be personal, in our line of business. It saves time.

"*He* doesn't know it was aimed at us," I offered instead.

Muscles answered the phone, despite it being well after midnight, and he and Callum had a whispered conversation that resulted in him agreeing to have a look for us the next day. Gabe was taking him to meet the pack for Sunday lunch, apparently, and was so nervous about the accidental were-wolfing that they were staying in eating pizza and ice cream tonight rather than going out. And as Muscles sounded extremely unwilling to give up an overdose of dairy products in favour of snooping on his new pack, there wasn't a lot more we could do right now.

"You should go home," Callum said to Pru, putting the phone back in his pocket.

Pru sniffed, and shifted on the seat. "I could do with a clean, I suppose."

"And do you really want Katja rushing home because the cat sitter lost you?"

"Good point." She got up, stretched, then said, "Don't do anything fun without me," and vanished.

Callum and I both looked at Tam, who stared blandly back at us. "Right," Callum said. "Home, then."

PARKING at our apartment block is "ample and convenient", providing you have a car of our quality and vintage, and you don't mind coming back to find someone's thrown up on the bonnet or fallen asleep underneath it. We found a spot under a streetlight a couple of roads over, the better to dissuade night-time nappers, and headed home, Tam and I scattering clumps of dried mud as we walked. Our building was as we'd left it – grey, stained, and, with a couple of broken streetlights on the block, only dimly lit.

The main door hadn't locked for as long as we'd been there, and Callum shoved it open onto the darkness of the scuffed foyer. He tried the light switch, but the bulb had evidently gone again, so he switched on the torch on his phone and we trailed up the stairs. Tam stayed with us, moving effortlessly, but her gaze flicked from the step ahead to the ones behind constantly, and her ears were back. I wanted it to just be the building's creaking walls and thin spots in reality making her uneasy, but she'd been here before. She hadn't been bothered then.

Callum let us into the apartment and went to flick the

kettle on, pointing at me as he went. "You need a wash. You stink."

I looked down at myself. The rain had shifted a little of the mud, but it had mostly just dried in patches to a dusty sheen, and my belly was still sodden and matted. "If you try to put me in a bath, I'll take your eyes out."

"You better come up with a plan, then. You're not sleeping in my bed like that."

"I don't sleep in your bed anyway. I have my own bed."

He dropped a teabag in his mug. "Sure. It must be some other cat that creeps in in the middle of the night and steals the covers."

"You should fix the door." I looked at Tam, who looked just as bedraggled as I did. "And what about her?"

Tam was ignoring us both, prowling around the apartment much as I had done last night. Even under the mud, I could see her hackles trying to rise, and mine were straining against my skin. I checked the door, suddenly sure it would be sealed against us, that we'd be trapped in here with ... whatever this was. This sense of horror rising like floodwaters.

Callum left his tea in our tiny closet of a kitchen and went to the desk, peering out the window as if catching the unease. "What is it?" he asked, the question not aimed at anyone in particular. "Seriously, what *now?*"

Neither Tam nor I answered. My nose was full of the smell of old mud and damp fur and Callum's cigarettes, but my whiskers were shivering. "Ms Jones?" I asked, as if she could hear me.

There was no response, but the world was thinning on the edges. My breath scraped at my ribs as reality *thinned,* and I couldn't catch a scent to tell me how to fight or which way to run. There was nothing I could place, no fingerprint of the familiar. There was only the creeping, cold steel reek of power and emptiness and indifference. Tam looked at me, her ears back, and jerked her head at the door.

"We need to go," I managed, and tried to think of a reason, any urgent excuse that would make sense.

But Callum just looked at us both, nodded, and ducked back into the kitchen to grab a couple of tins of tuna. "Let's go, then," he said, and a moment later we were back out the door. Callum pulled it hurriedly to behind us, the key clattering in the lock. Tam was halfway to the stairs already, her ears flat as she paused to look back at us, and Callum swore as he dropped his keys. I could barely hear over the noise of my heart, and murky spots pushed across my vision, glimpses of vast and terrible things that the eye made no sense of. I still couldn't get a fix on the smell, couldn't tell if this was something like the alley had been, or Ms Jones trying to make contact, or something else altogether.

The moment Callum turned away from the door I sprinted for the stairs, Tam already diving through the fire door that never shut to lunge down them. Callum thundered after us, the light from his phone bouncing as he ran, setting shadows leaping and flickering all about us. There could've been anything in there, and I leaped the broken stair more from memory than sight, streaking across the foyer and out into the night with Tam matching me stride for stride.

We didn't stop running until we reached the car. Tam's

eyes were wild, and her tail had shed enough mud that it was doing a respectable bottlebrush. Mine would've been doing the same, if it could. Callum was panting, and I could smell the fright on him. Even humans can feel when things get too thin. Either that or he really needed to cut back on the smoking.

"What was that?" he demanded now, both hands shoved into his hair as if holding his head on. "What the hell *was* that?"

"Something happened," I said. "Before Ms Jones. In the alley with the dog. Something – I don't know. I thought it was her, maybe, but now – it's not. It's *not.*"

"The Inbetween," Tam said, her voice a rasp of fright.

I looked at her, my mouth too sticky to even answer.

"What?" Callum asked.

Tam thought about it, and for a moment I wanted to leap at her, to slap my claws across her snout and snarl that this wasn't the time to be strong and silent, this was a time to use her damn words, but then she said, "Something's making the barrier thin. Or some*one.*" She hesitated again. "Maybe because if you can fall in – or be pulled – no one has to admit to pushing you."

I stared at her, spots swimming in my vision again, although I had a feeling these were less potential signs of the void and more potential signs that I needed a lie down and a large bowl of custard. "The Watch?" I managed.

Tam licked her chops. "Maybe. But they're not the only ones who have access to the Inbetween. And they're definitely not the only ones who know how to use it. You don't have to be able to shift to use it for ... other things."

I sat down on the cold of the pavement before I did

something unprofessional like fall over. "I think I like it better when you don't say so much."

"Me too," Tam said, and Callum hunkered down in front of us with his coat spread around him and his face ghostly in the dark. He put a hand on each of our backs, smelling of cigarettes and books and cold nights, and none of us said anything else. But his hand was warm, and the night felt a little less like it might suddenly swallow me. Which was nothing to be sniffed at.

IF IT HAD BEEN a week ago, we could've gone to the magician's house, but that was out for obvious reasons. We might've gone to Gerry, but we were now in the wee small hours, and even if we hadn't already been a bit worried about giving Gerry a bad reputation, I had no desire to see what a troll's nightclothes looked like. I already knew he used rollers to curl the hair on the tip of his tail, and that was enough intimate knowledge for me.

"Gertrude?" I suggested, as we sat in the car staring at our suddenly hostile building. Callum had the engine running and the heater on, but I was still chilled somewhere down around my bones.

"It's late."

I looked at him. "She's a *reaper.* When do you think they work?"

"Fair point." He persuaded the car into gear and pulled away from the kerb, swinging into a U-turn to head for the centre of Leeds. I put my paws on the back of the seat to watch our building until we turned the corner. I wasn't sure whether I was making sure nothing followed us, or just saying goodbye. It could've been either.

Then I looked around the car, blinked at Callum, and said, "Where's Green Snake?"

"What?" He put the brakes on, hard, and I fell on top of Tam, who growled.

"Some warning'd be nice," I said, rolling off Tam. She huffed.

Callum was checking his pockets. "He's not here. Dammit. *Dammit.* We didn't leave him in the apartment?"

We stared at each other, then I said, "Can't have. You didn't take your coat off, or sit down, and I'd've noticed if he fell out of a pocket."

"Where is he, then?" Callum demanded, scrabbling through the glovebox. "We can't just leave him."

"He's probably in the vents somewhere."

We both looked around the car expectantly, but no small green head slithered into view. The car just rumbled to itself, stuttering now and then.

Callum ran both hands back over his hair, then nodded. "I have to go and check."

"*No.* You can't go back in there."

"It'll be okay for me."

"You don't know that." I took a breath. "If you're going back in, I am too."

"You're staying here."

"No. I can sniff out Green Snake if he's there."

We stared at each other, then he said, "Fine. But I'm carrying you. That's final."

"So undignified," I grumbled, but without much heat.

Tam just looked at us both, then sighed and got up.

"You can stay here," Callum said to her, and she gave him a look that made him draw back against the door. "Or not."

We swung out into the night, Callum stooping to allow us both to jump from the car onto his shoulders, then hurrying down the street back to our building, his phone in one hand and the torch already on.

"Anything?" he asked, pausing with one hand on the main door.

"Nothing worse than normal," I said.

"Here we go, then." He pushed through into the foyer, shining the light around brusquely, then taking the stairs two at a time, not running, his breath even. We paused again at the top, but I couldn't smell anything in the dim-lit hall beyond the door, so we went through that one too, and a moment later we were staring at the door of our apartment.

I was straining to hear anything on the other side of it, my ears swivelling and my whiskers twitching. Or maybe not to hear, but certainly to *sense* something. Everything was darkness and must and slow decay, all half-drowned under that damn boiled cabbage stink. Callum turned the key in the lock slowly, the clack of the tumblers cacophonous in the silence, and when a siren went a couple of streets over, Tam hissed.

Callum pushed the door open with his fingertips, staying to the side as he peered in. The room was empty, the light still on from our sudden flight, and it lit the tattered paperbacks stacked on the desk and a couple of his T-shirts hung over the back of the client chair. All was still, and familiar, and yet not. It felt like it had been recreated from a photograph, technically correct but not *real.*

He stepped inside with us still clinging to his shoulders. "Green Snake?" he whispered, his voice low.

There was no response – not that we'd expected a shout, but there was no movement, either. Callum crossed to the desk quickly, checking my bed where it sat on one corner. It was empty. He went to the armchair, still unfolded from the previous morning, and scrabbled though the blankets quickly. Still no flash of green anywhere.

"Smell anything?" he asked.

"No," I said. "Or no snake, anyway." There was something, though. A cracking in my ears as of a pressure change, like a storm moving in fast from places unseen. "Something's coming."

Callum swore, ran the couple of paces back to the desk, and ripped the drawers open. Still nothing.

The pressure was in my chest now, swelling and groaning, and I had to raise my voice to hear myself over it. "We don't have much time."

Tam started growling, a low, rumbling sound that would've been terrifying if the *something* wasn't taking up every ounce of terror I had.

"*Green Snake!*" Callum yelled, loud enough that I squawked. "Where the hell are you?" He ran for the kitchen, and my vision started to blur. There was weight on my back, a prickling, crawling sensation of something trying to dig into my fur.

"*Callum—*"

Tam snarled, a sound that doesn't belong in the body

of your average cat, and swarmed across Callum's shoulders, lunging over me and pinning me down with her weight. She was hissing and spitting, and the muscled bulk of her was heavy enough that it ripped my claws from Callum's jacket.

I snarled myself, scrabbling for grip, something threatening to tear me away at the same time as Tam tried to trap me in place, and I spat every curse I've ever heard Callum come out with, each one raw in my throat as I fell. Not that I could hear them – the world had frozen again, the siren vanished, Callum stopped in mid-stride. I couldn't seem to get purchase on the coat, and it was more as if I were falling *away* than falling *down.* Tam was right with me, but she was frozen too, she couldn't do anything, and I could move but there was nothing to grab, nothing to hope for, what could *anyone* do against whatever this was? It was void. Nothing to bite, nothing to scratch, and nowhere to run. It had us, and the world was stretching out of reach, dimensions growing strange and dark as I fell.

Then, with the room still frozen about us, Callum spun with uncanny grace and snatched us both out of the air, clutching us to his chest like a child defending his favourite toys, and bolted for the door.

The world snapped back into movement and sound, and a large-bellied man wearing nothing but some very small, star-spangled underpants lurched into the doorway with a saucepan in one hand. "It's *two in the morning,*" he started, yelling loud enough that he'd evidently decided the whole building was awake anyway, and Callum just shouted back, *"Move!"*

The man staggered away with a squawk, and we plunged past him, racing for the stairs. Callum took them even quicker than he had on our last run down, and a moment later he was sprinting down the street, Tam and I squished into each other and him, eyes wide and tails pouffed to their fullest extent.

There was a kid just opening the driver's door of the Rover as we reached it, and Callum snapped, "Do *not.*"

The kid looked him up and down, taking in the tatty coat and wild hair, as well as Tam and me, then backed away and said, "Yeah. Crap car, anyway."

"It is," Callum agreed, dropping both Tam and me unceremoniously on the seat. He climbed in after us, slammed the door, and started the engine, moving jerkily, then scrabbled his cigarettes out of his pocket. There was a knock on the window, and he looked up, already tucking a cigarette into the corner of his mouth, then opened the door slightly. "What?"

"Can I have one?" the kid asked, gesturing at the packet.

"No. They're bad for you." Callum lit the cigarette, puffing smoke out the door.

"Right." The kid looked at us, then back toward the building, and said, "This guy with you?"

We all peered over the back seats, and spotted the man in the starry underpants striding down the street toward us. He'd put a woolly hat on in deference to the cold.

"See?" Callum said. "This is what smoking gets you." Then he slammed the door and pulled away from the kerb, while the kid took out his phone and started filming Underpants Man.

I waited until we were around the corner before I said, "If Green Snake's in the vents he better stay there."

Callum snorted, and fell back in the seat, reaching out to scruff a hand through my muddy fur. "We couldn't have left him."

"No. But still."

"Yeah," he agreed, and glanced at us both. "Let's not do that again."

Tam huffed softly, and I pushed my nose in among the debris that accumulated in the doorless glovebox, trying to think about where I'd last seen Green Snake, and not about the hungry darkness and the grip on my neck, disembodied and brutal and inexorable.

22

WE SHOULD HAVE A PLAN

Oddly enough, neither Callum nor I fancied chasing up a reaper in the wee small hours after that. Gertrude might be fond of doilies and cupcakes, but she was still a reaper, and we'd had enough near-death experiences for one night. So we turned to the PI's favourite pastime – waiting.

We wound our way back to the were club's neighbourhood through streets peopled by delivery vans and cars that were either filled with nefarious types or plain clothes police – or both – and pulled into the drive-through coffee shop we'd spotted the day before. It was a 24-hour spot, some chain place with a big, comfortably bright car park and a couple of people visible through the glass walls of the cafe, huddled over their tables. There was a delivery van just leaving the drive-through, and a few empty cars pocked around the shop.

Callum pulled up to the drive-through window and ordered something with extra caffeine and caramel syrup in it, as well as a bacon butty, which, after some whispered argument in his ear while he grinned unconvincingly at the young man in the window, I persuaded him to increase to three bacon butties.

"You only eat the bacon," he hissed, while we pulled around to the next window and waited for the order to come up. "It's a waste."

"But the bacon's the key part," I pointed out.

"You've got cat biscuits. And I grabbed some tuna."

"Your point?"

He sighed, and took the order from the woman at the drive-through, who looked at Tam and me sitting upright on the passenger seat, shook her head slightly, and said, "Enjoy your breakfast."

"You too," Callum said, then looked at the roof of the car. "I mean, have a good day. Night. Morning?"

She just waved us away, and we toddled off to park in the corner of the lot, well away from the building, and with a good view of the lane that led to the club. Callum peeled the bacon out of the two spare rolls and doled it out, then turned his attention to his own. I'd barely had time to do more than wolf one slice when there was a whisper of air parting in the back seat, and we all peered around at it. Pru stared back at us, looking distinctly cleaner than we were and dressed in a snazzy red tartan coat with a fluffy lining.

"You were quick," I said.

"Cat sitter was so stressed by how muddy I was that he drank a whole bottle of wine and is currently passed out on the sofa."

"I'm not sure he's suited to the job."

"No," Pru agreed. "One needs more fortitude to be a

good cat sitter. I see things have progressed from sitting in the car near the magician's house to sitting in the car near the were club."

"Consistency is important," I said.

"Evidently. What now?"

"Now we wait until Muscles turns up." Callum said, and leaned his seat back. He took a mouthful of coffee, making a face. "God, that's awful."

"How long'll that be?" Pru asked.

Callum checked his phone. "It's only three in the morning. It'll be a while."

"And what do we do once we get in?"

"Find the dentist and get him out," Callum said, taking another sip of coffee.

"Ah. Simple."

"It's important not to overcomplicate things," I said.

Pru wrinkled her snout. "And if the dentist's not actually there? Or if we get spotted before we get in?"

"We'll figure it out," I said. "Something always comes up."

"I'm still sure there must be more efficient ways to do this," Pru said. "You're both very casual."

"Do you have any other ideas?" I asked.

"I'm not the one calling myself a PI."

"Does anyone want any biscuits?" Callum asked, wedging his coffee cup between the seats. "I think you all need biscuits."

"Biscuits are not the solution to the faults in your investigative techniques," Pru said.

"They're a solution to many things, though," he said, and tipped his seat back a little further, crossing his arms over his chest and closing his eyes. "If you're going to fight, go and do it outside. Wake me if you see anything."

Pru and I looked at each other, and she leaned toward me. I pulled back, but she sniffed at my nose, then said, "What happened?"

I looked at Tam, but she was busy licking butter off the sandwiches. "Stuff," I said.

"Sorcerer stuff?"

"I don't think so."

"Watch?"

"Maybe." I shivered, cold fingers walking down my spine, and glanced behind me, but there was nothing there.

Pru watched me a moment longer, then said, "We could go and see if we can sniff out the dentist."

"It's too early," I said. "We need the place to be empty and the weres to be asleep."

She shifted slightly. "So … what? You want to just sit here?"

I looked around again, my tail twitching, and wondered when weres had seemed like the least of our problems. "No. We go and keep an eye on things." I pawed Callum's arm. "Let me out."

He opened one eye and looked at me. "You sure?" he asked, his voice low.

"No. But open it anyway."

He watched me a moment longer, then opened his door with one hand. We jumped across him and out onto the rough, chilly tarmac, and he swung his legs out of the car and sat watching us with his elbows resting on his knees, his shoulders tense. Pru and Tam looked at me.

"You go on ahead," I said. "I'll meet you on the drive."

"Is it a complete pain, not being able to shift?" Pru asked.

"No, I love having to go everywhere by paw," I said, and set off toward the road. "Don't do any fun stuff without me."

By the time I was standing on the edge of the pavement, checking for boy racers and car chases, they were both next to me, and we ran across the road together. I didn't argue the point. It seemed kind of ungrateful.

There were no pedestrians out, the car yards and timber merchants locked up behind heavy gates and flooded with security lights, and the night felt thin and damp and empty as we loped along the pavement to the drive. I could smell oil and exhausts and the crumbling edges of businesses just getting by. It was glorious after the cold flat scent of whatever had been in our apartment.

We left the sparse traffic behind as we turned down the lane and slowed to a more cautious walk. It was unlit, other than by the light that seeped over from the businesses to either side, but Pru's red tartan stood out against the pale gravel, and I don't think I was any less conspicuous. Only Tam, with her heavy tabby coat, passed as a shadow here.

"Reckon they're got CCTV on this?" I asked.

Tam looked at me, then tipped her head and veered off the drive, into the damp grass and down to the culvert that ran next to it.

"Really?" I asked, looking at the mucky, litter-encrusted ditch, but she was right. The cover was much better, and even if there weren't any cameras, anyone who stepped onto the drive couldn't fail to see us. Or smell us. So Pru and I followed, my paws soon wet with the remnants of the previous day's rain. I couldn't smell anything but old dirt and stale water, no whiff of weres or stronger charms. It was only as we reached the estate itself that I picked up the stern note of shift locks. Serious ones, not your cheap market stall varieties, or the amateurish ones at Muscles' place. These ones had been put on by someone who knew what they were doing. They were fresh, too – I had an idea they'd likely been re-done since our visit earlier, which meant the weres had someone on hand who knew their stuff for just such eventualities.

We paused where the weedy cover of the culvert was cut off abruptly by the car park, and peered across it at the long, low building of the were club. The pirate mannequin was gone, and there were only a handful of cars parked on this side of the building, but I could glimpse light around the doors still.

"Hardcore," I said, and Pru huffed softly.

"Let's find a good spot to wait," she said, and started cautiously up onto the potholed tarmac.

"Wait," I said, and she paused, looking back at me. "There might be tripwire charms."

"I don't smell anything."

"There's new locks on. They could be meshed with them." The smell would be indistinguishable if they were, but the tripwire would be set off by someone entering the perimeter. They could be adapted to whatever kind you were particularly worried about, so in this case they'd likely be tuned to us. And as to what was tripped – well, that was up to the individual charm worker. It might be nothing more than an alert, a gas lamp that flared into life in an office somewhere, or a pipe that clanged in alarm, or a tap that suddenly turned on by itself. Others were more interested in deterrents than alarms, and might set a bunch of pixie-engineered armoured hornets on us, or fill the car park with a writhing mass of toothy eels that might be real or might be imagined, but no one was going close enough to check.

"How are we meant to tell, then?" Pru asked.

"I don't know," I admitted. "But let's wait to find out until the place is empty, at least."

Pru looked around at the weedy culvert, and spotted an old bit of plywood that had been a sign at some point. She stepped onto it and hunkered down, curling her tail around her toes. It was starting to drizzle, and Tam and I looked at each other, noses wrinkled in matching distaste.

"Bet you wish you had my coat now," Pru said.

THE LAST OF the partygoers really did seem to be hardcore. Sunday traffic was building on the road behind us, and we were huddled onto Pru's piece of wood with our whiskers dripping by the time the last goblin clambered into his car and revved off down the lane, the bass thumping so deeply my ears trembled as they passed. But we still didn't move, not until the last of the light vanished from around the door. And even then we waited for as long as we could stand, while dawn crept reluctantly closer, but too far off to help us.

Finally I got up, my joints so stiff I was surprised they didn't creak, and shook myself off, stretching. "Alright. Let's try it."

"You think they'll be asleep?" Pru asked.

"No idea. But we can have a scout about, anyway." We all looked at the warehouse, low and dark and dripping in the rain, everything shades of grey in the city dark. The club looked half derelict, lost without the pound of music and feet. "I suppose we should have a plan of retreat for if there are tripwire charms."

We all looked at each other, and Pru said, "I realise you and lanky back there aren't big on plans, but this is your area of supposed expertise."

"Nothing supposed about it," I said, looking at the car park while I considered our options. Not that we had any, as far as I could tell. Cats have their own inherent magic, but we can't *work* magic. We can put shift locks in place, same as anyone, but breaking charms without being noticed takes some skill. So it was go in and risk it, or sit in a ditch and keep waiting. And I was sick of waiting. All I could think about was the pull of whatever was stalking me, and my back ached with the expectation of its grip when it found me again.

Then Tam said, "How about, *leg it?*"

Pru and I looked at each other. "I was hoping for something a little more specific," I said. "But that works."

"Of course it does," Pru said with a sigh.

We crept up to the edge of the tarmac together, and I lifted my chin toward the old garage to our left. "Let's get in there, smart-ish. Then we can see if anyone comes out to check on things, and use the cars as a bit of cover."

"Lead on," Pru said.

I led on, somewhat reluctantly. I wasn't convinced the tarmac wasn't going to suddenly transform into a tar pit, or the potholes birth giant ravening sea serpents, but as we scooted across the rough ground to the shelter of the shattered car hulks by the garage, nothing jumped out at us. I scrambled into a doorless Ford Fiesta and peered around the frame at the were club, Tam and Pru taking cover in a very old Volvo estate with a crushed nose.

The were club sat there blandly, the boarded-up windows giving away nothing. The car park stayed resolutely tarmacked and sea serpent–free, and all I could hear was traffic passing on the main road.

We waited.

No one emerged, in either wolfy or human form. Maybe they hadn't put any trips in. Maybe they'd decided we weren't worth the effort, or they just didn't know they could do cat-specific ones, and didn't want alarms being triggered every time someone turned up for a party. Although that seemed odd, given the power of the shift locks. Whoever had done them had more than a passing knowledge of such things.

Finally I jumped to the ground and looked up at Tam and Pru. "Come on," I said, and led the way around the garage, ducking behind it and into the gap between the back wall and the fence. The building wasn't double-sided like the one housing the were club, and on this side there was just a crumbling concrete apron with a rusting chain-link fence beyond it, leaving a human's arm span of space between it and the sagging walls. It looked as if it had been intended for the shops to put a chair out for lunch breaks or something, but I couldn't see that anyone would want to. The car yard next door had built their own solid wall right up to the fence, presumably to block out the view of the decaying warehouses as much as for security, so any lunch break taken here would be like eating in a cold, fusty wind tunnel. Everything smelled of rust and rot.

We took our time as we padded down the little alley, checking for any whiff of captive dentist or weres. But the whole place seemed unused, not even an abandoned bottle or the stink of an impromptu loo break. We paused at the end of the building and peeked around the corner. From here we could look down both sides of the were building, and there were a few cars parked around the back, near the door Yasmin had taken us in the night before. Nothing flashy, just a VW Golf that was well past its prime and a couple of dinky Peugeots, one with its front bumper held on with gaffer tape. Evidently the club didn't pay its resident employees particularly well.

The third row of buildings that made up the estate was set at a right angle to us, and the chain-link fence continued behind them. There was nothing to suggest it was any more used than these ones, no lights at the windows or cars parked outside, but I wasn't too keen on sniffing around the were club itself just yet. And it still seemed more likely that they'd hold the dentist in one of the outbuildings than in the club, where he might be heard. I glanced at Tam and Pru, checked that no one had appeared in the car park, then ran for the gap behind the building.

We arrived unnoticed, as far as we could tell, and

slipped into the narrow, concreted passage between the fence and the wall. It was no wider than the one behind the first building, but instead of a grimy brick wall beyond the chain-link there were scrubby bushes and tangles of weeds, a whiff of good dirt and small, furtive creatures and persistent wild places. Although that was almost drowned out by the stink of the passageway itself, which, unlike the one behind the first building, was evidently heavily used. It reeked of wolf urine and hasty encounters and spilled booze.

"Nice," I muttered, jumping a couple of empty bottles and padding along the passageway with my nose wrinkled. My hackles were prickling with the stink, but as I dodged an abandoned sock and skirted broken glass, part of me was still searching for that cold, deep magic whiff that kept touching the back of my neck. I didn't think I'd ever stop.

"This is recent," Pru said quietly from behind me.

"Looks pretty well used," I said. "Maybe the club toilets get a bit busy."

"It's more than that. Smell it."

"Rather not," I said, but I paused and tried to sort through the scents. Alcohol, yes, and desire, and a strange, ferocious joy, thick and rich and sharp on the edges. "They've been changing here."

"I thought so." She passed me, her tail flicking nervily, and paused, looking up at the fence. "It's open."

I followed her gaze and spotted the hole cut in the wire, the edges rolled back. It wasn't a massive gap, but it was more than big enough for a human to get through bent over. Or a wolf. I inspected the edges and found clumps of hair caught on the sharp corners of the wire. "They're running in the wasteland here. Right in the middle of town."

"No wonder they don't want anything to do with cats," Pru said. "If the Watch gets wind of this they'll ... well. I don't know. But it won't be pretty."

"You don't think Claudia was onto them, do you?" I asked. "She tried to warn them off before the Watch proper realised, and something happened?"

"I don't know." We stared at each other, then Tam gave a sudden, soft hiss. She'd been trailing behind us a little, checking back into the car park, and as we spun to look at her, I was certain we were going to see a were bearing down on us. But Tam just barrelled past us and dived straight through the hole in the fence, vanishing into the scrubby undergrowth beyond. Pru and I followed without hesitation. I had no desire to see what would make Tam run.

We didn't go far, hunkering down in a muddy hollow where we were hidden by a thicket of tall ragwort and the sort of broken bricks that always seem to populate wasteland like mushrooms after rain. I crept forward far enough to look back at the buildings, lit in the persistent glow of the city. I could just see the passageway through our green cover.

Angela emerged around the corner of the building and stepped over the beer bottles, carrying a takeout bag from the coffee place across the road. It swung from her fingertips easily as she walked past the gap in the fence, singing along to something that was playing on her ear buds, and stopped at a door a little further along. She knocked sharply and waited, taking her phone out and flicking through it. A moment later the door opened. I couldn't see who was there from this angle, but she held the bag out without looking up from her phone.

"Breakfast," she said.

The person inside said something I couldn't quite hear.

"Dunno," she said. "Anton's sleeping. He'll come see you later, I s'pose." The person inside said something else, and she shrugged, her braids lifting and falling on her shoulders. "I'm just food delivery, mate. You'll have to ask him."

Another murmur, and she rolled her eyes so impressively I could see it from here. It was a whole body eye roll. She put her phone away and stuck her hand out. "It all goes in the machine together. I'm not sorting your bloody tighty whiteys. I'm not your *maid.*"

A squawk of indignation from inside, then she snatched something before turning and walking away again. The door slammed behind her, and I stretched around the weeds to try and get a better look. The young were had a different takeaway bag with her, a shirt sleeve spilling from the top and the heavy brown paper still stained with grease from the meal that had been in it before. There was a collection name scrawled on the outside in thick black marker, bold enough that the shape was familiar and unmistakable.

"Malcolm," I hissed, without thinking. "It's the dentist, he's in there!"

And Angela's head swung toward the gap in the fence, her eyes wide and dark and horribly, furiously *aware.* Her chin lifted as she scented the air, and her lips pulled back from her teeth.

"Oh, well done," Pru whispered.

"Leg it," Tam suggested.

"Excellent plan," I said.

We legged it.

23

ALL THIS FOR A BLOODY NOSE

We all knew Angela had a soft spot for hairless cats, and seemed more inclined to want to cuddle them than tear them limb from limb. We *knew* that. But I challenge anyone to stand there as a young woman collapses into a formless mass, dropping the greasy takeaway bag of laundry to spill across the filthy ground, then reforms into a beast that's all teeth and muscle, scattering her own clothes behind her as she launches herself into the waste ground with a snarl that shakes the heart of even a seasoned PI. We weren't about to hang around and give it the old, *Excuse me, I think you've mistaken me for someone else.*

Pru was a flash of exuberant tartan, vanishing over the broken ground, and I pelted after her with my ears back and my haunches itching. Tam was right behind me, her eyes wide and her teeth bared, but even she wasn't hanging around to reason with a wolf-were. As has been noted previously, their human brains are in park when they've changed, which is a good reason for the Watch being less than keen on them changing anywhere around humans.

The ground was all torn earth and ragged edges, crowded with the undergrowth that springs up when humans walk away. It was a place of nettles and thorns, of twisted low shrubbery and spindly young trees, broken bottles and lost shoes and abandoned scraps of what had once been buildings, or cars, or some other debris of humanity. There was plenty of cover for those of small stature, but not when your pursuer has a nose that's basically a cat detector.

I slowed, letting Tam overtake me, then took off at a right angle to her, running parallel to the fence line. "Hey, Fido!" I yelled. "Or Fidette! Catch me if you can, pup!"

Angela snarled, much closer that I'd imagined, and I found that I had a speed somewhere above all-out sprint.

I was moving so fast that I lost my footing on what appeared to be the shattered remains of a toilet bowl and tumbled down a slope of crushed cans and well-worn rock and old roof tiles, coming to my feet at the bottom with the thunder of the were charging after me filling the world. I bolted without really looking at what direction I was going in, just aiming for some cover among the nearest thicket of overgrown grass. Angela snarled, a huge noise filled with rage and hunger, and I went zigzagging through some nettles with my eyes half-closed. Moment later I was rewarded with a wounded yelp, but the pound of her paws didn't slow.

I didn't even see the fence before I hit it. To be fair, it was hidden behind some sort of African savannah-level long yellow grass, and I was looking over my shoulder to see how close Angela was. I crashed into the fence hard enough to knock myself to the ground, gave a wheezy squawk, and managed to scrabble out of the way just before the were hit behind me. She rebounded with a yelp, shook her head, and swung it toward me.

"Stop," I managed, backing up. "*Stop,* Angela, it's us, you met us last night."

There was no recognition in her dark eyes, nothing but hunger and the joy of the chase. Her head hung low between her shoulders, and she took one slow step toward me.

"We're not here for you. We just want to talk to the dentist. That's it." I was still backing up, trying to keep enough space between us that I'd have time to run when she pounced. I hoped. She took another step forward. She wasn't even growling, her ears pricked forward and her mouth open just slightly. Her teeth were even larger than I'd thought before.

"We're not Watch. We're— *Gods!*"

She moved so fast that I never even had a chance to run. She was all youth and speed and raging instinct, and she pounced with both front paws, trapping me down with her teeth – those massive, immaculately clean teeth – resting right over my neck.

"Nice wolf," I whispered, trying not to move. "Good wolf."

She did growl then, a very low, small growl that reverberated all through my body. I closed my eyes, thinking that at least it wasn't going to be the Watch that killed me this life. Although mentioning them had probably hastened things along a bit.

And then Angela gave an almost human yelp of surprise, jerked away from me and spun around. I rolled up and leaped away, spotting Tam with her fur pouffed into a ball of fury, her ears back and her teeth bared, emitting the proper, approved, *do not mess* yowl of cats everywhere. Angela snapped at her, and Pru came out of nowhere and attached herself firmly to the wolf's hindquarters, a tartan, fluffy-collared limpet that was all claws and lashing, naked tail. Angela shrieked and spun again as Pru jumped free, and I went straight for the wolf-were's muzzle before she could so much as snap. She snarled, and Tam came in again from the side, so that Angela bounced around to face the new threat. But by that time Pru had launched another attack from *her* side.

Angela's eye rolled in alarm, and she backed up toward the fence, but both Tam and I went in hard, one from each side, driving her out again before she could reach it. She retreated, growling, trying to watch all three of us at once, and we kept advancing in a wide semicircle, matching her growls with our own. Everyone's ears were back, everyone's hackles up. Well, except Pru's, but they would've been if she had any.

It was that horrible sort of standoff, where none of us dared make the first move. She didn't want to back down, because we were *cats,* but cats have sharp bits and three at once was a bit much, so maybe she'd have let us go if we just backed down, and we *wanted* to back down, but we didn't dare because we couldn't be sure she wasn't going to swoop in and gobble us up as soon as we looked away. So we just all stood there growling at each other and wishing someone else would do something.

Then someone shouted, "Ange?"

The young were's head snapped around toward the noise. She raised her nose and howled, a wavery, elegant sound that sent my mouth dry, and Pru said, very clearly, something that she'd evidently borrowed from her human's vocabulary.

"Go," I said. "Get though the fence. *Run.*"

I didn't wait to see if the other two were following directions. I just launched myself forward and bolted straight past Angela's nose, leading her in a flat sprint straight toward whoever had shouted. I had no idea what I'd do when I got there, but if you're being chased by one were, you may as well make it two. How much worse can it be?

I ROCKETED STRAIGHT BACK up the slope of broken roof tiles, hearing Angela slipping behind me but not losing any ground, and sprinted for the gap in the fence. I didn't know how I was going to deal with two wolves, but if nothing else I could lead them away from Tam and Pru, and give them enough time to find a way out of the wasteland and beyond the shift locks. Then ... well, *then* I hadn't given much thought to. It's kind of hard to plan strategically when you can smell were breath parting the fur on your spine.

I swerved a patch of brambles, leaped a cracked bucket half-full of stinking water, and saw the gap in the fence. There was no sign of another were, and I ran straight for the building, urging my muscles to work harder. No one's made to keep up this sort of speed for any length of time, and I could feel myself lagging, my paws catching on clumps of dandelions and bricks emerging from the old dirt like buried fossils. I went through the gap still at as much of a sprint as I could manage, and bellowed, *"Walker! Walker, damn you, let me in!"*

Angela bounded after me, claws scratching on the stained concrete as she pivoted to chase me.

"Walker!"

I tore down the passage, painfully aware that there was no way out but straight ahead, and that the were was faster than I was, my legs exhausted and shaking with the effort of the flight.

"WALKER!"

I was past the door when it swung open, and I applied all brakes, flipping myself into a tumble and coming up sprinting straight back toward it. Angela, unfortunately – or fortunately, depending on your perspective – was not past the door. She slammed into it with a howl of pain, and someone swore as the door slammed shut again under the impact. I was still racing back toward the haven of the doorway, which had vanished as quickly as it had appeared, and I tried to stop before I hit the young were. I was fully committed, though, and all I succeeded in doing was running into her with all four paws extended just as the door swung wide again, slapping my rump before it hit Angela's shoulder, and sending us both sprawling. I was surrounded by the wolf musk of her even as the scent collapsed to a confusion of wolf and human. I yowled in horror, but it was mostly drowned by the crunching and tearing of reforming flesh and bone. I had one moment to wonder if I was about to be mushed *into* a were, then a young woman was kneeling above me with both hands held over her face. Blood trickled between her fingers while she swore in the sort of tone that said it was that or start crying.

"Ooh, *hairballs,*" I managed, my heart still going so fast that the words came out wobbly. "That must've hurt."

"Yes," she whispered, and someone grabbed me around the middle and hoisted me aloft. I hissed, twisting around and burying my teeth and claws into a warm, long-fingered hand clattering with bracelets.

"No," Yasmin said, and I eyed her for a moment, then let go.

"Put me down."

"Are you going to behave yourself?"

"You're the one's given Angela a black eye."

"Nose," Angela managed.

"I think you might have both, pup."

"Thanks," she said, glaring at me. It came out more like *thangggs.*

"That was Malcolm," Yasmin said, and glanced inside. "Throw me one of those robes."

I peered around her and spied the dentist, clutching a pair of disposable chopsticks like he thought he might use them to attack someone. "That's for vampires, not weres," I said, and he looked puzzled, then handed Yasmin a robe, studiously not looking at Angela.

"I'm really sorry," he said to the floor. "I didn't mean to hit you."

Angela growled, and caught the robe Yasmin threw her.

"Anyone else out here?" Yasmin asked

"No," I said.

"Two more," Angela said, shrugging into the robe. "Same two as last time."

Yasmin looked at me.

"Oh, you meant cats? I thought you meant anyone as in humans, other weres, magicians, that sort of thing."

"Where are the other two?" Yasmin asked Angela, not releasing her grip on me. I considered biting her again, but the longer I was here the more chance Tam and Pru had of getting back to Callum. Plus no one seemed about to eat me, which was frankly a relief at the moment.

"I don't know," the younger were said, pinching the bridge of her nose and tipping her head back to try to stop the bleeding. "They're still in there somewhere." She waved vaguely at the waste land.

"I did tell you to leave this alone," Yasmin said, looking at me. "Repeatedly."

"Yeah, well. The sorcerer's scarier than you, and she wants him." I nodded at Walker, who blinked back at me. He was dressed in jogging bottoms and a red T-shirt that said *If all else fails, panic,* and looked rather more relaxed and comfortable than pretty much anyone else in the room.

"Polly?" he asked. "You've seen Polly? When?"

"Eh. *Seen* is a loose term. But she's been in contact."

"Is she okay?" he demanded, lowering his chopsticks.

"She seemed to be. Worried about you, though." I looked up at Yasmin. "Can't imagine why."

"I've been trying everything to find her," Walker said. "*Everything.*"

"Except ask us, which should've been an obvious thing to do. Or at least answer your damn phone."

He scrunched his face up as if unsure he wanted to answer, then said, "I don't like that magician."

"Me either," I said, and Yasmin gave a small huff that might've been agreement.

"So where is she?" he asked.

"No idea, dude. We'd've been trying to figure it out, but *some people* set us off on a wild goose chase."

"What people?"

"*You,* you mouldy lettuce. Ms Jones needed us to find *you,* so we've been worrying about that. Plus you told Pru and Tam that she sent you a *postcard,* of all things—"

"I thought the Watch might've sent them," he said. "I wanted to throw them off the scent."

"A postcard?" Yasmin said. "That's a poor effort, Malcolm."

"I was very stressed."

"Why would *you* be worried about the Watch?" I demanded.

"Not for me. For Polly," he said, staring at his chopsticks. "That Claudia got her into some sort of trouble. I'm sure of it."

"I doubt that. And here we've been running around half the county looking for *you,* because Ms Jones said you needed help, and we found were traces. We thought you'd been kidnapped, or injured, or bloody well killed. Not … whatever this is." I tried to peer into the building, but I couldn't see very well from Yasmin's grip. "Can I get down, please? This is undignified."

"Why're you looking for the sorcerer? What do you

want with her?" Yasmin asked. She had one hand supporting me, the other resting on my scruff without tightening. I could smell the wariness in her.

"What d'you want with the dentist?" I countered. "You said you hadn't heard of him, but I've got it on good authority he's a regular, as well as apparently your current outhouse tenant."

"He came to us," Yasmin said.

"They're helping me look for Polly," Walker said. "Someone approached me at the surgery about her last week, then I was *attacked* at our house."

"Weres?" I suggested. "The stink was all over your office, which is why we've ended up in this lovely situation."

"No. I'd know if it was weres."

"Would you, though?"

"*We* were attacked at the house," Yasmin said. "Malcolm asked for help, and it was lucky he did. As it was, we lost Jorg."

I blinked up at her. "*You* were attacked? Who attacks weres?"

Yasmin looked at me for a moment, then said, "I want to talk to your human."

"Why? It's G and C London, not C and G London, you know."

She frowned at me. "That means nothing to me. Him being a North does."

"Ex-North. He's not been in the business for years."

"Doesn't matter. I want to talk to him."

"Well, Dental Dan there has his number."

She examined me, then said, "He's not going to come in here smashing things up, is he?"

I stared at her, as well as I could given the fact she still had me in a bundle in her hands. "Have you seen him? Does he look like he comes in smashing things up?"

"He's a *North*. And then there's that damn magician."

"You mean the one you were giving such a warm welcome to last night?"

She sniffed. "Some of us."

Walker had vanished back into the building, and as Yasmin eased her grip on my scruff, I saw it was furnished in the same student flat-meets-squatter style as the back rooms of the club. It made even our little apartment look refined. Walker reappeared, holding a phone out to Yasmin. "Just hit dial," he said, and went past her with something bundled in a tea towel in his other hand.

"Come in, Angie," he said. "I've got you some ice."

"Can I have a whisky to go with it?"

"You wouldn't like it even if I gave it to you."

"You don't know that."

"How about a Tango?"

"Ugh. S'pose." She took the bundled towel and pressed it gingerly to the bridge of her nose. "*Ow.*"

"Silly girl," Yasmin said, as Angela trailed past her, and the young woman gave her a murderous look.

"He opened the bloody door in my face."

"You shouldn't be chasing cats." But she patted Angela's shoulder with her phone hand. "Sit down. And tell Malcolm to give you some paracetamol with that Tango."

"Not whisky?"

"No."

"So unfair."

Yasmin smiled, and looked back at me. "Will he come without the magician?"

"I think he and the magician are on the outs."

"Good." She set me on the floor, closed the door, and hit dial while I shook myself out and had a quick groom. I heard the click as it went straight to voicemail on the other end, and she looked at me.

"I don't know," I said. "He probably forgot to charge it again."

"That seems careless."

"And I ask again, have you seen him?"

She tried to call once more, then shook her head and threw the phone back to Walker. "Well, I suppose he'll come looking for you at some point."

"I'm sure Tam and Pru will have gone to tell him of my heroics in distracting a ravening wolf so they could get away."

"I wasn't *ravening*," Angela shouted, from where she was lying on one of the sofas. "And one of you bit my bum."

"In our defence, you were trying to eat us," I pointed out.

"Still."

Yasmin shook her head, smiling slightly. "Come sit down," she said. "We've got things to discuss, once your North gets here."

"Such as missing sorcerers?" I asked.

"Such as the Watch," she said, and kicked off her trainers to walk across the floor barefoot, her trousers billowing softly around her like the plumage of a multi-coloured bird. "And the problem with Norths."

I stayed where I was for a moment, wishing I'd nipped out the door before she'd shut it, and wondering if I could get it open before one of the weres went all White Fang on me. But wishes are fishes and you can never get hold of the damn things, so I just followed the were to the sofas while outside the wind groaned around the old tin roof and my fur prickled with the fright of things to come.

24

RUNNING WITH WERES

I JUMPED TO THE ARM OF ONE OF THE SOFAS AND PERCHED there, staring at Walker. "So?" I said.

"So?" he echoed, blinking at me. He'd picked up his chopsticks again, fiddling with them anxiously.

"So what happened? Who attacked your house? Why're you hanging out with weres?"

Yasmin pulled the edge of an old sheet that was doing duty as a curtain away from the window that looked out into the car park. Daylight was arriving grudgingly, seeping around the edges of the sky and discovering colour in the shadows. "Where's that bloody North? You two seem to be pretty joined at the collar."

"Don't call him a North," I said. "He's not going to be helpful if you keep calling him that."

She looked at me. "He is one."

"Yeah, and you're a wolf, but I still call you Yasmin when I want a civil conversation."

She lifted her lip just slightly, showing a tooth, then looked at Walker. "Try his phone again."

Walker fumbled his mobile out, and I joined Yasmin at the window, standing on the back of the sofa that leaned underneath it and putting my paws on the thin wooden sill. It wasn't a big window – the place wasn't designed for its views. But it was enough, and from this angle we could see the cars parked at the back of the were club as well as part of the car park to the front, and the driveway in. There was no movement, and I wondered where Tam and Pru were. Hopefully they'd got out past the range of the shift locks on the wasteland and had gone straight to Callum to give him a heads up, although that didn't explain why he wasn't answering his phone, particularly as it'd come up as Walker's number.

"Are there any biscuits?" Angela asked. "I could really go for a digestive or something."

"I think I have some bourbons," Walker said, and wandered away to rustle through a grocery bag. I pressed my snout to the window and tried to spy movement in the culvert by the drive. The wind was rattling everything about, though, and from this distance I could only just make out the muddled greens of grass and weeds.

"You see anything?" I asked Yasmin, and she shook her head, not looking at me.

"I feel something, though," she said. Her mouth was slightly open, and I could see her canines, just that uncomfortable smidge longer than average. I shivered. "Do you feel it?"

I was about to say *no, is it a dog whistle?* but I did feel it. I didn't *want* to, mind, but it wasn't like I could get away from it. That tugging at the edge of awareness, a sense of something not quite fully formed. Something *gathering.*

And I couldn't smell it – you can't smell a feeling – but at the same time I could. Cold, raw magic. Steel as fine as a rapier. Always that sense of unease that seemed to keep following us. Following *me*.

"That?" I asked her. "You can feel *that?*"

"The thinness?"

Thinness. In a way I supposed it was, the world thinning to let something terrible in. "What the hell *is* it? Who's doing it?"

"We had the same thing at the sorcerer's house," she said, and there was a crash behind us. We both turned, and Walker was standing over a smashed cup of tea. Angela was holding the biscuits, looking from him to us in confusion.

"What's going on?" she asked.

"It's like at the house?" Walker asked. "As in – you think it's them?"

"I don't know," Yasmin said, and plucked at her long jumper irritably, as if it were scratching her. "I don't know that they're behind it, exactly. It smells different."

"*Them?*" I asked. "Who's *them?* What happened at that bloody house?"

Walker turned his startled owl gaze onto me, and Yasmin growled. "You should ask your damn *North*."

I matched her growl with one of my own. It was a bit small in comparison, but it was heartfelt. "My *damn North*'s the one who's been trekking around everywhere trying to find out what happened to both the sorcerer and this scented rice ball."

She blinked at me. "Scented rice ball?"

"What d'you have against Callum?" I asked, ignoring

the question. If she can't understand an elegant insult, that's on her.

She peeled off her leather jacket, throwing it on the sofa. "There's no point talking to you about this. I'm going to have a sniff around."

I jumped to the floor and stood between her and the door, glaring up at her. "No you don't. Not until I know you're not going to rip Callum's throat out just for being a North. You wanted to talk. Tell me about the house."

She scowled, taking off her necklaces and tucking them into the jacket along with her bracelets. "Or what? You'll shed on me?"

I opened my mouth, prepared to lie through my fangs and say I'd go to the Watch about their little were exercise yard out the back there, but Walker said, "I think it was mostly humans. But magic sorts." He waved vaguely.

I regarded him. "*You* sort of magic, or actual magic?"

He scowled at me. "I can do actual magic. But they were, you know. Better."

"How much better?"

"They got through the defences Polly put on the house and garden. And they were waiting for me when I got home. They'd have had me, too, if Anton hadn't got me out."

"We lost a wolf," Angela said. "And three were injured really badly."

"What were you doing hanging out with weres?" I asked Walker.

"I've been their dentist for ages," he said. "There aren't many dentists who can handle were teeth."

I sneaked a glance at Angela, who had her nose wrinkled as if remembering the dentist's drill. I had a feeling the weres weren't exactly delighted with their luck in finding him.

"I asked them to help me find Polly," Walker added. "She's never come back since that thing with your magician's dad."

"Not our magician," I said automatically, and looked at Yasmin. "You think the humans were from Dimly."

"I think they were either Norths, or sent by them," she said. "There was a scent on them, but there was also this other *thing*. That feeling." She waved at the window. "It made it hard to sniff things out. But no one else I know would be arrogant enough to take on a sorcerer, or have the strength to try it. And now who's sniffing around but a North with a pet magician? The same magician whose dad was working with *necromancers?*"

"Callum got out of Dimly years ago," I said. "We've been trying to find the sorcerer because we're worried about her."

Yasmin snorted, and I couldn't disagree with that. As if Ms Jones couldn't look after herself far better than we ever could. "I'm not waiting in here," she said. "I'm not going to be trapped by a bloody North and his pets." Her tone was dismissive, but there were new lines at the corners of her mouth, and her hands were so tight on her jumper as she folded it that the knuckles had whitened.

"But how can it be Norths?" I asked. "There's only Callum and his sister left, and they're just human. They're not *magic.*"

"I have to agree with that," Walker said. "I know power

when I see it, and Callum's …" He trailed off, waving vaguely. "Not."

Yasmin folded her arms across her chest. "You, I can understand not seeing it," she said to Walker, then shifted her attention to me. "You, on the other hand, are either scent-blind or just oblivious."

"I'm a PI. I'm the very opposite of oblivious."

"Sure you are. Do you even know who the Norths *are?*"

"Of course. They ran Dimly for generations. Dealt everything from unicorn dust to cheesy wot-sits." I returned her gaze flatly, but my hackles were crawling, and it wasn't from the gathering scent outside. It was from the memory of Callum spinning through the frozen world of our apartment, snatching Tam and me out of the air as if the brutal magic of the attack had no hold on him. I licked my chops. "They're smart, and hard, and know how to run a bunch of heavies, but they're not magic."

Yasmin tipped her head on the side, and smiled. It wasn't a nice smile, exactly, but it wasn't a *my what big teeth I have* one either. "And how do you know that? Or who do you know it *from?*"

There was a pause, while I tried to remember. But there wasn't much question. My previous lives were nothing but the vague memory of terrible deaths at the teeth of the Watch. And my memories of this life didn't begin much before meeting Callum. "Oh, come on," I said, thinking of the familiar whiff of dusty, buried magic on Callum's skin, so lost beneath cigarettes and old hungers that it was like the memory of sun in winter. "You seriously think he and his family are some sort of sneaky magic-workers?"

"Not exactly." She peered out the window again. "But they have power as well as influence. It's how they held onto Dimly for so long."

"Didn't help them when the Watch cleared them out," I pointed out.

"No," she agreed. "But they'd grown complacent and over-sure of themselves. And the Watch left one, didn't they? One who'd be helpful when needed."

Ez. They'd left Callum's sister Ez, with her contacts and her knowledge and her unicorn horn trade.

"You think the Watch is behind all this? They set Ez against the sorcerer?"

"I knew it," Walker said. "It was that Claudia. She's tricked Polly and now the Watch have her. I *knew* it!"

"Not Claudia," I said. "She's not that sort of Watch, or I'd be kibble by now."

"I don't think she is either," Yasmin said, and checked the window again. "But she's missing, your sorcerer is gone, and the Watch have backed *their* North, who seems to be intent on clearing out any resistance. So you see why having any North poking around in our business puts my hackles up."

"He's not a North anymore," I said, unable to keep the growl out of the words.

Yasmin turned to stare at me, and for a long moment no one spoke. Then she said, "Maybe, maybe not. But he still smells like a North. And I'm not waiting in here to find out one way or the other."

"So, what, you're just going to go out there and jump him? Guilty by genetics?"

"No. But I'd rather be ready. We can't have a repeat of the house."

"What if he turns up and you decide he's lunch?" I demanded.

"I'm not going to decide he's lunch."

"Sorry for the lack of faith, but you lot tend to get a bit …" I hesitated, looking for a tactful way to say it, but gave up. She was a wolf, she could take it. "All bite and no thought."

"*Undisciplined weres* do," she said, glancing at Angela, who huffed and took another biscuit. "Some of us, however, understand that every person of every kind has a little wild in them, and that it's only by embracing and ultimately controlling it that we become whole and free."

I tipped my head on the side. "Is that the gospel of the modern were, then?"

She snorted, and flashed me those teeth again. "There's nothing modern about it. Weres have survived for as long as we have by being smart about things. No thanks to you lot."

"Hey, I have no responsibility for what the Watch do. And I don't approve of most of it, either. They like killing me off every chance they get."

"Why am I not surprised?" she asked.

"Shouldn't this be a case of the enemy of my enemy is my bestie, or something?"

Yasmin grinned at me. "You're not my enemy. Or my bestie. Not yet, anyway." And then there was that horrible cracking, tearing sound again, setting all my hair in different directions, and a wolf rose up out of Yasmin's clothes where they puddled on the floor. She was lean and long-legged, her ears sharp, and I decided scooting backward a few steps was prudent. Out of snapping range, anyway. She glanced at me, tipped her head toward the door, and padded over to it.

I watched her go, and she stopped, looked at the door handle, then looked back at us, ears pricked.

"Open it, you muppet," Angela said to Walker, and he started, then hurried across the floor. He flung the door open onto the lightening day, which had grown windier while we'd been talking. Eddies and gusts scrabbled around the little alleyway, and the shrubs in the wasteland were shuddering with fright, while clouds gathered heavy and low above us, as if intent on pressing the dawn back. Yasmin shifted her gaze to me and waited.

"No," I said, but she didn't move. "Aw, come *on.*"

"She's not going to hurt you," Angela said.

"She's a *wolf.*"

"She's a were."

"Yeah, well, so are you, and you almost ate us."

She sighed. "I'm basically a pup. That's *Yasmin.*" She looked at me as if I should appreciate the significance of that, and Yasmin tapped one paw on the floor rather pointedly.

"Gods," I muttered, and stalked across the room to join the wolf. "If you eat me, I'm coming back in my next life to vomit hairballs all over your bar."

She half-closed her eyes, either in amusement or acknowledgement, and led the way out into the half dawn. I could smell rain coming, heavy and hostile.

"Hairballs with pumpkin gravy on," I said, and

followed the wolf into the alley. Life choices. I'd gone wrong somewhere. Again.

OUTSIDE THAT SENSE OF WRONGNESS, of *gathering,* was stronger. And it wasn't Callum, no matter what Yasmin said about Norths. So what was it? It set my teeth on edge and my ears back, making the wind feel too sharp and hostile, and the day too hard-edged.

Yasmin slipped long-legged down the alley, her own ears back against the wind, and stopped at the edge of the building, her nose lifted as she sniffed out the surroundings. I joined her, trying to keep my hackles under control. Between the wolf reek of her next to me and the threat of a storm in the air and the cold steel whiffs of something I couldn't quite describe, the sensible cat in me was advising a rapid retreat to somewhere warm and equipped with custard.

No one's ever accused me of sensibility, though, so I edged forward a little further, where I could peer around the corner at the club. There was still no movement from inside or around it, and the same dilapidated cars still sat there. Now that it was a little brighter out, I couldn't even see if anyone had put lights on inside.

"You got anything?" I asked her, and she glanced at me, her snout wrinkling. She didn't like it any more than I did, and her nose would be more sensitive than mine, more able to pick up the whispers of something incoming, the source of our shared unease. But what made a were uneasy? Trolls? Goblins? The Watch? Bloody necromancers? Super-charged Norths? Gah. I didn't know what I'd choose out of that lot.

Yasmin raised a paw to start forward, then stopped, her ears twitching.

"What?" I asked, and she gave me a look that suggested I should stop wasting my breath talking to her. But look, it's not my fault that dogs and dog-like things lack speech. All sympathy and whatever, but I'm not stopping talking just because they can't start. Most of them don't have anything to say, anyway.

She looked back at the drive, and we waited. It didn't take long. A Ford Ka with a hefty scratch down one side pulled into the car park and puttered around to the back of the club, where it parked in line with the other cars. There was a pause, then a man with thick blond hair got out of the driver's side and stretched. He was all long limbs and graceful movement, and Muscles looked like an army tank when he got out the other side. But they grinned at each other, and the were – I could tell that from here, I didn't even need to catch his scent – led the way to the building. Muscles caught up with him and they touched hands for just a moment, that furtive and uncertain touch that comes in the early days when no one's quite sure where things are going or how things will work, if they do, but when not touching seems impossible.

"Aw," I said.

Yasmin tipped her head at the two men then looked at me curiously.

"Muscles," I said. "Or Rav, if you prefer. He's an ex-necromancer heavy."

Yasmin had looked back at the men, watching them vanish inside, and now her head snapped around so fast that I skittered sideways away from her. "Ex! *Ex,* I said! He's alright, just got himself mixed up with the wrong crowd."

Yasmin growled, a breathy note.

"You're going to have to change back. I can't have a reasonable conversation with someone who's growling at me."

She rolled her eyes, which was blatantly unfair. How come wolves can roll their eyes but cats can't? She didn't change or growl again, though, and we both went back to watching the car park. Muscles and the wolf-man had vanished inside, and the whole place was empty again, a discarded plastic bag and the remnants of a newspaper rolling across the potholed tarmac like tumbleweeds. We waited a little longer, then I said, "Callum'll be here shortly. Muscles was meant to do a little scouting for us."

Yasmin gave me a sideways look.

"We were looking for Walker. We still thought you were holding him against his will, not hosting a sleepover."

Yasmin lifted her nose toward the drive and then the club.

"I'm not sure which way he'll come. But you're on this, right? No one's going to jump him?"

She gave a small, fluid shrug, and looked at the club again, her ears twitching.

"Oh, *gods.* Every were in that place thinks he's still a North, don't they? That he was behind the attack on the sorcerer's house?"

She tipped her head at me.

"They're all going to think he's here doing some North-slash-Watch heavy-slash-Dimly drug lord crack-down, and that the bloody magician's in league with him, aren't they? And now— Oh, deep fried broccoli with bean sprouts on. Now they're going to think an ex-necromancer's working with him too, only they don't know he's ex, and he does still have a whiff. *Hairballs.*"

Yasmin gave me a look that said very clearly, *Well done, got it in one.*

"Can't you stop them?"

She shrugged slightly, and I thought of Anton saying, *This isn't the time.*

"You don't have the authority to. Not unless Anton agrees."

A lift of her chin.

"Alright. Then we need to get to Callum first. Grab him before he gets in there, then no one needs to call off the d— guards."

She lifted her lip to show her teeth, but slipped away from our shelter and loped easily toward the long building that made up the garage and its neighbours. I followed, and we ducked into the passageway behind it, running single file across the crumbling concrete.

I just hoped we were in time.

25

I RECOMMEND A TACTICAL RETREAT

WE STOPPED BY THE GARAGE, OUT OF SIGHT OF THE CLUB, which seemed like a good call to me. No doubt Yasmin didn't want her reputation sullied by being seen with a cat, and I didn't want my coat sullied with teeth marks. We peered down the drive, but it was empty all the way to the road. The rain started as we watched, a sheet of it coming smart and stinging along the rutted gravel toward us. It looked like the advance of some rip in dimensions, and I shivered. I'd had more than enough of that recently. I took shelter under the hulk of one of the cars, but Yasmin just waited for the rain to pass into the car park, clouding the view of anyone looking out of the front of the club, then ran softly down the drive, her head low to the ground. I cursed the rain, weres, Callum's family, and then the dentist for good measure, and followed her.

I could mostly smell the chill dead oil scent of water on polluted earth, but I caught a whiff of cat, too – Pru and Tam, and my own faint traces, already being washed away by the rain. It was still coming in heavy sheets, helped along by the wind, and I had to squint against it. There was no fresher sign of Pru and Tam, but at least I knew they'd escaped the wasteland uneaten. Unless they'd run into another were, obviously, but one possible were attack at a time. Callum was the one most likely to get himself nipped, anyway.

"Anything?" I called to Yasmin, as loudly as I dared, and she shrugged, still casting about. I jumped into the culvert and tried to pick my way through the weeds, then realised I wasn't getting any drier. So I went for a full-body plunge, crashing through the undergrowth and avoiding the nettles, and never mind the unpleasant sensation of rapidly forming mud squidging between my toes. Yasmin gave a huff that might've been a laugh, but by then I'd already stumbled to a stop. Cigarettes and secrets, faint under the rain but still clear. And also a whiff of crappy, over-sweetened coffee.

"He's already here," I said. "He must've followed us in."

Yasmin trotted up next to me and snuffled at the weeds, finding Callum's scent. I wondered if she could catch the hidden parts that had taken me so long to notice – the low stain of magic, crushed almost to vanishing. It had been stronger since the thing with the necromancers, though, and I wanted to ask her more about the Norths. Ask her what made a were nervous of them, beyond the tenuous link to the Watch. Sure, they were the original crime family of Yorkshire and probably beyond. They'd controlled the flow of esoteric and more conventional goods for generations. But I'd never thought to ask *how*. How, when magicians and Folk magic-workers were around every corner, and sorcerers were rare but not unknown, a human family had held the north in its grip for so long. Had held it until the Watch deemed them no longer trustworthy. And even then, the Watch had less crushed them than *pruned* them, and to anyone that knew the Watch, that made no sense either.

I probably should've asked Callum before now, really, but I'm not sure how you drop that into conversation, especially when asking about his family tends to result in him reaching for his cigarettes and the nearest book. *So are your family in league with extra-dimensional beings, actual sorcerers of some previously undocumented type, or just plain good at recruiting the lowest denominations of the Folk world to act as your heavies?*

I was pulled out of thought by Yasmin breaking into a long-legged lope, chasing the scent along the culvert and back into the car park. I followed her at a sprint, my limbs still heavy after the desperate scramble through the wasteland, and we shot straight across the front of the were club, heading for the far corner where it butted up against the fence. Water splashed up off the pavement into my face and my fur was being plastered to my spine as the rain fell harder. It was cold enough to be verging on hail, and my paws stung with the chill of it.

We were almost to the corner of the building when the car came tearing down the drive. I spun to look toward it, its headlights splintering the rain and rendering the dark body almost invisible, and it thundered into the car park without slowing. The driver spun it around to the far side of the building, and we heard the brakes snarl as it came to a stop, followed a moment later by the heavy slam of an expensive door and, even through the weight of the rain, a muscular undercurrent of power.

"Aw, hairballs," I said.

The magician had arrived.

YASMIN ABANDONED Callum's scent and started back along the building, already breaking into a run.

"*Stop!*" I hissed, running a few steps after her, but she didn't even look back, stretching out into a sprint. I didn't fancy being Ifan when she raced around the corner. I hesitated, wondering if I should follow her. But I was less concerned by the idea that the magician might get himself nibbled on than I was by the thought that Callum could be walking straight into a were den with no idea that they considered him to be some sort of evil northern mastermind, out to rule the world with his troops of trolls and demons or whatever hanging on his every command. That was definitely a bite first, ask questions later type situation. So I spun back onto Callum's trail and sprinted for the narrow gap between the fence and the end of the were club, cursing the builders who'd decided that the roof had no need of gutters. It was draining all over my fur, by the feel of things.

I slipped into the little alley, finding no doors, just small, high windows the same as the one Pru, Tam and I had sneaked through last night. One was open, and Callum was standing on his tiptoes with both hands on the wall, peering up at it as if deciding whether he could get in or not. His hair was slicked to his head by the deluge, and his jacket was doing more to soak up the rain than it was to keep it off. I stumbled to a stop just as two large hands hooked themselves onto the windowsill from inside, and someone hissed, "All clear."

Callum started to peel off his jacket, regarding the window dubiously, and I hissed, "*Callum!*"

He turned, startled, and grinned at me. "There you are. Where're Tam and Pru?"

"Safe, I hope. Look, we've got to get out—"

I was cut off by a yelp from inside, and Muscles shouted, "Do you *mind?* Can't I get a moment's—" He was cut off, and even through the wall and the thunder of the rain on the roof I heard the crash of a heavy body crashing into a wall, and the sickening thump of a fist hitting its target.

Callum lunged for the wall, and I grabbed at his jeans. "*No,*" I hissed. "We have to get out of here!"

"We're not leaving him," he hissed back, and turned to reach for the window again as someone yelped inside, someone else growled, and there was a tearing noise that sounded a lot like a cheap toilet cubicle door being ripped loose, followed by some pounding that might have been the door being used to hit someone over the head.

"We can't go in there, either," I insisted. "The weres have been attacked and they think *you're* behind it. We have to get out of here *now.*"

"What about Malcolm?" He was hesitating, one hand on the windowsill, and from beyond it came more crashes and shouts and growls. If it was the same as the other toilets, it wasn't a big room, but it sounded like half the wolf pack was in there, trying to tear Muscles to bits. And *he* wasn't getting out the window. Callum would've been lucky to squeeze in, and his shoulders were about half the size.

"He's working with them."

"He's *what?*"

"He's fine, but we're not going to be if we don't leg it *now.*"

Callum still hesitated, looking up at the window, and maybe, *maybe* if he'd just listened to me the first time rather than being such a bleeding heart, we'd have made it, but maybe not, either. Because at that moment two huge paws and a snarling snout appeared in the window, and a very large, very angry wolf tried to launch itself out at us. Callum stumbled back, crashing into the fence behind us with a yelp and the sort of language I filed away for future use.

"*Move!*" I yelled at him, as the wolf's head vanished, leaving just its paws in place, then it launched itself up again, getting halfway out the window this time as a medley of howls and snarls washed around us, crashing off the walls and filling the world.

Callum shoved himself off the fence and sprinted for the back of the building.

"Other way!" I shouted at him, but the wolf was wriggling out of the window, front paws on the wall, so I just took off after Callum with my tail high and my ears back. Direction was less important than distance at this stage.

We burst out of the narrow alley into the car park, and Callum hesitated as he saw the magician's car. "Is that—"

A howl went up behind us, and there was nothing melancholy in it. It was an *I'm coming for you* howl, and

Callum kicked into high gear just as I wondered if I had any more sprint left in me. Where the hell was Yasmin? I'd at least hoped she'd give us some warning before we got eaten.

Then the wolf gave a startled yelp, and I risked a glance back. Tam was hanging from its ear, and it shook its head furiously, trying to dislodge her, as Pru attacked from the other side.

"Oh, *gods,*" I mumbled, skidding to a stop and racing back toward them. "There's more! There's more coming!" Even as I shouted it, two wolves burst out of the alley shoulder to shoulder, each struggling to be the first to grab a tasty little cat morsel. "*Cover!*"

Tam threw herself clear, Pru following her, and they both shot in opposite directions. Pru vanished under the magician's car as Tam dived under the nearest of the bangers. It wasn't as low-slung as the magician's car, but it'd be a silly wolf who stuck their snout anywhere near her. She was all pouffed fur and fury I could smell even through the rain and the dog stink.

Which left just me, staring at the three advancing wolves, and more coming out of the alley behind them. I tried out a couple of the phrases Callum had just taught me, but it didn't help the situation.

Then a stone bounced off the nearest wolf's shoulder, and it yelped, raising one paw in protest.

"Back down," Callum said, his voice calm. The wolf lowered its head, growling, and Callum tossed another stone. He wasn't throwing them hard, but his aim was good. It dinked off the wolf's head, and it spluttered. "Gobs, get under the car."

I considered it, but just retreated until I was next to him. "I suggest a tactical retreat."

"We can't leave Rav."

"Rav's *fine.* Rav's a were now, too."

"Doesn't mean he's safe."

The wolves were fanning out as they advanced, heads low and shoulders rolling, half a dozen of them already, their eyes fixed on us. Tam had emerged from under the car and jumped to its bonnet, eyeing the wolves as if deciding which one she wanted for dinner. Pru was edging out too, her eyes narrowed against the rain.

"Everyone stop," Callum said, raising his voice. "We're not here to cause trouble."

The wolves glanced at each other, and I felt the amusement pass through them before they looked back at us. Tam spat at one that veered too close to her, and it growled in return.

"Yasmin!" I yowled suddenly. "Yasmin, get your furry toes out here!"

There was no response, although the amusement vanished. I wasn't sure if that meant they didn't think much of Yasmin, or objected to me talking about her toes. There was no movement from the were club, nothing but the steadily advancing wolves. I glanced behind us. It wasn't far to the garage, but I didn't know how much that'd actually help us. Callum couldn't hide under a car like we could. He was too tall – bits would stick out.

"I did say no weres," I said. "I *said* that. It was company policy. But did you listen? No. You mung bean."

"We didn't know there were weres when we started looking for Walker," he pointed out.

"We should've quit at the surgery," I said, and one of the wolves made a little rush toward us. Callum flung a stone, hitting it between the eyes, and it snarled, slowing to a walk again. The ones to the sides had circled almost all the way behind us now, and Tam and Pru launched an attack on one of the trailing wolves, but it was over in a flurry of furious snarls, and the cats retreated under the nearest car with the were patrolling around it, growling but too wary to stick its nose within scratching distance.

"Get ready to run," Callum said, his voice quiet.

"Why? What're you going to do?"

"Just get ready, alright?"

"No," I started, but before we had any chance to argue, or Callum had a chance to launch some half-baked diversion attempt, someone rushed in front of us, waving his arms wildly.

"No!" he shouted. "Enough!"

"*Malcolm?*" Callum demanded.

"I've got this," he said, and waved at the wolves. "Stand down, there."

The wolves looked at each other, then kept creeping forward. The ones at the sides had taken advantage of the distraction to close in, and I eyed them warily. One showed me its teeth, and I returned the favour. It huffed amusement.

"I *said,* stand down," Walker insisted, and clicked his fingers. If he was hoping to produce some impressive flame or something, it did not go well. Nothing happened, and the wolves ignored him.

"Wonderful. Thanks so much," I said.

"This should work," he muttered, and pulled his chopsticks out of his pocket.

"Let's just keep backing up," Callum said, grabbing the back of Walker's coat and tugging him along. I looked at the wolves behind us and didn't move. Callum bumped into me and looked around. "Aw, man," he said.

"If you've got some dog repellent spell, now would be a great time to use it," I said to Walker. He ignored me, staring at the chopsticks.

One of the wolves from behind us rushed at me, and I rose on my hind legs to meet it, claws and teeth bared, but Callum's boot reached its muzzle first, catching it a solid blow that sent it scuttling backward with a whine.

"Sorry," he said, and I glared at him.

"It just tried to eat me!"

"Yeah, but kicking seems really unfair."

We didn't have time to discuss the ethics of kicking creatures that seem keen to eat your partner any further, though, because Pru yowled, "*Incoming!*"

We spun back to look at the wolves in front of us, and I whipped around again fast enough that I almost fell over, catching the wolves behind us rushing in as soon as our attention was turned. Callum was swearing again, snatching pebbles off the ground and flinging them, but there were no decent missiles to be had and the wolves were closing in regardless. I slammed a paw across the snout of the closest one behind us, and heard Tam and Pru kicking up a snarling, spitting racket as they tried to draw attention their way.

"*Stop!*" someone else shouted, and I risked a glance around to see Angela running barefoot toward us, her dressing gown clutched tightly around her. "Wait! Don't hurt them!"

One of the wolves ran to intercept her, shouldering her away from the group, and the biggest wolf gathered itself to leap at Callum. I threw myself sideways to avoid the charge of the closest wolf-were as it closed in from behind, feeling the snap of its teeth as much as hearing them. I rolled once and came up all claws and hackles, flinging myself after the beast as it as it lunged for Callum. He dodged sideways at my shout, dragging the dentist with him, and Walker said, "It should just—"

There was a *boom* that I think shattered vital parts of my ear drums, and I went flying backward, along with the wolves and Angela and Tam and Pru. Even the cars slid sideways across the car park, and the rain went with us, carried on the pressure wave. I fetched up against one of the broken cars at the garage, a good twenty metres away, and had enough presence of mind to claw myself behind the tyre, where a were would have a bit more difficulty fishing me out. I blinked at the carpark, where Callum and Walker were standing alone. Walker looked at his chopsticks and grinned.

Callum let go of the other man's coat and stared around, then yelled, "Gobs!"

"Here!" I shouted back, and peered out of shelter. The wolves were getting up and looking around cautiously, and Angela scrambled to her feet, her dressing gown liberally streaked in mud and her braids dripping.

"*Wait,*" she shouted. "Yasmin's here, she's going to sort this out—"

The biggest wolf snarled at her, his ears back, and she

flinched, but set her hands on her hips.

"Say that to her face, Johan."

"Look, we're not here to get in a fight," Callum said. "We were just looking for Malcolm—"

The big wolf – Johan – swung his head toward Callum, lips pulled well back from his teeth, and the other wolves started to regroup, a little more warily than before.

"I'll do it again," Walker threatened, waving his chopsticks. "I will!"

The wolves hesitated, looking at each other, then started their deadly, inexorable stalk forward. Walker clicked his chopsticks desperately.

"Stop," he insisted, and Johan gathered himself to leap.

And at that moment there was an explosion in the were club. A serious, proper, blow-the-windows-out, make-the-walls-shake-and-the-ground-tremble explosion. The roller doors tore from their tracks and flared out like stumpy wings all along the side, and dust and flames and shouts rolled toward us.

"*Anton!*" Angela screamed, and ran for the building.

The wolves wheeled toward it – we all did – and I shouted at Callum, "Tactical retreat!"

He ignored me and ran for the building, shouting to Walker to call the fire service. Because of course he did.

And I ran after him, because of course I did. Straight into a burning building full of enraged weres and magical explosions.

The only reassuring thing was that Tam and Pru were right beside me. If you can't be smart, at least be foolish with friends, I guess.

26

IT'S RAINING WERES

THE SOFAS IN THE WERES' RECREATION AREA WERE smouldering, and the old sheets that had hidden the windows were shredded, gone the way of the glass. Nothing was actively burning in here that I could see, but the haze of smoke was harsh enough to scrape my throat and set me wheezing. Chairs were overturned and the table tennis table had slid off its sawhorse stands, and the thin plasterboard walls between this room and the next, as well as the hall, were cracked and shattered in places, as if someone had hulked through them. Weres in human and wolf form struggled through the mess, and I spotted Xavier with a half-grown wolf-were under each arm and a small girl clinging to his back while he splashed through the water on the ruined floor and headed for the outside, shouting at everyone to stop playing silly buggers and get the cubs out. A wolf I recognised as Lani paused to snarl at me, then went back to threatening and cajoling a very old wolf who was more bald patches than fur. He had cataracts on both eyes, but still managed to give me a death stare as Lani guided him through the debris.

For a moment I thought it was raining inside, then I smelled the stale, grimy stink of the water. The weres had kept their club up to fire control standards, it appeared, and a sprinkler system had come on, drenching everyone and everything as thoroughly as the day outside.

I caught up to Callum and snagged his jeans with a paw. "What're you doing? We should get out of here right now."

"Rav's still in here." He hesitated. "And Ifan, too, I guess."

"Bollocks to Ifan," I said. "That was the same explosion as at Muscles'."

"We don't know that."

"I do." Or near enough, anyway. There was the same hot, raw magic taste to the charm. "He tried to bloody kill us."

"We don't know that," Callum repeated. "And even if it was him, he might not have known we were in there. And *this* certainly wasn't for us."

"I mean, there's loyalty and there's dog-loyalty," Pru said, and we both looked at her. "You get the difference, right?"

More weres were hurrying out into the car park and helping others across to the undamaged buildings, but Johan had followed us in, his head low and his eyes on Callum. Lani was on her way back too, the old were being led away by a young woman in a giraffe-patterned onesie.

"We need to decide what we're doing fast," I said,

eyeing Johan, who was creeping closer. "Before any of us get a nip."

Callum followed my gaze, and nodded. "Come on. We find Rav, and we get out again."

I didn't bother pointing out again that Muscles was already a were, so him getting nipped wasn't going to do any harm. He'd started a bathroom brawl for us, and we'd got his flat blown up, so I supposed we owed him something.

Callum broke into a jog, skirting toppled stacks of crates and their fallen cargo of broken, leaking bottles, and jumping stray cushions that had been blown off sofas and chairs. We followed him, scattering as we went to avoid the last of the fleeing weres and patches of broken glass. The lighting was dim and stuttering, half the bulbs blown out and the emergency lighting that was left apparently undecided about the wisdom of hanging on in the face of magic and water damage. The sprinklers were tamping down the dust of the demolished walls, but the filthy, ancient water mixed with the smoke to fill the air with a gluggy haze that pinched my nostrils and made sound carry weirdly.

The acrid scent of smoke mixed with the reek of angry wolves and the stink of smashed booze bottles, making it almost impossible to pick up individual scents such as lurking magicians or specific, nippy wolf-weres, and I resorted to trying to look over both shoulders as much as at where I was going. That resulted in a pretty unsteady path across the cluttered floor, but at least I'd have some warning before anyone sank their teeth – or charms – into my hindquarters. I could see Pru doing the same thing off to my left, while to the other side the faint shadow of Tam drifted in and out of sight, prowling forward with her head up and her ears forward, for all the world as if she infiltrated burning were clubs on a regular basis. For all I knew, she did, I suppose.

Callum led the way through the hallway, dimly lit by emergency exit lights and the gaping holes in the walls, and into the main room of the club. The explosion had evidently been centred on the back rooms, as it was less smoky in here, but it was barely any brighter than it had been the previous night. The lighting was sparse and the blacked-out windows didn't let any of the dark day in. Without the surging crowds and the heady, dizzying scent of joy and adrenaline and abandon, the place felt ragged and bereft. It was just what it was – a vast old building that should've been condemned and instead had become a place for the ignored and overlooked to unfold their wings and bare their fangs. With them, it was alive. Without them, it was just a shell.

The fire might not have reached the big room, but the pressure wave of the explosion must have, as the floor was tangled with fallen, twisted banks of lighting and the coils of cable they'd brought down with them. The bars were still standing, although the DJ booth had been crushed under some lights, and Anton and Yasmin stood glaring at each other in the centre of the floor, both in human form. Anton had one hand on Angela's shoulder, the gesture paternal, but he was keeping her at arm's length as if ready to push her away. He was still dressed, his shirt sleeves as precisely rolled as the night before, although his beard looked a little scorched at the edges.

Yasmin had wrapped herself in an old sheet, and her dark hair hung loose and tangled over her shoulders.

"I'm telling you," she said. "We need to let this go."

"A North brought cats into my club," Anton said. "And his magician destroyed it. Our *home.*"

Yasmin shook her head, giving an odd, half feral grimace. "I don't think this is as simple as it seems."

"You trust them?"

Yasmin didn't answer straight away, and Callum looked back at me, tipping his head to indicate we should slip back into the hallway and leave the weres to it. I turned to start picking my way back across the cluttered floor, and in that moment wolf-Lani burst out of the corridor with her teeth bared and her lean body stretched into a sprint, Johan on her heels. Callum spun away, already breaking into a run, and I launched myself into the were's path. She bowled right past me without slowing, a paw catching me and sending me tumbling across the floor before I could recover myself. I glimpsed Tam as she threw herself at Johan, but the weres weren't concerned with us. Johan kept going, Tam sliding off his haunches with a mouthful of fur and a disgruntled expression, and both wolves surged past Pru before she could even move.

"Stop them!" I yelled at Yasmin as Lani leaped at Callum from behind, her teeth snapping for his neck as her weight carried him to the ground. "*Call them off!*"

Johan lunged after Lani, his teeth bared in a growl of delight, and a wolf with the build of a cement truck appeared out of the shadows, moving far too fast for something of that bulk. He charged straight at Lani, dropping his shoulder as he hit her with an impact that sent her bowling across the floor with a squalling yelp. He went with her, moving too fast to stop himself, and they tumbled into Johan together as a leaner, paler wolf sprinted across the floor toward them, whining.

Johan managed to keep his feet, spinning away then turning back to lunge at the big wolf, teeth bared, but the lean newcomer was already there, launching his own attack on Johan. They crashed into each other, chest to chest, and surged across the floor, the smaller wolf struggling to hold his ground, and the huge wolf abandoned Lani and chased after them. Callum was already on his feet, brandishing a broken bottle he'd almost landed on. Lani snarled at him, her ears back, and glanced at Angela, jerking her head. More wolves were coming into the room, appearing from the shattered corridor, looking from Lani to Anton as if unsure who to take their lead from.

"Stop," Yasmin ordered, and Lani snarled at her, the noise pure, unadulterated fury, then turned her attention back to Callum.

Callum looked at her, then at the bottle in his hand, and dropped it.

"Bleeding heart," Pru said from beside me, and Tam huffed.

"The world needs them," she said, and trotted out into the floor. We followed her, aligning ourselves around Callum.

"He's not done anything," I said, speaking mostly to Yasmin. "You can see that. He won't even defend himself, useless cabbage."

"Thanks," Callum said, and looked at Anton. "Whatever you think I'm doing, I was just looking for Malcolm. That's it."

"Just like you were at the sorcerer's house? You *killed* Jorg."

"I haven't killed anyone."

"*Norths,*" Anton growled. "Norths, sneaking into my club, acting like you own the place. Norths and cats and bloody magicians."

"I'm not a North," Callum said. "I left all that a long time ago."

The were snorted. "You don't change your blood."

"But you do change your choices," Callum said. His hands were half up, the fingers spread and blood on his grazed palms. "You change your alignment." He glanced at Yasmin as he said it, and she just watched him, her expression uncertain.

Anton kept his eyes on Callum. His thick grey hair was dishevelled, and there was a bruise high on his cheek, but he stood without moving or fidgeting. His gaze was disconcerting, and Callum returned it calmly, his tatty coat dripping on the floor.

And it might have all been resolved quite amicably, but at that point the scrap in the corner, that I'd sort of forgotten about, escalated into some panicked yelping from one wolf, a furious snarl from another, and Johan came pelting across the expanse of floor with his ears back and his bloodied teeth bared, heading straight for Callum, and Walker chose that moment to run into the middle of the room and shout, "Everyone just calm down!"

Johan tried to swerve around the dentist, but he was going too fast, and he hit Walker with his shoulder, sweeping the man's legs out from under him as the bulky wolf and the skinny one tore out of the shadows in pursuit, the big one favouring one paw. Lani spun toward them, then jumped back around to face us, and maybe she was going for Callum or maybe not, but I wasn't waiting around to see. I threw myself at her, clawing for the sensitive skin of her snout, and Pru and Tam piled on after me. Lani howled, and I caught the crunching chorus of weres collapsing into wolves, as well as the thunder of paws as the hesitating wolf-weres rushed to join the fray.

Lani flung us off and lurched toward Callum, but Yasmin was already there, driving her back with snapping teeth. Callum grabbed Walker, hauling him to his feet and away from the scrapping wolves, and we cats decided the safest place was as close to the humans as we could get. There were way too many teeth going on out there, and all of them bigger than ours. Furry backs surged across the floor, browns and greys and whites, and teeth snapped, and heavy feral snarls and growls and the collision of powerful bodies shook the whole room. I'd lost track of who was who, or what side anyone was on, or if this had just degenerated into some wolfish free-for-all.

"We should go," I yelled at Callum, and he nodded, still with a firm grip on Walker. Tam lifted her head at the front of the club, and we started to scurry along the edge of the room toward it, keeping to the wall and trying to be inconspicuous. It wasn't far, and the fight was raging tirelessly behind us, drowning even the reek of smoke with the scents of fury and blood and rage. I could see the door hanging ajar, held half-closed by a damaged lock, rattling in the wind, and it seemed, for one perfect moment, that we were going to make it.

Then someone howled, the sound huge even in the echoing expanse of the club, and everyone *stopped.* It wasn't a sound you could ignore. We turned to face the fighters, and a great grey wolf with big shoulders and yellow eyes came stalking toward us with a slight wolf I recognised as Angela following him. The grey wolf gave an odd little half-howl, quieter than before yet still echoing and imperious, and the last of the scuffling stopped, the wolves pulling away from each other and coming to form a half-circle around us, pinning us to the wall.

Walker waved his chopsticks. "Don't push me," he said, but he sounded unsure, and Callum pushed his hand down, his eyes on the wolf.

Anton – it had to be Anton, because if ever a wolf looked like it should have shirtsleeves and tatts, the big grey one did – stepped into the semicircle and looked up at Callum, examining him.

Callum regarded him for a moment, then crouched down and held both hands out, palms up.

"Do not get turned into a were," I said to him. "The cigarette stink is enough. I'm not sharing with a wet dog."

"Can you smell it?" he asked Anton, ignoring me. "That I'm not a North? I don't count myself as one anymore, and I'm not your enemy. I'm not a magician. I'm not anything. See for yourself."

Anton stepped forward, his gaze not moving from Callum's. Their heads were level, and the wolf came close enough that he could have leaned forward and torn Callum's face off. Anton's mouth was open slightly, his teeth on display, and I could see his nose twitching as he examined the man in front of him. I wondered what he was smelling, how deep he could go on scent alone. Wondered if he could sort through that strange, latent magic scent to find the quiet centre of my partner, or if he'd hate him simply for the taint of what he had been. I tensed as Anton leaned even further forward, his nose almost touching Callum's face, and still Callum didn't flinch. He just waited, and I thought I'd never seen anyone as sure of anything as he looked in that moment.

Not that being sure of yourself matters when a were's just about giving you a snog.

And then Anton leaned back, his ears pricking up, and Callum smiled, and as the were turned to address his pack, a new explosion rocked through the building like the world was ending.

THE FORCE of it picked me up and flung me through the air, and I twisted as I went, as if I had any chance of seeing my landing when I had no idea what was up or down or if I was possibly dead already. My ears trembled with the blast, and through the under-blanket stuffiness of it the world was full of howls and crashes and the terrible crumpling of the roof being torn away and the walls smashed down. Then I hit a wolf, and another wolf hit me, and we all came to a crashing stop together against something hard while I wondered if I was more likely to die by explosion or being eaten.

The wolf on top of me was motionless, and the one under me was whimpering and twitching, so I added death by suffocation to the list of possibles while I squirmed around like a kitten in the pile-up, trying to find a way out. Someone was shouting, but between the fur and the ringing of my poor abused ears I couldn't tell who or what.

Then the wolf on top of me slid away a little, and I glimpsed light. I wriggled toward it and stuck my nose in the gap between the bodies, snuffling at the marginally fresher air. It smelled of burning hair and alcohol fumes and magic, and I clawed my way further forward, until I could stick my head out and stare around.

It was a battlefield. The were club was gone, utterly flattened, the walls falling away from where we'd been standing and the roof tangled up in the fence. Wolves were getting up and staggering around, shaking their heads, and as I watched some of them started to reform into human shape, the change slow and wobbly. Cubs were running from the far building, and I spotted a couple of older weres trying to herd them back. Someone was crying, sobbing so hard I could feel the hurt of it, and there was a lot of whining going on. I blinked around, looking for Callum, and the wolf above me gave a groan, then started to melt.

"Ew, *no.*" I lurched out of the pile-up as the wolf reformed into Angela, pressing both hands over her head. "Hey – you okay?"

"I don't think I like cats anymore," she managed, and a

girl of about twelve ran toward her, holding out a towel. The girl was crying.

"Lani," the girl said. "Where's Lani?'

"She'll be fine," the wolf that had been under me said, and I squawked, then realised it was Yasmin, back in human form. "You keep the littlies away, okay?"

The girl wiped her nose with the back of her hand. "But—"

"Send Nathaniel with more robes," Yasmin said, and sat up. There was blood on the side of her face, and she touched it gingerly. "Hurry up, now."

The girl turned and ran, and Yasmin moved Angela's hands, giving her head a cursory examination. "You'll be fine," she said, and gave the young woman's shoulder a quick squeeze, then looked at me.

"This was *nothing* to do with us," I said.

"No," she said. "It was the bloody magician." And she pushed herself to her feet and walked across the devastated shell of the club, stopping to check on other weres as they extricated themselves from the debris in both wolf and human form.

I looked at Angela, who was dabbing blood from between her braids. "You want me to lick that or something?"

"*Gross,*" she said, as if she didn't turn into a puddle of goo on a regular basis.

"I'm just trying to help."

She scowled at me and got up, tucking the towel tightly around her. "Yeah, that's gone well so far."

I couldn't really argue with that.

27

MOVING ON

SINCE ANGELA HAD REFUSED MY GENEROUS OFFER OF FIRST aid, I ventured out onto the floor in time to meet Tam, who was sitting on top of a motionless wolf and cleaning one paw. The rest of her was caked in debris, so I'm not sure why the paw mattered, but you have to start somewhere. The wolf twitched, and she looked down at it as if vaguely surprised to see it moving.

"Pru?" I asked her, and she lifted her chin. I followed her gaze and spotted Pru sitting next to a large woman with matted hair. They both looked as dust-encrusted and startled as each other, but neither of them seemed hurt. I padded on a little further, to where I could see Callum just sitting up. Ifan was leaning over him, his black coat unmarred by the dust encrusting the rest of us, and I broke into a sprint. Or would have, if I'd had any sprint left in me. As it was, I jogged clumsily toward them, shouting as I went.

"*Hey!* Magic boy! Back the hell off!"

Ifan looked around at me, startled, and Callum wiped

muck off his face, then pushed Ifan's hand away and got up, swaying slightly. A very large and very naked Muscles staggered over to steady him.

"Gobs – that's a relief. I hoped you were okay," Ifan said, and almost sounded like he meant it.

"What the hell was that?" I demanded.

"What?"

"Oh, I don't know – levelling the whole bloody building with a pack inside? With *us* inside?"

Ifan spread his hands apologetically. "I saw that wolf about to attack Callum, and I guess I just overcompensated a bit."

"A bit?"

"Gobs, enough," Callum said. He was using his sleeve to try to clean his face, but it wasn't working very well. "Is everyone okay?"

"No thanks to magic boy," Yasmin said, and I gave her an approving nod.

"Look, I panicked," Ifan said. "I'm really sorry."

"Anton wasn't about to attack me," Callum said. "Was he?"

"Not at all," Yasmin said.

"I didn't know that from outside," Ifan said, pointing to where the wall had once been. "I was looking in the window."

"What about the first explosion?" Callum asked. "What was that all about?"

"It wasn't me. I was looking for you, so I was kind of sneaking around. The explosion must've been someone else."

"Likely story," I said.

"It might've been me," Walker said. He was sitting on the ground, clutching his chopsticks. One of them had snapped, but was still holding together with a few fibrous threads. "Maybe it was like a chain reaction from outside."

"And maybe I set it off with a hairball," I said. Tam snorted appreciatively.

The old were with the dodgy eyes was in human form, stumbling around with an armload of robes and handing them out to anyone who looked vaguely human-shaped. He paused next to Yasmin, snuffled, and said, "Where's Anton?"

Yasmin turned sharply, her bare heels digging into the debris-strewn ground, and somewhere I heard a siren. "Anton?" she said, and a wolf heaved itself out of a pile of rubble, shaking dust from its coat. It swung its head toward her. "Anton," she said, more calmly. "Change back so we can talk."

The wolf looked down at himself, then up at her

"Change," she said, impatiently.

Anton whined, then swung his head toward Ifan as the sound of the sirens built.

"Anton?" Yasmin asked. "What's going on? I can't understand you."

The wolf gave a growl of frustration, then flung his head back and howled, setting my hair jumping in all sorts of directions and the cubs howling back as well as their human throats would let them.

Yasmin looked at Ifan. "What did you do?" she asked, every word as precise as a surgical tool.

He spread his hands. "Nothing, I promise. A concussion, maybe? I'm sure he'll be fine."

The old were stepped closer, still snuffling. "Liar," he whispered, loud enough that I knew Yasmin and Callum heard it as well.

Ifan shook his head. "The explosion wasn't designed to hurt *anyone*. Everyone else is okay, aren't they?" He looked around at the weres, eyebrows raised. No one answered. "See? I was just looking out for Callum." He glanced toward the road and added, "We need to get out of here if we don't want to answer any awkward questions."

The sirens were becoming a chorus, wailing from three different directions at once, and Yasmin wrinkled her nose, exposing her canines, then turned away from us. "Get the cubs together," she said, addressing the weres in general. "Leave everything – there's no time. Out through the wasteland and regroup at mine."

"Who put you in charge?" Lani started, and Yasmin snarled. It was a proper wolf snarl coming from her human body, and Lani took a step back, startled.

"Once we're out of here and safe, *then* we can discuss such things," Yasmin said. "Everyone out, *now*. We'll sort the details out later."

Johan grabbed Lani's arm and pulled her away, but other than a furious backward glance at us she didn't seem inclined to argue.

"Let's go," Ifan said to Callum. "We need to get out of here, too."

Callum gave him a level look, then turned to Walker. "You need to come with us."

"No," Walker said. "The weres are going to help me find Polly."

"So are we," Callum said. "And she told us to keep you

safe." His voice was flat, brooking no argument, and Walker blinked at him, confused.

"Why would she say that?"

"I wish I knew." Callum crouched down, pointing to his shoulder, and I jumped on. Pru took his other shoulder, and he looked at Tam, eyebrows raised. She snorted.

"I'd feel safer with the weres," Walker said. "No offence."

Callum sighed. "Look—"

"He can stay with me," Yasmin said, startling us all. The weres had mostly scattered already, but she'd claimed a coat from somewhere, and now she handed another to Walker. "He'll answer his phone." Anton stood next to her, his heavy wolf head hung low and his eyes fixed on Ifan. Yasmin's hand rested on his shoulder, a warning or a restraint.

Callum and I looked at each other. The sirens were getting louder, bearing down on us and tearing the dawn to pieces. There wasn't time. "Make sure he does," he said.

Yasmin nodded. "I want to talk to you anyway, North."

"Callum."

She examined him for a moment, then nodded. "Callum." She beckoned to Walker and turned away, striding barefoot across the car park with Anton prowling next to her and the dentist scampering after them.

"Cal," Ifan started.

Callum was already turning away. "I'll be in touch."

"I was only trying to help," Ifan said, catching his arm. "I didn't mean anyone to get hurt, but I really thought—"

"What were you really talking about with Anton?" I asked, as Callum shook himself free.

"I wasn't talking about anything. I was outside—"

"The other night," Pru said. "Inside. What were you going to come to an arrangement about?"

Ifan's expression didn't falter. He just spread his hands and smiled. "I don't know what you're talking about."

"And we can't ask Anton," I said. "Convenient, that."

The sirens had narrowed to the direction of the drive, and Muscles, who'd been lingering nearby while the slim blond were tugged on his arm, said, "We've got to go. I don't want the police thinking I did this as well as my flat."

"It does have certain similarities," I said, still watching Ifan, who ran both hands back over his hair, sending splatters of rain everywhere.

"My car's here," the magician said. "We can get past the police in it. It's got a few tricks for that sort of thing."

Callum nodded and said, "You do that. We're going to nip out the same way as the weres and circle back to my car."

Ifan shook his head. "Fine. Whatever. Look, in that case, I'll talk to the emergency services, let them think I called it in. Stop them looking for anyone else."

"Great," Callum said, and started after the weres, who had already vanished behind the third building, heading for the gap in the fence.

"Wait," Ifan said, and Callum turned back reluctantly.

"What?"

"Here." Ifan held out his hand, and I hissed at him, half-expecting some charm or magical binding, something that would stop us from leaving. But he just tucked

Green Snake into Callum's coat pocket. "He was in my jacket this morning."

"Right," Callum said. "Thanks."

"Sure," Ifan said, and I shifted on Callum's shoulder to watch him as we left. The magician watched us go, his face unreadable and rain collecting on the shoulders of his coat. He didn't look away for as long as I watched, and I watched until we were behind the building and hurrying down the alleyway, Callum ducking through the fence and scrambling into the patchy cover of the wasteland while the rain fell heavy and thick behind us, and drowned the scent of burned rubber and torched tin and hungry magic.

Our car was still sitting in the coffee shop car park, and people were still queueing through the drive-through, and only a couple of them were even looking at the dumpy plume of smoke rising from the industrial estate. From here it looked like nothing more than a bit of a bonfire that might've got a little out of hand, and the fire engines were already leaving again, with their lights quiet, by the time we piled back into the car. Callum pressed a hand to his forehead like he had a horrible headache, and glanced at us.

"Anyone in need of medical attention?" he asked.

"Does the application of custard count as a medical need?" I asked.

He considered it. "In this situation, maybe."

"Then yes."

Pru wriggled out of her dust and mud-encrusted jacket and shook herself off, pawing the soggy thing onto the floor. "Are we going after the weres?"

"I'm not sure we should right now," Callum said. "They need time to get sorted."

"We still don't know what happened with Walker," I pointed out. "They said they were attacked, but we don't have any details."

He looked at me, then nodded. "We do need to find that out. But they've just lost their home, and everyone'll be upset. We found Malcolm, and he's safe. That's going to have to do for now." He yawned suddenly, hugely. "And I need some sleep."

Pru looked at Tam, who shrugged. "Fine," she said. "I need a wash again, anyway. We'll come find you tomorrow."

"Give it a day or so," Callum said. "Your catsitter'll end up locking you in a box if you keep vanishing on them."

"I'd like to see him try," she said, and a moment later she was gone.

Tam got up, touched her nose to mine, and said, "Work on your rhymes a bit more," then she was gone too.

"Rhymes?" Callum asked, as he started the car.

"Long story."

"Aren't they all?"

The car groaned and grumbled its way out onto the road, windscreen wipers creaking and scraping, and Green Snake slipped out of Callum's coat and came to curl next to me on the seat.

"Traitor," I said to him, and he tilted his head at me, then wriggled about as if he had fleas. "You are."

"I suppose magicians have warmer pockets," Callum said.

"I still don't fancy them," I said, and settled onto my haunches. "Where are we going?"

Callum hesitated. "Home, I suppose. I want to make sure Mrs Smith's okay."

I froze, my throat suddenly tighter than the dust had made it. "We can't."

"We don't have anything with us."

"We don't have much there, either. Not to be worth going back for."

He hesitated again, and I almost asked. Asked how he'd moved when everything else had been frozen. How he'd pulled us out of the maw of whatever had held us. But he spoke first. "We don't even know what happened. We need to take a look."

"We need to stay alive."

He nodded, with more confidence than seemed reasonable. "We will."

That seemed groundlessly optimistic, but I just said, "Fine. You can go in first, then."

He grinned. "Deal."

I adjusted my position to put my chin on my paws. "Wake me when we get home."

"No you don't," Callum said. "If I have to drive, the least you can do is keep me company."

I started to complain, then looked at the shadows under his eyes, barely visible under the foundation of building dust, and spotted the muscle tightening and relaxing at the corner of his jaw. He might not have been almost gobbled up by a void last night, or treated to an out-of-body experience, but a couple of firebombings by his oldest friend probably didn't make for a great day. So I sat up again and said, "Yasmin's nice."

"You can't stand weres."

"I'm revising my opinion based on new evidence. I think she's the sort of person who'd keep custard about the place."

"Is that so?"

"Yeah. Just don't let her bite you. That was unfortunate for Muscles."

"I'm not going to be bitten by Yasmin."

"No?" I thought about it. "What about Xavier? He's alright, too. Likes cats. Although a bit too much, maybe."

"I've changed my mind. Go to sleep."

"Just don't take up with Anton. You'll end up drinking organic hand ground coffee made with unicorn milk and steeped in the waxing moon while discussing philosophy. I won't be able to stand it."

Callum sighed, and poked his phone until he got some music on, then turned it up until I gave up talking and tried to shout along to Sleaford Mods, which I don't have the accent for. Callum was better at it.

WE PARKED JUST down the road from our building, and sat watching it for a while.

"Are you sure this is a good idea?" I asked.

"No," Callum admitted. "But how else do we find out if it's just here, or if it's going to follow us? We need to know."

"That's far too reasonable for before breakfast."

"You just ate half a packet of biscuits."

"Before your breakfast, then."

He snorted. "Come on."

He climbed out of the car and let me jump back to his shoulder, my paws aching with all the running and rough ground. He lit a cigarette and leaned against the car to smoke it, both of us with our eyes still on the building and his shoulders tight with tension. His hair had gone grey, and his coat was about three shades paler from all the dust caked in it, and I wasn't sure I'd ever get myself clean, between the mud and the rain and the gunk of the explosion. Green Snake had evidently got himself hopped up on something in the magician's pockets and kept trying to climb up Callum's coat to join me.

"Anything?" Callum asked, as we watched an old man walking an equally old dog, both of them pausing every few paces, the dog to sniff things and the old man to lean on a stick and wheeze.

"It just feels off still." Off. *Wrong*. Wrong like fur rubbed against the grain. I sniffed the air, looking for a trace, anything that would tell me if it was remnants or presence. But whoever – *whatever* – held that power also had the power to hide. I couldn't tell who had been here, or if they were here still, but something was very, very wrong.

"Can you tell anything from it?"

"Not really." I hesitated, my eyes on our apartment building, waiting for the windows to blow out, or the sky to open above it, or *something*. I still had no scent to work from. The sense of wrongness was coming from somewhere else, somewhere deeper and more primal. There was just that taste of cold steel. "Old Ones take you," I whispered, not even sure who I was talking to.

Then movement caught my eye, and a small grey form detached itself from under the nearest car and scurried toward us. I blinked at it, and said, "Let me down."

Callum crouched, and I stumbled off his shoulder, my legs almost giving way with weariness. The grey shape resolved into a sleek-furred rat, and she tucked herself into the shelter of the car, peering about warily. "Susan, light of the sewers," I said, trying for jovial and not really pulling it off. "How's it?"

"Light of the sewers? That's weak."

"It's been a day."

"Well, it's not getting any better." She lifted her snout toward the building. "It's still there."

"What? Meal delivery?" I asked.

She looked at me for a moment, then said, "I know you're a cat and all, but don't go in there. I don't fancy picking bits of Gobbelino out of my nest."

"That bad?" Callum asked quietly. He'd stayed hunkered down next to us, watching the building. "Is Mrs Smith okay?"

"It's not after her," Susan said. "This is only for you. I saw you come racing out last night, so I went up to take a look this morning. And things are safe enough while you're not there, but there's no way I'm going in. The place is *wrong*, and it makes my paws itch. And whatever it is, it's still waiting for you."

Callum and I looked at each other. "Could you tell anything about it?" I asked. "Is it necromancers? Watch?"

"Couldn't say. But definitely not a user of your corner store level of spells. You've tweaked the tail of some major power."

"We don't like to do things by halves," I said, but my mouth was sticky, and the words fell flat.

Callum sighed. "Thanks, Susan."

"Sure. Bring me some fruit next time. A peach or something." She scuttled across to the nearest drain, then paused. "Although I'd recommend *next time* being at rather a later date."

She vanished, and I looked up at Callum. "What now?"

"We find somewhere to stay."

"Not Ifan's."

"No," he said slowly. "Not Ifan's."

WE WENT BACK to the car, since what else could we do? And then we left, because even hanging out in the same neighbourhood as our suddenly volatile apartment seemed like a bad idea. And, finally, we parked in a lay-by and called Gerry to tell him in a very careful and hopefully eavesdropper-proof way that we were having a small accommodation issue.

He listened gravely, then said, "You need to go on holiday."

"What?" I demanded over the speaker phone.

"Go and take some sea air," he said. "It'll do you good."

"What the hell," I started, and Callum poked me.

"Good plan," he said to Gerry. "You're right, everyone needs a break."

"Wonderful," Gerry said. "Send me a postcard of a dinkey – sorry, donkey."

"What—" I started again, but Callum talked over me.

"I'll bring you back some rock," he said.

"I prefer taffy," Gerry said, then added that he had to go, and a moment later the phone went dead.

I glared at Callum. "A *holiday?*"

Callum opened the fresh pack of cigarettes he'd just bought. The old ones were drying on the dashboard. "We're going to Whitby."

"*Whitby?* In the name of all small futile gods, *why?*"

"Because Gerry and I agreed on a couple of codes for if things got really messy in Dimly for him, or if he heard about anyone getting too interested in us. If it was about us, he'd suggest a trip to the seaside. Whitby's so overrun by people looking for vampires that most Folk avoid it. It's a good spot."

"*What?*"

"*Dracula*'s based there – you know, the book—"

"No, you book-addled parsnip. Bollocks to vampires. When did you decide all this?"

Callum waved vaguely. "Gerry and I talk. But the post-card – that means someone's looking for us. And prefer-ring taffy means things are getting dicey for him, too. So we're going to get out there, regroup, and figure out who's setting traps for us, and who's rousting Dimly." He started the engine again, and I stared at him.

"Whitby? Really? The *seaside?*"

"You might like it."

"I won't."

"There's fish."

"There're *seagulls*. And dock cats."

"Well, keep away from them. Low profile now. We need to vanish for a bit, Gobs." He glanced at me, the cigarette drifting smoke over his hand where it rested on the wheel. "Things are catching up."

"What things?" I demanded.

"North things. And Watch things."

I opened my mouth to protest that the only Watch *thing* was that they resented my free-wheeling way of life, then shut it again. It was starting to taste of nothing more than a way to avoid thinking about it. To avoid *remembering*. And I had a feeling the time for avoidance was gone. I *needed* to remember.

"What about Walker?" I pointed out. "And Ms Jones?"

"Walker's safe. Ms Jones found you once. She'll find you again."

"Well, that's reassuring," I said, and glared around the car. "Phone next time, yeah?" There was no response, and I looked at Callum. "I'm not sure she approves."

"We'll have to risk the disapproval of your invisible sorcerer."

I wrinkled my nose at him. There was a grin twitching at the corners of his mouth. "*Whitby*," I said. "Bet it all smells of seaweed."

"Probably," he agreed, and put a hand on my back. "Fresh fish, though."

"Better be," I said, and headbutted his fingers. He scratched the back of my neck, and gave Green Snake a little head rub, and we wound our way out of Leeds, the city falling away behind us as we headed north and east, away from the familiar and into wilder, stranger lands, where anything can happen.

But anything can always happen, and often does. The world is complicated, and unpredictable, and savage and beautiful, and it breaks all of us. But there's no shame in that. We're made to break, after all. We're made to break and heal and break again and heal again, and all we can do is keep moving forward, holding to those we trust and who trust in us. It's what makes life *living,* rather than just existing.

Plus, there's custard. I'll go through a lot for some decent custard.

Callum put the music back on his phone, and chopped and changed through the junctions, eventually sliding onto the A64 as we shed the city like a winter coat, on to stranger things.

And seagulls.

Gods, I really hate seagulls.

THANK YOU

Lovely people, thank you so much for choosing to spend some more time with Yorkshire's most dubious PI duo. Whether this is your first encounter with G&C London (in which case, welcome – and I hope you're not allergic to cat hair), or if this is your fifth outing (you glutton for punishment, you), it means so much that you've chosen to join us. I hope you'll now be keeping a close eye on Facebook vids for snake-tailed dogs ...

And if you did enjoy this book, I'd very much appreciate you taking the time to pop a review up at your favourite retailer.

Reviews are a bit like magic to authors, but magic of the good kind. Less blowing up childhood friends, more troll tea party, so to speak. More reviews mean more people see our books in online stores, meaning more people buy them, so giving us the ability to write more stories and send them back out to you, lovely people. Less vicious circle, more happy story circle.

Plus it keeps us in custard, which is the primary reason for anything to happen in life …

And if you'd like to send me a copy of your review, theories about cat world domination, cat photos, or anything else, drop me a message at kim@kmwatt.com. I'd love to hear from you!

Until next time,

Read on!

Kim

(And head over the page for more adventures plus your free sorcerer's house tour!)

STRANGE STORIES FOR A STRANGE WORLD

Old gods rise. A jewel thief falls. A late night wish is tragically granted ...

And somewhere, on the edge of the dark or in the belly of an unknown machine, stories are born. Stories of heroic chickens and lost demons, dangerous golf games and pies full of fury. Stories of magic and uncertainty. Stories of the unordinary.

Come on in and discover them. Don't worry, it's perfectly safe. This world is just like yours.

Well, almost. But there's nothing to fear here.

Except maybe the sheep. I'd watch the sheep ...

Grab your copy of Oddly Enough now!

Scan above to grab your copy, or use the link below:
https://readerlinks.com/l/2420325/g5bm

HOW TO HAVE A REALLY BAD IDEA

Possibly our last idea, to be honest.

When a good PI's dealing with a missing persons case, there's going to be some door-knocking involved.

But knocking on a sorcerer's door is very likely to result in said PI becoming a missing person themselves.

And letting oneself in uninvited?

Well, let's just say it's probably best to bring a bag for picking up the pieces ...

Find out just how wrong things can go for Gobs and Callum in your free download!

Scan above to claim your copy, or use the link below:
https://readerlinks.com/l/2420326/g5rm

ABOUT THE AUTHOR

Hello lovely person. I'm Kim, and in addition to the Gobbelino London tales I also write other funny, magical books that offer a little escape from the serious stuff in the world and hopefully leave you a wee bit happier than you were when you started. Because happiness, like friendship, matters.

I write about baking-obsessed reapers setting up baby ghoul petting cafes, and ladies of a certain age joining the Apocalypse on their Vespas. I write about friendship, and loyalty, and lifting each other up, and the importance of tea and cake.

But mostly I write about how wonderful people (of all species) can really be.

If you'd like to find out the latest on new books in *The Gobbelino London* series, as well as discover other books and series, giveaways, extra reading, and more, jump on over to www.kmwatt.com and check everything out there.

Read on!

amazon.com/Kim-M-Watt/e/B07JMHRBMC
bookbub.com/authors/kim-m-watt
facebook.com/KimMWatt
instagram.com/kimmwatt
twitter.com/kimmwatt

ACKNOWLEDGMENTS

Rather like a good troll tea party, books are better shared. They can't exist in a vacuum, either in the writing or the reading. And I am an exceptionally lucky writer and human in that I have many, many wonderful people around me, none of whom I can ever thank properly, because I am awkward and things get weird.

But I shall try.

First to you, lovely reader. For accepting that cats are selfish, snarky, and fickle, but living lives as complex and bizarre as our own. For reading, for sharing, for chatting on the social medias and via email, and for just generally being wonderful. Thank you.

To my beta readers, who are funny, delightful, and all-round exceptional. Thank you for never being afraid to say if something's not working, and always being quick to say if it is.

To my wonderful editor and friend Lynda Dietz, of Easy Reader Editing, who I'll never stop feeling lucky to have met. Working with you is just a bonus to being friends with you. As always, all good grammar praise goes to

Lynda, while all mistakes are mine. Find her at www.easyreaderediting.com for fantastic blogs on editing, grammar, and other writer-y stuff.

Thank you to Monika from Ampersand Cover Design, who makes creating perfect covers seem somehow effortless. Find her at www.ampersandbookcovers.com

And last but never, ever least, thank you to my friends and family, both online and off, who've helped me through a very weird and disrupted year. You are exceptional, and I am truly a very lucky human. I couldn't do any of the things without you, and I'd hate to have to try.

Thank you all for coming on this strange adventure with me.

See you next time!

Kim x

ALSO BY KIM M. WATT

The Gobbelino London, PI series

"This series is a wonderful combination of humor and suspense that won't let you stop until you've finished the book. Fair warning, don't plan on doing anything else until you're done ..."

- Goodreads reviewer

The Beaufort Scales Series (cozy mysteries with dragons)

"The addition of covert dragons to a cozy mystery is perfect...and the dragons are as quirky and entertaining as the rest of the slightly eccentric residents of Toot Hansell."

– Goodreads reviewer

Short Story Collections

Oddly Enough: Tales of the Unordinary, Volume One

"The stories are quirky, charming, hilarious, and some are all of the above without a dud amongst the bunch ..."

- Goodreads reviewer

The Cat Did It

Of course the cat did it. Sneaky, snarky, and up to no good - that's the cats in this feline collection, which you can grab free by signing up to the newsletter on the earlier page. Just remember - if the cat winks, always wink back ...

The Tales of Beaufort Scales

Modern dragons are a little different these days. There's the barbecue fixation, for starters ... You'll get these tales free once you've signed up for the newsletter!

Lightning Source UK Ltd.
Milton Keynes UK
UKHW040738160223
417122UK00003B/445